RIGHT

A PORTRAIT OF CONTROVERSY

In a 1980s America different from our own, both familiar and not, Congress passed and President Henshaw signed the Birth Cessation Act. Once it became law, no one would be allowed to have a child for 25 years, any woman under 24 weeks pregnant was required to have an immediate abortion, and all men were called up to report for a vasectomy.

"Conscious regulation of human numbers must be achieved." Dr. Paul R. Ehrlich wrote in his 1968 bestseller, *The Population Bomb.* By the early 80s, the government had statistical projections that population growth was outpacing the available resources needed for all in America to live a comfortable and secure life. A situation that would inevitably lead to the chaos and violence of extreme civil unrest.

Most Americans, liking comfort and security, supported the government's action. Most, but not all. And those who didn't—including a world-famous female billionaire entrepreneur inventor film producer; a TV salesman from Queens; a well-to-do Manhattan college radical; an unwed mother in Los Angeles who protests most horribly; America's premier pundit-columnist; and a young man who talks to his dead brother—became loud enough to start a fresh new controversy in America.
This is a portrait of that controversy.

PRAISE FOR
STEVEN PAUL LEIVA AND HIS BOOKS

"Steven Leiva not only promises but delivers. Bravo!"— **Ray Bradbury, Author of *Fahrenheit 451***

"*Traveling in Space's* humor and refreshing perspective is thoroughly enjoyable" — **Diane Ackerman, *New York Times* bestselling author of *The Zookeeper's Wife* and *A Natural History of the Senses.***

"Steven Paul Leiva is a master wordsmith able to take on any genre or blend them." — **Jean Rabe, *USA Today* Bestselling Author.**

"*Blood is Pretty* is a wonderful read, a highly entertaining and impressive debut novel." — **Richard D. Zanuck, Academy Award-Winning Producer of *Jaws, Cocoon* & *Driving Miss Daisy.***

"Many of the aliens' encounters with human beings are downright funny...much to think about, and I'm sure that *Traveling in Space* will play on my mind for some time to come" — **Russell Blackford, author of *Science Fiction and the Moral Imagination.***

"Bully 4 Love: A Rather Odd Love Story—a deftly crafted contemporary romantic comedy that showcases the author's genuine flair for originality and a distinctive kind of narrative storytelling." — ***Midwest Book Review***

"By the Sea: A Comic Novel is a delightfully engaging story about an eccentric community that resides in the foggy environs of Leech Beach...Leiva deftly interweaves characters' past and present to create a vibrant ensemble that is immediately engaging." — ***Literary Fiction Book Review.***

"A novel that delightfully throws out all the conventions of what a romantic novel should be like…part farce, part seriocomic story, and all sexually motivated, *The Reluctant Heterosexual* is a riveting tale." — **Stuart Nulman, *Montreal Times.***

"I've continued to enjoy thinking about the book long after reading it. *The Definition Of Luck or The Post-Modern Prometheus* certainly gets a recommendation from me." **— Andy Whitaker, *SFcrowsnest***

"This brisk and touching comic novel (*Made on the Moon*) has mysterious and profound things to say about the price of freedom. Highly recommended!" **— John Billingsley, "Dr. Phlox" on *Star Trek Enterprise.***

"*Creature Feature* is a weird, funny, twisty romp through the creepier parts of the American landscape. Highly entertaining and highly recommended." **— Jonathan Maberry, *NY Times* Bestselling Author of *Rot & Ruin* and *V-Wars.***

"Leiva is witty and engaging, stylistically striking an immediate generational middle ground...*Creature Feature*'s perfect mix of dynamic action and dry dialogue keep readers turning the pages." **— Areyon Jolivette, *The Daily Californian.***

"Steven Paul Leiva is a very bad man. His version of U.S. politics (*IMP: A Political Fantasia)* Trumps anything the real world has to offer. Hell, you thought the orange one was the only homunculus America had to worry about. You thought wrong. There's always the nuclear option." ***— Steven Savile, New York Times & USA Today* Bestselling Author.**

"*Journey to Where*—a truly wild trip. recommended!" **— Stephen Webb, Physicist, Author of *New Light Through Old Windows: Exploring Contemporary Science through 12 Classic Science Fiction Tales***

"Ray Bradbury will be remembered as one of the literary giants of the 20th Century. Steven Paul Leiva's book (*Searching for Ray Bradbury*) is a perfect tribute to the life and works of this great artist." **— Joe Mantegna, actor.**

"(Leiva's) true strength is in storytelling." ***— Amazing Stories Magazine.***

RIGHT

A PORTRAIT OF CONTROVERSY

RIGHT
A Portrait of Controversy

An Ahistorical Novel

Steven Paul Leiva

Los Angeles, California

Magpie Press February 2024

ISBN: 978-1-7352985-9-7
Library of Congress Control Number: 2024902859

Cover Design by: Juan Padrón https://www.juanjpadron.com/

Author Photo by Amanda Martin

Published in Los Angeles, California
Printed in the United States of America

DEDICATION

For Felix the Cat and Kimba the Lion
And That's the Black and White of It.

CONTENTS

RIGHT……………………………..….1

AFTERWORD………………...….341

ABOUT THE AUTHOR……………343

BOOKS BY
STEVEN PAUL LEIVA………………345

"Everybody is right I suppose, and the world is a rogue."

Vanity Fair - William Makepeace Thackeray

What If

In a 1980s America Somewhat Different From Our Own...

1

May 15—Washington, D.C.

As he crossed the line that separated that part of the White House reserved for the conducting of the nation's affairs from that part reserved for his residence, the first thing the president did was to take off his shoes. It was not a gesture to the growing power of Japan; it was just that once he crossed that line, the leather wrapping his feet became more like bindings than shoes. Release was his immediate desire, and relief was his immediate reward as he untied, loosened, and doffed. The socks went as well. Not just because of any offending odor but because they tended to air-cool his feet, now exposed and slightly damp with sweat—and he found that uncomfortable. Well-worn suede slippers went on, which allowed the president to pad around his residence. With such padded steps, he entered his private sitting room, private even from secretaries—those who took notes and those who gave notes. He padded his way to the bar, fixed, and then sipped a drink. He took a second to appreciate the effect. Then he turned and crossed the room to join three other men sitting quietly in a grouping of a couch and chairs.

These were particular men. Not one of them common. Not one of them less than brilliant. Not one of them shy of power. They were more alike than not, yet they never—absolutely never—had much to do with each other outside of the times they met here with the president. Any president. Every president, eventually, came to utilize them—or men like them. They were continuity. Presidents were temporary.

"Gentlemen," the president said as he sat down.

"Sir," two of them—one tall, one short— said in unison.

"Al," the third said. He was a senator—an old colleague of the president's. He was the majority leader who had always been re-elected by a landslide and a master manipulator of the power granted to him. Jovial on the surface. Grandpa to some. A celebrated wit. A killer if need be. To accomplish. To get it done. This was his number one task in life.

The tall man was from the Defense Department. Not noticeably high up. His was not a flashy position. But he had always been there through each succeeding administration. A good bureaucrat. A survivor. A pen with a punch.

The shorter man was from the National Security Agency. He had no title or position. At least none that any of the others knew. He was just there with the knowledge and to report the same. The NSA was about knowledge. Intelligence, some called it, but that had always been misleading. No one has ever said, "Intelligence is power."

"I have found these gatherings helpful," the president continued. "The knowledge is useful. The various possible scenarios are certainly eye-opening. But as you know, your suggestions for a certain action I've so far rejected. I know that's been frustrating for you. But I'm still fresh in the job. I still want to trust the democratic process a bit. And I haven't quite settled the old philosophical argument. Do events shape men, or do men shape events? Am I a product of history? Or is history to be my product?"

"Like all things, Al," the senator said, "it is a combination of both."

The president smiled. He was amused by the senator, a man so used to compromise. Then he turned to the NSA man. "What do you think, Skip?"

"We just supply the information, sir. It usually speaks for itself. It certainly does in this case. We are becoming dangerously overpopulated. The problem has affected almost every other country and is now inevitably affecting us. Please, sir, do not imagine science-fictional scenarios of people standing shoulder to shoulder, squeezing each other out. It is not a question of the ratio of land mass to the mass of the population. It only has to do with resources. Food. Fuel. Shelter. Remember, a ten-square-mile plot of land that is capable—for whatever reason—of supporting only one person becomes overpopulated once the census reaches two. It is as simple as that. Mr. President, we have laid out the facts and figures that show that we are reaching that point. With no action, we will reach it sooner than not—especially considering how volatile the flow of resources has become. Oil is a problem again. As is drinkable water. I'm afraid previous administrations have never helped much in that regard. The cost of producing food, the price to buy it, is up. The deficit has harmed us there. More and more, the basics will become scarce. That will drive prices up even higher—basic economics. The more things cost, the wider the gap between the haves and the have-nots. More tension then. More strife. More chance for disorder."

The idea made the tall man from Defense noticeably nervous.

"Yes?" The president asked him.

"Couldn't put us in a weaker position," Mr. President. Japan, Europe, Russia, somebody will take advantage of it. Not to mention certain factions of our people."

"Yes," the president said. "I know." He looked to the senator. "I need a miracle, Ken. I need legislation that will ban births in this country for a certain period. I need to bring the population down."

"How long?"

The president gestured for the short man to answer.

"Ten to fifteen years at least. With an option to go twenty-five."

The Senator shook his head. "That's awfully radical, Al."

"I know."

"Look, Al, I know Butchko's been preaching this. But who took him seriously? It was just a wild plan from an egghead. But the political reality, Al? To order something so against human nature?"

"That's why we need to prepare. That's why we four will be meeting more often in the coming months."

"Interesting you should mention Butchko." The tall man said. He and the others recognized that the president had already decided on a course of action. Now, they had to implement it. "Butchko's our key. He sees it all intellectually and doesn't see the political ramifications. But that makes him a very sharp spearhead. A very useful tool."

"But why a ban? The senator asked. "Why not a limit? One child per family." Again, the compromiser, the president thought.

The short man interjected. "That equation simply does not work. It's still too many new births. I suppose you could put a quota on the number of births—a certain number per month, for example—But who decides who gets a child and who doesn't?

Either scenario is also too much of a burden to enforce. They tried it in China. It never worked; it had the unfortunate consequence of female infanticide. A simple, non-discriminatory ban is much cleaner and easier to deal with. Later, resumption could be selective."

"And it is necessary, senator. Halfway measures will do no good here," said the man from Defense, never liking ambiguity in action.

"Who's the likely legislator for Butchko to work with?" the president asked.

"Senator Anderson, Al. They're friends. Anderson has been involved in the intellectualizing of this."

"So, drafting a well-conceived bill and its introduction is no problem?"

"None at all. It can be handled."

"And the control of its life in committee?"

"Oh, I'll take care of that," the senator said.

"And the House?"

"I think Parker will cooperate. Should we include him in this group?"

"I'd rather not if we can get the goods without it."

"Okay."

"Now," the president stood up, walked to the bar, opened the little refrigerator, and brought out a bowl of black olives. He loved black olives. "What about the people? Ostensibly, we are their servants."

"That's my main concern, the senator said. "Selling it on the Hill all hinges on the boys and girls selling it back home."

"I don't suppose we can rely on the normal apathy of the American public?" the president probed, knowing what power in the past had derived from this phenomenon.

"Huh! Not likely! You're talking babies here, cute, cuddly creatures! You're going to want the public, need them, truly behind us on this one, the senator said.

"We'll use the Roosevelt Gambit," the tall man said.

"What the hell is that?" the senator asked, jumping at the name of his political hero."

"Fear itself. A fearful public is a highly controllable public. Give them a bogeyman—communists, eroding moral values, higher takes, migrants, whatever—and you put them in a suggestible frame of mind. Now, the bogeyman, in this case, is quite real. If, as you say, the ratio between people and resources keeps tilting the wrong way at its current rate, or, worse, at a potentially faster rate, then we are going to be in deep shit. The people are going to hurt and hurt badly. Think of it. What are they going to do? If the almost invisible infrastructure of everyday life—the movement and delivery of the necessities of life—is suddenly broken, they wouldn't know how to take care of themselves. Outside of the few survivalists up in the hills somewhere.

But for the rest of us, if food—canned, frozen, dried, even fresh—were suddenly not on supermarket shelves, we wouldn't have the foggiest notion of how to get something to eat. Are the plants in our backyards edible? Do we even have backyards? Should, indeed could, we eat our household pets? Senator, if you woke up one morning and turned on your tap and no water came out, where would you go to get some? What would you do if it was the dead of winter and you turned on your heater, and there was no heat? Face it, we are no longer a nation of hardy pioneers. We rely so much on each other and the infrastructure we've built up to serve our needs. But that infrastructure is fragile. And we all know that. One oil embargo tells us that. The rationing of water tells us. Not to mention natural disasters, droughts, for example. Or deadly combinations of man and nature. Do you know the statistics of the lowering yield of edible fish the oceans have provided us lately? Pollution, of course, killing off a nice source of food."

"Yes, well, let's not get into political questions here," the president said.

"Sorry, sir, but my point being—"

"Your point being lost on me," the senator said. "I don't see panic in the streets over these things. I don't see a fearful nation. Not even a nervous one."

"Doesn't mean there shouldn't be. Because if we don't stop and—and this is the important part—and reverse population growth now, you will see panic in the streets. Plenty of it."

"No, I won't," the senator stopped the tall man. "I'm sure I'll be dead before that. You are projecting a situation ways off, aren't you?"

"Not as far off as you might think," the short man from the NSA said.

"Well, I'm a 67-year-old senator. If I live to be 87, will I see panic in the streets?"

"Senator, if we do nothing, you'll see panic in the streets on your 77th birthday. The only question will be, how long it had been going on."

"The point is, gentlemen," the president stopped eating olives, "if we take action now, we could live to be a thousand and never see it. And we would have a better America. The best America that's ever been. Lean, controlled. Each citizen living with an equal, or at least, a fair share of our bounty, whatever that might be. We've never really achieved that dream in America, have we? Too many damn people. The population too lopsided. The poor have all the babies, don't they? Poverty giving birth to poverty, an unending cycle. And each president elected is supposed to do something about it. And each president fails. But what can be done? Poor women having five, six, seven children each. Their children following suit. It's like having mercury in hand; how do you grab hold? Give them free birth control, and the morality squads will be down your back. Try to educate them, and they laugh in your face. They sap resources and give nothing in return. Can a society suffer that for long? Of course, it's not their fault; they're on a treadmill that is impossible to jump off. So it's just got to be jammed. It's just got to be stopped. Haven't you ever just wanted to stop, stop it all, cut away the deadwood, clean up the place, and reorder things? Start new. Start fresh. Don't you see, gentlemen, that, unlike any other time, we have that potential here."

The three stared at the president. He was rarely a man to ramble. Or to expose his true motivations. He was pacing, walking around the room softly in his slippers, yet he seemed almost to be stomping.

"America is a country disintegrating. It's not a concept one can use to win an election. But can you deny it? And outside forces are wearing away at it. Do you want to talk about overpopulation? Look at the Third World. It will explode, and that, gentlemen, will shake us to our foundation. Do you want a fearful America to get your way? Every night, on the news, you put on pictures from the Third World. And not from some damn desert, but from, say, Rio de Janeiro, where people are starving, masses of them, fly encrusted, bellies extended, backdropped by a once beautiful city, now virtually crumbling. It ain't Fred Astaire flying down for a romantic tango anymore. You show them a picture of that. You feed them the facts. Such conditions cause tensions harmful to America. For we are going to have to help feed those people. At the expense of our own? Maybe. Maybe to stem the tide. Maybe. For we are, after all, America. We are the world's guardian. It is the role that gives us our identity, our greatness—the greatest country in the world, the greatest country that's ever been. But we are only a little over two hundred years old—and disintegrating. If we don't survive, the world doesn't survive. Gentlemen, I will not be the president who presided over America's fall. If it takes scaring the shit out of the people, then do it. With my blessings. Whatever it takes. Just give me a lean, clean America."

The president strode back to the men. "Now I'm tired. I'm going to bed." He took the bowl of olives and left the room. The three men remaining look at each other.

"Jesus, we don't have another loony for a president, do we?" the warrior asked. The NSA man instinctively wondered if the comment was recorded.

"No, sir," the senator said. "You do not. That was a very calculated performance.

"Are you sure?"

"I've known Al for a long time. He's highly melodramatic. Comes from watching too many movies. He just wanted to make a point. Mostly to me, I suspect. Stop worrying about the people and what they'll think and start shaping that thinking instead. That's what he's telling us. Can we do it?"

"We have the means, yes." The man from Defense said.

"How?"

"By rushing the future. It's like a vaccination. You immunize by giving a little shot of the disease. We have worked out a scenario that will slowly and subtly place America in a condition that will begin to alarm people. Certain items will stop appearing on the store shelves. At first, items that are not basic needs, but the lack of which people will find damn annoying. The government, of course, will explain exactly why this is happening. Later, even a few basic things might come up scarce. The people will suddenly be faced with water flowing from taps only at certain hours. We will, as suggested, make sure that images from the Third World will pop up on the news. We'll batter people with images. We'll speed up the inflation of certain items. We'll widen the gap between the Haves and the Have-nots, making the Have-nots stronger in their anger, making them a nuisance to the Haves—mucking around with simple social dynamics there. We'll spread rumors—plenty of stories about the lack of plenty. Soon, lines will be forming. You know how the American people hate lines. Basically, we will pick the pockets of America. A gradual lowering of the standard of living—this is our bogeyman. It could be done in a year.

"Then we form a grassroots movement to call for action. We start letter campaigns, bombard Capitol Hill, and make the legislators think the people are ready to take to the streets, even if they are not. It's been done before. It's your basic squeaky wheel campaign."

"Then we will present the solution," the NSA man said. "A ten-year ban on births. Not a long time, really. We'll accomplish it through sterilization. That will solve the president's poor-women-having-babies problem. The middle class? They should see it as a welcome relief. Kids cost too damn much. The rich? Well, they are a powerful lobby. But they also have the power not to be bothered by it all. Certain accommodations can be made, such as falsified sterilization records. Also, long trips abroad are always an option. So, with proper handling, the rich are no problem. They will see the benefit of the ban. Particularly faced with the alternative."

"So, you're telling me," the senator said, "it's really a pocketbook issue."

"Isn't everything in the final analysis?"

"You feel that out of self-interest, the people will give up the right to bear children? To bear children is an awfully strong instinct developed long before there were pockets."

"Well, please remember, senator," the tall man said, "we aren't asking the people to vote for this. It's not a referendum. It's their representatives that vote. Convince them that the people support this, and you got it. Hell, we can fix polls if need be. And despite what you said, I do believe the normal apathy of the people works in our favor. Less than half of them vote anyway. Most follow. It's not quite that they won't know what's hit them, but many will really become aware of the ban—as a reality—only after it's law. We just enforce the law super quick, and we are home free. Okay, it won't be simple. But it can be done. And anyway, it's only for ten years."

"You think you can control the people that long?

"Yes, given the right authority, the right circumstances. The people are just a mass. Masses can be shaped. Look at Japan. They've never had any major natural resources. They lost a major war. They have half the population of the United States in a land area the size of California. But using mass effort, they are nearly as strong as we are. Stronger, some might say."

"Japan is a tribe. We are a nation of individualists."

"Oh, we gave up individualism years ago, senator. Even before TV."

"You know, there's something else maybe you guys haven't thought of. In 18 to 25 years, there will no longer be any young men around to be our soldiers to defend our nation. And there won't be for at least another ten years after that. Now, what the hell are we going to do without soldiers?"

The tall man from the Defense Department smiled smugly. He knew the senator thought he had them. He knew the senator did not. "Mercenaries, senator. Mercenary soldiers from the Third World. Lots of young men down there are going to need a job. It will be a buyer's market. We'll get them cheap, fatten them up, train them, make them loyal for their daily bread. Soldiers you buy are always better than those you must bend backward to recruit or conscript."

The senator stood up. He did not like these men. "I find your attitude cynical and sick. But I also find your facts to be irrefutable." The senator walked to the door. "prepare the people for me. I'll do the rest." He opened the door and exited, saying no courtesy goodbyes.

The tall man stood up, followed by the short man.

"I'm hungry," the tall man said.

"He never offers us anything. Not even an olive," said the short man.

They grabbed their briefcases and left.

The president's valet entered the room. He looked for and found the president's shoes. He picked them up and then left. They would be freshly polished by morning.

2

A year and a half later
Saturday, November 26th—Los Angeles

Large and elaborate weddings—weddings attended to by professionals for every little detail—are not so much displays of love eternal as they are nervous defenses of it. Or so thought Darryl Butchko, well dressed, standing stiff, waiting in the wings to be Edgar Handlin's best man on the day of his wedding to Vivian Pavin. "Absurd" summarized his opinion of the event. But it had been demanded by the bride, who was used to demanding, and not objected to by the groom, who was used to not objecting. Still, they had been lovers for years; they were both in their late thirties and so the pomp of this "teenage" wedding that hinted at states of virgin experience that no one could believe was—*Absurd.*

***

Vivian Pavin was the most important, successful, and famous female entrepreneur the nation had ever produced. But hers was not the classic story of poor fighting to become rich. On her eighteenth birthday, she inherited many more millions than she would ever need. Which, of course, made her accomplishments that much more impressive. She had been born into a warm, protected, and comfortable environment and reared and developed in that same—even improving—environment. She could have counted on that environment throughout her adult years with no effort expended at all. Except, of course, to let people see her as a princess, to admire her, and envy her. And to put her on a pedestal so that they might have an unobstructed view for their pot-shots. It was a stupid certainty that she did not mind. She was just determined to earn it for herself.

Vivian came of age and became a new woman when the New Woman was suffering setbacks. The war once thought won was raging again, and Vivian saw her duty. High school and college were years of soapboxing the cause of The Female. She was an angry young woman then: loving towards the shout, passionate towards the scream, tender towards the exclamation. If the literal beating of heads to drive her point into them would have worked—she would have done it. But then her verbal assaults were physical enough to give her the satisfaction of flowing adrenaline and pulsating blood. She never cared if, by her intense actions, she was liked or disliked, just as long as she wasn't ignored.

Then, one day, she suddenly grew tired. Not one symbolic day, but one specific day. One she would never forget and consciously relive for inspiration during times of doubt. Arguments were flaring within the group. The fine points of the philosophy of female psychology were being debated, dividing the group into two, then the two into four, then the four into eight. Each new group found a spieler; each spieler spoke their creed. Vivian was one of the best. Her knack at it, logically, should have brought success. Her lack of that brought her painful disgust.

"Look, I'm telling you... don't answer me before I'm finished... No! You don't understand!... You're not listening to what I'm saying... You're misinterpreting!"

Damn! Shit! Jesus! Was the cadence of her march back home.

A slam of the door, a flop on the couch, a sulk of the senses that set her up in thought. Forty-five minutes, maybe fifty. She felt and heard her breath as it tunneled in and out, raised and lowered her chest, finally slowing and quieting to a steady pace.

Like some dumb Greek philosophers, they are! Gray-bearded old craps, arguing over the universally dictated number of teeth in the mouth of the Horse without ever looking into the mouth of a horse!

Group effort is silly! Group action is ridiculous! Unless you run the group and the group listens and takes the measures you outline. But they don't!

To achieve on her own, to do it all herself, would do more for women, would prove more about women than any group action! She set her millions aside, laid her hands on only some bare thousands, and started a cosmetics company while still in college. Eventually, with a scent she developed in collaboration with chemists after fourteen months of twelve-hour days, Pavin Perfume became the bestselling perfume in the country three years after her college graduation. The scent went into all her products, whether based in oil, powder, cream, or water. Her picture went on all the packages; her calculatedly sexy image went on television. Soon, she had millions she could truly call her own.

Vivian was an example, and she liked that. She was pointed to as proof of female abilities, and liked that. But then some pointer pointed out—some defender of the home—that for a woman to succeed at a "woman's" business was hardly surprising. After all, *Madams* had always run the best *Bordellos.*

Another door slam and a decision to diversify. Her role as a model in her TV commercials linked her closely enough with the film industry to head in that direction, and by the time she was thirty, she had produced four films. Three received Oscars in various categories. More importantly, all four were money-makers the major studios would kill for. And she had fought the majors to achieve it. Independents, such as she was, rarely got the best exhibition deals, the major studios having—to put it gently—a bit more muscle. But through a glamour that she knew how to exploit, she made good deals, got the best theaters, convinced them to hold over her films, promised all would make money, and delivered on that promise.

It was a fantastic achievement tarnished by some Wall Street Wit commenting that women had always had an aptitude for the arts.

So she turned from *Barbie* to *G.I. Joe* and took up armaments manufacturing. She studied the craft intensely for a year, then assembled a team to design a new personal firearm of devastating capabilities. For Christmas the year of its debut, she had one sent—firing pin removed—to the Wall Street Wit.

Then, to prove that she was not becoming a mock man, she oversaw designing, manufacturing, and distributing a line of women's fashions that broke traditions and set styles and made another fortune.

Then, of course, she went into hi-tech. Computers, software, bio-genetics. She had the money to spread. She spread it.

People of such achievement regularly appear on the cover of *Time Magazine*. When Vivian Pavin was thirty-six, she *was* a *Time Magazine*. A special supplementary issue came out one week; its sole subject was *Vivian Pavin: Person of the Decade.*

Her groom, Edgar Handlin, had been mentioned in *Time Magazine* once. It was in the caption of a picture whose center of focus was the departing Secretary of State. The mention grouped him with "State Department employees" attending the Secretary's farewell address. He was in the back but visible. Vivian had his section blown up and framed, and she gave it to him as a Christmas present. It was a joke—

of sorts. Edgar Handlin had been her lover since college, although that word had never really applied. "Companion" seemed a better word, but it did not fully cover the situation. He was the only man she was ever seen with in public, although, if that was his purpose, he seemed inadequate for it. Those close enough to Vivian to know that she shared private times with Edgar speculated wildly but never came to a satisfactory base for good gossip. Some called it her charity work, while others hinted at a special love that few could understand. As far as anyone knew, neither had other relationships, even though Edgar spent most of his time in Washington at the State Department, and Vivian spent most of her time in Los Angeles at her corporate headquarters. While they were apart, they were alone. When they were together, time was found to share. It seemed a convenient relationship, although it was not fair to call it a relationship of convenience. So the announcement of a marriage, after years of the relationship, was a great surprise—and was not.

***

The bride and groom said their "I dos" with all the passion of "excuse me," and the ceremony ended.

The reception, where the solemn atmosphere of vow-taking was gratefully pushed aside, began almost as soon as Vivian and Ed walked back down the aisle and entered Vivian's house. The wedding had taken place outside, by the pond, with peacocks quietly observing. The weather had been cool but not unpleasant, and the scent of the imported orchids had been just right. But people are always pleased to stand and stretch after an extended sit, no matter how perfect the scene. And they wanted to get to the food. They wanted to see if it would be something special, which they expected, this being Vivian Pavin's wedding. Vivian did not disappoint. She had been determined that the food would be fresh in concept and fresh in fact. So she flew in a chef and his crew from Sula Island in the Molucca Sea about 700 miles east of Borneo (or so it was explained over and over to each inquiring guest), who had an incredible way with fish and other edibles from the ocean. The food was a triumph, and everyone applauded it. And as the first topic of conversation—as food often is at parties—it was an extremely lively one, conditioning the participants towards an afternoon of kinetic talk, often illuminated by the strobe lights of the press photographers pop-flashing around the room. But it was only the first topic of conversation. It was not the major one.

"What do you think about the No-birth bill?"

"Summed up easily, I think: Big Brother is aborting."

"A proper solution, I think. And with any luck, it will be an example to the rest of the world."

"If people had learned to conserve, it never would have come to this."

"What the hell, it's only for ten years."

"Don't kid yourself. The man's got an option for twenty-five. He'll take twenty-five."

"It's disgusting. The ultimate in governmental interference."

"Well, I'd stay away from stock in Johnson & Johnson. Ha ha!?"

"Of course, economically speaking, it has both good and bad consequences."

"Freedom is a precious thing, and easier to share the fewer there are."

"Freedom hell, food and fuel is the issue here."

"There are three films in various stages of production with no-birth as the subject matter. But, of course, mine started first."

"As long as it's not sex that they're trying to ban, I have very little interest in it."

"It's just going to kill the American Family, isn't it? The core of civilization is going to be wiped out. Not to mention Disney."

"Well, this is one thing the gays can't bitch about."

"It will mark the true liberation of women. Finally, our function in society will be as equal members, for none of us will have to stop and bear children. In essence, I guess I'm saying that we will now all be in the race, never having to drop out with this burden of *Perpetuating the Species.*"

"It's the goddamn fuss of those clinics that bother me. Jesus, another goddamn inconvenience. I'm going to check—does anybody know if you can have your own doctor do it?

"Mr. Butchko, what do you think? You're right in the thick of things there in Washington. Do you think the bill will pass, and President Henshaw will sign it?"

Butchko looked at the wife of the executive vice president of Pavin Productions. "I think—" he said, stopped and sipped some champagne. "I think it may be a subject of poor taste to talk about at a wedding reception." Then, with no further comment, he walked away.

Darryl Butchko was famous for such rudeness. The woman had half expected it and thoroughly enjoyed it. It would be a tale to tell. But for others, the Butchko sting was upsetting, and he had proved an "embarrassment" to the president on several occasions when remarks he had made found their way into the press. Of course, there were precedents and predecessors in other administrations, and the president seemed more than willing to carry on the tradition. For as stiff and stern, as arrogant and rude as Butchko could be, he was, for the president, a genuine source of amusement. Those traits and their effect on others were advantageous if well applied. The president himself, of course, never took Butchko's manner seriously. He reserved serious consideration for Butchko's mind. Butchko's mind was why the president had chosen him as his assistant for domestic affairs, even though they had never met. Physically, that is. Minds often meet long distance.

Butchko moved through the people, catching their glances. He ignored some. He acknowledged some. He returned greetings coldly or with a smile, depending. He stopped for some. He edged through others. He prided himself on not being a ready glad hand at parties just for social grace's sake. He did not sing and dance for anyone. He was a vigilant watchdog over his public face—it must *always* sync with his private one. "Genuine" was his preferred motto.

But it was a performance, nevertheless. His wife Bobbie knew it but never broached it; his staff members joked about it, but only among themselves; several members of Congress had noticed it more than once and were amused that in Butchko's attempt not to have his face doubled by Washington, a third had appeared, a somewhat credible compromise: A genuine effort to seem genuine.

We are all, at times, phony, Butchko was willing to admit to himself. *But if it is part of all our natures, it is natural, and what is natural is genuine.* Not purely Socratic, but certainly a satisfying line of thought.

Genuine attempts to be genuine were easier in a crowd for Butchko and more than easier in such a crowd as this: Beautiful people, beautifully appointed people, or people of such power that beauty was superfluous. For among these among the clouds, Butchko stood out. He was an advisor to the president. He was from the White House. And the White House—as a building and symbol—had a glamour and allure. Even if, in recent years, the once sacred Oval Office had been soiled, supposedly scoured, fouled once again, steamed cleaned by a hot-headed moralist, sullied by his incompetent successor, then finally settled into the comfortable arms of President Henshaw, it was still the object of America's curious affection. After all, it offered a substitute for the grand palace kept from us by that silly piece of paper. Like it or not, We the People gave it a royal bearing. And all attached to it also picked up a bit of the good posture.

Butchko knew this. And having once been but an academic—an activity of little allure except among some rare idealistic graduate students—he subtly enjoyed the change. But he was determined not to sing and dance just for that enjoyment. Or, at least, not to look rehearsed.

"Honey," Butchko's wife, Bobbie, came up to him. "Ed and Viv are about ready to leave."

"Oh, okay."

He had to go up to Vivian's bedroom to get from her the location of the honeymoon. It was a special request from Vivian. Only he would know, and only for emergencies. Not even her key staff people would know. It was for security. To keep away the world press that would love to invade the ritual and record it for all time.

"You know, Viv, I'm a bit of a busy person too. What if there is an emergency and your staff can't reach me?"

"Please, Darryl, don't argue. Just do this for me."

"Can I at least leave the information with Bobbie?"

"Does she gossip?"

"Viv! Please!"

"Well, I know how Washington parties are."

"Pious talk for one of the Hollywood crowd."

"All right. Okay. Of course, Bobbie can be trusted. It's only a week anyway."

"Thank you. You'll be recognized regardless of what you do or where you go. You know that, don't you?"

"Of course. But this will give us a head start. I owe that to Ed, don't you think?"

"Oh, sure. And it is exceedingly kind of you, a lovely thing to do for your new bride."

Vivian stopped her constant double-checking of the luggage. "Why have we been the very best of friends for years but never very friendly?"

"Because once we were the very best of lovers, and it was lovely."

"Two college kids fucking in the dorm do not make lovers, Darryl."

"Sorry. I guess I've always just been a romantic about the past."

"You've never forgiven my relationship with Ed, have you?"

"No, why should I? But it does seem more natural. A relationship between us would have been pure hell at times. I'm sure of that. I like to flatter myself, though, and think that a bit of heaven might have crept in now and then. But you are not a person for extremes, Viv. The nice, safe middle ground of purgatory suits you best."

Vivian had a way of staring, a closed mouth, teeth set, unblinking way to show that all her thoughts were trained—for better or for worse—on you. She stared that stare now and let some time pass slowly.

Then she smiled. "We're such good friends, Darryl, because we've been able to combine love and hate into a whole new emotion, one that allows for nothing but honesty. It's taken twenty years, but I think we've really accomplished something here."

"There was a cursory knock as the door simultaneously opened.

"Vivian?" said Ed as he entered. "Ready? Oh, hi, Darryl. You get all the information?"

"Yes, I did, Ed. I hope you two have a wonderful time."

"Well, we'll give it a shot. Listen, I want to thank you for flying in for this. Viv felt that you were the Best Man for both of us."

"If she felt that Ed, she would have married me in college. Viv, I'll go out and part your path to the car." Darryl walked out, quietly closing the door behind him.

"He's always been able to do that to me."

"Do what, Ed?"

"I don't know. Pull some zinger like that. You know, some sly little verbal assault on something I've said. Jesus, I hate that. Ready?"

"Yes."

"Okay. They're coming for the bags. Let's go."

There were the traveling goodbyes and thank-yous as they made their way out of the house, the quick squeezes, the hungry hugs, the once more congratulations. Darryl met them at the door and walked them down the path to the waiting limousine. Young men in blue coats stood around. These were the parking valets. There were several policemen on the grounds; the mayor was in attendance, and there had been a guarantee of protection and traffic control. Some guests followed the couple outside to be able to wave, grab one last second of sharing the occasion, and shout one final congratulations.

The sight of it all, the omnipresence of sounds, and the camera flashes quickly confused. Ed prayed that they could get out of the chaos and into the limo, get on the comfortable back seat, slump a little, and settle back into the enclosed calm. But before that happened, the chaos was suddenly scattered away by dead-stop screaming commands and high-pitched executive orders.

"What is that? Get it out of here! Move that thing! Get the police here! Get them to get that thing out of here!"

Ed and Darryl both recognized the voice and orders as Vivian's. There was a quick wondering eye communication between them, then a search for the source of her anger.

It was a bus. Big and black, with windows painted over. It had somehow passed the traffic control. It was parked across the street, with the driver clouded by a tinted windshield; its motor was running. On its side, painted neatly in red, was:

BIRTH = DEATH
NO BIRTH = LIFE

Police and blue-coated valets started moving towards the bus. Ed expelled a sound of recognition and slight laughter of relief.

"It isn't funny, Ed!"

"I'm sorry, Viv. But it is in a way. The No-Birthers are doing this wherever they find a wedding."

As the police got closer, the bus started to move slowly. There had been a rush of photographers out of the house to join the ones already outside, and the quick mechanical movement of auto shutters was the only sound for a few seconds.

Then the bus sped up and was gone.

"It wasn't funny, Ed!" Vivian emphasized again as she climbed into the limousine.

"Yes, well..." Ed was cut off by Vivian's scooting to the opposite side of the back seat. Before entering himself, he turned to Darryl. "Well, thanks for everything again, Darryl." There was a pause as Darryl nodded and slightly smiled an impatient, you're welcome. "It was kind of ironic, though," Ed continued. "That bus—it was obviously a painted-over school bus." Ed tried to expel a knowing little laugh.

"Have a good time, Ed," Darryl stated in a neutral tone.

***

Over the Atlantic

A quick burst of speed, a push back in your seat like gentle pressure from someone making a point by five fingering your chest, the nose up, the feel of the tilt, the glance out to see the receding lights, a tip to turn to set on course, then a steady state with a black view. Except for turbulence now and then, that was a jet flight at night.

Ed never really felt that he was flying. Encased in the fuselage cylinder, hearing only a low rumble, feeling only a slight vibration, but experiencing no significant resistance to wind or any other force of nature, he could never quite believe it was happening. He could have been in a simulator or an amusement park dark ride that gave the sense of flying but did not fly itself. It was, he supposed, the black, the lack of anything to see outside, to point to and draw on as a reference. But even during the day, when the visible ground and clouds below passed so slowly beneath—*and yet this plane is going incredibly fast, isn't it?*—there still was no sensation of flight, nothing to recall, to remember as "flying."

Ed was struck by the unreality of the real.

If the real seems an unreal attempt to seem real, then what is the unreal?

Ed had never wanted to know what the real was; his expectations of knowledge were not that high. He just wanted to know the unreal when he saw it.

Although there was nothing there, he looked out the window and faced Vivian's black-backed reflection. She was asleep. And she was ugly. Ed had noticed this often. That faces in sleep, unguarded during the unconscious, fall some, slump a little, find wrinkles not known when awake, find near jowls where cheeks use to be, find the eyes covered and cut off from making their impressions. Vivian's face now suffered from this, repulsing Ed just a little. For awake, in animation, Vivian was still the cover girl of her cosmetics, the image of young, sexy, dynamic, intelligent, tough yet tender. Hers was a face made for movement, beautiful when mobilized to express delight and pleasure. Or even disappointment or pique. Her face could be like stone, showing her to be stern yet still have some motion and thus be beautiful.

But asleep, she was ugly.

"Honey?" Ed said. He needed her awake.

Vivian moved and turned slowly as her eyes opened. Facing Ed, she smiled. Good, thought Ed.

"Hi," she said softly. "Have I been asleep long?"

"No, not long. I shouldn't have awakened you, but—guess I was a bit lonely."

"Oh, I'm sorry."

"No, don't worry about it. You were tired, I know. It was a long day. I'm the culprit for waking you. But I couldn't help myself."

"Well, that's kind of nice. I think I like that."

"Good."

'When do we land?"

"Ed looked at his watch, already reset for a new time zone. "In about two hours."

"Oh."

"You want to go back to sleep?"

"No, I feel fine now. You tired?"

"A little. Not much."

"You did arrange a car to pick us up?"

"Your office did that. I double-checked with them."

"Good. How about a drink?"

"Okay." Ed rang for the steward and ordered drinks, which came promptly. But then the plane belonged to Vivian.

They talked softly for the next two hours, ending with a conversation on politics.

3

Sunday, November 27th—New York

He signed his columns "Argus," but everyone was quite aware—had been for years—that they were the words and thoughts of Malcolm Kirkly. "Argus" was a pseudonym Kirkly affected in young manhood while brilliantly writing for the Harvard Crimson. It was done to follow a rarely followed tradition and to show that he had read his Bulfinch that week. Argus was the Greek Argus Panoptes, a giant of redoubtable strength who happened to have one hundred eyes, at least fifty of which were always open and seeing. What better image for a political, social, and cultural commentator? His eyes were never off the scene; he would never be caught unaware. He would be one "Who sees all," thus—he felt it was logical to assume at the time—one slightly more capable of being wise.

But now, in his 27th year as a professional columnist, he found the pseudonym a bit embarrassing. It was like being stuck with the nickname "Stinky" or "Pinky," derived from some prominent childhood attribute. But it was too famous to change. Besides, Kirkly still loved the image, still loved explaining it to all those around who had not—even to this day—read their Bulfinch. It was a nearly illiterate world. Kirkly recognized that as sad, regrettable, and shocking. But it did, in effect, put a higher premium on being literate, add a little more to the pride one could take, and confirm with strength that secret sense of superiority that all but a few did not mind feeling.

Kirkly was a snob. He never denied it. In fact, he declared it proudly and defended it constantly. "All men may be created equal, although I rather doubt it," he once wrote. "But all men certainly do not develop equally. And thank whatever creator there may be for that! For we would either have been all equally ignorant and have destroyed ourselves long before now; equally mundane, capable of survival, but condemned never to know great accomplishments, never to run after that which our daytime minds told us was impossible; or equally brilliant, so surrounded by the unique that we would have been unable to recognize it and apply it. Occasional brilliance is the mental mutation that guarantees our mental evolution to ever-higher forms. It must not come too often, nor in a multitude, but it must inevitably come, and it must come well, or growth stops. And where growth stops, decay begins."

Kirkly did not think he was brilliant but considered himself a great recognizer and appreciator of the brilliant and, thus, a man of great worth to society. He covered politics in his column, of course, but also art, science, society, and psychology. He wrote of nations, tribes, and individuals. He linked them all with the past, clarified their present, and pointed to their possible futures. He commented dispassionately or criticized resoundingly as the occasion demanded.

This occasion demanded something more than mere comment, more than even harsh criticism. It required something as simple as a warning shout of "Look out!" Yet also something as complex as a rational and calm explanation of the *whys* of that "Look out!"

And it had to be written now. The office was waiting for him to email the copy so it could be sent to all the newspapers to appear in Monday's editions. It had to be Monday's. It was the last chance, the last opportunity to have influence, to make a difference.

Kirkly turned all the lights off except his desk lamp. He put Beethoven on the stereo, left his study, went into the kitchen, poured a cup of coffee, returned, sat down, and stared at his lightly illuminated walls of books and, occasionally, the computer screen before him. He sipped the coffee and wondered once again why he, why anyone, liked coffee. He analyzed the taste, holding some in his mouth. One could not say it was a pleasant taste. It was a dusty taste. It was not bitter per se, but it certainly lacked any qualities that drive us to, for example, sweets. There are those who put sugar in their coffee, plus milk, maybe making an antidote to the taste. But Kirkly took it black. *If you're going to crave a taste you dislike*, he had always thought, it should be one *you dislike.*

Another sip. Then the cup had to be put down and the keyboard addressed.

This week, a bill may be passed in Congress whose effect, if signed into law, will eventually have a more devastating impact on this country and the world at large than that once always expected but never realized Third World War. The devastation may not be to ourselves, but it will certainly be to our souls.

There will be mass slaughter. Not within some mad inferno, some hell-inspired holocaust, but by action supposedly decided on in a calm, rational, and sane manner; action deemed necessary for calm, rational, and sane reasons; action labeled "Good" and "Right" for all—our country first, the world later. It is an action considered benevolent and merciful.

Like in a war, the young and strong will soon be at a premium. But where in a war the young and strong lose their lives in defense of something they believe in, the young and strong, in this case, will not even have the chance to defend themselves, much less lofty ideals they will not be allowed the existence to form.

I am speaking, of course, of the Anderson Bill, named after its author, California Senator Robert J. Anderson. The bill is better known and more appropriately known as the No-Birth Bill.

If the No-birth Bill—already passed in the Senate in a decision that seems to have hardly been noticed—is passed by the House this week, then the Congress of the United States will have said "Yea" to the destruction—destruction as sure as in any war—of one complete generation of future Americans. The president can still call out a decisive "Nay" and end this "calm, rational and sane" madness. But will he? We have no sure indication. President Henshaw has refused to discuss the legislation. He has refused to try to influence the Congressional voting one way or the other. It is evident that he has correctly assessed the historically sensitive nature of this bill and has decided to see what the country—the people—desire as indicated by the actions and votes of their ostensive representatives in Washington. In other words, he wishes not to commit himself until it is safe or, if the bill fails to pass the House until such a commitment becomes meaningless and thus disregarded. If this assumption is correct, the further assumption that the president will sign the bill if it comes before him is not unreasonable, for he will then be able to claim the act as acceding to the will of the people.

But is it? Do the people truly realize what they are getting with this bill? A solution to a problem? Hitler had solutions, too.

The cessation of all—all—births in this country for 25 years has been presented as the great panacea for all our ills. It is claimed that if the population decreases, there will be less to share the dwindling resources of oil, food, and uncontaminated water. And there will be less to fight for a share of the ever-dwindling dollar. The population, they claim, will come down to a level that will allow all to live as if there were no shortages of necessities and no economic crisis.

It's the old "lifeboat solution." Throw one or two overboard to keep the sharks happy, and not only is there more room, but fewer to divide the emergency rations. Of course, in a lifeboat, you must face the ones you choose to sacrifice. Even a furtive glance into their eyes may be enough to produce some guilt and remorse, which is always a disadvantage. The ingenious thing about this bill is that the sacrificed will never have to be looked upon as the sharks chew them up and drag them down.

But that does not make the act any less heinous in the eyes of God, nor should it in the hearts of men. But the hearts of men are being hardened by a new sense of crisis that can find its origin in too many people vying for too few resources, no matter where in the world you go. If this country does not "Literally crawl with people, like maggots upon a garbage heap," as some supporters of No-Birth have claimed, it is undoubtedly overcrowded. Had shortages not occurred, though, the only problem the overcrowding would have caused is the continuing practical problem of governing so many people that has led to such bungling bureaucracy. And that is the real genesis of this "solution." Not its logical rightness but its bureaucratic expediency. It is a "things-too-complicated-and-hard-to-handle-okay-throw-it-all-out-and-we'll-start-all-over" type of solution. It is the literal throwing of the baby out with the bath water.

And that is the tragedy. The genius, or the leader, or the leader of genius that it will take to point out the proper solution to our problems may just be one of the babies going out with the bath water. And so, the actual answer may be missed. But even if there was no such practical consideration, even if all babies born in the next 25 years were to be shockingly ordinary, not a leader in the bunch, how do we justify such an action? Because it will assure all of us living a greater share of goods in our pantry? But what then, I ask you, the House, and President Henshaw—will become of the good in our hearts?

Kirkly stopped. He read over the column. A bit long. A sentence here sounded off. A paragraph in the middle needed to be stronger. He re-read it, hoping that the bad sentence, the weak paragraph, would sound better the second time as if another reading could improve the writing. He read it a third time. Still dissatisfied, he clicked print. He would make his revisions on the hard copy. But first, another cup of coffee.

***

Los Angeles

The phone rang, and sudden consciousness reported the facts to Butchko: *It is late Sunday morning; you are in your hotel room at the Bonaventure in downtown L.A.; yesterday was Viv and Ed's wedding; Bobbie is beside you; the phone is ringing.* The report took no longer than his hand did to reach the phone.

Not sleepy sounding at all, wide awake and very aware, Butchko answered, "Hello?"

"Hello, Darryl. It's Bob Anderson."

"Morning, Bob. Any news?"

"Some. How was the wedding?"

"As grand and silly as weddings usually are."

Bobbie, now as awake as Butchko, slugged his thigh on the remark. She liked weddings. "Who is it?"

"Hold on, Bob. It's Bob Anderson."

"Oh. Say 'Hi' for me."

"Bobbie says 'Hi.'"

"Hi to Bobbie back. Listen, I think we have them whipped in the House. I just talked to the Majority Leader. It looks good, really good."

"That's good, Bob. When do you think?"

"Tomorrow, maybe Tuesday. But then we'll have the president to worry about. Have you gotten any better idea of how he's thinking?"

"None at all. He's a hard man to figure out. You served with him; what do you think?"

"No, I can't get a feeling. I never really got close to him. Nobody really did."

"I know only one thing. If the bill is passed, he's requested that it be brought to him in private, and he seems to indicate that if he signs it, it will be with no ceremony, no guests."

"You mean I won't be invited up for the signing."

"I guess not."

"Strange, it's a major bill."

"I know. But I've arranged to take it to him. I want to be the first to know. Listen, if he does veto, do you think Congress can override it?"

Well, I would like to attempt it, but we're dealing with a 'respected' president here. The Congress may want to let his decision stand. Of course, a lot depends on any public outcry following a veto."

"Well, we're lucky there. The public's behind it."

"It seems so. But, you know, Darryl, and this has been bothering me a bit, the, uh—the public is accepting this in an almost passive and uncaring way. I frankly expected a lot of opposition."

"You've had your opposition. Kirkly. The Church. Some from the other side. The Libertarians, of course."

"That's the typical opposition, the expected. I rarely worry about them. What I've learned is to be wary of the unexpected opposition. They usually have a point of view you're not prepared for, and they tend to be very determined and surprisingly strong. Who expected students to protest in the Sixties? Who would have expected them to make such a loud and effective noise?"

"Well, you should take the lack of your 'unexpected opposition' as a sign that most people are with us. I think this country has come to realize the danger we are in and are glad for a reasonable solution."

"I don't know Darryl. Do you ever backpack?"

"What?"

"Backpack. Hike in the woods."

"Hell no. The only camp I've ever been to is Camp David."

"Well, if you ever had, you would have noticed how weird the forest is when some sound is missing. You don't even know what it is, but it's missing. Then suddenly, there's a storm, or a fire, or dry lightning, or something, and all hell breaks loose. Well, that's the way I feel about this. I feel like some sound is missing."

"Yeah, well, I think I can understand that. But if the president signs, it's superfluous, isn't it? Your missing sound can remain missing then."

"A lot of that depends on you. You're an advisor, so advise him, give him our point of view. You're a persuasive man."

"Well, I've done my best so far. This is a very guarded man. I don't know why he has advisors at all."

"Nevertheless, you're there, and I'm not, so it's in your court. When's your flight home?"

"This afternoon."

"I'll call you tomorrow with an update."

"Okay, fine."

"Have a good flight."

"Thanks Bob, thanks for calling."

"Butchko hung up and turned to Bobbie, who was preparing to shower. "Bob thinks we've got the House. Now all we need is to get the president to sign it."

"He'll sign it."

"You sound surer than I can be."

"You all talk about not being able to *really* know him, to be able to read him. Well, I can. I only see him at social functions, but we have a good rapport."

"And just why is that?"

"Because I'm not afraid of him. I won't let him intimidate me just because he's supposed to be inscrutable. I treat him like the boy next door, and I think he likes that. He'll sign. He knows the hell this country is in for if he doesn't. He knows none of his predecessors have done any good or taken any action. I think he desperately wants to solve the problem, and I think he wants to be known as the one who solved the problem. He's 'played' at politics all his life to get into the White House to do some "grown-up" problem-solving because the White House is the most grown-up place to be to solve problems. I think that's what has always motivated him. Now he has the chance. It's the biggest problem ever, and he has the power to solve it. He cannot not sign it."

"But it's not his solution, Bobbie. He didn't push for this bill; he didn't work for it; he hasn't expressed one opinion about it. The most he can do is endorse it after the fact."

"He's not a stupid man, Darryl. It doesn't matter whose solution it is; he's the one who can implement it. It will come, literally, from his hand—or forever seem so."

"I don't know. I don't think he looks at things that way."

"There's no other way to look at it."

"There is always another way to look at it."

"Not for him, Darryl. Not for Albert Henshaw, whose whole life has been a trip down a road with this kind of destination, this quality of destination in mind."

"Well," Butchko said, unconvinced but unwilling to consider it any further. "It is sometimes illuminating to be married to a historian."

Bobbie smiled a not-totally-happy smile. "To a Pulitzer Prize-winning historian, you creep."

4

Tuesday, November 29—Washington D.C.

There was a famous photo.

Black and white, it showed the president at his desk, writing by the light of a small desk lamp, wearing one oversized, thick sweater to protect against the presumed cold. It was a stark and severe photo, black and white, not just by emulsion but by design, and it served him well as a testament to the president's sacrifices in a time of national emergency.

Which was true. The president had ordered the Oval Office cool. "Let's bring the heat down and cut energy consumption," he was heard and reported to have said. And he made it a dedicated habit to turn off all unnecessary lighting. Small gestures. But taken by his media advisor and nurtured into a glowing, healthy image, then harvested and distributed, those small gestures became the image that became the man.

But it was a sham. One that the president particularly enjoyed. It was his secret amusement that the media advisor himself never realized that the president's talk of energy consumption had been facetious, that he had ordered the thermostat down simply because he preferred a cool room to work in, and that had he preferred a warm room, he would have been perfectly comfortable ordering the thermostat up. His habit of working by one light was just *his habit* of working by one light. Had his habit been to work with all lights illuminated, all lights would have blazed in the Oval Office.

The president did like the photo, though, for it showed him working, doing the job, getting things done. A perception the media advisor never saw in the glossy or didn't want to see, for a *working* president was not a *sellable* president. The media advisor wanted for the window display a "Dynamic President" and so set about constructing one through pictorials, photo-ops, anecdotes, trivia, and bold quotes for the president's speeches.

Political freedom is meaningless to the economically oppressed. Yet riches cannot purchase the simple human dignity of freedom of thought. Therefore, we strive for a nation of DOLLARS AND DIGNITY!

"DOLLARS AND DIGNITY!" became the slogan, the catchphrase of the administration. The media advisor loved running around the White House, opening his shirt to reveal the slogan printed on the white cotton blend beneath. It was all—the artful image and the artful words—a brand of salesmanship the president had always seen the necessity and benefits of—having once been a salesman himself, having sold refrigerators and stereos part-time in his first days of college, having attended numerous sales training seminars where, besides the benefits of no-frost, he had been taught how to psychologically mold the customers to the point of readiness to buy, the moment where—as his trainer graphically stated—"You've got them by the balls!"

By the balls!

And what was he now about to do?

(Salesmanship had and would be of benefit here.)

He was about to—literally—get the country by the balls.

Two quick, sharp knocks on the door announced Darryl Butchko, his Special Assistant for Domestic Affairs. The president knew that for sure. No one knocked like Butchko. No one else could produce a sound so serious from wood, so matters-of-state. But then, the former professor of political science was now participating in the concrete, where before, he had merely played with the abstract. Like the 19th-century Eastern greenhorn lover of Western dime novels gone West, Butchko took the fact that a man wore a six-gun as a sign more dangerous than it was. Or, like a small boy in his first suit, he was, at times, too stiffly portraying his concept of "Grown-up."

"Come in, Darryl."

Butchko entered and spoke simultaneously. "I have the Anderson bill, sir."

"Yes, well, I assumed that. Give it here."

Butchko walked to the desk and handed over the multi-paged document. The president held it for a second, trying to sense the history. He liked history. He especially enjoyed making it. Finally, he placed it on his desk and looked up at Butchko.

"What's the media calling it, Darryl?"

"The No-Birth Bill, sir."

"Ah, yes. They can sum things up quite simply, can't they? Well, I suppose it looks good in a headline." The president looked down at the bill and read the first sentences, although he had read them more than once. "It's a rotten decision to have to make."

"I know, Sir."

"I've been sitting here thinking about it. I had Chapman and Bunkster in earlier. They gave some good advice for a more normal situation. But in a situation like this, I suppose I can only consult myself. I would like your opinion, though."

"I've been for this bill from the beginning, Sir. I'm sure you're aware of that."

"Yes. I am. Why?"

"For the survival of the nation, Sir. And, of course, eventually, the world. The depletion of our resources can only be offset by a serious decrease in the population. Nothing else has worked. Conservation has been a total failure. We're a country too conditioned to comfort, too in love with the material. Abstract arguments that food, energy, and water will run out have impressed no one. But lines are beginning to get longer, Sir. And people are noticing. Prices are creeping up. And people are noticing. When what has normally been considered staples suddenly become luxuries, the people's mood will become volatile."

"Yeah. The people are going to be pissed."

"Uh, yes. And the atmosphere for much violence will be thick. For once, sir, I would like to see society solve a problem *before* it gets out of hand. I think that's the mark of a mature society. Our only course is to bring down the population to a level that people can consume to everyone's content and to no one's deprivation. If there is going to be less to go around, there has to be less to share it."

The president leaned back in his chair. "So if you were the president, you would not hesitate to sign this bill into law and, after that, be prepared to enforce it?"

"That's right."

But then you're not the president." He leaned forward. "You're not the president, Darryl. Therefore, decisions for you are easy to make, and you make them easily."

Butchko felt insulted and slighted. "I have given the issue quite a bit of thought, Sir."

"Of course you have. But your decision, your conclusion after all that thought, does not affect the whole nation."

"Oh, I don't know." Butchko smiled slightly. "I believe that we can all affect the country and other people in one way or another. I feel a responsibility for my actions."

"Existentialism, Darryl?"

"I suppose."

"Okay. I accept your point. But there is still a difference between you and me—the *New York Times* is unaware of your responsibility."

"But I am."

"You are not as influential as the *New York Times*, Darryl."

"I guess you have me there, sir."

"Good, as long as I have you sit down. I feel like talking, and you were unlucky enough to walk in, so you'll have to listen."

"No problem there, Mr. President," Butchko said as he sat in the chair that faced the president.

The president leaned back again. "You know, Darryl, I had always wanted to be president. I had my campaign mapped out ten years before I ran. I gave my nomination acceptance speech hundreds of times in bathroom mirrors long before I gave it at the convention. I had always wanted to be president. And now I am." He smiled. It was the most unabashed smile Butchko had ever seen. "I rather enjoy it. It's the best job I've ever had. The pay's okay. Your housing is included. There's the opportunity for travel. The hours are a little rough, but you get used to it in time. And I'm a bachelor; no one worries what time I get in at night. It's a good job. I'm going to hate to give it up in five years. But I would hate it even more if I lost it a year from now."

"I doubt that will happen, sir. You're one of the most popular presidents the country's had in quite a few years."

"Popularity is fickle, Darryl. This bill has the potential to make me—Christ-like. Or condemn me as Herod."

"All the polls indicate that the country supports the bill."

"What about next year's country?"

"I don't understand."

"There's a reason why they call them the masses, Darryl. They're a mass, a very malleable mass, easily shaped this way, then that."

"Well, sir..."

"And what about history? How will this go down in history?"

"Are you worried about that?"

"Shouldn't I be?"

"No, sir. Quite frankly, I don't think you should. You should be concerned about the problem facing us today, not your historical image.

The president smiled a different smile this time. "You may be right, Darryl. It would certainly save energy."

"I'm sorry. I don't understand."

"Cutting the power off to all the goddamn presidential libraries we have in this country. Darryl, being the president is an absolute given that I will go down in history. The only question is, how? I could wind up as just one more name on a roster of American presidents. Or I could be tagged with lasting fame. Or lasting infamy." The president paused to breathe. A nice, slow breath in. An equally considered breath out. "I would rather be a Christ than a Herod, Darryl. I would rather be considered a savior of mankind than a slaughterer of little children."

"Embryos are hardly little children, sir."

"Some don't look at it that way."

"Then, sir, I suppose you could be a Pilate."

"And wash my hands of it? Neither sign nor veto? No. It is the same as signing in the end. The bill will become law, and I will have shown—weakness. I must make a decision. I must take a stand."

"Have you made your decision?"

The president stared directly at Butchko—and waited one well-timed moment. "I'm going to sign," he said slowly and clearly so that history could hear. "The danger is too great to risk. And anyway, a country in total chaos may care little for history and its particulars."

Butchko stood up and smiled. He kept it slight, subtle, trying not to make it sly, inwardly knowing that the situation was still grave. "You are a savior. It was your only choice."

"No, it wasn't Darryl. There is never only one choice. But this one just happened to be the most workable one."

"Pragmatism, Sir?"

"I suppose."

The president picked up a pen and quickly signed the bill. "Well," he said almost flippantly—how else could it come out?—"No more births for twenty-five years."

"It sounds bad, sir, but in the long run . . ." Butchko said as he started to leave.

"Darryl?"

"Yes, sir?"

The president stretched his arm out and pointed at Butchko with the instrument he had just used. "Would you like the pen?"

5

Wednesday, November 30—London

Ed Handlin rode down in the Hyde Park Hotel's elevator, looking at himself in the mirrored interior, and was happy to see what he saw. What seemed to be a well and comfortably layered, almost typically upper-class English man. He would have liked to have been English. He would have liked to have been typically upper-class English, not unlike other English gentlemen of clubs and Ascot and school ties. He would have enjoyed blending with the tweed. But he was not English. He was an American. Whatever the hell that was.

The elevator stopped, and the doors opened. As Ed moved out, he was greeted by John Gold—the hotel's guest relations man—dressed, as usual, in full tails.

"Good morning, Mr. Handlin."

"Good morning, John."

"Going into breakfast, sir?"

"Yes. We thought we would try The Park."

"Good. I think you'll find the food excellent. Any interesting plans today?"

"No, not really. Going to the theater tonight, though. I'm excited about that."

"Wonderful. What are you going to see?"

"Something at the National Theater."

"The Stoppard revival?"

"Yes, I believe so."

"It's quite good, I believe—an amusing play. I'm sure you'll enjoy yourself. Do you have your tickets?"

"Yes, booked them through here."

"Well, there you are then. Splendid. Do have a good time."

"Yes. I will. Thank you, John."

Ed loved John Gold almost as much as he loved London, for to Ed, John Gold was London or, at least, the Hyde Park Hotel, which was more London than what the slowly stranger city itself was becoming. Tall, thin, bright, boyish, and rarely unavailable, John was a servant to all but subservient to no one. He never failed to convince you that he was indeed happy to serve but, at the same time, was deserving of your extreme respect for this profession of his: To serve. Ed knew very well that the division of classes in England of a century ago and centuries past was never as gentle and genteel as romance would have it. But he couldn't deny that if one were of the upper class benefiting from the service of the lower class, any festering strife between the two would be easy to ignore, even if participated in. There was something about being served, about being treated as if your wishes for welfare were someone else's first thoughts, that made you almost obligated to strive for the superiority to deserve such treatment. But if you're not naturally superior—and who is?—then you're stuck with pretending, a pretense that probably leads to paranoia, a suspicion that the servant knows the truth, tells of it in the kitchen, laughs about it among his fellows, shakes his head, and clucks his tongue as he drinks his ale from an earthy mug; rather than sipping wine from fine French crystal. And you can't stand that, would say, "Can't tolerate that," and would turn harsh in dealing with the servant. It would all eventually turn sour. But you would have the upper hand and could ignore it until society and history forced their changes.

But to be served for a week's stay in London was fine and refreshing, and romance ruled. And John played the part well, and Ed applauded him for that.

"Ed entered The Park restaurant. The maître d' greeted him at the entrance and showed him to a table near the large windows overlooking Rotten Row.

"Have the Household Cavalry gone by yet?" Ed asked.

"Yes, sir. I'm afraid you just missed them."

"Well, maybe tomorrow. I'll have two orders of scrambled eggs, sausage, rolls, and coffee."

"Thank you, sir."

It was a lovely room. The high ceiling and the vast interior gave it a grand proportion that the well-laid tables, the fresh flowers, and the expansive view of Hyde Park through the massive windows could only add to and enhance.

Breakfast and Vivian appeared at the same time.

"Good morning," Vivian said as she sat at the table, grabbing a cloth napkin efficiently and laying it on her lap.

"Good morning," Ed responded.

Vivian took a near gulp of the coffee just poured for her. "Ah! Hot!"

"Watch yourself."

"Pass the rolls.

Rolls, croissants, and buns were lavished on china plates, more than either could eat. But just two or three placed on a plate would not have had the same visual effect and would not have added positively to a room with a high ceiling, tall windows, and more than ample space. Ed understood that. Things must be visually proper. As wasteful as it might seem in an era of shortages, from Ed's point of view, it had the advantage of butter. That is, they were as generous with the distribution of butter as anything else. On every truly fine English table Ed had ever sat at there was always a chilled silver dish containing many large balls of real butter, unlike in America, where you were lucky to get one pat of butter per bun. Only on a table of little care, Ed had always thought, would the butter be allowed to be consumed before the buns.

"These are the only sausages in England I've ever liked," Vivian said. "Any others I've had were putrid. It's not the taste, you know; it's the texture. They're—oh—soft—uh—that's not really what I want to say..."

"Mushy?"

"Yes, that's it. Mushy. And bland. I like tough sausages, I guess."

"Know what you mean."

"Did you get the tickets for tonight?"

"Yep."

"What's on for tomorrow?"

"The Royal Ballet at Sadler's Wells."

"Ed!"

"What?"

"You're pronouncing the R."

"So?"

"For a great Anglophile, you sure mutilate English pronunciation. The English pass over most Rs or, at least, don't make them so hard. Only Americans make their Rs hard."

"Well—I've always felt that if the R is there, you might as well use it."

"And show yourself to be the true *Ugly American.* Learn to say it properly; don't embarrass me."

"Okay, sure. How do you say it?"

"*Sadla's, Sadla's* Wells. Just pass over the R. Or it's there, but very subtle. Just don't go, *Sad-lur's*. Make the R very soft, sort of a, I don't know, sort of an R-ish A."

"An R-ish A?"

"Yes."

"Okay."

"Okay, try it."

"Now?"

"Yes, yes, now. *Sadla's Wells Royal Ballet.*"

"Okay. *Sadla's Wells 'oyal Ballet.*"

Vivian laughed a little snort of a laugh. Ed could make her laugh. That was what she always enjoyed about him.

"Right? Uh? Right? You said drop the R."

"Vivian laughed another little laugh or two and indicated surrender. "Okay, okay. How about a walk?"

They walked through Hyde Park, arm in arm and umbrella at the ready, along the Serpentine, the long club-shaped body of water that hosted ducks, geese, and humans in rented rowboats, weather permitting. Horses riders galloped along Serpentine Road, appearing as antique prints bought off Charring Cross Road might show them, with the green of trees and lawn to back them, traditional riding clothes to adorn them, brown, beautiful steeds under them, their fresh, full English faces sternly enjoying the ride. Ed rarely looked at them; he paid no tourist attention; he just let them pass and add to the general surroundings as if ordered up for that purpose.

A goose on the Serpentine began to follow their walk, never going slower and never going faster, yet seemingly unaware of them.

"He wants us to feed him," Vivian said.

"We should have brought a roll. Sorry guy, nothing today."

But the goose continued to follow until they left the bank of the Serpentine and began to walk on the grounds among the trees.

"Ed, have you enjoyed this?"

"Of course. You know I love London."

"I'm glad."

"A pretty fair honeymoon, I would say." Ed smiled. He was taking some delight in the trappings of being a newlywed. Over the past four days, the wedding ring alone had brought him much satisfying amusement. It was odd how the band and the simple placement of it on that particular finger could hold its symbolic sway over him. He woke up in the mornings anxious to see it as he brought his left hand up to wipe his sleepy face clear, washed his hands with a new intensity, and gestured with his left hand more often, getting it in front of his eyes. This infatuation would pass, he expected, and the ring would eventually become only something to fidget with nervously. But for now...

"Well, honeymoons," Viv said, "come to an end, then plans must be made and implemented. We must make some concrete decisions for our marriage."

"Shouldn't we discuss this with your board of directors first?"

"Ed!"

"Sorry, Viv, but you sometimes talk on a corporate level. Look, what plans should we make? We've had a relationship for twenty years as intimate as marriage. What has changed besides that at one of our parties, we said a few kind words to one another? If you're worried that I will become a demanding husband, you know that's not true. Nor am I in any position to ask you to give up your conglomerate and stay home to fix my meals. We will be seeing each other about as often as we always have. I still must live in Washington, and you seem determined to live in the harsh sun of L.A. What can we possibly plan for except the status quo?"

"If I wanted the status quo, I wouldn't have married you, Ed."

"Well, I don't at all understand what you mean by that."

"Look, there are many legal things, estate, wills."

"What's the matter? You afraid you won't get my government pension?"

"Don't be stupid, Ed! We are married now. That means a difference. Maybe I will move to Washington..."

"Christ!" Ed stopped. "You're going to run for president, aren't you?"

"No, of course not. Maybe I would move to Washington to be near you. Or maybe you should consider quitting government and joining me in L.A."

"Oh no. I have loved and married you but will not work for you."

"We could be partners."

"Viv, I don't understand nor want to understand any of your businesses." Ed started to walk again. "You know, in all the years we've been together, you've never quite gotten it into your head, have never really believed me when I've said that I like doing what I'm doing—for the doing of it. I love working for something greater than myself, Viv. That's the way I am. I'm a 'duty' type person. Had I been religious, I might have been a minister or monk more likely. Had I been a humanitarian, I might have been the power behind some charity. But being neither, nothing's as attractive as government service. You know I'm not motivated by money. I'm not motivated by fame. I'm certainly not motivated by power. I sometimes wish I were. But I'm not, and I can't help it. But I have nothing against people who are—obviously—or I wouldn't have married you."

"You're the only one I know who could say that and not make it sound insulting."

"Well, because it's not an insult, Viv. I have always truly admired your ambitions. I have been attracted to you because of them. You are more beautiful to me because of them. And I have shared them vicariously. But I cannot share them in reality. Look, Viv, I've always got a great kick out of watching your—what?—fight up the ladder, or what-have-you. Your energy, your drive. I've truly relished your success because—because I do love you. But I've never wanted to participate in all that. I certainly don't want to now. Viv, I can't dance, don't ask me."

Vivian stopped walking, stopping Ed. The stare was there. "Can you father?"

"What?"

"I want a child."

"What are you talking about?

"I want a child."

"Viv, I… A child? Viv, the No-Birth Bill..."

"Forget that for the moment."

"How can I forget..."

"Ed, don't argue right now, and listen to me! I have always been ambitious, it's true. I have always wanted to do things, to accomplish things. But it was never for the fame or money or power. It was never for any of those things; those were just fringe benefits. It was for the *ambition* itself. Can you understand that? I have always done things for the simple pleasure of proving that I could do them. I have taken special pleasure in doing things I was told that I couldn't do or wouldn't be able to do. I have always had to prove myself to somebody, to prove myself right and to prove them wrong."

"Them?"

"You know what I'm talking about, Ed. There are a thousand *Thems* out there. You've just ignored them. But I've challenged them. I was frustrated that they never had the same confidence in me that I had in myself. Why? I was obviously intelligent and talented. I obviously had the drive. Why didn't they show simple confidence in me? Because I was a woman? Because I was from the comfortable rich? Because of jealousy over my inherent talents?

"I could never figure it out, but it didn't matter. I just hated them for it. Then I realized one day that their lack of confidence, their jeering and snide comments forced me and gave me the energy to get it all done. I realized that my main motivation was to show those bastards up. Is that petty and mean-spirited? If so, I don't really give a damn because here I am, successful in all I have attempted, right in every course I have ever set out on. And in the process, I have built a—well, what else can I call it? An empire. Like Hughes. Do you realize that, Ed? Like Howard Hughes. But I don't want to end like him. I'm not going to go crazy. I consider myself above normal, not abnormal. That's why it was important to get married. That's why it's important to have a family. I don't want to leave my empire to a bunch of accountants, lawyers, and bankers, people I have always had to prove myself to. I don't want them to get one unearned dime off me. I want a child, boy or girl, to leave it to. Someone of my flesh and blood."

"I don't believe this. You're telling me you want a goddamn heir to the throne."

"Shut up, Ed! You make it sound ridiculous."

"Well, it is, damn it! If you had said you suddenly had this great desire for 'Motherhood,' maybe I could understand..."

I am not your suburban little housewife, Ed! I do not need nor desire Motherhood as a thing in and of itself. Maybe you don't understand me any more than I know you. I want Pavin Industries to stay with a Pavin."

"Well, then you blew it, *Mrs. Handlin!*"

"You know what I mean."

"This is absurd. Our country is about ready to ban births for the next twenty-five years."

"I'm aware of that, Ed. That figures into our planning."

"What do you mean?"

"I've been thinking about this for several years. But No-Birth made it urgent. I met with Harrison, and we decided to go ahead. If the bill fails, we have no problem. If it becomes law, we're in a perfect position to challenge it. Harrison figures we can keep it in court long enough to have the baby. Then it won't much matter what happens. As long as I have my child."

"Wonderful! You want a child, and you go to your lawyer before you talk to me."

"Ed, it's not as cold..."

"And why me? Why don't you just go to a stud farm?"

"Shut up, Ed! Damn it! You! You, because I love you, I always have. I know I'm not always terribly demonstrative about it, but I do love you. I know what people have said about our relationship. But you and I have always known the truth. I wanted you to be the father. I never even considered anyone else."

They started to walk again. Silent. The park faded a bit. The beginnings of rain were ignored. Each step contained volumes of thought.

Finally, Ed said, "You realize that if it becomes law and you go through with this, I will be forced to resign from the State Department. I will be a party to a Federal... Oh. That's why you were asking me to quit."

"It will be better if you do."

"Tell me—this was the whole rationale behind getting married? Was all that other stuff we talked about just for argument's sake? Strange. You've always been so unconventional, yet your child can't be a bastard?"

"Yes, it could have been. I wouldn't care any more than anybody else would. That ought to prove to you that I am sincere."

"Well, it doesn't really matter now. You can't have this one, Viv. I won't go along with it. It's a stupid plan. The motivation behind it is stupid. Your thinking on this one is stupid. This is just another case of wanting to do what you're told you can't. Of proving them wrong. Of being right. But what's at stake? Any test of the law by you might very well kill it. Yet maybe that law is our country's salvation. Are you willing to destroy that? And are you willing to bring to life one human being born for all the wrong reasons? Not for love or joy, but for ego and dynastic considerations? You do have an empire, Viv; that's more than true. But unlike the old days, that does not set you above simple moral considerations. If you want a child, find another buck. But if you're sincere in wanting only me as the father, you better forget your plan."

They stopped at the statue of Achilles.

"It's too late—I'm already pregnant."

The rain was heavier now. Ed handed the closed umbrella to Vivian and walked off alone.

***

Ed crossed the Carriage Road and entered the Hyde Park underground station. He bought a ticket, descended on the wide STAND-TO-THE-RIGHT escalator, and then went through a tunnel with turns to the platform.

PICCADILLY LINE NORTH

People were standing, waiting, smoking, reading. Ed could only read the large and uniformed curved billboards on the tunnel wall across the tracks. He stared at one for Oxtail soup. He had never eaten Oxtail soup. As much as he loved things British, he figured he never would.

There was a wind. It raced past those waiting, disturbing hair and clothes, perpetually ahead of the train. Out of the dark, close, curved walls into the lighted open tunnel, the train followed and stopped and opened its many doors in unison. People flowed out, people flowed in, grabbed seats, grabbed handholds. The doors closed, and the train moved forward progressively faster, evidenced by the illusioned flip of the curved billboards until the tunnel became a black tube fitted for comfort.

The next stop, GREEN PARK, some out, some in.

The next stop, PICCADILLY, Ed was out, up the wide escalator, and onto the street. It was still raining as Ed began to walk up Shaftesbury Avenue. Open umbrellas were everywhere, moving and darting within and among, through and by each other. Some people crowded the entranceways of stores, waiting for the rain to stop. With rain washing his hair down, Ed continued until a familiar corner, then turned. Two known blocks down, then another turn, and he entered one of the adult entertainment-oriented streets of Soho. He headed for a building proclaiming a PEEP SHOW, a HOLLYWOOD PEEP SHOW, reached it, and entered.

The girl at the change box, who sometimes danced, gave him pound coins for his twenty-pound bill. Two rows of connected private booths were cornered to form an L. Ed picked one and entered, locking the door behind him. At eye level was a window—covered on the other side—rectangle in shape, a foot and a half by maybe a foot, the length running side to side. Ed found the coin slot and put in a pound. The wood flap covering the window on the other side mechanically flipped up. A curtained, narrow area was revealed four to five feet from the booths. Inside, a nude woman danced to the sound of the latest popular music. Noticing Ed's booth now occupied, she moved towards it, to it, up close. She put her hands on the raised flap and gyrated slowly, letting Ed see all. One hand went down to her right breast. She cupped it, stroked it, pinched her nipple. Down further, she gently grazed her pubic area, all the time her hips moving to the beat of the music, music Ed hated; music descended and decayed from rock & roll, rock, disco, all music of one uncomplicated note, but music now—and for Ed, only now—appropriate to the occasion—basic music for basic feelings. The woman backed away, back for all to see.

The flap came down with a bang.

Ed put in another pound coin.

The flap opened again.

The woman was on the floor now, spreading her legs, affording a proper view, feeling where the rest would have felt, given the chance.

She was not ugly. Nor sleazy. Nor fat. Nor did she have pimples on her bottom, nor arms too hairy. She was, in fact, beautiful. Her figure was perfect, her breasts of an attractive full and firm size, her skin smooth and soft appearing. Her hair was nicely cut, and her well-featured face took well the sensual looks she provided.

Another flap opened. She got up and headed towards it but remained in Ed's view.

She was attractive. Ed was unattractive. Not in the physical sense—Ed was more handsome than most—but for some other reason that Ed had never been able to comprehend. He simply did not attract women. No woman that he knew of had ever looked upon him with lust in her heart, only a generalized liking and acceptance that Ed was a nice guy. That's how he felt; that's what experience pointed out to him. Vivian did not count. He knew the reality of his relationship with Vivian; he was not stupid. What sex there had been between them in the last twenty years had been handed out by Vivian almost in gratitude for services rendered or maybe for periodic proof of her constant, calm argument that Ed was, indeed, an attractive man. She even encouraged him to have other women. Misplaced energy, Ed always thought—she should have encouraged the women. But he tried and failed. He had made many great female friends in twenty years but never one lover outside Vivian.

It was simple; he finally concluded after years of manhood worries. He simply did not attract women. He did not send out the right signals, he did not have musk, he did not reek of masculinity, he did not know, and couldn't seem to learn, the mating call. He was unattractive. But being unattractive did not stop him from being attracted; it did not stop his needs, wants, and desires, maybe put there by nature, maybe put there by society. So he knew the London peep shows, he knew the Los Angeles adult bookstores with their booths and loops of videotape, and he knew that every city had its "area" where he could go, where many went, where those who lacked the power to stimulate could themselves be stimulated, for they still needed that, no matter what, and they would get it where and how they could.

But was he now being stimulated? Was his body reacting? Was his mind forming fantasies, those little cathartic, erotic playlets that had kept him sane? No. The attractive woman was only a naked person, a human unclothed, zooed for the moment in his mind, not much more interesting than any other species on display. He tried to help; he unzipped his pants and played with himself, but it remained flaccid, almost foreign to the touch.

Damn! he thought. *Goddamnitshit!* He had thought things had truly changed between him and Vivian, that it was finally over, this being unattractive to everyone. He had thought, maybe, their strange, subtle love-like relationship had heightened, had reached a normal and known level. He had thought, maybe now, that Vivian was truly beginning to desire him, that perhaps she always had, but her uniqueness and ambition had put it aside to allow her accomplishments. But now, accomplished, settled, she was giving herself the luxury of feelings, and her feelings went out to Ed. Why else had the relationship lasted? Why else had she always kept him around? Why else did she now want to be married? If this were true, if it just could be true, he would no longer have to worry about all the others—or the lack of them. He wouldn't have to care; he wouldn't have to be concerned. He had his; she was on his arm. *See! Look!* That was the answer, maybe, the reason for "true" love. It was easier, simpler, calmer, and more comfortable to settle for one true one and not be concerned about a legion loyal to your male secretions. But the point was the accuracy of "true." A course could not be retained without it.

The flap came down. Ed contemplated one more pound but knew it was no good. He re-zipped, unlocked the booth, and walked past the change girl and out onto the wet street.

The rain had stopped. People were moving about again without their protective domes.

"Hey, mister!" Two young boys were addressing him. "How is it?"

Ed looked at them, saw their sly smiles, saw them ready to elbow one another, saw their near future of private, excited talks in one or the other's bedroom, away from the parents, away from those who punish.

"Depends," Ed confronted them. "On whether you like that sort of thing or not."

Back to PICCADILLY STATION, onto a train, this time to KNIGHTSBRIDGE STATION, a bit closer to the hotel entrance. Up the stairs to the street itself—Knightsbridge—so named, so it is told because once two knights fought till blood ran over who would cross first. Into the hotel, up some stairs to the main foyer.

"Good afternoon, Mr. Handlin," John Gold greeted him. "Did you have a nice walk? Bit wet, though. I hope you didn't get too soggy. Have you seen the Telegraph yet? I had one sent to your room—some American interest in it. Your No-Birth thing seems to have been signed by your president."

6

Tuesday, December 6—Washington D.C.

The reporters waited with slight movements: A few steps to a colleague, a handshake, an adjustment of glasses with the hand that held the pen. Most were familiar to each other; some were familiar to the nation. Some gossiped, some prepared questions, some told the latest joke. Some—mainly the newer ones, still fresh to the occasion—watched the doorway for the first sign that the president was coming.

Technicians were adjusting lights, microphones, video cameras.

Photographers were double-checking the settings of their cameras.

Pundits were waiting somewhere else for all these recording instruments to rewind and regurgitate.

Sudden activity in the doorway. The president came through, various suited personnel in his wake. He reached and ascended the podium.

"Good afternoon. I have some statements and an introduction to make. Then we'll have questions.

"As you know, I signed the Birth Cessation Act into law last week. It provides for a cessation of all births in this country for the next twenty-five years. The signing of this act into law was not an easy decision. Even after the Senate and House, after months of careful consideration, had both, in their collective wisdom, given their overwhelming approval to birth cessation, it was an action on my part that came only after much soul searching. Ultimately, I decided to sign the act for one fundamental reason: The retention of the American Dream. For far too long, we have ineffectually cried that that dream is dead. But such a dream—a dream that created the greatest country in the world and gave to that country the most incredible ideas and ideals with which to manage it—such a dream does not die. But the dreamers sometimes become disheartened, discouraged, and disappointed when that dream buckles under the tremendous weight it is, at times, burdened with.

"The great mass of population that this country has had to support for too many decades now, the administrative complexity of governing that population, and, most importantly, the thinning of resources available to that population, has been the most significant weight the American Dream has ever had to bear, the most substantial pressure it has had to endure.

"Birth Cessation has been designed to lift that weight, to relieve that pressure.

"Ten years ago, we suspended all immigration; we closed all our borders to relieve the pressure. As you well know, it had some effect, not always to the good. Its worst effect, for me, was always the feeling that we were being unfaithful to our forefathers, that we were being untrue to our original purpose for being, that great goal that brought America into existence: To be home and haven for all freedom-loving individuals. When I came into office, by executive order, I allowed controlled immigration to return, and we regained pride in our purpose. But the pressure was still there. With this new law, we believe we have found a way to relieve that pressure without compromising our principles. A way, in fact, that reaffirms our principles.

"What's the best analogy for this action? I think it is the peach tree. When the peach tree's branches are full and green and overflowing with new life in the Spring, it is pruned. Some of its branches are cut back; some are cut off. What is left looks like a bare and ravaged tree. But come the fall, those branches left will support a fuller and sweeter fruit than an unpruned tree could have hoped to have achieved, even if it had been watered and fertilized with the most excellent care, for it is only the branches, never the *roots* of a tree that are pruned. The roots provide sustenance no matter how many branches there are on the tree or how many peaches are on those branches. But the fewer the branches, the fewer the peaches, the greater the share of sustenance each receives, and the fuller and sweeter they are for it.

"It is the same now with our nation. We are pruning a few branches. But our roots—Democracy and the American Dream—the roots that provide our sustenance, remain untouched. And we will eventually all be the fuller and the sweeter for it.

"Now, under the Birth Cessation Law, an agency of the government is to be formed to implement its provisions, and a director is to be appointed by the president to oversee that agency. I want to announce and introduce the individual whose name I will submit to Congress for confirmation as the first director of the Birth Cessation

Agency, Mr. Darryl Butchko. As you know, Darryl Butchko has been my Special Assistant for Domestic Affairs since the beginning of my administration, and he has served not only ably but brilliantly in that capacity. So brilliantly, he has, at times, been rated—by those who feel the need to rate—higher than me as far as a job well done is concerned..."

Some laughter. Finally. One always waits for the customary levity.

"... but he does deserve such a rating. Before my administration, Darryl Butchko was a political science and social behavior professor at the University of California at Los Angeles. While there, he wrote numerous articles and books on contemporary American problems, whose brilliance is so enviable that one feels compelled to plagiarize them. I resisted the temptation to steal his ideas by hiring his head—so to speak."

A little more laughter.

"Darryl Butchko understands America's problems as well as any man living today. He is the perfect candidate for this post and will fulfill his duties with competence and compassion. I want to introduce him now and have him make a statement. Darryl?"

The president stepped down, and Butchko stepped up, shaking hands while passing.

"Thank you, Mr. President. I would like, at this time, to outline the basic provisions of the Birth Cessation Law, which I, if I am confirmed as director of the agency, will be responsible for. First, all births in this country will cease for a period of twenty-five years. To achieve this, all males over puberty will be required to undergo a simple vasectomy at one of the special clinics that will be set up across the nation. The cost of the vasectomy will be minimal. The technique to be used is the new König technique that will allow for a resumption of reproductive capacity in those males so wishing after the end of the twenty-five-year cessation period. In other words, a vasectomized male of fifteen today will be able to impregnate at the age of forty after another simple operation.

"A second provision of the act dictates that all females whose pregnancies are currently no farther along than twenty-four weeks will be required to have that pregnancy aborted, also at special clinics and a minimal cost.

"These two programs will go into effect almost immediately, with notices already in the mail.

"For the next twenty-five years, any woman who happens to become pregnant through accident or subterfuge will be required to have that pregnancy aborted if, when discovered, she has not yet reached twenty-four weeks. If her pregnancy has carried on past twenty-four weeks, it will be allowed to come to term, but the resultant child will be forfeited by the mother and placed into a foster home at parental expense. There will also be a possibility of five years imprisonment and/or a $50,000 fine for both the mother and the father of record if there is one.

"At the end of the twenty-five-year cessation period, providing our goals for population reduction have been reached, the cessation of births will end, and regular reproductive activity will resume.

"I think that covers it. Mr. President?"

President Henshaw came back to the podium. "Are there any questions?"

"Mr. President!"/"Mr. President!"/"Mr. President!"

The President to the White House Correspondent from NBC News. "Bill."

"Mr. President, how soon will these clinics be open?"

The president turned to Butchko, "Darryl? And I think most of your questions should be directed to Darryl."

Butchko returned to the podium. "The clinics will open next week. Information will appear in local newspapers, television networks, and all the news services."

"Mr. Butchko, how will you enforce the provisions that all males have the vasectomy?"

"We don't anticipate there will be much enforcement involved. We will call forth people based on social security numbers and school records. We are assuming that people will come forth on their own accord. After a while, though, certain records will be checked to see if anybody needs reminding that they have not yet had their vasectomy."

"Mr. Butchko, what is the need for the twenty-four-week and under abortions?"

"We wish to start reducing the population as soon as possible. The situation is that critical."

"Mr. Butchko, why are there stiff sanctions against future birth? Surely, if all males have the vasectomy, there will be no future births."

"We do not rule out the possibility that we will miss some people or that others, in defiance of the law, will seek out preserved and stored sperm for artificial insemination."

"You expect some defiance then?"

"No, not really. But the Congress felt it prudent to prepare for any no matter how little."

"But if there are only a few pregnancies, why not let them all come to term and let the parents keep them?"

"A law without sanctions is no law at all."

"What about the moral issue, Mr. Butchko? For some in this country, abortion is still a mortal sin."

"Have you read the Constitution lately? We have a separation of Church and State in this country. Moral issues are the domains of religions, not civil law."

"But civil law allows for conscientious objectors in times of war. How about in this case?"

"According to the recent draft reinstatement law, the conscientious are allowed to object but are still required to serve. It will be the same here. If any pregnant woman conscientiously objects to an abortion, she will not be required to have one, but she will also not be allowed to keep the child."

"Why not?"

"Again, it would rather defeat the purpose of the law, wouldn't it?"

The president took the mic. "I think most of this is hypothetical. All indications are that the people of this country realize the importance of this great national effort. We expect nothing but cooperation from the citizens of this country."

"Thank you, Mr. President."

***

New York

Malcolm Kirkly stared at the enemy. His VHS machine was on *pause,* and the image of Darryl Butchko that it had caught and carved through an electronic and digital process still unfathomable to Kirkly was appropriate. Butchko's teeth were bared. His mouth was open, lips back, teeth prepared to penetrate. The awful animal descent of man came to Kirkly in full force. Sad, he thought, that the mud still clings to our feet.

He had not known that Butchko was the enemy—the *particular* enemy—until an hour after that morning's news conference, which he was now reviewing. Jack Cuthbert had called. Johnathan E. Cuthbert, it said on the masthead of *The Washington Wash*, Publisher-Editor.

"Malcolm, how are you?"

"I'm fine, Jack. What do you want?"

"Same thing I've always wanted. How would you like to do an article for next week's *Wash*?"

"Same answer, I'm afraid Jack. I don't do dirty laundry."

"Yes, I know Malcolm. You're the political, social, and aesthetics philosopher of our age and wish not to sully your good name with an association with my little blow for the public's right to know."

"Jack, you have just managed to flatter both you and me in one breath and, in both cases, through abominable, if attractive, falsehoods. I am not a philosopher; I am a mere journalist who takes pride in his work. And the only active blow you've ever made is for your private right to profits."

"Free enterprise, Malcolm. You have supported it in print yourself."

"I have also supported truth in advertising. Now, may I know what you really called about?"

"I'm serious, Malcolm. I've got an article for you to do, and once you learn the facts—and I do mean facts, Malcolm—I think you'll want to do it."

Okay, Jack. Make your pitch."

"It concerns this morning's TV star."

"Henshaw?"

"No. Butchko. Your opposition to No-Birth is well known, if ineffective. Well, I've got some info on Butchko that puts a whole new light on it. It's enough to make you effective if you use it right."

"It's the law now, Jack. The effectiveness would be a bit late."

"Laws are overturned daily, Malcolm."

Of course, Kirkly thought, a fundamental in the American system. Simple. He hated that Cuthbert could so quickly bring it up, and he could so easily forget it in the slight depression of defeat.

"Okay, let's have it."

"Not over the phone. I'll take the next shuttle to New York. I'm only going to give you the bare facts. You must agree to write the article if you want the material to substantiate them."

"Let's hear the facts first."

"Okay. Hold tight, I'll be there soon."

The phone went dead.

Kirkly did not like it. *The Washington Wash* was a rag, a gossip-laded, yellow-colored rag, which was low enough to find pride in its work as evidenced by its name and its masthead motto—It All Comes Out In The Wash. It was the well-to-do bastard child of all those supermarket tabloids that attracted the attention of plump housewives and pimply-faced teenage girls with stories of screen stars, astrological stars, and the star diet of the week. All Cuthbert did was treat the politicians of Washington like the stars of Hollywood. It was not an original concept; a strange glamour had come to Washington years ago, and there had always been those willing to gossip about it. Cuthbert just had the industry to make such gossip very profitable for himself through a product cheap enough to throw out with the rest of the garbage after what little nourishment it had was assimilated.

But Kirkly was quite aware of his failing (if it was a failing) of rarely listening to those he looked down on. Occasionally, he should listen to them, he had once reasoned. If for no other reason than to substantiate through experience his intuitive feeling that he should never listen to them. He might as well make this one of those occasions.

Had he not known what Cuthbert did, Kirkly would not have taken the time to find fault with him. On the surface, Cuthbert was reasonably acceptable. Having money, he used it well to make it plain that he had money. The house was the right size in the right neighborhood and rightly decorated to be magazine-perfect. The wife looked correct. The clothes were chosen and worn well. And Cuthbert's nighttime pleasures placed him among others with houses and wives and clothes that seemed similarly suited. He went to the Kennedy Center—a lot. His cultural trips to New York were frequent. He was a benefactor of symphony orchestras and important museums. But Kirkly had always felt that Cuthbert's appreciation of the arts was more an appreciation of the advantages of an appreciation. Kirkly did not doubt that Cuthbert was well amused by this play or that ballet; he just doubted if Cuthbert had any idea why he was amused, leaving only the appreciation of advantages as the matrix behind it all. Or, maybe it was more to the point—yes, perhaps this was it—that once you achieve enviable professional and financial success, despite the particulars of that success, to have such things, to behave this way, to attend these types of cultural activities, were just the things that such people did. Maybe it was as simple as that.

It was like a Hollywood television producer Kirkly had once met. He was a charming and cultured man, well-read, well-moneyed. "Civilized" was the word that applied. Yet he had achieved his life (he had been born poor of ignorant parents) by creating calculatingly conceived, cliché-ridden, pat and simple-minded, mass-directed formula entertainment. He was a patrician who rode about in luxury on the backs of plebeians seeking simple amusements.

Strange, thought Kirkly.

Or maybe not.

***

Cuthbert arrived in the late afternoon.

"Do you know much about Butchko?" Cuthbert asked.

"Only what I've read in the news magazines, papers, what mutual acquaintances have told me. I've read some of his writings. He seems able, competent, and maybe as brilliant as they say. A good choice for a presidential advisor."

"Do you think he'll make a good director of the Birth Cessation Agency?"

"Well, nothing about that agency, in my mind, is any good. But will he make a good administrator? I assume so."

"I think he will be able to handle the job *very* well. But then he understands the Birth Cessation Law. I mean, *truly* understands the particulars of it."

"Okay. Why?"

Cuthbert smiled. "Because he wrote it. Every word, every word that supposedly came from Anderson's fertile little mind."

Are you saying he's the actual author of the law?"

"Everything. The whole idea, the entire concept, was his. And now he's the director of the agency. *Very* interesting, don't you think?

Kirkly thought for a minute, trying to decide if, indeed, it was very interesting. "What proof do you have?"

"I got one of my researchers to start dating his secretary."

"Why?"

"What?"

"Why did you get one of your researchers to start dating his secretary?"

"Are you kidding? Butchko is an advisor to the president."

Did your 'researcher' like this woman?"

"Yeah, luckily, she's quite nice. I mean, *very* nice."

"Okay. What else?"

"She doesn't like Butchko much. I guess his manner leaves her cold. I also think she made a play for him and got rebuffed. Anyway—once she got comfortable with my researcher, she started running Butchko down and venting her frustration about working for him. During one of these bitch sessions, she gave up the secret that Butchko had written the bill. My researcher asked her to prove it, and she returned the next day with a file of evidence, including the first handwritten draft of the bill—in Butchko's hand. Plus floppy disks with computer files with all the drafts she did for him."

"Do you think he drafted the bill at Henshaw's behest?"

"No. I think it's Butchko's alone."

"Why? To get a new job? Probably at less pay."

"No, of course, that's not logical. But my readers may think it is."

"Maybe he truly believes in the concept of No-Birth and just went about the business of government?"

"Why did he keep his authorship a secret then?"

"Was it a secret?"

"Come on, Malcolm, you know it was always presented as *Anderson's* bill."

"Maybe he just thought it wasn't proper for him to be doing it. I mean, if Henshaw was not behind it."

"But that's part of the point, isn't it? It wasn't proper. It was Butchko playing secret god, or at least secret president."

"It sounds bad, but..."

"There's another thing to consider. Possibly the real thing. Butchko had a child once—a little girl. Several years ago, his wife and his girl were in a car accident. The girl died. The wife was badly injured—and came out of it having to have a hysterectomy. She's now sterile, of course."

"Look, I see what you're getting at, and it's nothing but cheap psychology, you know."

"Cheap psychology sells damn well in *The Wash.* Plus, cheap psychology is not necessarily wrong psychology. Can't you see it? The loss of a child, his wife becoming sterile. Then, suddenly, he's placed in a position of power and uses that power to force his personal tragedy on the whole country. Share my grief; share my tragedy. If I can't have children, then nobody should!"

"That's an almost unbelievably childish point of view."

"Hey, Washington is crawling with kids."

Kirkly got up, walked around, sat down.

"Okay. Maybe you've got something. Write the story. Why do you need me?"

Don't be so damned childish yourself. I can improve my profile and ad rates with this story. I can up them even more if it carries the 'Argus' byline."

"Then you would have to pay me a substantial amount."

"No problem."

No, I'm sure it isn't. But I still don't want to write for *The Wash,* Jack. I think it is a pile of shit, Jack. I hate it. I even hate your typeface. I don't wish my name to be associated with it."

Now Cuthbert got up. "Can I fix myself a drink?"

"Help yourself. Sorry, I didn't offer."

"No, that's okay. I don't expect courtesies from you."

Vodka. Tonic. Ice. A sip. "You know Malcolm, I used to be a snob like you. My mother hated it. So, of course, I was always twice the snob around her. Didn't faze her. She would say, 'Come down off your high horse, young man.' So, come down off your high horse, Malcolm. My 'pile of shit' has gotten rid of three very incompetent congressmen, it stopped Baldwin from becoming a serious presidential candidate last time, and it has forced some substantial cutting of waste in Washington. So we gossip a little. So we sing and dance for our readers. That's the sizzle. But we do have steak now and then. This Butchko thing is steak. Look, you do hate No-Birth, don't you?"

"It is the most disastrous mistake this country has ever made since the Civil War. I can't begin to imagine the consequences. It is immoral, eventually demoralizing, and—well, wrong."

"So, we show it up as one man's attempt to equalize all to his predicament, as a law born from the mind of a disturbed individual. We taint the law, make it suspect; then maybe we can defeat it. Maybe *you* can set things right."

It was an opportunity. It was as simple as that. Kirkly did not like the circumstances or the tone of this opportunity; it certainly did not meet his high standards of debate. But as he looked into the face of Cuthbert, the ultimate image of pragmatic reasoning, he was suddenly struck with the lightheaded thrill any co-conspirator must feel. Yes! We have found the weakness in the enemy's defenses. Strike! Strike now! Strike hard!

"Yes, fine, go ahead and do it. But *I* don't want to do it for *you*. But reveal all the facts. Play it for all it's worth, and I'll commend you in my column, I'll call you a great man, I'll praise the piece, I'll call you the most courageous gadfly of our era, I'll even give your typeface a good notice. But I don't want to do it."

"Then it won't get done."

"What?"

"You write it, or I sit on it. You do it, or nobody does it."

"You must be joking? You can still increase your ad rates without me."

"What the hell do I need to sell more ads for?"

"You're kidding? You would do this?"

"Yes. I want you to write for *The Wash*."

"You cannot withhold this story. It is too important."

"Then write it!"

"I..."

"You're the one that sees it as a duty, not me. I don't give a damn. What the hell? I've already got two kids. I don't want more. So, no more screaming, bratty, shity-pants kids for twenty-five years. Wonderful! A little national peace and quiet.

"You're quite the bastard, Jack, aren't you?"

"Yes, well, I'll take that up with my maker when I die."

"Don't be so flippant."

"Damn it, Malcolm! I know you; you have no choice. Now say yes, and I'll give you the documents. Your deadline is in two days. I'll send a courier up to get it."

Cuthbert pulled a file out of his briefcase. "And if you dare use this in your column first—I'll destroy you."

Kirkly stood up. He took the file from Cuthbert. "I want a hundred thousand dollars to write this."

"You've got it."

"And I'm going to take every dollar of it and donate it in your name to some charity for shity pants brats."

"Malcolm, that's kind of you. I would be honored."

7

Friday, December 9—Los Angeles.

The silver and white piece of wrapping paper lay crumpled under an antique table by the front door in the foyer of Vivian Pavin Handlin's house. It had been on the foyer floor since the wedding, now almost two weeks. It was the only bit of trash the staff had missed during the cleanup after that rather hectic yet exciting wedding.

Ed and Vivian opened only a few ceremonial gifts that day while photographers blocked most guests' views. Why gifts at all? Ed had wondered. They were hardly a couple starting out; they wanted for nothing. But Vivian had decided that it was a tradition she liked. The guests were requested to go for the unique, and they mainly came through. Now, the staff had an odd assortment of things to find places for.

A week ago, the paper had been in the open, in the middle of the foyer, not under the table at all. A resident there for a week, it had not moved during Ed and Vivian's absence and the staff's surprise vacation. In the middle of the floor, while tiny particles of dust fell on it, it had stayed as immobile as all around it except for the hands and pendulum of the foyer clock.

Yet it had had an active existence before that, having been manufactured from wood pulp, having had birds and bells in silver and white printed on it, having been rolled onto a tube of cardboard, shipped to this warehouse, then to that, then, finally, to some more than expensive little shop on Rodeo Drive in Beverly Hills where it was rolled off the tube, cut to size, creased to hold and formed around a box. A ride in a Mercedes, a ride in a Rolls, placement on a table, separation from the whole piece, crumpling, trashing, escaping due to an accident of gravity, landing and resting on the foyer floor.

Stillness.

For a week.

Accompanied by all the other stillness—save for the swinging of the pendulum in the clock and the measured movement of its hands.

Until…

The door opened swiftly, and Vivian entered with force. The air, disturbed, pushed towards the piece of paper, reaching it, lifting it slightly, moving it along a path to a point just by the table. Ed followed, walking in and by the table, brushing the paper under it with an unintentional kick from his right foot. He noticed it; he heard the little pop of a sound, the slight scrape of the paper across the floor. He looked down quickly and saw the paper. But he didn't feel like bending over to pick it up.

"I'm going upstairs to rest," Vivian said.

"Fine," Ed answered as he entered the den to fix himself a drink.

They were just back from London, from a honeymoon over.

After his drink, Ed went upstairs to Vivian's room. She was sitting on her bed, nude, legs crossed, reading some mail that had been left for her. He stood in the doorway, not yet noticed, noticing the scene. He looked at Vivian nude and thought of the peep show girl naked. Vivian was concentrating, and her face was set; it was stern. Her eyes moved slightly back and forth as she read the letter. The peep show girl had moved her eyes up and down—up to the customer, up to make contact through the glass, down demurely, down to see, down to indicate, to lead to certain pleasures. She had held her breasts, cupped them, massaged them, and raised the nipples through manipulation. Annoyed by an itch, Vivian scratched her left breast as she continued to read.

Why, as an early teen, had he thought he would die if he did not see a real live naked girl? A natural urging that leads to offspring? An unnatural urging that leads to peep shows?

***

The piece of wrapping paper was still there, Ed noticed. Even a week after he had accidentally kicked it under the table. He bent down and picked it up. *Oh, from the wedding.* He held it and balled it up as he went upstairs to Vivian's room.

Like the week before, Vivian did not notice him in the doorway.

She was stuffing a pillow up her dress. She rounded it out, formed it with her hands, and domed it over her stomach. She stood in front of a floor-length mirror, looking at herself from all sides, turning to the left, to the right, straight on. She studied herself.

It charmed Ed. It was such a young woman's thing to do—trying to visualize your pregnant self. Maybe No-birth was, at the very least, a shame, if not a sin, if it could take away such a simple pleasure.

"Well," Ed said, only slightly startling Vivian. "Maybe you do desire motherhood."

"Don't be stupid," Vivian said as she pulled the pillow out. "I'm working on designs for my maternity clothes. It could be a new Pavin line."

"Oh."

"Did you talk to Harrison?"

"Yes."

"Well?"

"He said to be the loving husband and proud expectant father standing at your side, with my arm around you in support, would be an 'important media image factor' in your case."

"Which is what I've been saying."

'But not in such lovely language."

Ed walked over to the bed and picked up the pillow, the designer dummy, and the dress (fetus) form.

"You know," Ed said, placing the pillow back down. "I truly understand what this is all about now."

"Good."

"No, not good. I don't understand to your advantage."

"What do you mean?"

"I mean, at first, I couldn't understand; why me? Why didn't you use artificial insemination or hire some Adonis to impregnate you? I have always been too grateful for our relationship to question it, afraid that trying to bring logic to the dream would destroy it. But I always knew, without admitting it, that it was some strange dream that just happened to suit you, so you continued with it. Then, you proposed. Remember? Remember the concert, the dinner, and then drinks before the fireplace. All that romantic stuff you're usually too impatient for? Then you proposed. 'Look,' you said. 'Why the hell don't we just get married?' As if it was the logical next step to take after a twenty-year courtship. 'Let's merge,' you could have said, and I would have understood better. The tone in your voice wouldn't have been any different. But I thought, Well, it is logical, but not quite in her usual way. Usually, she would acquire instead of merge. But her request is for a merger. Maybe, just maybe, she has finally succumbed to my charms. Maybe after twenty years, I have finally swept her off her feet. You almost had me convinced when you started making wedding plans so enthusiastically. I hadn't seen you that excited since you designed that damn gun.

"But I see it all now. Harrison made it clear. It was all just preparation for the big campaign. You couldn't just be Vivian Pavin pregnant, civilly disobeying the law, and winning your case through the efforts of high-priced lawyers. For that would just be the triumph of the rich, like being a billionaire and never paying taxes. That would be no good as far as the 'media image factor' was concerned. The common person couldn't relate to that. Of course, *you're* allowed to have *your* baby. You're *Vivian Pavin.* You would never have made college students' dorm rooms as a poster that way. But Vivian Handlin, wife. Vivian Handlin, expectant mother. Vivian and Ed Handlin and baby Handlin to be, symbolizing the American Family under siege, that would ring well in the ears of the grassroots, wouldn't it?"

"Ed, you're angry about realities that can't be changed. Your reading of Harrison is correct. But all it means is that we carefully considered this move. We felt it was important enough to do it with as little risk of loss as possible. Do you want to see No-Birth ruin this country?"

"I thought No-Birth was here to save this country."

"That's what they would like you to believe. And maybe they believe it. But to me, any democracy that sanctions the robbing of the basic freedom of human reproducibility is a democracy on the first step towards totalitarianism."

"Wonderful! Is that a quote from your first speech?"

"Stop being so goddamned sarcastic! Look, you decide. Do what you want. I've tried to explain it to you. Harrison has tried to explain it to you. If you're not convinced, then go your own way. But we do need you. *I* need you. And—and I do love you, Ed. I always have. Marriage is just a piece of paper. If I had married you for all the 'right' reasons, would that have proved my love for you any more than our twenty years together? Love isn't proved by what you vow but by how you act. If I didn't love you, you would have known it long before now."

"But why the deception? Why do all this without telling me?"

"You said it yourself, Ed. You don't understand or want to understand any of my business."

"This is not business, Viv; this is our personal life!"

"No! This is business! The last twenty years was our personal life. But this is business. The business of trying to effect a change, of saving this country. It is the most important business we will ever do and will be brutally public. So decide now, Ed."

It was quiet for a moment. Ed stared at Vivian, who was beginning to undress. Other clothes, something for the evening, were on the bed.

"You are going out, Viv?"

"Dinner meeting."

She was nude. "When are you going back to Washington?" she asked.

"Next week."

"Are you going to resign?"

Ed still had the balled-up wrapping paper in his hand. He unfolded it and smoothed it out. There was half of a bird, the top of a bell visible. "Do you love me?"

Vivian grabbed the evening dress. "Yes, Ed, I love you."

"Put the dress down then."

"Ed, I've got to get dressed."

"Do you love me?"

"Ed…"

"Love me!"

"Ed, I'm going to be late!"

"Fuck me!"

"Ed!"

"Now Viv! Like a good little wife, resign yourself to your fate and share our conjugal bed."

He stood there, wrapping paper in his hand, standing as straight as he ever had. Vivian stood straight, nude, with the dress in her hand. Only her eyes moved, quickly darting to the clock, gathering information to calculate the time remaining and how it could successfully be divided. That done, she laid the dress smoothly over the chair of her dressing table, grabbing a look at her image on a box of one of her own Pavin perfumes. It was a seductive, wind-blown, revealing look. She took it deep within her, re-lived the flash of the photographer's strobe, turned around, and walked to Ed, coming close enough to allow her nipples to graze his shirt. She took the wrapping from his hand and balled it into her own. It made the only sound in the room as she kissed Ed. Her other hand raised and started to unbutton his shirt. She probed Ed's mouth with her tongue and made little sounds in her throat. She crushed her breasts into his chest.

And she took the balled-up wrapping paper and massaged it around and around Ed's crotch.

***

Over-the-air

"This is the NBC Nightly News. Tonight's anchor: Eric Stearns."

"Good evening. NBC News has learned that next Monday's edition of *The Washington Wash* will carry an article that may be the first serious blow against the government's Birth Cessation program. Here with the story is Jane Woods in Washington."

The face of Eric Sterns was electronically replaced by the face of Jane Woods, backgrounded by a view of the bold logo of *The Washing Wash* bolted onto the side of an office building.—

"These are the offices of *The Washington Wash*, a news tabloid self-proclaimed to be more interested in gossip than government. Its brand of muckraking has set off several controversies in the past, and this Monday's issue is bound to continue that tradition. The difference is that for the first time, *The Wash* will carry an article with the byline of a respected writer, Malcolm Kirkly, better known as Argus.

"The article concerns the government's new Birth Cessation program. The 'gossip' to be revealed is that the true architect of the program is not Senator Robert Anderson of California, who sponsored the bill and—it had been assumed—authored the legislation that instituted the program. Instead, the author is presidential advisor Darryl Butchko, who Congress has just confirmed as the first director of the Birth Cessation Agency.

"Johnathan E. Cuthbert, publisher and editor of *The Wash*, claims that complete documentation will be provided in the article. But one point that there can be no documentation on is the clear implication in the report that Birth Cessation is nothing more than a psychological revenge for a personal tragedy, namely the death of Butchko's three-year-old daughter five years ago in an auto accident and the infertility of his wife due to injuries resulting from that same accident. Cuthbert is willing to admit that this point is pure conjecture, but conjecture, he says, based on the known facts. It can also be assumed that the Argus byline is expected to give the charge some validation.

"So far, the White House has not commented on the matter, preferring to wait until the article is published and they have had time to study it.

"Jane Woods, NBC News, Washington."—

Eric returned with his practiced, serious demeanor.

"In related news, today was the first day of mandatory abortions under the Birth Cessation Act. As provided in the act, all women twenty-four weeks pregnant or less must report for an abortion at a designated clinic. For a report on this first day of state-ordered abortions, we go to Tom Kline in New York at one such clinic."—

Over a view of a line of women on a New York sidewalk, Tom Walker narrated, "Women started lining up at this clinic on 54th Street in Manhattan just after eight o'clock this morning. There has been a slow but steady stream of them ever since. Some came alone. Husbands or family members accompany others. One woman in the line had three of her six children with her—

—"How do you feel about having to come down here this morning for an abortion?"

"Fine. Just great. I don't need any more kids."—

—"Any feeling about your abortion this morning?"

"Just want to get it over with, that's all. I was planning one anyway."

"Why?"

"Well, you know, I agree with the whole concept. We really need to take care of our problems, you know, before we bring any more children into this world. I mean, it will give us some breathing space."—

—"Some though, one woman in particular, one month pregnant, did not seem happy to be here."

"I'm here because I was told to be here because that's the law now."

"But you don't want the abortion?"

"No, of course not. It's my baby they're killing. My baby, not theirs! What right do they have?"

"But you seem to be here willingly."

"Better they kill it when it's just, 'tissue' than when it looks, you know, like a baby. I mean, they would kill it or give it away eventually, wouldn't they?"

There were tears. The camera zoomed in close to pick up the tears.—

—"Tom Kline, NBC News, New York City."—

The picture faded to break for commercials as an announcer stated, as did graphics superimposed on the screen: "Coming up—crisis in Chile."

8

Monday, December 12th—Washington, D.C.

He had been sitting in his office at U.C.L.A. outlining his next article, really getting no work done, for it was raining.

The clouds were those wonderful, quilted clumps of black and dark gray, swelled with the moisture that becomes the downpour, which strikes loose leaves from their trees, felling them to fall on the vibrating, water-pocked texture of the sidewalks and black paved roads. The sound of the rain was a fast-dripping hiss, and the air was cool, washed, and fresh and could be smelled with pleasure as it came through the open window.

Such times were Butchko's favorite. The nasty sting of sunshine was out of the environment; the light was subdued, giving all—buildings, trees, cars—the chance to conceal what certain grit they might not like revealed. It was a time that allowed thoughts to go deep, thinking to sound clear, and life to seem immediate. Butchko always knew—for a fact—that his blood flowed when it rained, that his heart pumped, that every part of his body was waiting and willing to respond to the impulses of his brain.

In the summer, when the sun has a clear passage to the face of the earth and comes directly on, more than willing to thousand-times prick the skin, settle in, and burn, the action of a man is hindered by drag as if the hot air grows thick enough to restrict enough of the movements of a man and his mind to make each day a sweated waste, a sunbaked bit of past useless for memory's sake.

But in the winter, in the cool, in the wind and rain, in a time when the sky is complex, textured, and inconsistent instead of a dull, smooth, roller wipe of blue, or more often in L.A., brown, there is no resistance. A man can move through the cool, always forward he hopes, but, at least, around to interesting stops of contemplation.

So Butchko thought. A minority sentiment, he knew, traitorous to those who saw tragedy in the rich being washed down the side of the Hollywood Hills.

He was waiting during the rain for the sound of her. He knew they were coming. Bobbie and Erin were coming to pick up the car. They would come on the Westwood shuttle bus to U.C.L.A., walk quickly, even in the rain, to his building, up the elevator, and then down the hall, Erin in the lead, running towards his room, yelling

"Daddy-Daddy-Daddy-Daddy-Daddy" in a perfect, musical staccato.

"Daddy-Daddy-Daddy-Daddy-Daddy."

She was here! Butchko got up and went out into the hall, down on one knee. The rain-coated, rubber-booted, hooded three-and-a-half-year-old came running towards—to—into his arms.

"Hi, Daddy!"

"Hi, beautiful. Huh! Hug! How are you?"

"Good."

"How was nursery school today?"

"Good. We made cookies!"

"Cookies!"

"Uh-huh."

"Did you bring me any?"

"No. Ate them."

"Bobbie came up to them.

"Hi, honey." They kissed. Erin liked to see that. He gave Bobbie the car key.

"Be careful, will you? Rain slick streets."

"You're a worry wart, you know that?"

"With good reason. People in L.A. don't know how to drive in the rain."

"Okay, I will."

"I'll see you later tonight, beautiful,"

"Okay, Daddy.

Erin's hair was in two side ponytails; her round cheeks were flushed, and her face was still wet. He hugged her. As small as she was, there was still so much to hug, so much to love. He hugged her again. They parted. Bobbie and Erin went to the car. Drove to LeConte. Left onto Hilgard. To Sunset. Left, just after the green.

Why the hell didn't she see that son-of-a-bitch coming?

He could only imagine the sounds—the wet squeal of tires, the metal crumpling impact, the shattered tinkling of glass, headlights smashed—but he could imagine it very well. Too well.

Erin was killed instantly. Bobbie was so harmed, so hurt, she could not attend her daughter's closed-casket funeral.

There was a return of the shudder of grief, and the copy of *The Washington Wash* slipped off Butchko's lap.

He opened his eyes. He reached down and picked up the tabloid. He looked at it analytically. What color was newsprint? It was not white—*there it is in black and white*—no, not white. And certainly not black. Not gray. Brown? Maybe, but very light or very off, not a brown you would choose to decorate with. But, yes, maybe brown, as some eggs are brown instead of white. Did that make a difference? He tried to remember. Was his mother always buying brown eggs because of some difference? Brown? No. No, not really, but—ah! Dingy! Dusty! Soiled! Yes! White, but white needing washing, needing to have its brightness brought out. Like a shirt. Like sheets. It was a sheet, wasn't it? A scandal sheet? Was this a scandal? Could they make a scandal from a father's grief? Or was it a fact sheet? Was this the truth? Was it anywhere near the truth?

The phone rang.

Again.

The answering machine clicked on. Bobbie's voice sounded: *This is the Butchko residence. I'm sorry, but we cannot answer the phone right now. But if you leave a message, we will gladly return your call. Please leave your message at the tone.*

The tone sounded.

It's Monday, 6:15 pm. Mr. Butchko, it's Donald Carr from the Post *again. Just checking on your reaction if you've read* The Wash yet. *Look, I would love an exclusive if that's possible. You can call me at the Post tonight. I'll be there until ten."*

"Well—what is your reaction?" Bobbie said, standing in the doorway. Butchko looked up.

"That possibly I deserve this. Maybe I should have been more up-front about my participation in the bill. But I didn't ask for the directorship. I never even considered it. Somehow, the president... I think he knew I wrote the bill. He gave me the pen. That's what that meant. He's putting it all on me. If this thing goes bad, he's putting it all on me. I get silent credit or noisy blame, whichever it's to be. He said he didn't want to be a Herod. But he signed the bill anyway because he was damn sure that if History decided to judge harshly, it would be me on trial and not him. He is not a stupid man, Bobbie. You were right; you said it. He is not just 'The Great Administrator.' He's a politician, alright."

"Why didn't you refuse?"

'How could I? I conceived Birth Cessation because I believe in it. How could I turn down the opportunity to ensure it's done right? As his advisor, I figured I could keep my eyes on it. But this, this was being able to have my hands on it. It just seemed the right thing to do."

"Don't take it. Resign."

"No. That would be taken as an admission that the concept is somehow underhanded and sneaky, some kind of evil plot. It would ruin the whole program. No. I can fight this. It all sounds bad, 'Darryl Butchko, devious mastermind, conniving luster after power' and all that. But it's not really. I can explain it. I think the president will be willing to help me explain it. If I continue to take the 'credit.' It's this other thing, this thing about Erin."

"I know, honey."

"Christ! It's the kind of emotional stuff they can really milk. It's the kind of 'facts' the 'people' like to hear, the kind they can understand and really get mad about."

"With any justification?"

"No! Do you think so? Do you think I'm that petty that I would be so motivated?"

"Grief has—its powers. Hatred has its powers."

"Hatred? For whom?"

"Me." She could feel the filling of her eyes with tears.

"Bobbie!"

"Me. For killing our child. For being barren."

"That's absurd. I don't blame you, I don't—"

Darryl stood up and crossed the room to Bobbie. "Why are you letting this trash upset you? I thought we settled all this. We had a tragedy, a personal tragedy. We dealt with it."

"You loved Erin so much."

"Of course I loved her. I loved her deeply! She was precious to me. But so are you."

Butchko cried whenever his wife cried. He was not so much an emotional man as one touched by emotions. And there were now the beginnings. "But I would not—I *do* not hate the world for my loss to the point of plotting its pain. That's melodrama! That's hokum! What I'm doing is damn serious. You've got to believe that. I thought you did."

"Yes, I do. Are you going to answer all of this?"

"I'll have to. And you? They'll ask you questions, too."

"Yes, I know. I'll handle it."

"Bobbie, have you seriously ever thought I blamed you?"

"Yes."

"Don't, ever again!"

"I can't."

"Bobbie!"

"I've blamed myself."

"Bobbie."

"I'll be all right. I've been all right.

"You've never once talked about it."

"I'm a dispassionate scholar, Darryl. I handle facts well.

Butchko smiled. "Then why are you starting to cry, you cold academic?"

She laughed. "I don't know. Why are you?"

"I don't know. Maybe, right now, I want to."

"Me too."

"Together?"

"Yeah."

The next day, they laughed about their crying.

***

Cleveland

He had decided to walk to the hospital. He had decided that that would be best. It was a fine day, and the sidewalks would be crowded, but then so would the buses. So there were pros and cons. Sitting on a bus, he could hold the bag tight, maybe steady. Walking it would necessarily jiggle. But on a bus, someone might ask, "What's in the bag?" Walking, he was open to accidents; someone might knock into him, or he might drop the bag, exposing or destroying. Then, he would have to do it over again.

But he would risk walking. He felt more alone while walking.

He could see the hospital in the distance and wondered what entrance he would use. He began to worry; he could see himself lost in the hospital, going from floor to floor, wing to wing, trying to find the right place. Complex buildings intimidated him. They were all labyrinthine mazes, puzzles, and games to find your way around, and he had always hated games because he had always lost. He reached into his jeans pocket and felt for his brother's knife. It was there. At least he felt it. But what did that mean? He brought it out and looked at it. Now, he was assured. He had done this two times before during his walk; he did it before he left. His brother was dead. The knife was one of the few things he had that had been his; he never went anywhere without it. Yet he still had to check; he still needed assurance. Everything had to go right.

Entrance ceased to be a problem when he found it marked clearly with an arrow.

FEDERAL ABORTION
AND
VASECTOMY CLINIC

Along the line, a smaller sign with another arrow.

A & V CLINIC

Finally, at the clinic, another sign.

AUTHORIZED FEDERAL
ABORTION & VASECTOMY CLINIC

There was a line of women on one side of the large room. A longer line of men on the other. They were waiting, processing, being instructed, being led down corridors and into rooms. He had to pass through people, excusing himself, while looking for a suitable empty section. There was a waiting area with uniformly colored couches and chairs and a table covered with magazines. He walked over to the area, sat down, and rested the bag in his lap, feeling for the knife again.

He was disappointed. No one took notice of him. He should have done as he had first planned: run in screaming, commit the act, throw down the papers, and run out. But when he walked in, there was such a businesslike atmosphere to everything that he had just gone along. So now he sat on the couch, unobtrusive and not quite knowing what to do. He saw a magazine that listed an interesting article and almost picked it up, but no! He had to do it. *What will they think when I do it? I'll do it on the count of ten. Then I'll jump up and do it. One—two—three—four—five—six—seven—eight—nine—ten—huh—eleven—* He picked up the magazine. The article wasn't interesting, but he read it fast, mingling it with his thoughts, reading a sentence on a subject far from his immediate concerns, thinking a word or two unrelated to the article.

He read a second article, comprehending none of it

Okay, now, I must do it. One —He reached in and grabbed the knife—*two—three—four—five* —He reached into the shopping bag and wrapped his fingers around the end of a large, clear plastic bag sealed tight at one end—*six --seven* —He opened the knife with one hand—*eight—nine* —He was ready to pull the bag—*ten!*

He got up.

"Hey!" he shouted. "Hey!" He looked for everyone, looking, seeing. Heads turned. Faces closed quizzically inward. He pulled the plastic bag out, letting the brown paper bag fall to the edge of the couch and then to the floor. The plastic bag was filled with a dark red liquid with a mass of something floating inside. He took the knife and poised it over the bag.

"Stop Butcher Butchko!" he shouted.

He slashed.

"Stop the abortions!"

The red liquid came pouring out, spilling on the floor, splashing on the couch, and others sitting there. They recoiled their bodies to escape the soiling. Some screamed. With assistance, a slight push, and a small squeeze of the bag, the mass was forced out, falling to the middle of the red puddle with a slap.

It was the fetus of a pig.

"No more No-Birth!"

He stepped over the puddle and out of the room, throwing behind him some papers he had drawn out of his pocket.

"What the hell?" A doctor said as he walked over to the mess.

A nurse picked up one of the papers. On it was crudely printed:

BAN BUTCHKO NOT BIRTHS!
STOP THE ABORTIONS!
STOP THE VASECTOMIES!
STOP BUTCHER BUTCHKO!
The BCA (Butchko Cessation Agency)

The doctor wondered if this would get on television.

9

Tuesday, December 13th—Washington D.C. News Conference

"Mr. Butchko, how do you answer charges made by Malcolm Kirkly in *The Washington Wash* that you conspired in secret to draft the Birth Cessation Act and that you did this to gain the job, and the attendant power, of director of the BCA?"

"Well, first of all, Mr. Kirkly, our friend with the hundred eyes but hardly 20/20 vision, has not made charges; he has merely speculated a little. I'm sure even he would not argue with that. He may argue with the statement that his speculation is based on little understanding of the facts, but that is my statement nevertheless."

"But does he have his facts correct?"

"It is true that I was involved in drafting the legislation. But in collaboration, not 'conspiracy,' with Senator Anderson here. And it was certainly not done to gain a job. I never even considered that the president would offer me the job. It is an administrative job, and I am not much of an administrator."

"Then why did you accept it when it was offered?"

"Because once offered the job, I realized that, due to my intimate knowledge of all facets of the law, I would be the best qualified, outside of Senator Anderson, to see to its implementation."

"Were you offered the post, Senator Anderson?"

'No, I was not."

"Any reason why?"

"I'm sure the president knows I'm very happy being a U.S. Senator and would have refused any such offer."

"Mr. Butchko, not being an administrator, do you foresee having a problem doing a competent job?"

"No. I believe I will rise to the occasion."

"Senator Anderson, were you just the messenger of the bill?"

"Absolutely not! Darryl and I have known each other for a long time. The ideas that served as the basis of birth cessation are ideas that we have both discussed on many occasions. We both firmly believe it is the only solution to this country's current and future problems. Darryl and I were prepared to put these ideas into a book at one time to make our proposals in that form. But three years ago, I was elected to the Senate, and Darryl was made a presidential advisor. We suddenly saw that we were now in positions to offer our ideas, not in the abstract form of a book, but in the concrete form of a bill before Congress, open to public debate by the people's representatives. A debate, I might add, that convinced an overwhelming majority of those representatives that our ideas were sound."

"It should be mentioned that had I not been appointed a presidential advisor, I probably still would have aided Senator Anderson in drafting the bill, as many people aid many senators and congressmen."

"But you were a presidential advisor, Mr. Butchko. Did the president know of your involvement?"

"Not to my knowledge."

"Then he may have known?"

"Well, I did not consciously keep the information from him. We just never spoke of it one way or the other. Since my staff and others knew I was working on it and no secrets were trying to be kept, he certainly may have found out about it."

"If he did know, don't you think he would have brought it up?"

"Not really. President Henshaw gives his staff great liberty to participate in the democratic process. Besides, as we have seen, the president supports Birth Cessation. It was obviously a job he wanted to see get done. He saw it was getting done, so he concentrated on other matters. That would be my guess, anyway."

"But do you think it was proper for a presidential advisor to be drafting legislation without the *active* knowledge of the president?"

"Why didn't you ask me that question a year ago? We could have saved ourselves this afternoon. It is a question that has been currently on my mind, though, and I must admit, after some reflection, that I don't think it is at all proper to be drafting legislation if you are a presidential advisor without the active knowledge of the president. So, a slight impropriety is, I feel, my major offense here."

"Mr. Butchko, what will be your salary as director of the BCA?"

"Lower than my current salary if that's what you're getting at. And I must say, I resent the question. That I would dream up such an elaborate method of putting a few more coins in my pocket is crediting me with a far more devious imagination than I have.

"Look—in any outrage people are feeling over this so-called revelation, are they stopping to ask about the basic logic behind Birth Cessation? This country is in the middle of a genuine crisis. We are rapidly reaching the point of far too many people and far too few resources. That is indicative of dangerous times. A simple reading of history will inform us that all do not generously share limited wealth but greedily and viciously fight over it. In a world of too many people and too few resources, the most horrible of inequities would arise as the strong would slowly push the weak out over the sides. The weak, the non-privileged, and the newly oppressed would soon rebel and revolt against those who have hoarded the resources, and you would then have a whole new form of class warfare. I know that sounds outlandish, too horrible to happen in this country. But do, please do, read your history, and you'll find such horrible outlandishness far too commonplace. We have often ignored history in our plans for the future. I have been determined and dedicated that this time we would not, that we would act against the seemingly inevitable flow of fate. That we would take command of our future.

"I hate to sound too academic here, but—it is an American tradition to reshape, gain control, and command history. Democracy, framed in our constitution, is a perfect example of that. It was not a preordained outcome of the human story that *our* America would be created. It happened because of *exactly* who the leaders of America were at that time and from where they drew their inspiration, an inspiration to change. Any other group of leaders may have formed a completely different kind of government, probably one more like those that had always been. Our constitution is almost a freak of history. But it is a freak that protects us against our human nature, our tendency to want freedom for ourselves—and for others only if they agree with us. What else explains why democracy was so slow to become a leading form of government on this planet? I can almost guarantee you that if we allow our country to degenerate into one boldly divided between the Haves and the Have-nots, then either the Haves will bring a dictator into power to control the unruly Have-nots, or the Have-nots will bring a dictator into power to overthrow the Haves. And that will be the end of the American experiment in democracy. If this country grows too big for its resources, if it gets out of control—we will never regain it."

"Mr. Butchko, what are your feelings about Kirkly's suggestion that you may have conceived of Birth Cessation as a sort of revenge against the nation for the loss of your daughter?"

"I consider such irrational musings to be too absurd for comment."

"What do you think of the incident in Cleveland yesterday and that you are starting to be called 'Butcher Butchko'?"

"I am not starting to be called Butcher Butchko. One disturbed young man looking for attention pulls a stunt and calls me a name. Then the press puts it in all the newspapers and broadcasts it on all the TV stations, and suddenly, it seems as if the whole country is calling me that name. You know, I believe in a free press. It is fundamental in our democracy. But I must admit that I wish the press had a sense of proportion. Thank you."

"I'm afraid that's all the time we have for questions." Said the gentleman from the White House Communications office.

"Mr. Butchko?"

"Mr. Butchko?"

"Mr. Butchko?"

Butchko left, leaving the calls unanswered.

"Jesus!" one reported said to another. "He really comes off as pompous, don't you think? That's going to hurt him. They don't like that out there."

"Yeah," the other said. "I think you're right."

***

Over-the-air. All Three Networks. And Then Some.

The screen revealed the landing of Air Force One

The taxi.

The complete and full stop.

The door opening, and President Henshaw emerging, arm immediately outstretched, hand at the end metronoming hello.

It was a remake. Screens had seen the scene before but with the part played by others.

It was a rerun. Henshaw himself had played this part before.

It was a rehash. Even played back fast forward, it would seem sluggish.

But the reporters ran to the man's side nevertheless.

"Mr. President!"

"Mr. President!"

"Mr. President!"

"Mr. President, did you see or hear Darryl Butchko's press conference this morning? And if so, what did you think of his performance?"

"His performance? Well, I did not hear a song nor see a dance, so I don't know what performance you are talking about."

"Mr. President, what did you think of his comments?"

"Why don't you ever ask me what I thought of the press and their questions?"

"Okay, what did you think of the questions?"

"Well asked, gentlemen and ladies, well asked."

"And the answers?"

"Straight and honest. I think Mr. Butchko clearly explained his actions and motivations."

"You have no qualms over his authorship of the Birth Cessation law?"

"None. It only gives testimony to my ability to choose the right people. I stand by my choice of Mr. Butchko. It was obvious from what he said this morning that he was the right man for the job. He believes strongly in the concept. It will not be just a job for him. To get that kind of man in government these days is rare. I believe the country can be as proud of Darryl Butchko as I am."

"And the revelation about his daughter?"

"I agree with Mr. Butchko; it's an absurd thought."

Then the president was in his limousine, and all the reporters turned to their cameras, and all said:

"President Henshaw, arriving here in Boulder to address the Western Governor's Conference, but with matters of more national importance on his mind."

***

Los Angeles News Conference

"Excuse me! Excuse me! Please! Mrs. Handlin will be out in just a second. She will give a brief statement and then answer questions.

Uh—is she ready? Yes? Okay. Uh, ladies and gentlemen, Vivian Pavin Handlin."

Vivian walked to the table on the platform and sat in front of many microphones.

"Uh—Ed? Ed, honey, could you come up here? Come on, Ed. Ladies and gentlemen, this is my husband, Ed Handlin. I think it appropriate that he be by my side."

"Ed stepped forward, leaving the impression of moving backward, reached and ascended the platform, sat next to Vivian, received a kiss and a smile, and smiled slightly at the crowd.

Vivian turned to the audience and made it clear on her face that she was ready to begin.

"As you may know, I come from a family that flourished under the American system of government. My grandfather made a fortune and was added to by my father by exercising their rights within the political, personal, and economic freedoms granted by our constitution. I put much of my inheritance aside, started fresh with the American Dream, and found it lacking nothing of its promise. I am a patriot—a word not often used anymore, but the one that clearly defines my love for this country. But I am not, and I refused to be, a passive patriot! We have a tradition of protest in this country that has kept our constitution from becoming a stodgy and forgotten document. Protest guarantees that our constitution will be referred to settle questions of the day. When it is necessary, protest is the most patriotic of duties.

"I believe that certain current events demand patriots to arise in protest and demand that we refer to our constitution and realize the freedoms it guarantees and how some have conspired to abridge those freedoms.

"I am talking here, of course, about the recently established Birth Cessation Law, that hideous plan, that 'Final Solution' of a man beginning to be known as, and indeed, he will be known by history as, Butcher Butchko.

"This slaughter of children that Butcher Butchko has instituted goes against everything the constitution stands for. It goes against the constitutional guarantees of life, liberty, and the pursuit of happiness. It goes against individual choice, the cornerstone of our system. Birth Cessation is a threat to the fundamental American way of life lived in freedom. How this country was blindly led into Birth Cessation, I have no idea. But we must walk away from it with our eyes wide open.

"To aid in accomplishing that goal, I am prepared to put my resources behind an organized and orderly protest of Birth Cessation. I am willing to fund a challenge to the law's constitutionality, which we believe condones the most violent of unreasonable seizures. I am willing to do this because I believe this must be done, for no government has the right to invade the sacred domain of birth. That is the domain of individuals, of families, of men and women concretely expressing their love.

"The foes of freedom must understand that my dedication to this cause goes beyond the financial resources at my disposal. I am more than willing to put *myself* on the front lines of resistance. I am more than willing to lead the vanguard personally. I know only one way to enter the battle in this fight for freedom. Ladies and gentlemen—" Vivian paused for the drama, for the drum roll "—I am proud to announce today, *happy* to declare, that I am pregnant—"

The press moved on that. Mouths opened, bodies bent forward, pencils scratched. There was a sudden hum.

"—That I am pregnant and have no intention of following the recent marching orders from Washington. I will not willingly submit like a passive lamb to an abortion. I *will* carry my child to term. I will *not* willingly give up my newborn for State adoption. I will *not* allow my family to be broken up like some Southern slave mammy of long ago in another era of national shame! My child, *our* child—"

Vivian was kind enough to place a hand on Ed's. It almost embarrassed him.

"—if a boy will be named George Washington Pavin Handlin. If a girl, she will be named Susan B. Anthony Pavin Handlin. Names symbolic of the ongoing fight for fundamental human rights. For what right is more essential than the right of birth?

"I enter this protest backed by the history of America and its tradition of protest. My protest is one of civil disobedience. I expect to be arrested, charged, and brought before a judge and twelve of my peers. Although, my only true peers would be twelve pregnant women. At that time, a light will be shed upon the Birth Cessation Law and its constitutional weaknesses, and that light will defeat it. Butcher Butchko is going to lose his shop. I guarantee it!

"Now, I would like our attorney, Mr. Harrison McNeil, to join us, and we will be happy to answer any questions you might have."

10

Wednesday, December 14th—Downtown Los Angeles

The quiet seemed to go with the cold, the cold with the quiet. The dark formed an equal third. All three surrounded her; she was very aware of that, of being centered within all three elements of being precisely centered, nowhere near an edge, no turn a shorter way out. At three a.m., she stood on the grounds of the Music Center.

She placed the heavy metal can down, and its clang radically disturbed the quiet. She unhitched her sleeping baby from the knapsack, papoose-like carrier she wore, and brought her around to her arms. She sat at the edge of the fountain centered with Lipchitz's sculpture of the Dove of Peace bringing its wares to mankind.

She was tired. It had been a long walk. It had been a struggle to lug it all.

She adjusted her oversized, baggy, green and brown striped, wrap-around sweater that had been much of what warmth she had known for the last three years. She sniffed the air to clear a path, scratched the side of her face, and tightened a blanket around her child.

She had been to the Music Center only once before. Just the year before. With Duane, who knew she wanted to be an actress or artist or something and tried to impress her. They came to the Dorothy Chandler Pavilion, "Where the Academy Awards are given out," Duane told her. They saw a big, awful revival of some lumbering, old, stupid musical that people like to come in from The Valleys to see. She had struggled to put together something dressy, although it was almost against her principles. But Duane was a nice guy. He had been very nice to her, giving her much moral and even some financial support, and seemed not to demand sex in return. But maybe it was only because he was too shy or reluctant to come off as aggressive. Perhaps he was demanding love instead—that's what he seemed to ask for anyway—and that was impossible to give as payment. But she could at least dress up for him; she could put on the blue dress that clung that he liked to make him feel good while standing by her side. She could do that and bear it for a while because he had always been such a nice guy.

They arrived, parked underground, and rode up the elevator with an older group of people she immediately disliked. Like her parents, they looked, smelled, and tasted like her parents back in Milwaukee. Once out of the elevator, she made her dislike clear, not far enough out of earshot, in Duane's opinion. Later, she ridiculed the play and the performers during the performance, irritating Duane. However, later, at a coffee shop, he claimed he admired the guts she had to express herself and her independent mind.

Her independent mind had her living in a shabby little single apartment with two cats that crapped in a litter box in the bathroom. As they kicked to bury, they propelled the tiny white sand onto the floor. It would crunch under Duane's feet when he went in, and the crap smell lingered and merged with the general cat smell as he went back into the main room. She would be sitting there with a cat in her lap, loving it, stroking it. Duane would come up and pet the cat and make a nervous, crude joke about "petting your pussy."

She had had the cats for two years. She had even taken them back to New York when she had followed an old boyfriend there who had gotten a job doing kiddie puppet shows for a burger chain. He was an actor, as she thought maybe she was. Or perhaps she was a costumer—she had a flare for making do with clothes—or, eventually, a writer—she could come up with pretty good ideas now and then, better than what she saw on TV. They had met at a small theater in L.A. where she was employed to organize the prop room, and he was "starring in" their Christmas kid's play as a giant, mean rat. He was not quite tall but was well built and probably had, Duane was sure, a big one.

They broke up in New York. The puppets went south for the winter, and he followed, instructing her to return to L.A., get an apartment, he would send money, and return after the summer season. She packed up the cats again and came back. She was not followed by money, nor him.

Duane heard the story and helped, gave his opinion of "macho studs," confirmed his belief in feminism, and was rewarded with the title: Just like a brother. Duane hated that. He tried to counter it by declaring his love. She loved him, yes, she said, she loved him, but not *That way*, and she could never have sex with a man she did not love in *That way*.

Nevertheless:

He drove her to blood banks, where she sold hers. He gave her an old radio of his so she could have some music. He listened to her politics, her philosophies, her plans. He told people about her in case they needed to hire somebody. She worked now and then and knew how to wait on tables, but she never got along with bosses. Or, rather, with being bossed. Duane would listen sympathetically to her tales of the stupidity of the bastards and try, through verbal wit, to prove to her that she had done the right thing in quitting.

Eventually, she got a job at another theater company. A small one, a not very important one, one with egos large and fragile, nonetheless. She took tickets, arranged props, and sat in on drama lessons. Duane got a new job around this time as well. They began to see little of each other but talked on the phone now and then. Duane got to hear all about Mike, two years younger than her, a theater company member, really cute and tall, of course, somewhat taller than Duane. "But then," Duane would say, "Who isn't?" She was happy now, she said. "Good," said Duane. "I'm glad," he continued politely.

She called him at work one day to tell him that she was pregnant and that she and Mike would get married. He didn't say much beyond that he was in the middle of a meeting, so talk to you later, good-bye. Months later, she walked over to his apartment, big with child, to return his radio. No, she and Mike were not married yet, but they would be soon, and her mother would come out for it if not her dad. "Good," said Duane, then, "Goodbye." He walked her to the door and did not offer to drive her home. Finally, he had found the courage not to be a nice guy.

By accident, Duane later talked to someone who had been in the theater company with her. No, she didn't marry Mike; he went off somewhere. She had the baby and brought the baby to the theater all the time, to the rehearsals, lessons, and set decorating. It cried and shitted and disrupted and got on people's nerves. "She left, you know, one of the member's fathers has an electronics company or something, and she's there now, on the assembly line, dredging away.

"And after she fought like hell to be an actress."

"No," said Duane. "After she *thought* like hell to be an actress."

"What?"

"Never mind."

She stared at the Mark Taper Forum, its round, relief surface now dark, the decorative spotlights that illuminate it having been automatically extinguished at midnight. When she had been here before they were on, they had reminded her of her little brother—the little snot—who used to put a flashlight under his face in the dark and try to scare her.

The baby farted—or worse.

Julius Caesar was playing at the Forum, so the glass-encased poster in front of her said. The next attraction was a new play, a docu-drama comedy about Ronald Reagan. The socially conscious artistic director of the theater was trying to make a statement in his programming.

She could hear the few cars passing on the Hollywood freeway, hiss-humming so clearly in the early morning cold, their sounds stretched and thus altered by the Doppler effect, although she didn't know that this was what science called it. She hated science. It destroyed flowers and trees to put up tall buildings.

The baby was stirring, sensing the problem in its pants. She laid the blanket down on the concrete, then placed the baby, still in its carrying sack, on the blanket. She got a folded piece of paper and scotch tape from one of her large sweater pockets and walked to the glass case containing the poster for *Julius Caesar*. She unfolded the paper and taped it to the glass. It read in red ink, in her tight handwriting:

I take my life and my child's life to assert my individuality. I am the master of my life. The government should not say yes or no to anyone's life. They have no right to say no to millions of the unborn. I take my life and my child's life to wake people up, to cause them to think about what is happening. The mass murder and slaughter by Butcher Butchko and his henchmen must be stopped! Congress must do something, or the president, or the Supreme Court. If not them, then the people.

PEOPLE ARE PRECIOUS

JAN LAWRENCE

Jan walked over to the large red gasoline can she had lugged. She picked it up and unscrewed the cap. The odor came to her immediately. She reached into her large sweater pocket and took out a book of matches.

She poured gasoline on her child. The baby awoke gagging, coughing, crying. Jan hurried to light the match but was hampered by still holding the can. It slipped; it dropped out of her arms to the ground, flat down on one side, with gasoline starting to pour out. She jumped back slightly, screamed a little, felt panic, and struck feverishly a match against the back of its book.

Finally, flame.

She threw it on her child, pushing aside the dark and chasing away the cold.

Sudden awareness of the consequences of her act came to her as her child was first obscured and then consumed by flames.

"Oh god! Oh shit!"

She screamed, cried, looked at the can, and saw the gas flowing. She quickly jumped to it, fell to it, kneeled in the puddle, and poured what was left on her all over her frantically as the dark crept back and as the cold began to return. Somehow, she had managed to keep the matches dry and tore one out of the book.

Strike!

Strike!

Strike!

The dark was pushed aside; the cold was chased away.

***

Transcontinental—Washington D.C. to Los Angeles

'Ms. Pavin's office."

"I would like to speak to *Mrs.* Handlin!"

"May I say who's calling?"

"Darryl Butchko."

"Yes, Mr. Butchko, please hold. I'll see if Ms. Pavin is available."

"Good morning, Darryl."

"Just what the hell do you think you're doing?"

"You saw my news conference?"

"I saw a circus; a God damn Hollywood PR circus."

"Don't question my sincerity, Darryl!"

"I question your sanity. Do you realize that you are jeopardizing Birth Cessation?"

"That's the idea, Darryl."

"God damn it, Viv! What right do you have to meddle in this?"

"You pompous ass! What right do you have ripping babies out of women?"

"I'm trying to save this country!"

"I'm sorry, I didn't know you were Jesus Christ."

"Viv!"

"Shut up, Darryl! I am opposing you on this—that is what the hell I am doing. Your plan is vicious, stupid, immoral, and just plain *wrong!* You are a Fascist, Darryl. Do you realize that? You think the State should do all and be all. You've always had this naive belief that the State is somehow wiser and smarter than the *people* themselves. And, of course, *you* are wiser and smarter than even the State, and so, suddenly, you are 'Lawgiver,' you are suddenly God, the wrath of God, the hand of God, and the will of God, all wrapped up in—"

"Oh, cut it out! You don't understand a thing and have no right to lecture me on overweening pride."

"Go to hell, Darryl!"

"Speaking of which, I hated your wedding."

"Thank you."

"Why did I have to be the Best Man?"

"Call it a preemptive political/PR. strike."

"I'm having you arrested, you know."

"Good! Thank you, that's what I want."

"You're not going to get what you want."

"We'll see."

"Vivian!"

"Don't yell at me, Darryl! Don't ever yell at me!"

"Vivian!"

"Good-bye!"

***

Washington D.C.

"Shit! Why the hell did I get into a shouting match with her?"

"Sounds like she started it, sir."

"Yes, but—God damn it! I never figured on this. What's happening here, George?"

"George Mays, Butchko's administrative assistant, poured him a drink.

"I don't know."

Darryl took the drink and sipped. "I thought it was all settled. I thought everybody agreed. Maybe I am naive, but I thought everybody could see the necessity for Birth Cessation. Everybody certainly seemed to be behind it. Why wasn't anything said before it passed? Why didn't Vivian protest this before it passed? Yes! Why? Make a note of that; we've got to ask her that.

"I can't believe all this. Kirkly, then this. That idiot in the hospital. Well—I guess we might have to fight after all. We can't let them stop this. That would be like signing the country away.

"Call the president, George, then Bob Anderson. We've got to get organized fast, and we've got to get our strategy down. What do you think? Do you think this could be a battle?"

11

Thursday, December 15—New York

A TALE OF TWO MARTYRS
by Argus

I suppose it is inevitable that any cause, any campaign, any struggle for justice and for what is right must have its martyr. Somewhere down the line, one person's struggle within a larger struggle is suddenly thrust into the open, and the collected eyes of like thinkers see a simple symbol that will stand nicely for complexities they have been desperate to articulate. It is, in a way, regrettable. Better all struggles could be won through intelligence instead of images, reason instead of rhetoric, and minds instead of martyrs.

But intelligent reason by minds can be, at times, dry and dull, no matter what the subject. Symbols—thoughts dressed up and eager to perform—can act as entertaining conveyers of messages. That is, of course, the purpose of the parable and those more complex forms of symbolization: the novel and the play. That is why a good work of fiction usually outsells a good piece of nonfiction, and the short story is more fun than the essay. Symbols—martyrs—have their purpose.

The growing struggle to strike down the recent Birth Cessation Law has been blessed—if that is the word, and if it is, it is painful to use—in its early stages by not one but two martyrs. One is genuine. One possibly not. At about three a.m. on December 14, Jan Lawrence, who by all indications was a lovely young woman, chose to take her life and the life of her infant child with a can of gas and a book of matches. It seems she could not tolerate the thought of living in a society that condoned the mass slaughter of millions of innocent unborn children. It was her only way of expressing what she felt. It is a strong possibility that it was not a moral act, especially because she reached beyond her life to end the life of another. But who has the wisdom to judge? What is clear is that she was reacting to an irrefutably immoral act, that she felt shocked and ashamed for her country. Such strong emotions can lead one to make morally ambiguous choices. The taking of lives has always been part of unjust acts, just as they have been a part of people's reactions to them. Men have died because of crude conditions of labor. Other men have been killed during violent strikes protesting those conditions. Men have died due to the tyranny of governments. Other men have been killed during the rightful opposition to that tyranny. I do not pretend to know whether the different deaths can be balanced on scales of morality. But some deaths do seem more morally motivated.

I cannot condone what Jan Lawrence did. But I can understand it. I can have compassion for the pain she must have felt over realizing what her country was trying to do to her and all of us. It wasn't a weak act. In its way, it took great strength. To sacrifice yourself in the light of day and in such a way that you remain around to reap the glory-filled pats on the back is one thing. To sacrifice yourself in the dead of night, alone, quietly, yet with the hope that someone will hear your tiny voice, is something else again.

I have never trusted Sunshine Martyrs. Is that what Vivian Pavin is? The day before Jan Lawrence took her and her child's lives, Vivian Pavin announced through the loudspeaker of the world's media that she intended to give birth to life—despite the current law. It is a grand and noble gesture, to be sure. But then Pavin is a millionaire—maybe much more than that—and can certainly afford the grand and the noble. I do hope she's sincere and not just a dilettante martyr. For if the government does prosecute—and how could they not?—then her case could be the test case that challenges the barbaric Birth Cessation Law. But who will side with her? She is a woman of great talent and means, if she wants a baby badly enough, she could leave the country—as I assume many of the rich will. Vivian Pavin is not really under the thumb of the government, and therefore, she is not one of the oppressed. To play-act as one is an insult to those genuinely burdened by this law. And will she, at some point, grow tired of play-acting? Will she leave us in the lurch and cheapen the struggle? Vivian Pavin has always been a woman who enjoyed the limelight. I hope this is not one more attempt to get into it.

The phone rang.

Kirkly slowly put his pen down, keeping his eyes on the text, reading the last few sentences over. He reached for the phone and picked it up.

"Yes?"

"Mr. Kirkly, this is Roger downstairs. We have a young man here who wishes to speak with you."

"What's his name?"

"Uh—Gerald Downing."

"I don't know him. Can you ask him what he wants—wait, no, put him on the line."

Kirkly could hear an exchange and the change softly over the phone.

"Mr.—uh—hello, Mr. Kirkly."

"Yes, Mr. Downing, what can I do for you?"

"Well—uh—I kind of wanted to talk to you—if that's okay."

"About what?"

"Well, yes—um—it's about a thing I want to do, uh..."

"What kind of thing?"

"Well, it has to do with—uh—it's like a club, well, no—uh—an organization I have an idea about—uh—you know, Birth Cessation and all."

"Mr. Downing, I'm afraid I'm trying to finish work on a column."

"Well, I just want to take a little time—uh—what I want is, really, some advice on, well, sort of a protest organization against No-Birth."

Kirkly recognized the voice. Not Downing's voice, but a voice he shared with many. It was a voice Kirkly did not like but one that commanded sympathy from him.

"Okay, Mr. Downing. Put the concierge back on the line, and I'll ask him to let you up."

"Oh, okay, thanks, Mr. Kirkly! I'll—uh—I'll see you in a few seconds."

The physical Gerald Downing kept faith with the voice. Kirkly could see that as he opened the door. He was a young man, not short, but of no stature worth noting. He wore a white shirt, tie, slacks, and sportscoat, but in that disheveled manner that indicated that he worked in these clothes rather than, say, administered in these clothes.

"Mr. Kirkly?"

He was nervous and simply scared.

"Yes, yes, Mr. Downing, come in."

Kirkly led him to his study, somewhat enjoying Downing's wide-eyed taking in of the surroundings.

"Sit down." Kirkly placed Gerald in a chair before his desk. "Would you like a drink or coffee?"

"Uh—no, thank you."

Kirkly sat at his desk. "Well, I guess you better proceed."

"Uh—well, Mr. Kirkly, I—um—well, I've always been a fan of yours, if—uh—that's the word. I mean, I've always read you since I was in high school. We had a teacher, Mr. Roach, who really liked you. So I read you, and I got to like you a lot. Not just what you said but the way you write. So—um—so, of course, I've read your recent stuff on No-Birth, and I got just as mad at it as I guess you are, and I thought that, maybe, something could be done, you know, like an organization or something. So I thought I would come to you and see if you have any advice about something like that."

Kirkly remained silent and still. He looked attentive but made no effort to talk, to give aid and comfort.

"My idea, I guess, is—um—getting people together who are against No-Birth and make a public protest, and send out letters and telegrams to the president, and—uh—get, you know, on the news with our story. An activist group, I guess."

"Who would organize this group?"

"Well, I guess I would. I mean, I'm willing to."

"What do you do now, Mr. Downing?"

"Um—I'm a major appliance salesman at a store in Queens."

"Major appliances?"

"Yeah, you know, refrigerators, washing machines, TVs."

"Are you married?

"Yes. Well, separated. And I have a little girl."

"Did you go to college?"

"Yeah—uh—for a couple of years. But then I got married, and Sharon got pregnant, so I dropped out. I probably would have anyway; I didn't care much for it. Not the learning, I love that, I read a lot, it was the teachers and the whole academic thing. I didn't care for it at all. And I was an English major, and I wanted to be a writer, at—um—at that time, and I found that if you want to be a writer, you should major in anything but English."

"Possibly so. Now, what kind of advice do you need from me?"

"Well, I thought, knowing how you feel, that you might help in the organization, maybe write about it, or get some other people behind it, or something like that."

"Well, thank you for thinking of me, Mr. Downing, but I've always made it a policy to remain the unattached observer."

"Yes, I know, but this group is going to need help."

"Yes, indeed, you are. It will take money to organize properly."

"Uh, yes, I know. But I think we'll get our supporters. But what it's really going to take is a lot of hard work. And I'm willing to do that, even to the point of quitting my job, if a, you know, a small wage can be—uh—got. But even without that, I'm ready to work hard and organize this. But I'm not, obviously, anybody special. And we need somebody like that to, well, I thought you would like to get involved."

"What exactly do you see yourself as in this organization?"

"Uh—what do you mean?"

"Who are you going to be in this organization?"

"Oh. Well. I'm willing to—uh—head it up, I guess."

"I see. Well, Mr. Downing, I don't know what to tell you. I know an organization, such as you're talking about, may be needed. But I also know that one, possibly more, will pop up shortly, organized, most likely, by people much more in a position to do so than yourself."

"Well, yeah, I know, but—"

"But that is no reason for you not to try. I don't think I can be of much help. Like I say, I try to stay out of such things. A columnist should comment on the passing parade, not join it. But I certainly can give you my moral support."

"Well, I thank you for that—um—though, I—uh—wonder if you could—well—I've got some essay-like things here that I wrote, which kind of explains, I mean, puts down how I feel. I mean, I tried to really show what's wrong about No-Birth. Maybe you could read them and tell me what you think. I mean, should I try to get them published? Uh—could they do any good in fighting No-Birth?"

"Yes, I could read them. Just leave them."

"Oh, okay. Uh—should I call you then, in a week or so?"

"No, leave your address, and I'll send them back with comments."

Kirkly walked Gerald to the door.

"I want to thank you again for this, Mr. Kirkly. It's really been good to meet you."

Thank you, Mr. Downing. I'll read your essays. Don't be concerned if it takes a while before I get back to you."

"Oh, no, of course not, don't, I mean, at your leisure."

"Goodbye, Mr. Downing."

Gerald held out his hand and offered Kirkly an awkward handshake, not quite coming forward enough, nor at the right angle. "Goodbye Mr. Kirkly." Their hands parted, and Kirkly shut the door.

Well, thought Gerald as he stood in front of the shut door. *Well.*

He went down the hall to the elevator, looking at the plush Old New York, chandeliered, gloved elderly lady decor. There was a mirror across from the elevator, and Gerald looked at himself. He liked the coat he had on; he thought he looked good in it.

Well. Think. How did it go?

He went down the elevator.

"Goodbye," he said to Ralph the concierge.

"Goodbye, sir."

Gerald went out the door and stood facing Central Park. It was a short walk to the 72nd Street-Central Park West subway station, but he needed a long walk. It was early afternoon, but he had called in sick anyway, so he crossed the street and entered the park.

Well? How did it go?

He turned left at the fork and started to pass joggers, bike riders, roller-skaters.

It wasn't quite what he wanted. Kirkly was not as enthusiastic as he had hoped. It wasn't quite as he had imagined it, the imagining that had first excited him, but…

But he listened. It wasn't—I wasn't—God, I was nervous. I was an ass, really. But…

The combination of the park's wildness, the country of it, with buildings to be seen in the distance, that extraordinary New York evidence of civilization lining the park was an incredible sight. He loved it. He got to Manhattan as often as possible to view it. He hated Queens.

But I think I got my ideas across. He wasn't too negative, anyway. But how can I organize without him? Just do it, I guess. Maybe I can get on a talk show to do it. But…

It was cold. He stopped and thought it might be best to head back. He sat down on a bench. He wanted the park some more.

But that's hard.

But he would be good on a talk show; he knew that. As he would be when speaking to crowds anywhere. He had several speeches written already, basically, in his head. He had given them more than once in that ethereal region above somewhere, just on top of reality. He had even heard the amplification of his voice and saw how he looked from the audience.

If only. Look—hell—goddamn major appliances!

It wasn't closed, though. Kirkly was going to read his stuff.

Hell, that's something.

Kirkly would like his writing. That could do it.

Or at least—gee, yes, God!

Kirkly might then really encourage him or know how to get him a column, maybe. Or recommend him. Good columnists are needed; we don't have good ones like we used to.

He reached Fifth Avenue and the even fancier park-facing apartments.

Gerald looked up. *Yes!* he thought. *Yes!* With some enthusiasm.

12

Monday, December 19—New York

Vivian had expected her arrest to be the first reaction to her news conference. She found, instead, the first reaction to be several offers to speak in person and more than several to appear on television. Two had appealed to her. One was to speak at the graduate School of Law at Fordham University in New York City and the other to appear on one—the highest rated one—of the early morning network news/talk-gossip/entertainment shows that originated from New York.

Vivian liked speaking at universities. Ever since her days as a college student, when she was not listened to as often as she would have liked, she loved any opportunity to capture an audience in the unreal world. There was something about going up to the lofty top of the mountain to tell the wise ones a thing or two. It gave her an enjoyably different, if not better, feeling than even noisy success in the real world. And television! Vivian had always loved herself on television. But only in ways unique. Her first exposure as the sexy symbol of Pavin Perfume was unique because she was the reality behind the symbol, the producer, not just the promoter. In subsequent appearances, she always demanded a difference. It could be subtle; it could be slight, but it had to be satisfying.

This time? "Yes, Mrs. Handlin will appear on the show, providing she is the sole guest for one half hour. She will not talk on this matter for a quick seven minutes, then be replaced by a series of thirty-second commercials for mouthwash. The question of No-Birth is far too complicated—Mrs. Handlin is far too complicated—for that."

Yes, they agreed, yes, that would be fine. Did they agree reluctantly? Eagerly? Vivian did not know; Ed took the call.

They had an apartment in New York, across the street from the Metropolitan Museum of Art on Fifth Avenue. They had gotten in on a Saturday, and the phone had been ringing since arrival. Ed took all the calls. All the calls were from reporters asking for interviews, TV talk show talent coordinators asking for an appearance, and columnists asking for clarifications.

There were YESs for some.

There were NOs for others.

"No, Jesus, of course not! The Christian Network of Stations? Good God, no!"

"Hold on, Viv," Harrison McNeil said. "Do you know how many people they reach? Do you know what control they have and how persuasive they are? Hell, Viv, they're the god-damned Bible personified, the video image of God. They say God wants you to jump, and millions of people jump! And these millions have money. All kinds of money that can be donated to a worthy cause."

"Yeah, but Harrison, do I have to go on like some Born Again freak? I'm not going to go out there and pray and confess my sins or something.'

"No, of course not. But we've got to use this!" Harrison turned to Ed, who had been tightly capping the mouthpiece on the phone. "Look, Ed, tell them that Vivian would love to, but the discussion must remain on the subject of No-Birth, and on that subject only, no discussion of religion."

"And they've got to send a remote unit to me," Vivian added. "I don't want to go to their studio."

Ed discovered he could say "yes" with conditions and "no" with grace. But it was hard. He had not been a diplomat at the State Department; he had had no practice. He had been one of the ones who looked at questions of international importance, picked them up, turned them around, prepared statements explaining all sides seen, and then watched the diplomats go on their "instinct" anyway. But he had enjoyed it. His job was to know the world like one gets to know a play: the characters, the plots, the developments. Seated in the audience, whether high in the balcony or front row center, he enjoyed the performance.

"I don't understand your resignation at all," Ed's immediate superior had stated one week earlier. "If there was ever a career State Department man, you're him."

"Well, George, as you know, I just got married."

"Ed, secretaries quit when they get married, not more-than-competent analysts."

"George, that's not quite it. My letter of resignation explains it for the record. I would though like to—uh—I feel I owe you a further explanation. But off—off the record."

"Okay. Go ahead." George Midland sat back in his big chair. He was a big man, the former football player Ed always found in these positions. He was the type of man who would get more seriously agitated over football playoffs than a border war among oil-rich countries. He was the type of man who looked like he had shoulder pads on under his three-piece suit. He was the type of man Ed could get along with but could never really like or imagine being liked by. They had not liked him in college, they had not liked him in life, and they had almost always been his immediate superiors.

"George, Vivian feels very strongly about this Birth Cessation thing."

"For or against?"

"Uh—against."

"I see. But that's a domestic matter."

"Yes, I know, George, but Vivian is going to announce tomorrow that she plans to protest the new law."

"Look, Ed, your wife is a very visible person who will always be doing things like this. But it's American. Protesting, I mean. The fact that your wife can do it louder than most should not affect you, as long as there is no conflict of interest."

"Well, I guess that's true, but—uh—the thing is, Vivian plans to protest through civil disobedience."

"Oh God. Are we going to have that again? How?"

"She's pregnant, George. And I guess she plans to stay that way."

"Christ! I guess you're the father?"

"Well, of course!"

"And you're going to support her in this?"

Ed needed air. He breathed in deeply. "Yes."

"Reluctantly?"

"No, not really. I—well, I'm supporting her and will be legally liable. I don't want to cause the department any embarrassment. So my resignation is, I think, the correct thing to do."

"Yes, of course, you're right."

***

Ed was tired of the phone, making notes, asking reporters to spell their names, and explaining that he was *"Mr. Handlin."*

Why wasn't Vivian's assistant doing this?

"Ed, we want the press to know you are behind this a hundred percent," Harrison explained. "We want them to get to know you. For God's sake, don't be shy about it. Speak! Give some statements. You know the text by now. Vivian will call you on stage tonight, and we'll try to get you on camera tomorrow."

"I need some air. I'm going for a walk."

"Okay. Fine."

"Viv, do you want anything? I'm going for a walk."

Vivian was at her desk, working on her speech. "No, thank you," she said to the paper before her. "Thanks anyway, Ed."

Ed descended. The elevator doors had opened, and he had entered, nodding to the operator as the operator nodded to him. Down, open, out, out again onto the street, down 83rd to the corner, onto Fifth Avenue, across the street to a place in front but to the side of the Met.

The Met. Massive and solid and sculptured, imposing, implying mass as monument. Never view it straight-on. Get a slanted perspective, get the avenue in on it, and get the Empire State Building to make its point at the end of the view. Storied buildings lined up; the park stretched, spreading for blocks. It's all a mingle of brown, off-white, and some green. Civilization. Man and his stamp. But, better, later, Ed knew. As ruins. As all that's left of glories long past. He could see the Met as a ruin, a thousand years from now, a grand indication of people who must have been great to have such a grand indication.

There is nothing petty about grand ruins. There is nothing of the human about them, only the humanities. Left are only the bones that held them upright, maybe the hair that adorned them, but never the flesh, the tender, wound-able, sear-able, wet human flesh that decays as it dries, falls apart, then off and down into the dust—petty little particles of no note. Ed loved the luxury of ruins. Man was past, but present were the worthiest things he ever did.

Down Fifth Avenue to a bundled, gloved, and capped vendor and his steaming hot pretzels: the big, tough, chewy ones, salt prominent on the top.

"One, please."

"Yeah, okay," the vendor said. He prepared the pretzel as he continued a conversation, a dialogue on the merits of something he damn well *knew* the values of, as opposed to the other guy who knew from nothing. Ed felt like an intruder and that he should apologize. But he got the pretzel, paid for it, and ate it as he continued down Fifth and into the park at 79th.

Down a path passing trees with leafless limbs now matching trunks, curved and crooked lines intersecting, intertwining, informing on the season and telling of its harshness. Ashen gray, color not native now. Stark, standing there, rigid, ready to snap at a look. Quiet and calm, not dead, but deadened. Open to interpretation through contemplation, a scene to stare at, fix a gaze on; eyes steady, but mind wandering.

Ed liked his face to be cold, his skin tightening, and his lips slightly cracking. He expelled a long, visible breath, moved down paths a little faster, and got to *it* quicker.

Alice was at the toadstool. The Mad Hatter looked on. The intelligent little girl was as still and cold as the trees. Ed walked around the statue and read the metal quotes on the ground, as he almost always did when visiting Alice, then sat on a bench. What always drew him to the statue? He had never read the damn book. "Oh, you should, oh you must!" he had been told for years. "Yes, yes, I know. Well, I'll get around to it someday." He felt guilty about it. He bought a copy, a deluxe, original illustrations edition, and put it in the bookcase. He stared at the binding and admired the color of it but never got around to it. Yet he felt he knew the story. He had seen the films. He had looked at the illustrations more than once. He had read the allusions to it in many other writings. He knew what a Tweedledee and Tweedledum were. He knew that the time had come to talk of many things, of shoes—and ships—and sealing wax, of cabbages and kings. He understood the mockery of a strident shout, "Off with their heads!" He knew the feeling of a mad tea party, the look of a Cheshire cat grin, and the horror of a Jabberwocky. He felt as if he had already gone through the looking glass. Or was it down a rabbit hole? In either case, he thought he knew Alice, the little girl with stunning blond hair, a blue dress, and a white apron, who grew too tall for any good and shrunk to a size made for adventures.

He felt. He felt as if. He felt like. Could life be lead as a simile? He had never once before asked himself such a question. But he had stated something the night before that called him to question. He said it as an obvious matter of fact, a thing of record. Yet—being a fact, he assumed, essentially of no note—one he had never come across before.

They had tickets to a Broadway show. He and Vivian and Harrison. They always caught a play while in New York, and they were treating Harrison. But Vivian and Harrison continued to work late into the afternoon and beyond into dinner. Maybe, they had said, you should go without us. We've got this speech to get done.

Ed went and sat with an empty seat on either side. The impression is, maybe, he thought, here's a man who hates being pushed next to people seated next to him so much that he buys three seats to guarantee elbow room. Eccentric and expensive, but when you've got it...

The play was fine. A colossal production, well-staged. A large cast well moved. Moving in what it had to say. Colorful, of course. Rousing, a bit, offering that lift you express in rounds of applause, beating out your appreciation. The actors bow, the actors direct your attention to the orchestra, the actors bow again, the actors direct your attention to the stars, they bow, smile, you applaud some more. At this point, it is a teamwork effort between them and you to make the feeling right, to make it theater. The curtain comes down. People pick up their coats, umbrellas, purses, and programs and break in the middle of rows to exit right and exit left. They go down the stairs together, chattering, expressing opinions—loving, hating, accepting without prejudice—vibrating off into pairs or more, out into the street flowing with taxis.

Ed did not go for a taxi. Why fight it now? Why be in such a hurry? He walked alone down 45th to Broadway. He walked to Times Square, to the concentrations of light deliberately formed to form emotions, move you this way or that, and direct your attention. Ed walked with sureness. Always in a place like this, walk with sureness. He did the first time he came here, and he always did since. Take it in, but take it in subtly. Never stare, never show signs of awe, look like you have business to attend to, and give no hint that you do not belong.

Ed turned in when he reached it. He went down the stairs to the room with the booths, decorated in reflective materials and lights, which gave and received and gave and received to create a wet candy, licked color look that Ed liked. The man stood near the center of the room with a handful of quarters and a handful of bills. He watched the six or seven men mill around, looking at the booth doors, reading the signs, grabbing glances at each other. "Come on guys, no loitering," the man said. "Spend your money, come on." Ed walked up to him, handed him a five-dollar bill, and took quarters in exchange. He walked over to and entered a private booth, placing two coins in the slot.

The panel slid up, opening on a curved room, walled on one end by the connected booths with identical panels—some open, some closed. Soon, a live nude girl was dancing in front of him. There was another to the side dancing in front of another open panel. There was no glass, as in London, no impediment. Ed stared, and the girl in front of him, who stared right back, pushed her pelvis close for a better view and an easier fantasy. Her partner was doing much the same. "Hey, you like that?" She said to the man in the other booth. "Betcha you'd like to reach right out and touch it?" "Yeah," he said. "And what would happen if I did?" He had read the signs—NO TOUCHING OR PROCURING ALLOWED BETWEEN EMPLOYEES AND CUSTOMERS. She smiled. "Why I'd cut the fucker off!" The man laughed.

Ed's girl was not bad, but another panel opened, and she moved on. However, he could still see her and leaned in slightly to watch her work the other booth. Then his panel slid down; the bought time had expired. He quickly put two more quarters in, and the panel slid up again. The girl saw that she had a loyal following and gave Ed a look, sticking out and moving her tongue in a classic bit of signaling.

Time was called again, so Ed left this booth for another. Another live nude girl. But behind the panel, glass this time. She was alone in her private connecting booth. Alone just for Ed. Alone with a phone, a means for an intimate conversation—if one so wished. No dancing, she sat on a stool, caressed herself, and looked at Ed lovingly. This was not cheap. This cost two dollars to raise the panel.

Ed picked up the phone, a little nervous; he never knew what to say. She picked up her phone. "Hello," Ed said while looking up and down, trying to show his admiration. Why not? Give her something. Do something for her.

"Hello," she said.

"How are you this evening?"

"Oh, I'm just fine, honey. How are you?"

"Oh, okay. Especially now."

She smiled. She ran her hand over her breasts, stopping to pinch and play with her nipples. Down more, five fingers wide, down to—

"You like cunt?"

"I uh—do find an occasion now and then to like it, yes."

"She stared at Ed's crotch. She lifted her head slightly and made eye contact. "Let me see yours."

"What?"

"Let's see it."

"No—no, I don't think so."

"Why not?" she said with a practiced pout.

"Because I'm a voyeur, not an exhibitionist."

Time was up, and the panel slammed down...

***

Ed stopped looking at Alice. He got up off the bench and walked around the conservatory pond, passing a class of schoolchildren, all speaking French. He eventually returned to 5th Avenue and returned to the apartment building.

***

The limousine slowly passed Lincoln Center. The light-enhanced white buildings made a festive statement, as the noted of New York turned out for a benefit performance of a new opera, pulling up, getting out of their cars, passing between the New York State Theater and Avery Fisher Hall, and towards the Metropolitan Opera House, to end up stopping, and possibly greeting friends, under the murals of Chagall. The air was cool, and the laughter sharp as the world concentrated for these people, as the black not reached by the lights of Lincoln Center became borders, beyond which the temporarily obscured rest of the world ceased to exist.

Vivian viewed this from her limousine and thought two thoughts. First, it was an occasion she should be attending, usually would be attending, but now, because of her speaking engagement at Fordham, she was not. Strange. She had a funny and petty paranoid feeling as if she was viewing the lights and spirit of the "prom" from the parking lot, having not been invited for not being liked. Second, why are they carrying on so when I am speaking tonight, practically next door? The world is coming to a crazy end. I have something to say about it, and these dressed-up dolls are mechanically going to the opera.

Stupid. Stupid thought. Egocentric. But still...

"I didn't realize this thing was tonight," Harrison said. "It really ties up traffic. But we've got plenty of time."

"Where are we supposed to go?" Ed asked.

"Don't know. Some girl's going to meet us. "Um," Harrison took a slip of paper from his coat pocket, unfolded it, and read, "A Shelly Clarke. She'll direct us."

Vivian felt some regret. Maybe she was missing something. Perhaps night illuminated by man's sense of fun was fine, was all right to deal with, enough for life, for it was recorded with smiles, under the best conditions, hair in style, clothes on straight, pleasure well placed. SNAP! It's in the papers, and everyone who wasn't there reads and sees it, bringing a little of the illuminated into their own lives. No! Now and then, yes, on occasion, for effect, but always? No! It's illuminated but not important.

"I think this is it, ma'am," the chauffeur said as he pulled up to the curb in front of Fordham. Standing there waiting was a young woman in jeans and boots, a thick turtle-neck sweater, and a bulky coat. She had long, straight hair parted in the middle and a slogan-bearing button pinned boldly on the coat's lapel. She was the image of the activist, Ed thought. A standard item, carried for some time now, the stocks rarely depleted. She looked eager to be angry. Ed hated that.

"Ms. Pavin? Hello, I'm Shelly Clarke. I'm honored to meet you."

"Thank you, Shelly. But, please, call me Vivian. Ms. Pavin was my mother's name. And please have me introduced as Mrs. Handlin."

"Oh yes, of course. I'm sorry, I—"

"That's okay. By the way, this is my husband, Ed Handlin, and our attorney and good friend, Harrison McNeil."

"Hello."

"Hello."

"Hello."

"Well, we've got a huge crowd. The whole campus has been excited to see you."

"That's very gratifying."

They walked hurriedly in the cold, following Shelly, even though she insisted on walking among them. It made steps uneasy and direction hard to predict. But it was normal. Shelly was afflicted with the common condition of VIP Proximity—an instinctual move to worship in conflict with a calculated determination to stand on equal ground. It was worse when you truly admired the person and their actions so well defined your thoughts. You want them on high, but you also want to be worthy of being on high with them. Shelly felt giddy but fought it. She wanted to smile stupidly but suppressed it. As they entered the foyer, where some of the students still milled, she knew that all eyes turned to them because of Vivian, but attendant to that was the fact that she—Shelly—was within their vision as well, linked, in their view, with Vivian. So, she acted accordingly, taking straightforward and straight serious steps from important point A to equally important point B.

Shelly took them to a small room to wait and have coffee. They sat on a couch and caught their breaths.

"Once this No-Birth thing started," Shelly, who felt the need to provide conversation, said, facing Vivian and addressing her directly, "several of us grouped to protest. We wanted to get active, you know. We don't believe you can sit around when this kind of thing happens. We felt the great need to do something, so we discussed it, and..."

Returning to college was like returning to college, Vivian suddenly realized.

Ed sat and drank coffee.

Harrison was on his feet.

"… nobody listened much, but when the truth about Butcher Butchko came out, it got better, and then your news conference, and wow! That really had an impact! So we..."

Ed got up to get some more coffee.

Harrison sat down.

"...well, we didn't have a name, you know, we were a very loose group. But with all these things going on, we got organized, so we needed a name for an identity, so we chose *The Jan Lawrence Society!*"

"I'm sorry," Vivian pulled her mind off Ed at the coffee machine. "The what society?"

"The Jan Lawrence Society."

"I—who?—I don't think I've..."

"The woman, you know, who took her and her baby's lives in protest of No-Birth."

"The woman who killed herself," Harrison further explained, "At the Music Center in Los Angeles."

"Oh, I'm sorry, I've been so busy. I guess I hadn't read about it."

"Yeah, we thought the name was appropriate and would honor her. Look, I'll go see if they're ready for you. I'll be right back."

Vivian turned to Harrison after Shelly had left. "If my news conference had such goddamn impact and helped get them all together, how come they didn't call themselves The Vivian Pavin Handlin Society?"

"Because," Ed answered from the coffee machine, "Vivian Pavin Handlin is not dead."

13

Tuesday, December 20—Queens

Sleep, like death, is no relief.

You had gone to bed, you were tired, the sheets felt good, and it had been a hard day, but it was at an end; that's the only thing good about days: they eventually end—ahh! You have some thoughts; you pass stuff by yourself, you try to be satisfied with the situation, the possible solutions to the subjects of your thoughts; you move a little, you turn over on your side, maybe; suddenly you remember something you forgot to do—DAMN!—it was important, it will be a bitch tomorrow. Oh well, you breathe deep. I can't do anything about it now; you might as well...

You are awake. It is light, the alarm is screaming; that thing you couldn't do anything about is now ready to declare itself urgent and within your grasp, or rather, it is grasping you, pulling you out of bed...

Gerald Downing reached over in rapid reflex and turned the alarm off. He left his bed, marched into his little living room, turned on the TV, switched to the right channel, retreated to the bathroom, and urinated. When he got back to the living room, the morning news and information talk show was just getting started. He kept the sound low as his mother, whom he lived with, was still asleep.

"... appeared last night at Fordham University, speaking to a rally sponsored by the newly formed organization, The Jan Lawrence Society, named for the recent political suicide victim. One week ago, the now Mrs. Handlin declared that she would defy the government's Birth Cessation Act by not aborting the child she claims to be carrying. In what can only be described as a rousing speech, she called upon the students and others to follow her example."

The newscaster—young and neat of hair with a cleft in his chin—faded from the screen, and the taped image of Vivian Pavin Handlin took over.

"... both sexes can do their part. This is not women's struggle alone, but the struggle of all free people who wish to remain free. Men! Stop agreeing to the state-ordered violation of your reproductive rights! Stop submitting to the unconstitutional vasectomies. Women! Stop aborting your children! They are not the state's but *your* children. Men! Impregnate your loved one *now!* Women! *Get pregnant!* The whole of the childbearing population of America should GET PREGNANT! If we all got pregnant, what could they do? Who would they attack first? Could Butcher Butchko use his bloodied blade on us all? No! Our sheer numbers would defeat him. I say, GET PREGNANT! I say, GET PREGNANT! I say GET PREGNANT!

"GET PREGNANT!" the crowd responded.

"GET PREGNANT!"

"GET PREGNANT!"

"GET PREGNANT!"

The newscaster returned. "Mrs. Handlin will be our in-studio guest in this half hour, talking to Frank. But first, these messages."

Jesus, Gerald thought as he got up to make some coffee. *God, that was great!* He felt as he returned to the living room and turned the sound down on the commercials to think.

Get pregnant!

Get pregnant!

I must support her. I must give her my full support. What other course is there? What other weapon do we have but the weapon of our bodies? The very bodies our government is so desperate to control.

She must need, reason told him, assistants—at least, an administrative assistant, certainly.

"Hello? Yes, this is Gerald Downing, Vivian Pavin Handlin's AA..."

I could note it all down, could...

"Look, you'll need an official biographer. You're a great woman. You probably don't realize that, but you're critical to this country. And now, with this..."

...could get to know her intimately, not just as her biographer, but as a friend...

"I would say that I knew her as well as any man alive..."

...weep during the eulogy at her funeral. Give the eulogy! Tears came easily to him.

"...for whom was Vivian Pavin Handlin, but a person with the clarity of vision to see a danger that others saw as just some pretty panacea to the country's problems. Was she not, then, the Paul Revere of her time? As well as the Minute Man, putting herself on the front line of battle? In the quiet moments, she often said to me..."

The whistle blew on the kettle for the coffee; the commercials were coming to an end. Gerald ran to the kitchen, turned off the fire, then ran back to the TV.

Frank came on—the host. Sincere and straight-backed, Midwest and intelligent and easy to know with a wry thought always edged at the corner of his eyes. Now, though, he seemed slightly confused, looking for a quick and appropriate summary of the events.

"We spend our time on this show reporting and commenting on the news. It isn't often that we get to make it. But I think we've made it now. Vivian Pavin Handlin, the most successful female industrialist of our age and recent challenger of the Birth Cessation Law, has just been arrested by FBI agents here, in our studios, just before her scheduled appearance before our cameras. It has, to say the least, thrown us all into a bit of confusion, but we'll try to report the facts of this extraordinary incident as accurately as possible. Seated here next to me is Sally Hemmings, one of our associate producers, who was with Mrs. Handlin when the arrest occurred. Sally, can you tell us exactly what happened?

"Well, Frank, I was with Mrs. Handlin in the green room—"

"For our viewers, the green room is where our guests wait before coming on camera."

"Uh, yes, thank you—anyway, we were in the green room, having coffee, when three men entered and identified themselves as FBI agents and announced that they had a warrant for Mrs. Handlin's arrest in connection with alleged violations of the Birth Cessation Law. Then, well—then they led her away."

"Well, now, let me try to understand this. Were you alone in the green room with Mrs. Handlin?"

"No, her lawyer, Harrison McNeil, was there with her. And, of course, he did all the talking when the agents arrived. And, also, there was Ed Handlin, Mrs. Handlin's husband."

"And, presumably, the father of her unborn child."

"Yes, that's right."

"Was he arrested as well?"

"Uh—yes, they also had a warrant for his arrest."

"Do you have any idea, Sally, how the FBI agents got into the studios and the green room?"

"Well, that was a simple matter of their authority. Our network security people had no reason to deny them access."

"Well, this certainly must be, as far as we know, the first time that a controversial individual set to appear on a television show has been arrested before doing so. We also have no idea why the government decided to arrest Vivian Pavin at this time. After all, her defiance of the law has been known for the past week. We have no indication if this was planned as a grandstand event, in which case arresting her on camera certainly would have been more dramatic. Or, since we are live, it might be assumed that government officials woke up, like most of you watching, to the information that Ms. Pavin would be our in-studio guest and decided to take that opportunity to come down here and arrest her. We will endeavor to clarify the situation and report it to you as soon as possible. Now, Sally, one last question. It is obvious, of course, that Vivian Pavin expected to be arrested for her actions, for she was taking those actions specifically to be arrested, setting her up to challenge the government on the issue of Birth Cessation, but did she seem at all surprised by the arrest, and especially its time and place?"

"No, Frank, actually, just the opposite. She seemed very accepting of it. She offered no resistance, of course, and, as I said, let her lawyer speak for her. There was one small moment, though, when I did perceive in her reaction a particular look, a—it's hard to peg down—well, I would say it was a look of realization that your opponent had just made a very good move indeed."

"As in a chess game?"

"If you like. Or hand-to-hand combat, for that matter."

"Well, she may be right. Time will tell. Thank you, Sally, for that report. As I said, we will keep you updated on this story, which we seem to have become involved in. But now, let us break for some commercials. We'll be back."

Gerald was quick to the phone (*quick to action*, he thought of himself), quick to call Malcolm Kirkly.

"Hello?"

"Uh, hello, Mr. Kirkly?"

"Yes."

"Uh, Mr. Kirkly, this is Gerald Downing, remember? I came by the other day last week."

"Yes, Mr. Downing. I'm sorry, I haven't read your articles yet, but once I do, I promise I'll call and—"

"Well, I'm not really calling about that, Mr. Kirkly. It's something different, it's—well, did you just see on TV the arrest of Vivian Pavin?"

"Yes, I did, I was just watching it."

"Well, I was just wondering, uh, I know you said you couldn't get involved in any protest organization, but things are a little different now. I mean, she's been arrested merely for being pregnant, and I think we ought to do something about it and quickly. So, I thought that if maybe, through your column, you could help get something started. I mean, I think we ought to form a defense fund for Mrs.—uh—Handlin. You know, solicit money to pay the legal costs because, I think, obviously, this will probably go, you know, to the Supreme Court, so I thought, well, I mean, that's basically it."

"Mr. Downing, you may not be aware, but I doubt Mrs. Handlin needs a defense fund raised on her behalf. She has, I would guess, a few million to spare for the job. She is probably protesting simply because she knows she can afford to."

"Oh."

"I'm sorry, Mr. Downing. But do get back to me later about your writing."

"Oh, okay. Thank you, Mr. Kirkly."

"You're welcome. Good-bye."

"Good-bye."

14

Wednesday, December 21—Syndicated

GUEST EDITORIAL THE FINAL, FINAL SOLUTION?

By Rabbi Bernard Behar

Antisemitism is a creature at times brazen and foolish and, at other times, subtle and sly. Jews have been both clubbed and excluded from clubs. Epithets against the Children of Moses have ranged from "murderers!" to "merchants," both stated with spit. Hitler, the fool, in a hate-filled and shameless action, tried to wipe us off the face of the earth. The Arabs tried for years to drive Israel into the sea, whether by military action or Petro Dollar blackmail.

But despite all of this, the Jews have survived. For 3000 years, we have survived. But that is no assurance that we will survive another 3000, 300, or even 30. For, as everything else in our time has become sophisticated, so has antisemitism.

Consider Birth Cessation. A concept passed into law with hardly any protest. An idea designed—its architects state—to lessen the burden of too many people crowding the nation. But what burden are they trying to ease? People in general? Or, possibly, some specific people? Who among the various minorities in this country will be "lessened" the most? The Jews, of course.

Between 1970 and 1980, the population of Jews in the United States decreased by 100,000, dropping to 2 1/2 percent from 3 percent of the U.S. population. After 1980, the decrease, while less dramatic, has undoubtedly been steady. We Jews have been combating the decline by increasing our proselytizing, something that does not come naturally to us. We have become, out of necessity, missionaries. Not to convert some far-off islanders but to bring back into the religion Jews who make a point of claiming the title by biological circumstances alone. We wanted to put the spirit back into the genes. It worked. We became less, but we became more robust.

Antisemites must have found it a horrible dichotomy. A cutting down in the number of Jews—their hearts' desire—and yet, stronger, more apparent, more visible Jews. How does an anti-Semite respond to that?

Is Birth Cessation such a crazy answer? Every group's population will decrease. But ours may fall to a point where we become negligible to the nation. Our population may drop to a virtual point of no return.

The anti-Semites may have found a way to wipe us out, drive us into the sea, and destroy our race—finally.

This is a much smarter plan than Hitler's. His actions, as horrible as they were, were, by the fact of their horror, the progenitor of the State of Israel. But who will see Birth Cessation as a horrible act against the Jews? Who could even recognize it as such?

If we do not do something, and soon, we Jews in America may fade away—unnoticed.

***

Washington, D.C.

THAT WILL TEACH HER NOT TO MESS WITH DARRYL BUTCHKO!

It was the statement Butchko wanted to make, almost for medicinal purposes. It would have relieved the past week's pain, frustration, and mental congestion. It would have been satisfying. It would have been sweet. It would have been a broad-smile, self-soothing statement to shout like something out of a Broadway musical. An emotion made strong and solid to withstand a great effort to project to the back rows. But no real emotion is solid. Emotions are layered, can flake, can separate into more than one.

THAT WILL TEACH HER NOT TO MESS WITH DARRYL BUTCHKO!

It was, ultimately, more sad than satisfying. Butchko knew that, hated knowing that, hated being denied the simple pleasure of revenge by the more complex knowledge that revenge itself is no finer than that which motivated it.

Partly motivated it, Butchko thought. This is official; there are objective concerns: she broke the law, she has endangered the future of this country, and she is doing this to the *country*, hurting the *country*, not me. We have somehow arrived on the same field at the same time to play before the same crowd.

Butchko liked that—he had to admit—finally—maybe after talking to the president. He, too, realized and enjoyed that this was history here, visible enough to be written down someday. Despite the conflict, the fact that Vivian had been a close friend, despite their close connection, and the hurt he felt at her opposing him, at least this was the essential drama of the day, not just one of the many petty little stories progressing to ends butted up against, and almost indistinguishable from, a million new beginnings all laying around, off over there, tucked into that corner, or this one, central only to those tucked away with them. This was the final, the ultimate story of the day. Opposed by Vivian or not, they were linked, for they both remained part of the *Brethren of the Focus,* standing together to be seen, seen often, and recognized, seen as offering the same thing to the world, disagreements apart.

That could exhilarate—the thought of it, Butchko had to admit. But he was no more willing to show it than to shout:

THAT WILL TEACH HER NOT TO MESS WITH DARRYL BUTCHKO!

They used to make love. Years ago. "Fuck," Vivian would say. Butchko had always insisted on "Make love."

"We don't make love, goddamn it! We fuck, Darryl, we fornicate, we screw! We do it because it's fun, because it feels good, because we come to climaxes, our bodies tremble, and we make silly sounds of delight because we're having such a goddamn good time."

"There's no tenderness there? Is that what you're telling me, Viv? No love? No passion for the person, as well as lust for the body? Are you telling me that those quiet moments, those nice calm, non-climatic times when we're just lying in each other's arms, gently stroking each other, mean nothing, have nothing to do with it?"

"Those quiet moments bore me stiff."

"Well, thank you!"

"I mean it. I mean, what the hell, we've done it, it felt great, but now it's over, damn it, there are other things to do; what the hell are we just laying around for?"

"Well, yeah, sure, I guess you're right. I guess I shouldn't be surprised. What the hell, you fuck like a man anyway."

"What's that supposed to mean?"

"You know what I mean. You always expect me to do this, that, and the other to make you feel good, to get you there, but I got to fight like hell to get you to do a few simple things for me."

"Well, I do them."

"Yeah, but with that sense-of-duty smirk on your face. I tell you, you can make someone feel just like shit."

"Oh, go to hell!"

Yet Darryl proposed to Vivian—more than once. There was something about her eyes. Hard was the impression some first got. But Butchko saw them as firmly set on goals, backed by intelligence. Shining, not with liquid, with a light. Illumination, not reflection. It had been his curse to fall for women intelligent enough not to fall—in a giddy, stupid way—for men. What he had always loved in women was independence. But their independence meant that they had no real need for him. For somebody, he supposed, but not for him. But then, of course, there was Bobbie, but—

"Sir?" George Mays walked in.

"Yes, George?"

"They've arrived in Los Angeles."

"And was court time found?"

"Yes, sir. In about two hours. Judge Ramírez. Ninth district."

"What do you know about him?"

"The Justice Department says he's a 'tough guy'—their words—on violations of things like environmental standards, integration stands, civil rights and immigration cases. They seem to think he believes that Birth Cessation gives his people—that is, Spanish surnames—their best chance to finally get their share of the pie."

"Sounds good."

"Yeah."

"Manipulative as hell, but good."

"Well, it achieves the goal, sir."

"I just think we've got to get it done quickly. She's becoming a goddamn example—uh—a model for people. That whole crap, her calling for—her calling for women to get pregnant and all. Jesus, that's dangerous! Because she's right, isn't she? If everybody did that, we couldn't control it; we'd have no way. What would we do? Send in the National Guard to abort pregnancies? Then, the whole thing would be lost. Women would have twice as many babies as they normally would, just out of spite. Our resources would deplete just that much faster. Hunger would increase here, worse abroad. And the worse it got abroad, the angrier the rest of the world would get at us. There will be no fuel; industry would grind to a halt, mass unemployment, idle, angry people out there, leading to anarchy, the weakening of our freedoms, a climate for some dictator to—sorry, George. I'm lecturing again. It's the teacher in me. Sorry."

"No need to apologize, sir."

"It's just—it's irritating that they can't see that! That *she* can't see that! What she is doing is tantamount to treason. Only here, the enemy is our future selves. Well, with luck, we've stopped her."

"Looks like it."

"Will you get me the president, George?"

"Right away."

It took twenty minutes.

"Darryl."

Mr. President, good afternoon, sir. I thought I would give you a brief report on the situation."

"Fine. Go ahead."

"She's in Los Angeles now, sir, and will be in court in an hour and a half. Judge Ramírez."

"Yes, I know him. A hard worker during the campaign. He's a good man."

"We're hoping for a positive decision. We feel confident about getting it. That, then, should diminish her influence."

"Good. Sounds fine. However, on a personal level, Darryl, will your past relationship with Pavin cause you any embarrassment? Will Kirkly, for example, find anything in it? Can he use it like he used your daughter?

Blunt, Darryl thought. Brutal in his lack of delicate embellishments.

"No, I don't think so, sir. If anything, it's a plus. Friend or not, we're prosecuting because she has broken the law."

"How close are you to her?"

"I've known her since college. While I was teaching at U.C.L.A., we socialized with her and Ed Handlin.

"What's he like?"

"He was a lower echelon career State Department employee. I think that about says it all. I've also known him since college, but I can't say I know him well. He's not someone you care to know much about."

"Do you think he strongly supports his wife? Do you think he truly understands that this could mean jail for him?"

"Well, I think he would support anybody who would feed him, sir."

"Okay. On another note, what do you think is the potential of our action making a martyr out of her?"

"No, I don't think so. That's why we're getting it done fast, to prevent that sort of thing from building up."

"But you are almost attacking her with a vengeance. Don't we come off as the bad guys here?"

"No, sir! Definitely not! Maybe if she was some poor housewife from Iowa who wanted to be a mother. But this is one of the richest women in the world, a famous businesswoman, and a person known for enjoying the limelight. I don't see how she can get much sympathy from the average citizen. I think they'll see her as a spoiled rich bitch playing little games for her own amusement."

"That may be too quick of an assumption, Darryl. All hate of the rich is born from envy. And all envy is just the love of the unattainable. But love nevertheless."

There was a pause.

"Darryl?"

"Yes, Mr. President?"

"We talked briefly once about the potential of a Herod in all of this. It was, on my part, a selfish conversation. I suppose I initiated it to gain your assurances that I would not become the Herod of our age. I no longer need those assurances from you, Darryl. But it is also true that I could not give them to you."

"I need none, sir."

"Well, good, Darryl. Self-assurance is always good."

***

Los Angeles

"Your honor, I respectfully request that the bench reconsider its order. Since we are dealing here with a highly controversial law, which will be tested in this court, it seems to the defense that any decision on the application of the law should be withheld until its future is decided."

Judge Ramírez knew exactly how Harrison McNeil felt. His well-planned and professionally admirable legal maneuver was surprisingly failing. But did McNeil realize how Ramírez felt? He had blocked the maneuver with a swift move of his own and deserved the allowance of a hidden broad grin, an unseen bow acknowledging the unheard applause, which is probably what McNeil was expecting. But this time, it was a different satisfaction than that; this time, it was not a question of gaining points for his side (the unofficial side of the judge). Points didn't seem to matter; little victories held little appeal. There is no time for satisfaction in the right applied techniques of saving a drowning man—there is only the rush to save.

"Mr. McNeil, while the bench recognizes that this law will have to stand the test of this court and most likely others, it also cannot ignore the fact that it is a law now in force and a law with clearly stated demands."

"But, your Honor, we have not pleaded guilty, nor has my client been proven guilty. And yet this court is applying the punishment."

"Mr. McNeil, I resent that statement for its implications, and it puts you very near contempt! If your client is proven guilty in this court, the sentence will be handed down at that time and not before. And I remind you that it will be a sentence dealing with a mandatory fine and incarceration, as the law provides. It will have nothing to do with this court's current order, and thus, this court's current order has nothing to do with it. Mr. McNeil, if your client was a burglar and had the presumably stolen goods in possession at the time of apprehension, would you object to their being impounded for evidence?"

"Your Honor, you can hardly—"

"Would you, Mr. McNeil?"

"No, your Honor."

"Then I see no reason for your objection on this occasion. The law clearly states that all women less than twenty-four weeks pregnant at the time of its inception shall report to an authorized clinic for an abortion. Those disobeying this Federal law shall be taken into custody, and their pregnancies shall be aborted involuntarily if need be. Then they shall be brought to trial with all deliberate speed."

"But, your Honor, we are challenging that very law."

"And I don't deny you that constitutional right. But until the law is reversed, I shall follow it to the letter. Your client is to report for an abortion at her designated clinic within seventy-two hours. I will release her into your recognizance, Mr. McNeil, and charge you as an officer of the court to see that she acts according to the law.

Court adjourned."

15

Friday, December 23—Pasadena, California

Sparky's Family Coffee Shop on Colorado Boulevard in Pasadena, California, like Sparky's Family Coffee Shops everywhere, was interiorly decorated in sort of a whore's lipstick pink and shades of purple, such as her pimp might wear. Or possibly they were candy colors, the hard kind displayed in clear glass jars with glass lids that eventually get chipped on the rim. The pink and purple color scheme encompassed the walls, the trim, the booths where people slid in to claim their transient family dinners, and the dresses—the uniforms—of the waitresses: light pink blouses with puffed sleeves, flared, ridged skirts of light purple, a dark burgundy over-apron. The menus were laminated and caught the glare of the bright overhead lighting. They featured such items as the *Sparkyburger*, the *Sparkydelux* (roast beef and American cheese grilled); *Sparky Jones' Locker* (fish and chips), the *Sparkymelt* (your choice, tuna or ground beef and cheese, grilled again, the *Sparkysteak*, and Sparky himself, a poorly illustrated little plump pink and purple boy with freckles, who bowed and presented color photos of the various Sparky meals on plates. And, of course, there were tempting desserts, which included a *Sparkyshake* and Sparky's specialty, *Strawberry Sparkycake.*

In the corner of the coffee shop stood a pink Christmas tree with purple ornaments.

The public address system was softly playing, "God Rest Ye Merry Gentlemen," and Karen Winfield was humming along with it as she poured coffee for the customers who had just come in and sat down in booth 15.

Karen liked Christmas. She was looking forward to it. She lived with her parents; they were more or less close, and they always put on a big thing, and she had gotten the day off. After three years here, she had seniority, and the manager said yes to her request for Christmas off, even though they would be open that day, with a special *Sparkyturkey* dinner offer. Karen took the coffee to her customers, who were still looking at their menus as they talked.

"Can I take your order now?"

"Umm..."

"Umm…"

"Umm…"

They all said.

"How about if I give you a minute or two, then come back?"

"Yeah, sounds good. Uh, could we have some ice water, though?"

"Oh, sure. Be right back with it."

"They were regular customers, although Karen did not know their names. *Your neighborhood Sparkys* stood somewhere between a real neighborhood eatery and just a cold link in a hard chain. She knew people by sight, enough to smile warmly and say, "Hi!" how she liked to, but not enough to mean the "Have a good day" she would leave them with. But that was okay; she held no nostalgia for small-town America. Her parents did, some, but only from old movies seen on television. They had been born and raised, and their daughter had been born and raised in the Southern California suburbs: flat-landed stretches of houses, schools, stores, parks/houses, schools, stores, parks/houses, schools, stores, parks divided into areas called cities, with interchangeable names, if not totally indistinguishable.

"Hey Karen, you're up!" the cook called out. The three *Sparkyburgers*—one with cheese—that booth 17 had ordered were ready. She went to them, checked them, added garnish, grabbed them, and ran them over to booth 17.

"Here you go. More coffee?"

"Please." She rushed back behind the counter, grabbed a pot of coffee, took it to booth 17, poured, then moved to booth 15.

"More coffee?"

"Sure."

"You ready to order?"

They were and did. Karen noted it all, ran back to the kitchen and slapped the order form onto the little carousel of hooks that served as the conduit of communication with the cook.

Three men in booth 15 drank their coffee and waited on their orders. They came here often after work, when they worked late, and they often worked late. As students from Pasadena City College came here often, and women from the beauty college across the street, and clerks and salesmen from the discount department store next door.

The three men worked at an appliance repair service, taking in and fixing toasters, blenders, and coffee machines still under warranty, which guaranteed free treatment for their ills. There was the manager, a middle-aged, tallish, diluted Dutchman (born of a pure Dutch father but also of a mother whose family managed to mix Anglos and Latins and, possibly, American Indians into their blood), who, nevertheless, was always referred to as that "stubborn dutchman." He took no little ethnic pride in that. There was the head repairman, a short, stocky, near-bald sixty-year-old who looked like he could fix anything he got his hands on if he cared to, but he rarely ever cared to. And there was the young, newlywed kid who worked the counter and was rude to the customers as if they had no right to bother him with all this broken shit.

"Jack?" The kid addressed the manager. "I need next Wednesday off."

"What? What the hell for? We're closed on Friday; you'll get that day off."

"Yeah, I know that. But I'm supposed to have my vasectomy on Wednesday."

"Oh shit! You gonna go?"

"Well, sure, I have to."

"The hell you do. With all this crap starting up, you'll be just as well not to."

"What crap?"

"Jeez, man, don't you watch the news or anything? What do you think of that, Sam? Goddamn young people! Look, people are starting to protest this No-Birth stuff. People burning themselves, holding rallies, that thing Vivian Pavin's doing."

"Who?"

"Oh, Christ! Well, it don't matter. I just wouldn't bother with it right now."

"You mean you're not going to have yours?"

"Don't need to."

"Why not?"

"Already did it. Years ago. I had one kid. Sure didn't want any more after that."

"Then why don't you want me to get mine? Jane and I got one kid, too."

"That's not it. It's just that if this No-Birth thing is going to be reversed, then it will be a waste."

"How do you know it's going to be reversed?"

"I just do, kid, because it's obvious. Hell, whenever protesters start bitching, things just flip-flop around. I've seen it all my life. It's the squeaky wheel law of life. You know about the squeaky wheel?"

"Yeah, I guess."

"People are getting mad over this. It's just the government telling them what to do again. They hate that."

"Oh, I don't know. It seems to me it's for our own good."

"Oh shit! What the hell do you know? You're still wiping snot with your sleeve. Listen to me, damn it! It don't matter if it's for our own good. 'We the People' don't like the government mucking around with us. Why the hell are they telling us that we can't have kids? Right Sam?"

"Yeah, sure."

"But you can't have kids anyway."

That's not the point! Maybe I don't want kids, but I also don't want them telling me I can't have kids if I do want them.

"Even if it's for the good of the country?"

"Oh fuck the good of the country! It's only for the good of the rich bastards and the politicians. They're the ones who are going to get something out of this. Not us little guys."

"What are they going to get?"

"What? Well, shit, it's obvious if you'd just think about it. They want to take the pressure off them. I mean, an over-populated country of angry people who can't get what they want leads to revolution, right? Well, they don't want no revolution, so they're going to cut down on the population—make us too small to do anything. That's the whole plan."

"How do you know? I mean, who told you?"

"Oh shit, anybody with half a brain can see it!"

"Which half?" Silent Sam asked.

"What?" Jack looked at Sam with no affection.

"Which half of the brain gave you this insight?"

"Shut up, Sam!"

Sam smiled and took a sip of his coffee.

"I don't know," the kid said. "I think it's a good idea. They want to make it easier for us to live."

"It will never be easy for 'us' to live, kid. And it will always be easy for them to live. Do you think cutting down on the population is going to change anything? Shit no! Thems that got will get more, that's all. And you and I will still just be struggling along. It's the corporations, you know. They own everything, they run everything, they are everything."

"What do you mean?"

"I mean, it's the corporations. They're conspiring to do all this. They've got ol' Butchko in their hip pocket. All that crap about his dead kid, all that psychology crap, was just a smokescreen. He's just doing this in the pay of the corporations."

"I don't understand that, Jack. How do you know all of this?"

"I know."

"Oh, bullshit! I bet you don't know any more than anybody else. If the corporations are so powerful, how come a few people protesting is going to change things?"

"Look, kid, don't argue with me. I've got double the years on you."

"What the hell does that have to do with it?"

"Well, you'll know when you get to be my age. A little experience in life is what you need."

Their order came, and fresh coffee and a bottle of catsup for their fries.

"Well, what do you think of all this?" the kid asked Sam, the repairman, who shrugged his shoulders.

"What do I know? What do I care? That Vivian Pavin got all kinds of corporations, but she's against No-Birth."

"Oh Christ, Sam, she doesn't have corporations like I'm talking about. I'm talking about the big ones. She's just an attention-getter. Always has been. She just goes into things for the glory. She's a big show off."

"Oh, I don't know." Sam countered. "They said on the news that they're going to make her have an abortion. That's going pretty extreme for a little glory."

"Well, if you think she'll have to have that abortion, you're dumber than the kid here. Somebody that rich don't ever have to do what they're told."

"I still don't get this corporation thing. I think that's nuts," said the kid.

"Look, they've been running this country for years, hell, the world! Everybody knows that, right? There's no real governments anymore. They just decided they wanted less people, so they press a button, and boom, there you have it: a law is passed. Hell, man, all that stuff about Butchko really writing the bill? Of course, he did! Under orders from the corporations!"

"But why?"

"Why not?"

"That's no answer, damn it!"

"The corporations don't need to give any answers."

"I don't want answers from them; I'm trying to get some from you."

"Look, *kid,* I don't have to give you no answers. What I'm telling you is right. If you would use your brains a minute, you would see that."

"Oh, fuck!"

"Oh yeah, young mister, know-it-all here. You can't be told anything."

"Well, what the hell are you? You say the corporations are doing all this, but you don't say why."

"You don't need a why."

"Why don't I?"

"Look, kid, just believe me. I know what I'm talking about. I've got a few more years on you, and there's some things I've learned that you can't even imagine. So just shut up and listen!"

"Oh, you're full of shit, Jack."

Jack smiled. "Well, you can say that. But someday, you'll know. And then you'll come to me, hat in hand, and say, 'Well, Jack, I guess you were right.'"

"Like hell, I will."

"You can't teach these young shits anything, Sam. Goddamn, look at that! You're already done with your food, and I've hardly got a bite in here."

"That's because I haven't been spouting off about nothing. I eat when I'm hungry. That's my goddamn old age wisdom."

Karen heard some of this conversation as she periodically checked on their coffee cups and condition. It was getting usual. Many people in the coffee shop having breakfast, lunch, or dinner were talking about No-Birth, about the vasectomies and abortions and Butchko, and what the news said about him; about that girl who killed herself and her baby, about Vivian Pavin, who used to get talked about all the time anyway. It was all getting kind of boring for Karen. She didn't like hearing about such things. They used to do it in school, social studies stuff. She didn't like that either. They used to make her read the newspaper and watch the news so they could discuss it the next day, but she didn't want to discuss it, hated being called upon by the teacher, for it was so embarrassing because she didn't understand all that political stuff, all that "current events" stuff, which really didn't have much to do with anything. That's the way she felt, anyway. She hated the look of newspapers, all those columns and little letters. And she didn't like hearing the news; with things said and words used, she didn't quite understand. She admitted such deficiencies, but with no shame, for she didn't like any of this stuff, so it didn't matter. She liked the weatherman at one station; he was funny. And the sports guy was kind of cute.

No-Birth just meant she couldn't have babies. She didn't like that; she wanted someday to have babies. But since she was fat and not too pretty, and shy because of it, even though smiling and pleasant even in the worst of times—also because of it—she never figured to have babies anyway. She never dated in high school; she hadn't in the three years since, so even the fact that men would be unable to impregnate her unwillingly didn't hold much relief for her. Anyway, that astrologer in her favorite paper predicted a major upheaval that would divide the country, which meant, to her, that that gigantic earthquake everybody always talked about would soon happen. Then, all kinds of people would be killed. And that's a more important thing than this thing. The earthquake scared her. She hated it when small ones happened; she was always sure that this one was going to be the Big One. According to what everybody said, California was not the best place to be, but she didn't know where else to go. She was sad about that girl and her baby but didn't understand why she did it; she just thought it was awful and hated to think about it. Vivian Pavin didn't mean much to her. She was pretty and all. And rich, but that didn't mean much to Karen, who did, though, have a box of her Pavin bubble bath in her bathroom with her picture on it; it was last year's Christmas gift from some of the guys at work. She wasn't sure who Butchko was, except something in the government and she had seen him on TV.

"Hey Karen, you're up," the cook shouted, and she went to collect her order.

"What are you doing for Christmas?" the cook asked.

"Oh, gonna be with my parents, I guess."

"That's nice, families are nice."

"Yeah, I like my family okay."

"Sure you do. Got them all good presents?"

"Yeah, I guess."

"What are you gonna get from Santa?"

"Oh, I don't know."

"What'd you ask for? A man, I bet."

Karen laughed a little high-pitched laugh.

"No, look, really, that's what you should ask for."

"Oh sure, fat lot of good it would do."

"Ah, you shouldn't put yourself down."

"Ha, ha, you're very funny."

***

Los Angeles

It was a beautiful house, Vivian Pavin Handlin's house in Hancock Park. It was large and brick—red brick—and solid, designed along some English way, with trims of dark wood. The grounds—where diverse green pants grew—were well ordered in an open display of the rationally creative mind. The house's interior was a true expression of the resident, layered with looks, textures, designs, colors, and feels that formed comfort. Physical comfort, of course, for what was the object of "home" otherwise? But, more importantly, there was also a very personal comfort deriving from the coordination of likes, similarities, and agreements. This "personal" comfort did not exist for visitors, no matter how much they might admire what they saw. Visitors can never really feel at home. Being surrounded by so much presence, not your own, is always uncomfortable.

Parker, a medium-sized man who seemed to consist of one virtually square muscle, a great fan of the L.A. Dodgers and beer in cans, and Vivian's on-call pilot, had always felt suddenly stiff in her home; starched, or something, into an unnaturally good posture. He had been there rarely, and rarely was the way he liked it, even though it was fun to talk about it afterward, and his wife loved to hear all about it. But the rooms were just too big, and things looked too fragile, and there were some immutable laws about this place that he couldn't grasp. Such ignorance was sure to lead to a mistake, an infringement of some kind, and then sirens would blare, and the cuffs would snap on—or so it felt to Parker as he stood in the foyer, which was larger than his whole living room.

"Can it be done?"

Parker looked at Harrison McNeil. He didn't like him. He never had. Other people who traveled with Ms. Pavin in the jet always expressed fascination with the plane and admiration for him for knowing how to fly it. The dream of flight—dreams of flight—still affected many people. But not this guy. Parker always felt like a bus driver when this guy was on the plane.

"Yeah, I guess, but—"

"Let me know now. I must have the facts. And let me know if *you* can do it."

"Well, it is risky. And I don't know, but I would think it's illegal. I mean, beyond FAA stuff."

"I won't lie to you, it is illegal. But it is a good bet they won't find out how it was done. And if they do, you'll have me as your attorney at the company's expense. So don't worry about it."

"Where would you want to go?"

"I'll let you know later."

"I don't know..."

"Look, you'll be taking off from a private field and landing on one. You are just ferrying a new plane to its buyer."

"But I've never done that sort of thing. I mean, they know I work for Ms. Pavin."

"I got you the job. The manufacturer is a client of mine. He had to send this plane over, and his best pilot got sick. I was playing golf with him and suggested you."

"I fly it there and come right back?"

"No. You're going to get a two-week vacation out of this."

"What about my wife?"

"We'll fly her down commercial."

"Well, what if, I mean, suppose somehow I'm stopped before takeoff, and they find her."

"I don't think things will get that dramatic, Parker. But in such a case, the story will be that she snuck on, and you didn't know a thing about it."

"Well, okay. I'll do it for Ms. Pavin. She's been a good boss."

"Good. Now, when you get out there, you ask for Jim Stein. He will act and talk like this is just the ferry job. He won't mention a thing about what's happening, nor should you. You'll have coffee with him and then take off. Mrs. Handlin will already be on board."

"I could lose my license over this?"

"When you come back, Parker, I promise you will still have your license. There will also be a bonus for you. It will be paid, it will seem, by Stein. It's all perfectly safe. Okay?"

"Okay, Mr. McNeil."

Parker left, and Harrison went upstairs.

"Okay, it's all set," Harrison said as he entered the bedroom. Vivian was packing. Ed sat by the window. "But I still think it's a mistake, Viv. You're going to ruin your case. You're going to lose your support."

"I'm going to lose my baby if I don't go Harrison. Try to think of that, will you, damn it! They want to rip my baby out!"

"Of course not, Viv, but I know—"

"Can you stop them? Can your appeals and legal tap dancing stop them?"

"Maybe Viv. The weekend and Christmas give us more time than the seventy-two hours. I might be able to get something done."

"And if not?"

"If not—you will be forced to have the abortion."

"Well, I'm not going to take that chance, Harrison. I'm going to have my baby."

"But, Viv, that kills everything. We don't have a fight then; we can't get this issue into court. You will be a fugitive. You will hand the justification for everything they're doing to them on a platter. Birth Cessation will be stronger because of it."

"I'll fight it from there. Don't worry. We can turn it to an advantage."

"You'll be seen as a coward by everybody. You'll prove to the average person that the rich never have to suffer punishments, and you'll lose them. Have the abortion, and we'll get the people on your side."

"What's the use of going to court if I have to have an abortion?"

"You will still be liable for the fine and imprisonment. Vivian, we are fighting the government's infringement on your body. It's going to be a lot easier, it's going to be a lot clearer to people, if there is an actual infringement, an actual suffering."

"Do you know what you're saying?"

"I'm saying, let them abort the fetus. Then we'll go on and win this fight. Then, you can have another pregnancy in total freedom.

"I want this baby, Harrison. *This* child."

"Damn it, Viv, don't pull this sentimental crap on me. We entered this thing to knock down this law, to destroy it. What you are now doing jeopardizes that."

"I didn't think they would do this."

"Well, they're doing it. Now, let's use it. Have the abortion. Prove you're in this fight to stay and committed to it. Even though you could easily run away to have your baby in safe surroundings, you stay to fight them. You'll be one with all women, you'll become the extreme example, we'll get massive support, and either win in court or get Congress to reverse the whole thing. For God's sake, Viv, for the good of the country, stay!"

"You don't care about me, about this baby!"

"You're right. I don't. I *care* about this country instead. I'm sorry for that. But I'm more concerned about this country being on the right path than I am about your little personal hormone-controlled needs and wants. We have got to stop them, Viv. They'll soon be telling us how to live each second of our days if we don't stop them. You have got to see this through."

"Harrison, I am going to have this baby. I don't have the time to think up rational, political reasons why. I just am. It's what I want. And you know damn well it's a waste of your time telling me what I can't do or what I should do."

"Excuse me." Ed was passing through them.

"Where are you going?" Vivian demanded to know.

"To the bathroom."

"Are you going to pack after that? We haven't much time."

"Uh—no, I don't think so. I don't think I'll go with you."

"What? I suppose you agree with Harrison?"

"No, not necessarily."

"Ed," Harrison said. "They'll try to convict you if you stay, even if Vivian is gone. They're crazy to get someone on the block. If not Viv, then they'll be happy to settle for you. If she must go, then it is best that you go too."

"Ed, you must come. I committed this so-called crime, not you; you know that. What's the good of staying? I don't want you hurt."

"You don't?"

"Of course not!"

"Well, thank you for your consideration. But I don't feel like traveling right now."

"That's no reason."

"I don't want to be running all around the place."

"We're not going to be running. I know where we're going."

"Well, I—look, I have to go to the bathroom."

"You're going to be the father of my child, Ed. I want the father of my child there when he's born. That's important to me, Ed. Please?"

"I'm sorry, Viv. Can we talk about this after I get out of the bathroom?"

"No, damn it! I want this settled now. You're going with me! I don't want any argument, Ed. I need you with me, you're going, and—"

"Look, do you want me to piss right here? I'm telling you, I'm not going anywhere!"

There was some slight panic in Ed's voice. It surprised Vivian. But no more than it surprised Ed himself. "Except to the bathroom," he said, recovering his calm. Then he broke away and left.

Vivian stood still for a few seconds, not allowing the anger more room. Finally, she returned to her packing and said to Harrison as she addressed her suitcase, "Do your best to protect him."

16

Wednesday, December 28 — Queens, New York.

At his estranged wife's request, Gerald Downing had moved in with his mother.

"I have to put Laura in a nursery school, Jerry. That's the only way I'm going to get this job. So I was wondering—um—if you would consider moving back with your mother and then paying for Laura's nursery school. I know you like your apartment and all, but with the money you save on rent, we could pay for the nursery school."

Gerald said yes without hesitation. His apartment, the first residence he did not have to share with his parents or wife, never proved to be the excellent center for sexual activity that he somehow had assumed it would become once he re-entered the "bachelor life." It had become, instead, simply a place to be alone in. He woke up and dressed for work there, went to work, went to bars, came home late, found what was frozen in the freezer to eat, heated it, and ate it. He would, at times, dream there, plan there, pretend there. But such activity is portable.

He didn't mind his mother much. Or, rather, mother was not much of a problem. She was not a motherly mother. She was not a gray-haired, cuddly, little old dear who sometimes found it hard to accept her son as a grown man rather than the little boy whose nose she used to wipe. She had gray hair and was potentially cuddly and, indeed, older than young, but she was nobody's little dear. And she had rarely treated Gerald as a little boy, even when he was a little boy. She was an individual, not quite like any of his friends' mothers. So, he never thought of her in the classic sense. She was a woman who once had potential for great things or, at least, self-satisfying success. But this or that, or a combination of the both, or possibly a more personal candidate for blame, directed her, under orders, to a simply suburban life of housewife/mother. Because of the unused potential, she was never comfortable in the role. She kept the house well only if it was urgent—routine housekeeping in the sense of a day-to-day duty felt basis held no appeal for her. She found no pride in spic 'n span and no shame in dust and disorder. She mothered well but very practically, with realism instead of bedtime stories. She gave a clear and precise love, never clouded with sentiment but sincere, nevertheless. Her life's main, honest, actual occupation was as a thinker. She much preferred to sit and think than stand and sweep. She was a person who liked to mull, ruminate, meditate, consider, and contemplate. She wanted to give it—it being almost anything—some thought. And she liked to come to conclusions.

"I used to think that environment had a lot to do with people's personalities. But now I think it's more biology. Look at Ross and John Spencer. They grew up in the same family and environment but turned out to be opposites. It must be biology. Look at your sister and you. You're not anything alike."

Gerald always resented such pronouncements. Somehow, he took them as her attempt to "teach" him something. He was glad his mother never wanted to mother him, but why must she try to teach him? So he would always answer back. Actually—he would always argue back.

"But that's not quite it, Mom. Sara and I did grow up in different environments. I grew up in a family with an older sister. And she grew up in a family with a younger brother."

"Yes, but I think people are born the way they are. I mean, two people can grow up in the same house, and one can be bad, and one can be good. Or, one can be outgoing, and one can be shy."

"Yeah, but, Mom, listen. I just told you, it's not the same house. There are other factors—"

"But it seems set. Ross and John had the same parents raising them; they grew up in the same economic conditions. I mean, one wasn't a victim of poverty, and the other a spoiled rich brat—"

"But you're not listening to me, Mom. Granted, biology might have something to do with it. They're discovering all kinds of things about our genes and how they affect us. But, still, the environment is all around us, pressing in on—"

"But the environment is the same—"

"But it's not the same, goddamn it! I just told you that. You don't listen to me."

"Why do you have to argue? I just made a statement. I'm not asking you to argue. A person can't make a simple statement?"

"But you made a statement that practically said that everything is preordained, that it's all fate or something. And I don't think it is. What do you want me to do? Just let that pass? There are other things to consider."

"I just made a simple statement. I don't want a lecture."

"Well, what were you giving me? What did you make the statement for?

"I don't know. Don't I have the right to make a simple statement in my own house?"

"But you make it like the damn thing should be engraved in gold."

"I do not! I just made a simple statement."

Despite the debates, it was a close relationship. It had a routine to it. Every greeting by her on his daily homecoming was a replay of the last and a rehearsal for the next. The door to the house was always kept locked, and when she heard his car pull up, she would get off the living room couch, unlock the door, open it, unlock the screen door, and hold it open, almost stepping one foot out. She would then stand there the minute it took him to take his coat off the hanger in the back, lock the car, and walk up the driveway to the house.

She stood there—as if in a vigil—holding the door open, waiting to see him safely in.

As he came up to her, she did not release. She continued to hold the screen door open, standing in the doorway. He was always forced to slide through, brushing against her body. Then, she would close and lock the door.

"And how was your day?" she would want to know.

"Oh, fine," or "great," or "not too good," he would say and then continue with the details. He always detailed his days. She would sit back down on the couch, and he stood before her and performed, acting out his day: the main humor in it, the most significant pain. He embellished to impress, trying to convince her that he was getting somewhere, having an exciting life, doing important things, being more than mundane—as the very young manager of the major appliance department in store number 36 in a large chain of discount department stores.

She liked that. She was very proud that he was a manager of a department that could lead to a store, that could lead to a division. All it took was hard work, drive, and realistic ambition. She never said that—that would be interfering in his life—but she encouraged him when he would talk with some enthusiasm about the future of the job, which was not that often and was done— she never realized—for her benefit. His enthusiasm was usually spent on talk of writing, success at something one can't apply for, and "head-in-the-clouds-nine-feet-off-the-ground" ambitions.

"You have to be practical," she would say, and they would argue. But not for long; that would be interfering in his life. So she would stop, hold back on it. It's his life; he should lead it. But she's led a life. Are lives so different that one going on now shouldn't learn from one that had gone before? Yes, he would say. She just knew he would argue the point. But maybe he would soon see and suddenly recognize how her example could replace some experience and save him some time. But you can't push it. Just show it and hope he picks it up. And not argue about it.

***

"Do you have to read that rag, Mom?"

Gerald hated supermarket tabloids. Their lines of type contained everything irrational, non-thinking, and biased. Core things that fulfilled wishes for easy answers and comforting facts. He hated the headlines that spoke loudly as you stood in line to check out bread and butter. He hated the articles that promised cures, in 750 words or less, to ills that kill. He hated the eyewitness accounts of UFOs, ghosts, reincarnation, and life in Atlantis. He hated the portraits of old and new, living and dead stars as mean, greedy, unhappy, fallen on hard times, and having miserable times. Why do people want to read that? They envy stars, worship them, practically deify them, but, eventually, want the satisfaction of "knowledge" that proves the stars are really "no better and no better off than me."

Whoever said they were?

And he hated the cute animal pictures.

His mother *loved* the cute animal pictures. And some of the more "interesting" human interest stories. Not the questionable stuff, of course not! But there was more to the paper than that. She wished he could see that: here, see, let me show you this, read this...

Exhibit number ___

Evidence placed before the court.

Evidence was important to his mother. She was a presenter of evidence. When she liked something, she wanted to present it—show the picture, read the joke, explain the wisdom—as evidence that it was as good as her liking it declared it to be—or not as bad as he seemed to think it was. It was not supporting evidence. There was no need for supporting evidence; this was foundation evidence, the thing itself. The thing itself should be enough.

"Here, read this. Don't worry about what it's in; just read it."

"Read what?"

"The article in the left-hand corner."

DOCTORS FIND SAFE DIET PILL

The article went on to state that a safe diet pill was now on the market—non-prescription—under various brand names, and it quoted various authorities as stating that these pills—which curb your appetite—were somewhat near a miracle for dieters. Safe, natural, and effective.

"Well, what do you think?"

"Wait a minute, I'm not finished."

He was finished. He didn't know what to say. It was not a very important item, nor very interesting. He reread it, trying to figure out why she had him read this "evidence" of the paper's goodness and rightness. They were both overweight—he, like her—but they never searched for new diets. If one were made clear and easy by certain relatives, they would try it, but otherwise... And this was not news. These pills had been on the market for years, selling at discount drug stores and hawked on daytime-old movie-local talk show television:

TAKE ONE JUST ONE-HALF HOUR BEFORE MEALS, AND YOUR CRAVING HUNGER WILL DISAPPEAR. YOU'LL EAT LESS BECAUSE YOU WILL WANT LESS. THEN YOU WILL BE ON YOUR WAY TO A SLIM, NEW YOU.

He could see that the tabloid was heading in a new direction. From taking the false and making it seem true to taking the old and making it seem new. He turned to the front page.

SAFE DIET PILL FOUND!
Details on page 37

He wanted to snort and declare disbelief. But the fact was he could believe it. It was logical for the tabloid to pick off all those fat people waiting in line to buy their "last, definitely the last" frozen banana cream pie. He turned back to the article. Why did she have him read it? Then he saw it. End of the article. Small boldface type. Credits for the authorities quoted.

Dr. ____________is chief of staff at___________ Hospital. Dr.

____

is a professor of medicine at __________ University. Dr. _________is a diet specialist for _________ Labs.

He had criticized the tabloid for misquoting sources or even making up quotes and their sources. "What are their credentials? Who are these people?" he would ask to win arguments.

Here it was.

Proof.

Evidence.

Seeeee!!

He told his mother his feelings about the article that it really wasn't news.

"Did you notice the, uhm…"

"What?"

"At the bottom. I don't know what you call it. The list there of the doctors and what they do."

"Oh, yeah. But that doesn't mean anything, Mom. It's still not news. Don't you see what they've done? They've taken common information and presented it as if it's a great big exclusive story. Just so a bunch of overweight housewives will get all excited at the checkout stand and buy the paper."

"I didn't get all excited about it.

"I didn't say you did."

"Nobody said it was world-bending. I just thought it was interesting."

"But it's not interesting, Mom, that's the point. It's not news."

"No, I mean the other."

"What? The credits? So now they're trying to legitimatize themselves. That's easy to do in an article that says nothing.

"Look, I don't want to argue."

"Then why did you make me read it?"

"I just wanted you to read it, that's all. I thought it was interesting."

"But why? You know it makes me angry; you know I can't stand this shit!"

"You don't have to swear."

"I'm sorry, but you're always doing this to me. I wish you would stop. Just don't bring that paper up to me again."

"Okay, I won't. I won't ever show you anything again!"

She started to cry. Started. His mother always only started.

"Why do you do it to yourself? You know I'm going to get angry. You know I'm going to shout. What are you trying to do? What are you trying to prove?"

"I'm not trying to prove anything. I just wanted you to read it, that's all."

"But why? You don't answer why. You know I don't want to read it. Every time you do this, we argue. You are not going to convince me that that paper is any good. You are not going to win me over to it."

"I'm not trying to convince you of anything. I just wanted you to read it."

"BUT WHY?"

"Okay, I won't do it again. Never!"

***

The next day, as he left for work, his mother asked:

"Think you'll need a coat today?"

"Got one in the car."

"Okay. Have you got everything else?"

"Yes."

"Your wallet?"

"*Yes.*"

"Keys?"

"Yes!"

"Everything?"

"*Yes,* mother!"

"I'm just asking."

"Okay. See you later."

He left.

He was back in four minutes.

She greeted him at the door.

"What did you forget?"

"My sales book."

"Oh."

"He ran into his room, grabbed his sales book, put it in his coat pocket, and went out the door she was still holding open.

"Drive carefully," she said as he got into his car.

***

Washington D.C.

Darryl Butchko ached. It irritated and annoyed, was a bother, and dragged. His neck, of course, had pain, and his back felt the stiff pressure of it. His arms felt numb—if you can *feel* numb if that wasn't a contradiction. It was a very energetic numb, a sort of active weakness, a radiating listlessness. He found himself getting clumsy, dropping the damn phone, slipping, tripping; reaching for and missing. He would swear then, sometimes sharp, sometimes guttural; half loud, half controlled in the middle and brought down. It was a sway, a veer off to one side. Not the usual smooth, straight ahead, the humming along, the sailing along. Resistance was felt.

He had no idea why all this was happening. Why could a plan planned not then just be implemented? He had no idea why the idea was being corrupted. But he knew that the corruption was the cause of the resistance. They did not seem to understand. And yet, they once did, they had understood, the logic was clear then: laid out even, edges in line, angles matching. Butchko thought back to Anderson's perception of "something missing." Something missing implies something existing. Was the protest there before but just missing? Or unseen? Or unheard? No. Real protest, by its nature, is always heard, with righteous protest eventually becoming the loudest sound. Or does the volume make it righteous? Was there protest? Maybe there were some slight sounds. There was Kirkly—but who reads him? Who would have listened if he had not gotten dirty about it? There was the Church. But they're always protesting to no effect; they ban films, and their congregations still go to them. And a few small fringe groups had made disparaging remarks in various newsletters. Altogether, it is a weak minority opinion. The majority, though, seemed to have clearly seen it. *Too many versus too little.* The danger announces itself. They had done without. They were tired of that. Tired of lines and delays, and the once commonplace becoming a luxury. Butchko knew very well that bringing the masses up to virtual affluence, compared to centuries of material poverty, had kept revolution away from the Western world. Even the most ordinary present worker lived much like the most ostentatious past lord, complete with steeds and servants, although of steel, plastic, and engines. Rebels are not born from the comfortable. Rebels come from those who never had, finally becoming fed up with those who had always had. Or they came from those with a little wanting more. Or—the most intense and angry ones—from those who have had and have had it taken away. Butchko had feared that and felt that a plan to give back somehow what had been taken away was urgent. Nobody seemed to have argued. Then. Why now?

It was the corruption. The corruption of an idea by those who did not truly understand it. Kirkly. And stupid burning girls. And college students. And—and Vivian.

"Where's Vivian?"

"Sir, we just don't know," George Mays reported. "She failed to report for her abortion and has dropped out of sight. We don't know if she is in or out of the country. But with her resources, she could be just about anywhere."

"Why the hell didn't that judge lock her up?"

"Sir, you don't lock up millionaires on a first offense."

"You're a real egalitarian, aren't you, George? Couldn't he have assumed that she might try something like this?"

"It's all such a new thing."

"I suppose. What about Handlin?"

"He showed up in court at the appointed time with a certification of vasectomy. His trial date is being set."

"I want him in custody."

"I don't think we can get away with that. I don't even know if we can charge him. The evidence is no longer available. We only have Mrs. Handlin's word that she is pregnant."

"Isn't Handlin accepting paternity?"

"He's not talking much now."

"Shit!" Butchko shut his eyes. Brief relief, barely adequate. "She's gone overseas, I know it, George. Like you say, she has the means. She's going to pop up somewhere and become a real pain. We could have had her; we could have diffused her. The public would have loved to see one of the rich handed some justice. But now, she's a fugitive, giving up everything for a 'cause.' Damn! They'll be writing damn folk ballads about her soon. Stupid songs. To be swayed by stupid songs instead of reason. Stupid songs, mob psychology, charismatic symbolic leaders. George, these are the enemies of reason in a conflict such as this. I hate it. How do you fight stupid songs? You want to stand up and be clear, concise, and logical with your arguments, but they won't listen; that's not entertaining enough; there's no hummable tune, like in a stupid song."

"Sir, if I may, I don't think things have gone too far off the track. I would say that the majority is still behind Birth Cessation. It's just that a few well-placed protesters have been given some publicity."

"That's the danger, George; well placed. But I'm sure you're right. The majority is behind us. For now. But what are the statistics, George? The level of response to abortion and vasectomy calls has dropped, hasn't it?

"Well—slightly."

"Have you ever seen a slight drizzle turn into a downpour? You go out without a hat and coat and then get awfully wet.

"Look, this thing about Handlin. We must use him. I mean, we have to get him. Hard! What about—I don't know—some charge of obstructing justice? Or withholding evidence? I mean, he won't tell us where Vivian is. Isn't that withholding evidence or something?"

George considered it—or counted beats to give the impression of consideration. Finally, "I don't know. Suppose we could try. I'll call the Justice boys on it."

"Good. Do it. Get him for me. I want him. I want them to know we're not fooling around. I want them to know we're tough and mean business."

Silly talk. Even Butchko knew it. Yet it fit, it was right. He was mad. He had a right to demand. They broke the law. They conspired to undermine it, to destroy it. They sat there, wide-eyed, looking long but not seeing, realizing, or understanding. Like some dumb child that you say something to repeatedly: *look, I've told you once, I'm not going to tell you again, can't you get it through your head?* God! You can't reason with these people!

Darryl disliked the feeling of conflict. It was a certain feeling, well-defined, sharp-edged feeling of shock at being stunned, of dismay over the disarray the question had fallen into. It was bad enough in academic conflicts of theories, but that was all game anyway: players positioning for advantage, advancing through good moves, retreating, grumbling when the action had been matched or bettered. There was discomfort when suddenly facing opposition where none had existed before. Before being that more pristine plain when your position was but a statement as yet un-stated, a thought just thought about, considered, and enjoyed privately for its own sake—was tempered by the knowledge that that's what academia was for: Games of one sort or another. But this? This was literal life or death! Why must there be a game here? A game with players always intense and loyal to their colors? This was not dealing with the murky "truths" of the classroom, studies, and labs. This was facing the facts of the day, the problem here and now before you, trying to edge you out. You don't move back, you don't stand aside, you don't let it ease through—you stand still and push! Then, you glide through when the problem has fallen and smile as you pass. But when you're prevented from pushing, when someone says "Don't!" or obstructs the straight path of your push—then there is little to smile about. So you close your mouth, jut your jaw; you close ranks and charge. And you win, or you lose. If you win, you can push at the problem, smiling again. If you lose...

"Get Handlin for me, George. Let's put him on a spit and roast the bastard."

17

Tuesday, January 3 —Des Moines, Iowa

Everybody thought the damn job was easy. That was the problem. Everybody thought he just came to work, fiddled around, read a little, watched some TV, drew his one cartoon, and then went home—even though he never left before his scheduled time. Everybody thought he was privileged somehow. Especially the reporters who had to "sweat and slave," so they said, to get the facts, assemble the facts, report the facts. As he walked across the city room each morning, he felt he was on some degrading parade through self-claimed superiors. He felt rotten fruit would be thrown at him. He felt jeers, even if he didn't hear them.

That's bullshit!" Crosley, his editor, said. "They like your cartoons."

"I didn't say that. I said they think I have it easy. It's not easy, you know."

"What do you think? You're the only editorial cartoonist that's ever been? These guys have seen a dozen of them. You're just new, that's all. You're just experiencing the out-of-college-out-into-the-real-world blues, that's all. Don't think too much about it."

But Rusk did because Crosley was right. He did one editorial cartoon a week for four and a half years in college, sometimes calling out the comedy of campus stuff and sometimes of local, national, and international issues. There's always something in a week. But this daily assignment, daily getting an idea, drawing it, writing a caption, daily having a point, a clear statement, daily saying something, was a scramble up the hill, an effort to the top before nightfall. Yet it's the only thing he ever wanted to do. He started drawing as a kid; it came easy—especially caricatures. In high school, he began doing caricatures of his teachers and got in trouble. But he also amused some people and won the admiration of others. He peeked out of adolescence to see if big people did this and discovered that cartooning went on everywhere and that some people made very good money at it. From that point on, he would sit smug and snug during career planning sessions as the other kids were nervously trying to decide if they could get through life without breaking their backs or refused to pay attention, thinking it was all too far away or felt the anxiety of adult decisions being forced on them. For he knew what he was going to be: A Cartoonist! He would draw a few drawings, and they would pay him big money. He would live in a fancy townhouse like Jack Lemmon in that movie and be admired.

But what *kind* of cartoonist? Some stupid counselor had to ask. Well, you know, in the comic books or funny pages or something like that. That was too frivolous for the counselor. Too silly, too inconsequential. How about editorial cartoons? What? The counselor made him start reading the editorial pages in the two local papers and encouraged him to draw things up for the school newspaper. And he did, making fun of football players and how they got all the attention and money when hardly any went to the art department. Then, on to college with a major in art and a minor in journalism. He was taking it seriously. The counselor had always informed him about who won the editorial cartoon Pulitzer Prize each year.

But now! The scramble. Every damn day! The reading. The thinking. The lookout for the wicked little truths behind the righteous lies of politicians, big business, religious leaders, fanatics from various ends of the spectrum, and, at times, the people themselves. And he was on a trial basis. The old guy had died suddenly. He had been alright and somewhat known, and Rusk walked in with his portfolio at just the right time. They needed somebody, of course; they never considered that they could get along without one. Somehow, having their little daily one-shot visual opinion seemed essential to wave in people's faces. Rusk sat silent in the interview as the editor-in-chief flipped through his drawings—not laughing. Jesus Christ! Chuckle a little or something. Smile, nod your head, or even shake it. Disagree if you must! Anything!

"Well, yeah, I guess they're okay. Can you start Monday?"

Rusk smiled. Hell, this is going to be easy.

***

"How you coming on the cartoon, kid? Look, we can't have a white square in the space, for Christ's sake, so hurry it up, will ya?"

Crosley, the OP-ED editor, said that—or some equivalent—every day.

"Oh, not bad. A few ideas here. Look, here's something on New Year's. I didn't do anything on New Year's Day, but it's still the new year, right? So how's this?"

Rusk held up a sketch of Father Time—looking very much like Darryl Butchko—lopping off the head of the Baby New Year with his scythe.

"Gruesome. Do you always have to be so damn gruesome?"

"Well, what do you call abortion?"

"Okay, fine, why don't you do one with him castrating some guy?"

"Hey, that's an idea!"

"Stop right there, kiddo."

"No, I knew it wouldn't wash. I was just doodling. But look, I want to do something on Butchko. I like this one, but maybe it's a bit gruesome too, huh?"

It was Butchko again, as the Statue of Liberty with a sword instead of a torch being held up and a baby impaled on the blade.

"Shit, Rusk, cut this crap out. Can't you be a bit more subtle? Please? You did that Jan Lawrence thing with some restraint, do something like that."

That "Jan Lawrence thing" had been four successive drawings arranged in panels of a fire with a gas can sitting nearby and a baby carriage. From panel to panel, the fire goes from large, hot, and fierce to weaker, to ember, to a pile of ash. The caption read:

THE FLAME OF MOTHERHOOD EXTINGUISHES.

"That was good, you know, you didn't show a body or crap like that."

"Yeah, I know, but this is different. Look, how about Butchko in a straw hat and apron with a meat cleaver? And, um, he's behind a meat counter full of fetuses."

"Pretty damn obvious, don't you think?"

"Well, they're calling him Butcher Butchko, see, and—"

"So what? It seems kind of low to me. Look, think for a while what Butchko's position is. Try to understand it. Not that you have to agree with him, but you should get to the heart of what he's saying, I mean what is his position? Then attack that if you want. Don't just play on what others call him. And be careful about that anyway. Just because he's suddenly attacked doesn't mean that that attack is right. You might wind up making a fool out of yourself."

"Hey," Rusk smiled broadly. "What's an editorial cartoonist anyway, but the court fool?"

"Well, I don't know if you're the court fool, but you better be a fast fool."

That's what's wrong with editors, thought Rusk; they always want to edit. Hell! Gruesome? So what? If I was an old bastard and established, had my anthologies out, he wouldn't dare change a thing. So why give in? I should fight!

Bold! Tough! Strident! Pungent! He wanted such words to be on the cover of his first anthology. Maybe—*A strong voice for a challenging decade.* But not if they're going to handcuff him all along the way. Hell!

He walked around the city room, down a hall, into the restroom, and over to the Daily Arts section.

"Hey, Rog. Do you have any passes to movies?"

"Yeah, sure, here."

He walked back, poured himself a cup of coffee, and returned to his drawing board.

Position, he thought. What is Butchko's position? Huh—this resources thing. Resources? What? Energy. What does energy get us? Electricity, cars. That's nothing but luxury stuff. Luxuries? Well, pioneer America had no luxuries. Real America. Hum...

Pencil hit paper. Butchko came out with a statue again, but this time, it was of "Justice." Instead of blindfolds, he wore designer sunglasses. And on one tray of the scales of justice he held were several infants looking scared. On the other scale—the weightier one, thus the one Justice was tipped towards—there was a new car, a big screen television, a mink coat, bottles of wine, and a stack of steaks. He felt fevered drawing it; the lines went down fast and, it seemed to him, true. He had to be careful; it had to be delicate and well-defined. The infants had to have character, and the resources, the goods, luxuries—everybody's fair share—had to be immediately recognizable. He stopped. He looked it over. Yeah, it was right. But words were needed. Under the infants, he wrote THE UNBORN. Between that and the other scale, he wrote US. Under the luxuries he wrote, THE AMERICAN DREAM. And under the whole image, in large letters, he wrote: JUSTICE *IS* BLIND.

Yeah. He was happy with it. Gleeful, almost. He signed it. His signature. Just "Rusk," of course. A distinctive—he hoped soon to be recognizable—signature with a large R, a small u, a small s, and a large K. He laid it down—boldly.

Rusk

***

Chicago, Illinois

"Comedy is hate; it's as simple as that," Willie, a mentor of sorts, once told Stan, his prodigy of sorts. "And don't give me any of that bullshit about you having to love your subject, or you wouldn't find humor in it. Even in a gentle spoof, you point out, you attack, all the things that you really hate about what you're spoofing. You may not think of it as that, but that's it. It's hate, not love, that motivates laughter. Self-hate, hate of parents—you know, the old Jewish mother stuff—hate of wife; that's pretty typical, you know. The old comedians used to do all those old wife jokes. Fifteen minutes of wife jokes make her out to be the dumbest broad in the world or the biggest bitch or something. Fifteen minutes of unrelenting exposure of all the faults you hate in your wife. Fifteen minutes of the audience laughing their heads off at your wife's expense. Then, one last minute saying, 'But, seriously folks, I love my little Marge. She's my strength. The mother of my two darling kids. A beautiful woman. Truly, the light of my life. And if I have had a little fun here at her expense, well, it's because I truly do love her.' Then, if they could sing, and even sometimes if they couldn't, they would launch into some sappy song about the woman in their lives. Bullshit! Hates the bitch! Fifteen minutes of truth. One minute of covering up the tracks. Sure, it was exaggerated. But, you see, the hateful things were there to exaggerate, that's the point. And sure, he probably loves her too, but there's no laughter in love, kid. And laughter is the commodity. We can both hate and love at the same time. But not in the same breath.

"So, let's see, what else is there? Oh, the old mother-in-law stuff, of course, and all the political stuff and stuff people hate about everyday living. You know, little things like appliances that don't work, or big things like the IRS or something. You see, what I'm saying is that, essentially, all comedy is put-down humor. Some of it can be brilliant, like when the comedian talks about things that he *really* hates and not just about things that irritate him. Do you see the difference? When he gets truthful about his hates, then his comedy will take on a, well, uh, shit, a truth, I guess, that is so recognizable that the audience will fall in with it. Simple, good comedy, on the other hand, is just that which deals with the more general and universal hates of everyone, you know, not anything personal with the comedian. Uh—traffic cops and waiters, for example. Hack comedy, although it can be funny, is just a joke designed to attack things the comedian assumes the audience hates, things he assumes the audience wants to hear being put down. Brilliant comedy is art. Good comedy is talent and craft. Hack comedy is prostitution. But, like that unhallowed profession, hack work can sometimes pay very well. So, Stan, you've got to decide where you're comfortable. Do you have things inside you that you hate and are dying to attack? Or do you think you clearly see all the general faults of the world and think you have the talent to point them out in a palatable manner? Or are you just on the lookout for this week's scapegoat that you can throw the first stones at to get the crowd's applause? Where you fall will define the type of comedian you will be."

Jesus, thought Stan, if Willie is right, then this comedy club is a little hall of hate we're in here, and all these people are here specifically to have me do their attacking for them.

Stan looked around the small comedy club, an establishment featuring food, drinks, and barbs. The audience was mostly young, with a sense of possessing the world and a right to kick at it. They were mostly well dressed and well off, relative to the times. They were attractive and more or less self-confident, showing the "more" right now, shelving the "less" to be dealt with when home alone. They were laughers. Big laughers. The chuckle was a joy to them; the howl a pleasure; the guffaw near nectar; the sustained, tear-inducing, breathtaking, chest-hurting belly breaker was Nirvana, a sort of raucous state of grace. Couples together would continuously make eye contact on the getting of a joke, swinging their heads to face each other, mouths open, gasping breath between laughs, showing teeth, nodding in agreement that they did indeed recognize the idiotic thing this joke was pointing out; being thrilled, having their hearts leap, having their pulse apparent over this coming together in agreement. Laughter is romantic. Maybe erotic. It is easier to love someone who laughs at what you laugh at, who ridicules what you ridicule, who hates what you hate, than it is someone who, for example, takes seriously what you take seriously.

So they sit and hold hands and laugh.

"And their laughter," Willie had said, "is like a positive reinforcement for the comedian. Do you know what that is? Once a comedian gets laughter out of people by his own doing, it feels so good; I mean, man, it feels so good; he'll do anything and do whatever it takes to get it again. That's why there are so many hacks. They want the laughs so bad that they'll look for the easiest route; they'll try to find out what the audience wants to laugh at—right now—and go for that instead of looking into themselves and discovering what makes *them* laugh, you know, laugh honest and hard. But if they took the time, you know, to look inside themselves and find some *things*, man, they would get better laughs. You know what I mean? I mean, what's deep in one is probably deep in all. It's biological, genetic, or something. To truly touch the audience, instead of just tickling them, you've got to connect with age-old human things. You got to draw them up and put them out there for your audience.

"But maybe that's instinct; you got it, or you don't. If you don't, you can't get it. If you do, you can't get rid of it. And I've known some who would've liked to have gotten rid of it."

Stan now knew that he probably didn't have it. He once thought he had. He would probably think so again when self-realization became a bore. But for now, the knowledge was his, and it depressed. So—he would deal in daily particulars, period, instead of timeless universals; he would be a man of his age instead of for all ages. But—who cares? Death will end his concern with reviews, which is the case against immortality. The laughs he can experience today are better than the laughs unheard tomorrow. And if there are laughs, he's good—the laughs prove it. Easy laughs or hard laughs, it doesn't matter. If they are loud now, followed by applause now, then he's good; he knows delivery, timing, how to get it across, and how to deliver. He's good.

You can't argue with that, can you, Willie, you old bastard?

He was up next, and he had new material to try out.

"Ladies and gentlemen," the owner-host announced. "Next up, we have a new young comic as fresh as today's headlines and a hot bagel, Mr. Stan Factor!" And his two hands closed on an applause of enthusiasm, leading the audience in a show of pre-appreciation. Stan jumped up on stage, grabbed the microphone, and looked down in another quick assessment of his audience.

"Hi, how's your sterile little selves? Have you all had your vasectomies, guys? Now, I know most of you guys have been telling girls for years that you've had a vasectomy, right? 'Hey babe, don't worry about me. I can't get you pregnant. I'm clean, I've had it cut, babe!' Remember that line? But how was the girl really to know, right? I mean, it wasn't like a vaccination mark, right? Where, as kids, we could all lift our sleeves and show it off, right? 'Hey, man, my vaccination spot is bigger than your vaccination spot, nay, nay, nay, nay, naaaay, nay.' Right? No, but this was different, right? How could a girl tell? Accept the guy's word for it? Believe him, just because he wore that little pin? Or maybe, take a good hard look at the area concerned? Perhaps she could see a little scar, huh? Look, if it got that far, it was a bit too late, one way or the other, right? No, ladies, you almost, to a man—so to speak—took their word for it. He, he, he. And if you weren't on the pill because it gave you liver spots or something? Well—balloon time! So you go to the guy, right? And you give him one of those old knock-knock jokes.

"*Knock, knock!/Who's there?/Hugo/Hugo who?/Hu-got me pregnant, you son-of-a-bitch!/What?!/You heard me!/But it can't be me, I've been VA-SEC-TO-MATED. Who else have you been screwing around with?/Nobody, you bastard!/Then it must be—oh my god!—it must be an IMMACULATE CONCEPTION!*

"Then he gets all excited. He says he'll run downstairs for a pack of apostles and be right back. And then you—never—see—him—again. Right?

"Well—all that's over with now. Now, the problem won't be to find a man with a vasectomy but to find a man without one. Actually, you'll be able to find them easily. They'll all be in the Federal Penitentiary. Right? Public enemies, to say the least, right?

"MAD VIRILE! MAD VIRILE! GET THE MAD VIRILE, LOCK HIM UP!

"But, what the hell? It's for the good of the country, right? Look at it this way: do any of you have children? Ah, there's a few here. Well, you know those times when you've got the sniveling brats—uh—sorry, I mean, the sweet little dears, in bed, *finally*, and the house is quiet and calm and relaxed, and you can do what you want—you know, *adult* things? Well, that's all the government's done—just sent the kids to bed for twenty-five years. 'Night, night, sleep tight, don't let the bed bugs bite.'

"And really, who's going to be hurt by it? Well, there is one small minority that might suffer a little bit.

"Baby-sitters! Right? I mean, they're pissed about this thing. I mean, what the hell are they going to do for twenty-five years? Raid their *own* refrigerators? Well, I'll tell you, the government better watch out for this crowd. They're already planning organized sit-ins. Or 'Baby sit-ins,' as the case may be. Their slogan will be: WE'LL SIT HERE UNTIL WE CAN—uh—SIT HERE! But they're a small minority; they don't matter against the common good, so I wouldn't worry too—oh, wait, there—I just thought of another minority. Has anybody—in their headlong rush to decrease the surplus population considered the plight of the most put-upon minority in this whole affair—child molesters? No, really, it's true. Have you given any thought to what child molesters are going to do? Fool around with those little cupid statues that, you know, piss into your local fountain? Or maybe there'll be a run on those little Kathy-does-everything dolls. You know, the ones who eat and wet and sweat and say mama and roll over and crawl on their knees and suck on a real—bottle. Can you see a child molester going into a toy store and buying one—just a little bit embarrassed:

"'Uh—ah-ha—I'm—uh—buying it for my granddaughter, yeah, for my granddaughter.'

"'Sir, there are no granddaughters.'

"'Oh, well, they'll come back, and I'm shopping early to avoid the rush.'

Then he stuffs it into his raincoat and runs out, right?

"Well, again, a small minority, right? Who gives a shit, right? Doesn't really matter. So says Butcher Butchko—Oh! That's not nice. To repeat names like that. Unfair, I would say. We have *no* evidence that Mr. Butchko is a butcher. The fact that he has the only office in Washington with sawdust on the floor hardly constitutes hard evidence. And the fact that if you go into his office for a meeting, his secretary doesn't say, 'Take a seat,' she says, 'Take a number,' is purely coincidental.

"And all that 'psychological profile' stuff they've been pulling on him? It's pretty theoretical, I would say. Take, for instance, the recent revelation that Butchko once admitted that he thinks the height of American culture is that old TV show, *Leave it to Beaver*. You remember the kid, Beaver, his brother Wally, and their two cute parents. Most people would think that if Butchko admired this show so much, then he must have some affection for the American Family, right? I mean, it was a show about an *intact* American family! Not like all those later shows where one of the two parents was always dead, right? But, no, uh-uh, say the psychologists. Butchko's love of this show is proof positive that he is a man bent on aborting the world. Why? Well, say the collective shrinks; it's simple. The lead character's full name was—remember—*Beaver Cleaver!*

***

"Well, what did you think?" Stan asked the owner-host-bartender after his set.

"Not bad, at first. That pregnant bit that's pretty good. They all related to that. The baby-sitter bit was cute. The child molester? I don't know. May have been in bad taste."

"They laughed."

"Doesn't mean it wasn't in bad taste. I don't know about that Butchko stuff, though. Who remembers sawdust on butcher shop floors but old small-town bastards like me? I mean, have you ever been in a butcher shop with sawdust? Do they even have butcher shops anymore?"

"Yeah, but it's sort of a racial memory."

"Well, maybe, maybe not."

"I wanted to make some kind of play on Butchko's name and—"

"And that *Leave it to Beaver* stuff. Who remembers that show?

"There I got you. That's a big deal for my generation. We grew up in re-run heaven, you know."

"Yeah?"

"Yeah."

"Well, okay. I guess it's a funny payoff. A bit crude, though."

"Yeah—but that doesn't mean they won't laugh."

18

Wednesday, January 25 — near Oodnadatta, South Australia

It was a Victorian house of recent construction and so as large and grand as fancy would have it. It sat atop a hill, somewhat close to a mountain, between Lake Eyre and the hardly populated town of Oodnadatta. Of its seventeen rooms, ten were as Victorian as the exterior design, with all modern conveniences cleverly disguised or designed with that romanticized era in mind as if Jules Verne lived there. The other seven rooms housed unadorned, extremely functional, and well-equipped scientific labs. They were two worlds strangely mixed.

As the guest of Dean Harry, the "Master" of the house, Vivian Pavin Handlin was welcomed to travel between the two worlds. But she had felt far more comfortable in the Victorian rooms and remained in them. The shock of her quick departure from Los Angeles, the upset of her plans, and the strangeness of days re-patterned along unexpected lines were all somehow buffered by the plush, the red, the marble, the dark wood, and leather, all of which were beautifully illuminated by the imitation gas lighting. She would walk from one room to another and up and down the graceful stairs. She would touch and feel the ornamentation, the furniture. She would study the paintings hung in each room and read the leather-bound "classics" in their leather furniture library. She would even invade the kitchen and bake pies and other pastries. For the first time in her life, she wasted time and didn't care. The leisurely pace that some might feel was the hallmark of the Victorian Era was the pace she desired, causing days to go slow but weeks to pass quickly, in an odd but true relativity of time.

Somehow, it all seemed simply right for impending motherhood. She never would have thought of it that way before, of course, and she tried to avoid thinking of it that way now. For she was only too aware of her true opinion and, like some dumb movie you find completely enjoyable, she wanted the present beyond criticism.

But...

Had she retreated? Worse, deserted the field in the face of fire? Was she hiding, avoiding the law? Had she given up, taken the rich person's prerogative to be able to leave the field of battle? Or was she in self-exile? A more politic, romantic, better-shaded way to express it?

She went to her bedroom and put her hair up, then dressed up in a shiny green silk gown with frills of lace from Dean Harry's collection. An old, beveled glass mirror reflected it all to her. Was she trying to find some image of Woman? Of Mother? Silk and lace and a time when a woman was intensely present as a vision rather than highly visible as a presence.

What task was it to be a vision? Silk and lace and powder and hair ordered to appeal.

What task was it to be a presence? Thought and work and conviction and points ordered to convince.

Silk was smooth, and lace was delicate, white, and pretty. The dress rustled a song as she moved with feminine grace. Shadows were soft, the light low, the feel of things lush with texture. Things were agreeable.

Thought was compelling, and work fulfilling. Shadows delineated, the light defined, things always seemed differentiated and clear, except to others. Things were not always agreeable.

She needed a cat. She could see that. She needed a cat to sit in her lap and complete the picture. Maybe an all-white one, brilliant against her green silk, that purred as she petted it. A cat responds to a stroke in kind. Give a cat warmth; you get it back. Love it, it will love you. A cat is more a mirror than a beveled kind.

"It doesn't fit." Dean Harry walked into the room. "Oh, as far as measurements are concerned, it's obvious that the dress is long enough, the shoulders are right, and you certainly fill it out amply. Your hair is correctly styled. Your face even seems the proper heart shape. But the gown and you do not fit one another. The play acting is strained. It's too artificial. I'm afraid, Vivian, you could never truly participate in my little Victorian fantasy here."

Vivian turned with a glide, calling up the coquette. "Are you so sure?"

"Yes. But not as sure as you are."

"You're right. It's the damnable truth. Hey! 'Damnable truth.' sounds pretty Victorian. Maybe there's hope."

"No, Vivian, my dear. Words alone won't do it. Take off the dress, let your hair loose, come down to dinner, and I will enter your world briefly, as you have lingered too long in mine. And I will explain how I intend to aid you."

***

Dean Harry was like Verne's Captain Nemo without the hostility. A genius, an inventor, no lover of mankind—for he had little respect for anyone's intelligence compared to his own—but a fair man willing to allow all others the right to achieve whatever height of mediocrity they might. He was not a cooperative man, a community man, or a collaborator of any sort. He worked alone, allowing others only to assist him and faithfully carry out his wishes and desires, orders, and instructions. He discouraged questioning, for no one could ask anything more perceptive than he had already asked. His first urge upon any question was to lash out and strike. But he was socialized, if not sociable, and that prevented him from landing blows upon his "opponents." Which is what his questioners became upon the questioning.

He was pompous. "Pompissed," an old lover used to call him. He was sure of himself. He wore an untrimmed beard, smoked a pipe, and dressed in a flamboyant Victorian manner to fit his flamboyant Victorian manor. Sometimes, he would stand at the top of the stairs and cut a figure. He would stand there momentarily, enjoying the stance, feeling strong and invincible. But, despite all this, he was a coward. He was afraid—indeed, it was a near-cold fear—of anyone unsure of him. Whether phobia or fact, he had felt the fear since childhood. It had been the cause of his first tantrum, his first school fistfight, and his first sexual rejection after philosophy intruded on the physical.

He had found isolation helpful. As a child, that meant time stretched out over his bed with comic books—panels of colored other worlds, luxuriant in powers dispensed, making heroes super and so right. As an adolescent, it meant a fascination with the future, where all things were clean, clear, well-ordered, new, fantastic, sensible, better, wiser, and brighter—or so told the illustrations in magazines and pulps. As a young man in the world, a self-aware budding genius suffering the proximity of too many other budding geniuses, it meant finding a time to place his imagination. A conducive era where he could seed the quiet with his thoughts. He found the period of Queen Victoria, where geniuses could be solitary, somehow funding themselves to invent their flying machines or earth borers, time machines or submarines or spaceships propelled by anti-gravity paint, any of the past wonders of the future. In middle age, it meant facing facts. A fondness was not a foundation. Something concrete, natural, and dimensional had to be built.

Vivian had provided the foundation. She had the empathy.

As he was known then, Dean Haroldson, an employee, came to her one day with his heart pounding furiously. She was puzzled and perturbed at that—bothered that she had to be bothered by reasons unknown. But she had patience, for she knew the value of this man's work in one of her labs.

"Ms. Pavin, I've worked in your lab for a couple of years now, and I'm sure you are aware of my work."

"I am Mr. Haroldson."

"Right. I feel it could have been better, more innovative, certainly more creative."

"Well, Mr. Haroldson, if you're saying that your work could have been 'more,' then obviously you consider it at least somewhat innovative and creative."

"That is correct."

Vivian paused before answering. It was the question of a child innocently familiar with the obvious. "Yes, Mr. Haroldson, I believe it probably was."

"I have never doubted that, Ms. Pavin. I'm quite confident that I'm a genius."

"Although not very modest about it."

"I've always felt that if a man is a genius, he should be smart enough to know it."

Vivian laughed. "Yes, Mr.—. Look, I'm going to call you Dean."

An affirmation was nodded.

"Good. Dean, you're right, of course. And the greatest talent of a 'modest' genius is fishing for a compliment, wouldn't you say? I suppose all of this leads to a request for more money, which you are worth. But you could have taken this up with your immediate superiors."

"No, it's not money. At least, not all of it. Look, I don't work well on a team. My best work can be done only alone. That is why my work could have been more creative. I am pulled back too much by the others. They argue too much with me about silly things and won't let me get on with it."

"Dean, teams are set up in the labs to get the best work out of everyone, to challenge each of you through collaboration and competition, to have someone express caution when needed."

"An understandable corporate desire. But it is not needed in my case. I know exactly what I'm doing. I know when to do what. I don't need anybody telling me anything."

"You know, your ego is almost insufferable."

"You cannot accuse me of something I gladly admit to. This is my point! I know I have an ego. I am aware of it. I live with it daily and am comfortable with it because it is justified. It is other people who are uncomfortable with it. And that is what I am trying to do here: get away from other people."

"You want a lab to yourself, I suppose?"

"Yes. But—but more."

"Again, more?"

"I have some land I inherited in Australia. It is remote. I want to build a lab on it. I want to build a home on it. But I do not have the financial wherewithal. If you fund it and leave me alone, I promise you can patent everything I come up with."

"Well—it's an interesting idea, Dean. I appreciate your bringing it to me. But I don't know. Exactly what are you asking me to spend?"

Dean Haroldson pulled out a slip of paper and handed it to Vivian. "I've worked out the figures." Vivian took it and looked.

"Pretty steep, Dean."

"It is a special house. Special labs."

"And the staff?"

"Mere assistants."

"If I spend all this money on you, what assurances do I have that you won't develop something amazing and patent it yourself? Short of placing spies among your assistants, of course."

"I am incapable of duplicity.

"No one is incapable of duplicity."

"I am. I hold it up as no virtue. I consider it a fault. If I could do it, I would now be in a position similar to yours."

"Not much of a flatterer, are you, Dean?"

"No. Because I am incapable of duplicity."

Vivian chuckled. The man before her was amusing, if nothing else.

"Do you truly think your endeavors will be profitable?"

"It is inevitable."

"And what do you get out of it?"

"Comfort, Ms. Pavin. Simple comfort."

***

Dean Harry pulled the chair out and seated Vivian at the dinner table. "We'll be served now," he said to the attending servant. He moved with strong grace as he sat with a straight, but not stiff, back, took command of his napkin, and looked at Vivian as if to say, *See what a wonderful thing you have wrought!* He smiled.

"You're an even more confident man than you were three years ago, Dean. Of course, you were extremely confident then, but now you are at a level I've never experienced in a person."

"It is much easier in a world of one's creation and control. You feel safe to flaunt your confidence."

"Well, that's my trouble then. I've never felt so weak and helpless and ready to rest my head on the chest of a strong man."

"Exactly. But no man would truly be safe with your head on his chest. And this man is not about to put himself in that jeopardy. So what I'm about to tell you to do is what you should be telling yourself. However, I do not agree with a word of it. "First, are you sincere with this campaign to reverse the Birth Cessation Law?"

"Do you doubt it?"

"I doubt all things."

"Don't be so presumptuous.

"Don't take offense. Consider me to be you. This is you talking to you. You are asking yourself questions. Consider me your cricket."

"What?"

"Your conscience."

"What's wrong with my own?

"It seems dormant at the moment."

"Dean, you're being rude."

"When have I not been? Look, I do not want to do this. But you have invaded my world. I do not like it, and I want you out. And the only way to do that is to get you back to your world."

"I pay for this world!"

And that is precisely why I want you out. It is like living with your damn landlord. You remind me of my indebtedness, and I would prefer not to be reminded. I pay my rent in full to forget it. So if I can aid you in fighting in the hopes that you will win, then, my dear landlord, you will be free to go and leave me alone. Now, why are you against Birth Cessation?"

"Are you for it?"

"I have never been pregnant."

"Don't be asinine."

"Stop avoiding my questions. You are against Birth Cessation?"

"Yes."

"You have laid your 'body' on the line against it?"

"Yes."

"Why?"

"Because I believe it to be evil."

"What? The simple act of not having children. What used to be called birth control?"

"No. The act of government control. It is not the cessation of births. It is the government-ordered cessation of births that I fight. What right has the government got to invade the body of a woman?"

"The right of power."

"In our system, Dean, the government gets its power from the people."

"So? Power is power."

"But power abused—"

"Is power usually affecting an outcome you are personally opposed to?"

"This is something the *people* are against."

"But the people give the government power?"

"Yes."

"And the government, using that power, ordered Birth Cessation. Therefore, the *people* ordered birth cessation."

"The people give the power; they don't necessarily give the orders."

"Then they are using the power unwisely."

"It is the government that is abusing the power. You seem confused about this. But then, Dean, you've chosen to isolate yourself. Possibly you're just not qualified to make judgments?"

"I am isolated physically. That is true. Maybe spiritually as well. But certainly not intellectually. I am isolated from nothing intellectually. I have installed a communications room here, second to none. I get news broadcasts from all over the world. I read. All the magazines, all current social criticisms of note. How do you think I know what needs to be invented? You pay for that knowledge. You profit greatly because of it. Do not question it. My real point is simple. I have seen no real lack of support among the American people for the concept of Birth Cessation. Neither did the Congress, so they voted for it, exercising their people-given power. You have no right to call upon that easy defense of a position, 'The people are for it,' because quite obviously, they are not. Admit that you hold the minority opinion, Vivian, and then show some pride in that. But, let me ask: if the government has the civil right due to proper power to 'invade a woman's body,' then what possible objection can you have to it?"

"Maybe the people have been misled?"

"You mean, maybe they do not agree with you."

"I wouldn't state it that way."

"Of course not."

"I am against this kind of 'Big Brother' government control over private matters of private individuals."

"I wondered when that term was going to come up. It always does, you know."

"Maybe because it's valid."

"Maybe."

"Damn it, Dean! We're talking about abortion here; we're talking about the government ripping babies out of women."

"And we're now talking in highly emotional terms. You are not against abortion."

"I certainly am."

"You fought the right-to-life movement, didn't you? You were for abortion then."

"Okay. Let me clarify it. You're right. I'm neither for nor against abortion. But I am against the government ordering a woman to have an abortion or ordering her not to. That's why I fought the right-to-life movement. Because they wanted government control over women's bodies, and that is why I fight No-Birth; because it gives the government control over women's bodies."

"Not to mention men's potency."

"Yes, that too, of course."

"Why did the right-to-life movement fail, Vivian?"

"Because we put up a good fight. We showed the fallacy of their position."

"I believe that is a wrong assessment. Abortion was the most emotional of all questions. You do not destroy emotions with cool logic. Positions based on emotions are never destroyed, only supplanted. The right-to-life ideal faded under the stronger philosophical concept of right-to-consume. More people became concerned with their daily bread and the number of lips smacking for it than the rather pristine luxury of life for the unborn. That is why most people see little evil in robbing the cradle to stock the larder. Your enemy, Vivian, is not the power-hungry government; it's the simply hungry people."

"I cannot accept that, Dean; there is support for my position."

"Yes, some. But not majority support."

"Then what are you saying? I should give it up?"

"By no means. But if I could have my druthers here, I would want you to admit that you are against Birth Cessation—despite the majority being for it, despite the democracy that brought it about—simply because *you* happen to think that *you* are right about the evil of it."

"There are many others who feel the same way."

"That's not the point."

"Whatever I can do to give them support, strength—"

"Vivian, what if absolutely no one at all agreed with you? What if you were completely alone in your point of view? What then? Would you fight just as hard?"

"Yes!"

"Why?"

"Because..."

"Yes?"

"Okay, Dean. Because I happen to think that I am right."

"And everybody else is wrong?"

"I suppose that follows, yes."

Dean smiled. Vivian hated his white teeth. "And you would hold on to that lone position with no support from anyone else?"

"Yes."

"Simply because you happen to think that you are right?"

"Yes. What else could I possibly do?"

"Have you considered that Butchko may be right?"

"Of course not."

"He is, you know."

"That's your opinion."

"America is busting at the seams. There is no material left to let out the garment of the nation. The body cannot expand; it must reduce. Even though millions of individual cells will not be allowed to multiply."

"And why must the nation reduce? For simple, vain, cosmetic reasons?"

"No. For the health of the body. That the body will become more attractive is a mere side benefit."

"I notice that to state your position, you must rely on a clinical analogy. Why don't you just say it? Some must die, and some must not even be allowed to exist so that others may live. That's not an issue of weight reduction, Dean; that's a moral issue. Where's the morality in your position?"

"Where's morality?"

"Hovering over the head of any two people gathered! Once one has the chance to affect the other, his choice to do so is a moral choice. If his choice is to try to assert control over the other, then he is evil."

"To stop a man—to assert control over him—from murdering another is evil?"

"Yes! Definitely! But a lesser evil than the control the killer was trying to assert."

"There are gradations of evil?"

"Of course."

"Birth Cessation is very evil?"

"Yes."

"Even though it may save the nation from total economic ruin, social chaos, and physical destruction?"

"That's a matter of opinion."

"I said, may."

"Yes, despite that."

"You helped break the anti-trust laws?"

"Yes. Another example of control I was against."

"You profited greatly once the laws were repealed."

"I profited greatly while the laws still existed."

"You've never quite stated your views in this manner before, have you?"

"No, Dean. You have a way of leading people to high philosophical plains."

"You are *truly* against Birth Cessation?"

"Yes! Are we going to go through this again?"

"You got pregnant to test the law. You have life growing inside you for a court case. Bold action. But on the first threat of opposing action, you ran away."

"Following in your footsteps."

"No, not at all. I made no pretenses that I was concerned with anybody else but myself. You wish to be the great liberator."

"Are you accusing me of cowardice? Well, if a coward feels fear, then I am a coward. I felt an immense, sudden fear. It confused me. I wanted to get away from the confusion, the threat. They were going to kill my baby!"

"Your baby is important to you?"

"Of course."

"Why?"

"I don't know. I can't explain it. Motherhood was never a joy I looked forward to. But—I feel an intense need to recreate. Sounds silly."

"Not really. But is that need to override your opposition to Birth Cessation?"

"It was once the same thing."

"Now?"

"I won't let harm come to my child. I will have my child!"

"And to hell with the rest of the world?"

"No! You bastard! Dean, what do you want? Just let me be. Let me have my child! I ran away, okay? I'm off the field. The mad aborter wins. You win. Now leave me alone, damn it!"

"But you don't want to be off the field."

"I want my child!"

"There is a fire in your eyes, Vivian. Have I succeeded in stoking you? Are you now ready to fight!"

"Damn you, you pompous son-of-a-bitch! You don't want to be my cricket; you're a perverted little Geppetto."

Dean Harry laughed a big, bellowed, hardy Victorian laugh. "Yes! Yes! A fair assessment! But only to finally cut your strings. I do not want to control you, Vivian. I would not ever want to be *that* evil. I want you back in control of yourself. *You* want to fight to win. *You* want your opinion to prevail. Not me. I think you are completely wrong. I think if you win, you stand a chance of destroying America. Your moral stand certainly seems right. *Laissez-faire* for one and all. Unfortunately, that is only going to give one and all the right to kill each other over silly things like space, food, water, warmth—and life. But, wrong or not, you once gave me the gift of—I was going to say freedom, but that is not it—of my individuality. I owe you more than patents and profits for that. I owe you the opportunity to fight—which you dearly and individually wish to do—and the protection you desire for your child. You should not need my help for this. You should have figured it out for yourself. And once you see it all, if you wish to remember it as your idea, I am more than willing to remember likewise. For history is not so important here as truth."

***

After dinner, Dean took Vivian to the communications room.

"As I said, I have not escaped from the world. I have merely gained complete control over my relations with it. All relations are based on communication. So I communicate. But on my terms."

It was a white and silver room, hard and harsh to view. It was unpleasant. There was a bank of video monitors, some lit up with images, some not, each connected to a recording device, each on orders from a computer when to play and when to not.

"My array of disk antennas can pick up just about any signal being sent from any number of satellites. In effect, I have world television and radio coverage, both public and private. I can see anybody's drama, everybody's comedy, the sports of every nation, and, of course, their news. Except for language, it's all about the same. A sitcom is a sitcom is a sitcom. Physical competition on the field, any field, differs little except in the size and shape of the ball. There are the players. There are the fans. And they are all the aggressors. But the news is different. There are differences there. In simple comedy or sports, people are just trying to express themselves. But in the news, they are trying to express opinions despite the objectivity they profess. Of course, the news from some countries tows the party line in their opinions. But the news in other countries tows other, more subtle, lines. There may be only one way to report the facts. But there are a thousand ways to express the facts. And I think by now I've seen them all. The curious thing is, I usually find myself in agreement with the 'facts' as they are being expressed while I'm watching newscast B, even though I agreed with the same but disparately expressed 'facts' I heard on newscast A but a moment before. I do not agree with a round of applause, as I would say, at my party's political convention. Rather, I agree as I would agree with fresh air, warm breeze, and swaying trees, that it is a beautiful day. I find that a bit disconcerting. I suppose it is because it's the video equivalent of, 'It's all there in black and white.' Completely illogical. But despite that, I think there is something here we can use to your advantage.

"What I propose is simple. I do not merely receive here. I can also transmit. I can beam a signal up to a satellite and spread it around the world, like spider web lines, reaching into whatever corners I desire. If I could then force reception on the whole world—in other words, if I were not at the mercy of millions of on-off switches—then I could talk calmly, casually, personally, and friendly to just about everyone who has a TV set, which, in America, is 99 percent of the population. I could talk to them in a very agreeable manner. I could become fresh air, a warm breeze, a swaying tree—the essence of a beautiful day.

"But I have nothing to say to them. Not even a friendly, 'How-cha do?' But you, Vivian, you have a great deal to say. You have 'facts' to express. So, let us put you on the air. You remain safe here, a womb for your womb. But you also return to the field. Powerfully."

"And the on-off switches?"

"Oh, I am sure every station in America will want our signal. You are—what do they call it, Vivian? Pre-sold? Yes, that is it. You are pre-sold, Vivian. You are now, and you are news. They will take you because they feel it is their social duty. But really, it is because you will bring in ratings and deliver bodies to the front of the nation's TV screens. We will leave gaps in the broadcasts for their commercials. They will like that. And it will assure that they will run us a second time. And a third. Unlike politicians, we do not need to buy time. Unlike Hollywood, we do not need to sell our product. It will be an open sluice."

"Can they track back here, though? Can they figure out where the signal is coming from?"

"I have ways of masking it."

Vivian considered. She looked around the white and silver and saw the changing images, the little protrusions of control here and there.

"You're right. I should have thought of this myself. I owe you for this."

"You do not. I have explained my reasons."

"When can we start?

"Soon. I have a few details to work out."

"Dean, this makes me very happy. Almost giddy. I can feel it. I mean, physically feel it."

"Of course. The recovery of self is always euphoric."

19

Thursday, January 26th — Woodland Hills, California

Her soap opera was coming on, and she was damn glad. For the past three days, they had pre-empted her show—she always called it "My show," and she did, indeed, feel ownership of it—for coverage of a presidential trip abroad. It was one of those pomp and circumstance trips with a lot of reviewing of troops and guards, and visits with wreaths to graves of unknown soldiers, and brass bands and marches, and everybody looking solemn, taking it all much too seriously, like high school graduation, she thought. It was colorful, of course, and travel log-like, and she had always liked travel logs. And it was an important event, they told her—world leaders together trying to diplomat their way to solutions and peace, together for the first time in ten years, together after near misses at war—but, still, to take up all that time, to show all those boring slow marching soldiers on parade, and tell you little anecdotes about the country, and what-have-you, for three whole days, was a bit much, was duty done to death.

Especially when her show was coming into a crisis period (but then, when wasn't it?), things were coming to a head. Certain baddies were due to get their comeuppance; love would finally see the light because of it; major, instead of just minor, alterations were due. She could feel it. She could always feel it. Part of the fun was trying to figure out how it would go, to pre-plot it.

She hadn't, of course, missed anything. The news reports did not replace the show; they just delayed it. But this putting off till tomorrow—or the next day or the next day—what should be gratifying you today was disturbing, nonetheless. Her day was ordered because of the show, giving each hour its particular character, that character somehow predicated on whether it came before or after the show. Maybe the cool of the mornings, the high sun and heat of noon, the calm lowering light of late day contributed also, but that was all like flesh on soul—apparent and changeable, maybe even attractive, but not the truth. Truth was the hour the show was on each day, five days a week, five hours each week, all about the Harrison family and friends in their community of no secrets. Two hundred sixty hours a year, making the show a family saga that bested the Russians by far. Not that she was aware of Russian family sagas.

The show came on at 12:30. At 12:15, she would always make lunch for herself. Bill was at work. The kids were grown up and gone. She was almost always alone. The air conditioner would be on in the summer; the heater would often be on in the winter. She would get into a rut now and then and have the same thing for lunch for several days. But, eventually, tiring of that, she would change—surprise herself. At 12:30, the very familiar voice of an announcer would declare the time, and then another announcer would state the show's title with a flare. They were Pavlovian voices, signaling pleasures. Then the first scene commenced, and she was engrossed for an hour, breaking concentration only during the commercials to grab a quick progression into her household chores. Her children, who lived locally, had learned never to call their mother during this hour. A woman generally given to phone conversations the length of summer vacations, if called during this hour, she became a spokesperson for the reticent. The child felt like a phone solicitor—*Hello? No, sorry, we don't need any today. Thank you, and good-bye.* Avoidance was better than such filial confusion.

This day, she dreaded the possibility of yet another special report, even though she knew the president was on his way home. But what if his plane crashed? Or if there was a flood, fire, or something else with destruction that might send the news vultures out? No! They couldn't, they wouldn't. She had to have faith, simple, calm faith. She had to believe that the world would return to what it once was, that, once again, her mornings would be anticipation, her noontime fulfillment, her late days a contemplation on it all.

She was trying to figure out Brad. That was the main thing. Why, if he no longer loved Valerie, now knew the folly of love for one so inherently evil, why must he continue to agree to see her whenever she cried out, whimpering, simpering bitch that she was? It would destroy his relationship with Susan, who was sweet, sharp, beautiful—no, maybe better said, lovely. Valerie was beautiful; that could not be denied. But Valerie was evil. Joan was so in love with Sal; why was she giving him up? Okay, he was a lot younger, but she had striven so hard to get him educated after recognizing his potential. And he didn't want to lose her; he wasn't asking her to leave. It was just dumb! Why did she have to be this way?

The twin announcers announced. She was relieved. The familiar had returned. She took a bite of her lunch and settled into the couch. The images came on and captured her eyes.

The doorbell rang.

"Damn it!"

She struggled off the couch, keeping a watch on the screen, keeping her ears open to dialogue, and went to the front door.

The doorbell rang again.

"Yes, coming!"

She opened the door, not happy, expecting to see a salesman or a religious fanatic—the kind in white shirts or cotton dresses that prowl suburban neighborhoods, looking for prey to pray with—or a long lost relative, all equally unwelcomed.

It was Darleen, a neighbor of nine years, mother of three, wife to a butcher in Culver City. A bit on the plump side but cute, she was also a great viewer of the show—Oh, she thought, her TV must be on the fritz.

"Jean?"

"Oh, hi, Dar. The show's on, you know."

"Yes, I know. I'm sorry. Listen, I've got to talk to you."

Darleen came into the house and crossed to the living room. Jean followed, annoyed and anxious to check the TV.

"What's the matter?"

"I just got a call from Mike."

"Is everything okay? Is he hurt?" Jean always imagined Mike being a butcher, chopping a finger off.

"Oh, no, he's fine. It's just that he's heard something. At the store. He said everybody's talking about it."

"About what?" Jean said as *Brad* entered the room to find *Susan* in tears.

"The food shortage. He said it looks like it's started."

"What?" *Susan* slapped *Brad* hard; you could hear the sting. She immediately regretted it.

"He heard it from the truck drivers. They said they're being laid off next week. Well, some of them. Half of them. Because there won't be as much food to deliver."

"Darleen, I don't understand." The commercial had come on, and Jean hit the mute button on her remote control.

"It's the food shortage. They don't have enough food to stock all the markets, so they're rationing it, sending only part shipments. Everything. Meat, vegetables. Even can goods. Mike said they've been running out of canned goods for a while, but it's just now beginning to show."

"We've never had a food shortage."

"What does that mean? They've been warning us. It's just that I never figured it would happen so soon. I mean, we've been worried because Mike's a butcher, and his union's been talking about it, but—"

"Well, how long? Do they know how long?"

"No. Forever, I guess. Mike said to get to the store quick and stock up on canned goods and frozen foods. We have that big freezer. He's going to do the same at his store. But he has the car. So I got to get a ride. Can you take me? I'll give you some space in my freezer, and Mike will bring home some meat for you."

"Well, I guess, yeah. Let's finish the show, then we'll go."

"No! No, Jean, we've got to go now! "

"Now? What's wrong with waiting? I want to see the show."

"No, now, really! Mike said people are finding out. They're all going to go down there."

"But, Darleen, the show—"

"Jean, please, I haven't done any shopping this week. If they run out, we'll starve."

It was a pleading voice. Strange and off, odd and unusual. It was not fitting to Darleen somehow. Darleen had never pleaded before, strained her voice this way, concentrating it into a direct, thin line, except, maybe, once at thirteen, begging for permission to go on her first date. Or, perhaps, at eight, pleading for that doll she had always wanted. But this was distinct and not at all trivial. It was hysterical.

"Well—okay, I guess. Let me get my purse," Jean said.

Reluctantly, Jean slipped a tape into the VCR and hit the play button. She could see the rest later. But it just wouldn't be the same. Then she snapped off the TV just as *Joan* kissed *Sal* goodbye.

It was a bright day washed by the rain of the night before. The trees were freshly green. White, full clouds presented themselves boldly against a very blue sky. It was a rare day for Southern California, more used to shades of polluted gray. But Darleen, sitting somewhat forward in the passenger seat of Jean's car, noticed only the street ahead, the constant flow of asphalt, like a river passing underneath, a river of importance and destiny. She kept her eyes just a little forward, hoping that would speed things along. She didn't talk. Jean liked to talk when she drove, but when she turned to Darleen and saw her stare; saw her eyes fixed on an unknown future, she could think of nothing to say.

When they pulled into the supermarket's parking lot, things seemed normal. Sort of. Like a good supermarket shopper, Jean immediately entered the parking ritual of driving her car to the row closest to the front doors, hoping to find a space. Then, seeing no space, crossing to the next row for a cruise down it, looking for empty spaces. Finding none here either, she moved on to the next, prepared to continue row by row to find that one blessed, open, oil-marked, white-line boarded space for your car as close to the front doors as humanly possible.

Darleen quickly looked in as they passed the wide, glass front door.

"Jesus, it looks busy!"

"Always is on a Thursday.

They traveled down the rows, finding no breaks. Darleen's head was darting quickly back and forth, looking for an empty spot, noticing only other cars—more cars—pulling into the lot. They passed car—car—car—truck—car—van—oh! There! No—damn! Motorcycle.

Jean smiled. "Let's try out a bit."

She drove the car to the side of the lot while Darleen, a bit frantic now, kept her eyes wide open, looking everywhere, even through the windows of cars, to get an advance look at the next row. But there were no empty spaces at all, anywhere in the lot.

"I have never seen it this packed, Jean. Maybe more people know about it.

"I don't know. But what do you want to do?"

"Well, park somewhere."

"Where? There's no spaces." Jean felt helpless, rolling along at four miles an hour.

"Over there. Anywhere. I don't care."

"But there aren't any parking spaces!"

"I don't care, just park. Look, they're doing it."

Darleen pointed to other cars beginning to park anywhere, letting out passengers who ran into the store.

"But I don't like—"

"Jean! Please! We've got to get in there. Let me off if you want to.

"No, I guess..."

Jean found a spot on the side of the store reserved for delivery trucks. There were none. Darleen jumped out of the car, leaving the door open behind her, and ran. Jean sat there for a moment, not quite knowing what it was she was feeling. Darleen was hysterical. Should she also be? This was strange. It was almost a TV drama; it seemed so serious. She got out of the car, locked her door, and crossed around to shut and lock the other door. She then walked slowly to the front of the store. She wanted to walk slowly; it seemed important to her to walk slowly.

Jean entered the store and saw that things were not quite normal. It was far more crowded than usual mid-day, but people seemed to be trying not to notice it. People seemed to be making a conscious effort to be only inconvenienced and not irritated by the blockage of carts in the aisles, the clumsy maneuvering around each other, saying "Pardon," "Excuse me," "Sorry." Everyone seemed to be trying not to let on, trying not to show worry. Even as the shelves started to thin and the baskets began to fill. There were long lines at the check-out stands, and the cashiers seemed nervous. The young checkout crew bagged the food as fast as possible. For the crowd, for the business, for the activity, it was much too quiet in the store. Hushed, almost.

Jean passed through the turnstile into the central part of the store and looked for Darleen. She sidestepped her way past people and carts and boxes of goods just opened, just emptied. She saw several women and one man struggling to push one cart and pull another, causing mild clashing against other carts and display shelves. Another man, a customer, was cutting open newly brought-out packing boxes with a pocketknife. Inside was canned macaroni and cheese. Several other customers watched, waited, and finally reached in and pulled out cans in an almost systematic group effort. Jean stood on tiptoes to look over heads to find Darleen. But, by doing so, she sacrificed balance and found herself falling forward after a sharp bump in the buttocks. Only the fact of aisle-wide shoppers prevented her from falling.

"Oh, jeez, I'm sorry! Are you okay?" the bumper said. Others also showed concern in their eyes but also a bit of inconvenience.

"Yes, it's okay. I'm fine." There would be a big bruise; she knew it.

"Gee, I am sorry." The bumper was being far too polite, forcing concern and remorse.

"No, that's okay. I'm fine. Excuse me." Jean found herself having to say as she edged between the carts, bodies, and boxes. She found Darleen, with a cart nearly full of boxes and cans, wedged in by some other customers but calm even if caged. Jean squeezed over to her.

"Jean, where's your cart?"

"Uh—I didn't get one."

"Well, I'm not shopping for both of us. This is just my stuff."

"I know Dar. I mean, I didn't think of grabbing a cart. I don't even think there was any when I came in."

"Well, let me finish up. We'll hang on to this cart. Then you can shop. But we've got to go quickly."

"I don't see how we can."

"Just move along. That's what everybody's doing."

The wedge had parted, and Darleen began to move out as she would from a stop light. "Look, I'm not getting any meat because Mike said he would take care of that." She was, as she had been, whispering. "But maybe we ought to pass through and get some for you now?"

"Yes—okay—I guess so."

Jean was tagging along. That's the way she felt. She wanted to hang on to the back of Darleen's blouse. She was stepping in short steps; that's the only way the crowd would allow movement. She felt childlike. She felt like she was at the store with Mommy when people were bigger than they really were and more threatening.

The p.a. broke in. *"Mr. Morris, we need more change up here,"* said the voice on high. *"On my way,"* said another.

Jean now noticed that she was warm, and what a strange feeling that was in a supermarket. From childhood, supermarkets had always meant coolness to her. They were air-conditioned and had long refrigerated bins of frozen food that you would lean into on hot summer days, watch your breath, and cool your bare arms. But now she was warm. And she found breathing hard. Yet supermarkets had always been airy to her. And well lit. Yet today, so many bodies caused shadows.

The meat counter was jammed with near supplicants, all having made requests of the butchers for specific cuts of meats, cuts now being hurriedly done.

"Oh damn, we'll be here forever," Darleen said. "Why don't you get in line, and I'll go check out and bring the cart back to you."

"Oh—okay—I guess so."

"Good." Darleen, after taking Jean's car keys, left.

But Jean did not stay by the meat counter. Instead, she moved on, edging and excusing her way down one aisle and up another. She wanted to see the faces. She felt a need to isolate and look at the faces. She understood nothing from the crowd: the flow of arms, legs, torsos of various shapes, enviable figures, sloppy fat bellies, desirous chests. She wanted to see faces up close, as if framed by a screen.

Full, yet fallen, with folds, one woman's face sucked in its lower lip and seemed to be biting down. The eyes darted from shelves—now getting sparser—to her basket. The lip would pop out when she reached to select.

Thin and pointed, one man's face was set, as if decreed, into one expression of hard forward. The eyes did not dart with questions but were still with answers.

Another face, a woman's, more pretty than seemed her due, kept commenting on those around her, and the situation in general. It was not happy; it was annoyed.

The red, freckled face of a box boy, clean and slightly silly looking, had dropped from its usual grin-provided upturn to a slide down into part confusion, part concern. The boy had little plastic numbers tightly held in his hand, some of which he had taken out of a shelf groove, some of which he was putting in.

"Hey, what are you doing?" a customer asked.

"Uh—changing the price. There's been a price change on these pork and beans."

"What do you mean?" The customer was the thin-faced man.

"Well..."

"You just upped the price?"

"Yes..."

"Hey, what are you trying to get away with here?"

"Uh..."

"Son-of-a-bitch!" The thin-faced man was beginning to shout. "Hey, they're starting to raise the prices on us!"

"What?" The boy was scared and had no ability to explain.

"Look, they're trying to take advantage of us!"

Other people were starting to look and beginning to listen.

"You fucking son-of-a-bitch, put back the old price."

"Look, mister, I..." The boy was seventeen and crying.

"God damn it!" The thin-faced man pushed the boy hard with his right hand. The boy banged against the shelves and fell to the ground. "Look, I'm going to take this shit, and they better not charge me the higher price!"

"Take it easy, guy," a voice said.

"Damn it! They're trying to screw us, don't you see?"

"That's no reason to—"

"I'm not going to take it! They're trying to pull one over on us."

Someone was trying to help the boy up.

"Look, I think we ought to get them first. Just take what you want and leave. Damn it, that'll show them." The thin-faced man was throwing things in his cart now.

"Hey! Don't take it all!"

"Fuck you!" A woman kicked the thin-faced man hard in the shin. He pushed her face in retaliation.

"Someone, call the manager."

"No, what the hell, he's right. We got to get it before they stick it to us."

"Hell, they've probably been raising the prices all along."

Someone dropped a plastic water bottle. It split and flowed.

"Hey, watch it!"

Many people were now grabbing at boxes and cans, not knowing what they were getting. People in other aisles now knew of this, but not what started it. They saw only what looked like a panic and, in seeing, felt. Suddenly, the crowd became a mass. Movement that had been slow but progressive was now energetic but went nowhere. The people at the check stands knew what had happened and froze. Then, some started to move out of the store, grabbing bags of food or not. It was no longer hushed; a din arose. There were cries, shouts, and curses—the sounds of metal on metal, of things spilling, of glass breaking. People were being pushed now and shoved. There were no *excuse mes*, no *pardons*. Store employees wanted to do something but didn't know what to do, so they settled for a run to the office and a call to the police. People were leaving now, escaping with bags and carts full of food. Some went straight for their cars. Some just ran pushing carts piled with food through the parking lot, forgetting about their vehicles, out onto the street, down the street, away—just away.

Inside, a vast metal product case had been tipped over. A child of four had been crushed beneath it; her flowing blood made the floor slippery. Jean was there, staring at the scene, her mouth open, not moving until she was pushed. Pushed hard, down and to the right, into a semi-spin, her head—at the temple—striking the exposed corner of an empty metal shelf. She seemed suddenly very much awake, then—

Jean fell and thumped to the floor, and her sliced temple poured forth blood to meet and mingle with that of the child.

***

New York City

Gerald Downing looked at his coat and was sorry that it was second-hand, although he remembered his delight at having found it at a YWCA thrift store. He tried to buy clothes that one could strike a pose in, model in essence, instead of just wear. And this coat—probably that of someone's suddenly dead father—was dynamic in ways that Gerald had never been able to afford. It was a statement-making coat that quickly and silently communicated things that one couldn't shout effectively.

Gerald put it on and stood in front of the mirror. He turned to the right. He turned to the left. He gestured with his right hand. He smiled and nodded, agreeing with a statement he imagined someone would say.

He loved the coat. But could only wish he had been the original owner. The fact that second-hand was prevalent in most people's lives these days, that thrift, bargain hunting, and conservation were widely learned techniques of survival, took no edge off it; sharpened the pain, in fact, for most would naturally assume the truth of the coat, and would never credit it to his discerning taste, only to his common thrift. But he looked good in it, nevertheless, he hoped. For he had somewhere to go. He had been invited, and that delighted him.

The envelope was addressed to:

Mr. Gerald Downing

And the invitation read:

THE JAN LAWRENCE SOCIETY
Cordially Invite You To A
CONCEPTION RECEPTION
Buffet Eats And Action
Oriented Conversation On How To Stop
Birth Cessation.
Jan. 26, 8:00 P.M.
At The Home Of
Mrs. & Dr. William T. Kurtz
Donation: $500
RSVP

The Jan Lawrence Society had been growing. From the first group at Fordham University, it had spread to other New York area colleges. Meetings were called often and announced in the small student appeal papers, inviting all, not just students, to join. Gerald had read, had decided: yes, he would. He had been excited by the Vivian Pavin speech they had sponsored. He agreed with their goals. Or—actually—they agreed with his goals, for hadn't he tried to organize first, hadn't he gone to Kirkly? Kirkly had not helped, but maybe they could. He still liked his ideas; he still thought they were good. Perhaps the Jan Lawrence Society could help put them into action. They should have a publication, of course. He would suggest it, offer to edit it, and powerfully carry the philosophy and point of view across in his editorials—stinging, pungent, well thought out, and eventually influential. Kirkly would see that and soon congratulate him.

How about Point Conception for the publication's name?

Was that something geographical? Did he see it on a news report or something? Doesn't matter. It works as a name for the publication. The point *is* conception.

Birthright!

That's good. The right to birth. That's even better than *Point Conception.*

Gerald Downing, the editor of BIRTHRIGHT! *The official publication of the Jan Lawrence Society, stated today...*

He combed his hair again. Finished, he put the comb back into his back pocket, feeling his wallet, thinking—no. The bulk of it was, well, thick, a lump almost, a big bump on his butt, kind of klutz-like. He took it out and placed it in his inside coat pocket. It was heavy there, dropping one side of the coat. Shit! He adjusted his coat to compensate, but the wallet still had its effect. He took it out and took everything but essential ID and money out of it. He put it back. Better. Yes. He took it out again and opened it while watching himself in the mirror. Yes, better than reaching back to his butt like a spastic, more...

***

Gerald had gone to his first meeting, sitting in the back a bit shy, allowing himself to be impressed by some he had seen interviewed on television. It was a small group, maybe 25. But it was right after Christmas, before New Year's, vacation for most. They discussed it all. The whole concept of No-Birth. How it was all Butchko's mad plan. Vivian Pavin. Her protest. Her rich coward's flight.

"I don't know," said Shelly Clarke, who had organized Vivian Pavin's speech. "Maybe she's planning something we don't understand."

"Doesn't matter. We've got to act. We can't wait for others."

Gerald listened hard, nodded hard, and even chanced a throat vocal acknowledgment of agreement, sending a small signal into the room's atmosphere that he was there. Obviously, some in the room were old friends, or, at least, classmates, so friends forging. They had words and secret codes and looks that meant something that naturally excluded Gerald. No one had yet asked him who and what he was, which bothered him. Not that he wanted to mention major appliances instead of college courses, but he would like to have been noticed. He thought Shelly Clarke glanced at him now and then, which pleased him. She was pretty. But was it interest, suspicion, or mundane curiosity? Maybe he could be mysterious. Did he look like a graduate? Perhaps someone finished with school, set in a profession, rather than one incomplete, stuck in work. But he wasn't really, no, he didn't like college, that's all. Found it too sterile. He had learned more and studied more since being out than he ever did while he was in. He loved to learn. He read a lot. It was school he hated. That's what he would say—

if asked. Work? He worked to earn money. To have time to write. Fascinating things you can learn about people as you try to sell them refrigerators, ha, ha. Here tonight? Well, concerned, of course. Have been against it since the beginning. But pretty much cut off from things, working, then spending off hours writing. I thought I would search out some like minds for the stimulation.

Someone mentioned children—the joy of and the sin of being denied them. Gerald saw the way. "I have a daughter," he announced. Shelly Clarke looked at him. "Uh, I'm divorced. But I see her every other weekend. She's four, and, and precious to me. You're right. It is a joy to have a child. I guess that's why I agree with you."

"You are…?" Someone asked.

"Uh—Gerald Downing."

Some noted that, and then the conversation continued along various lines, finally leading to action plans.

Shelly Clarke said: "We're getting to the point where we need money more than talk."

"How about a fundraiser?" Someone asked.

"Sure. But what?" Someone else answered.

"I don't know. A concert or something."

"You need money first for something like that. We're starting with nothing."

"Well, I've got sort of an idea." Shelly Clarke said. "How about something like a cocktail party? That wouldn't cost much. I think I can get my stepfather to host it. We'll have a donation and invite people who can afford it. We'll make it sort of half party, half planning session. Get all kinds of advice on how to protest. I mean, I know some professors who would come. They're against No-Birth. And there are other people; some prominent people might or have come out against No-Birth. Maybe Malcolm Kirkly, possibly we could get him to speak at the party."

"Uh…" Gerald sat up straight. "Do you know how to get in touch with him?"

"Oh, I'm sure that's no problem. He lives here in Manhattan."

"Oh—well—I thought maybe I could help there. I mean, I have his address in my book. I could—uh—if you wanted—uh, get in touch with him.

"You know Kirkly?"

"Well, yeah. He helps me with my writing."

"Great! Okay, fine. If you could do that, that would be wonderful. Let's talk about it after the meeting."

They decided on the party. The CONCEPTION RECEPTION, Shelly named it, and they all agreed with laughter. They decided on the donation amount, which Gerald was proud he did not flinch at. Those who still needed to be members of the Jan Lawrence Society were asked to join. Gerald signed up, leaving his address for an invitation to the party.

Shelly Clarke approached Gerald briefly as people left and reminded him to contact Malcolm Kirkly. She gave him her number. And he gave her his.

He had seen her on TV, being interviewed. He had listened. He was interested in what she had to say. But he saw as well, seeing her severe beauty, quick and exciting futures—if only he could meet her—which now he had—incredulously—putting himself on the line about Kirkly. It had been sort of easy, not too many barriers. He talked to her easily, as he would to a customer. But with a little stir inside. He thought of futures. He had been vocal against marriage after his broke up. But, maybe with one more compatible. It's evident that they agreed on things. She was a law student, thus bright, so perhaps she could understand his thoughts. He had always wanted the best—beautiful, smart—women to fall in love with him. He had always wanted to be that highly complimented.

He walked to the subway, realizing that he was being romantic. Overly romantic, most likely. But so what?

***

...more professional, more natural for a man in a sports coat. His dad, he remembered, had always carried his hefty wallet in his back pocket. His dad had been a laborer. He wore tan work pants, and the tan faded around the outline of the wallet after much wear. He always had a handkerchief in the other back pocket, which he would take out to wipe his brow, maybe blow...

***

He had come home from the meeting late to find that his mother had put his mail on his bed. Two bills, a book club notice, and—

Gerald's mouth went dry—an envelope with Malcolm Kirkly's return address. It must be his writings back, the few essays he had left with Kirkly. Kirkly had said he would read them and comment. Kirkly had told him not to worry about how long it might take to get them back, but it had been well over a month, and Gerald had begun to think Kirkly wouldn't answer. That would have been his excuse for calling him about the Jan Lawrence party. To check up on it, to see...

Previous thoughts came back to Gerald. Thoughts of Kirkly liking his writings, getting him a job, a column somewhere, maybe, or what? Well, maybe, at least, a start? Gerald opened the envelope sloppily, tearing it nearly in half. He pulled out several pieces of paper; most were his writings; one was a letter from Kirkly. He read it in one look, as if looking at a picture instead of words, and received a strange, mixed feeling of disappointment and joy. For Kirkly was not discouraging yet offered nothing concrete.

Dear Mr. Downing:

I enjoyed your essays. Although they are not publishable, I see quite a bit of potential for you as a writer. Outside the controversial aspect of No-Birth, which you handled competently, I was impressed with your well-thought-out use of words, which show great promise. Keep up the good work. And keep writing!

Best,
M. Kirkly

Gerald now read it word for word. Then he read it a second time. It sounded great! Then it sounded like nothing at all, like a nice way of saying, "Get lost, kid, you're bothering me." Then it sounded great! Or, at least, not too bad. Why? Because it was back in Gerald's hand, his to do with as he wished.

***

... his nose. He did not dislike any of this about his father. It was just the idea that a son should go beyond his father.

***

He was ready. He picked up his invitation, put it in his coat's inside breast pocket with his wallet, and left his room.

"Oh, you look nice!" his mother said as he said goodbye.

"Thank you.

They talked for a few seconds. He reiterated how important this party was and his part in it. She expressed some concern that it was dangerous.

"I mean, have you checked out what you're doing? Is it illegal or anything?"

"No, Mom, of course not. We have the right of peaceable assembly in this country, you know."

"Well, you don't have to get so smug and snide!"

"I didn't."

"Yes, you did. You can sound really smug sometimes. It's not very attractive, you know. If you want people to like you, that's not the way to do it."

"I don't want people to like me."

"Oh, don't make silly statements."

"I—well, whatever. I know what I'm doing."

"I didn't say you didn't. I just asked a question. Can't I ask a question in my own house?"

He left and walked to the subway station. Why couldn't she take what he said and be proud of it, just simply proud? He would love to have known. Not even everything about Kirkly got much more from her than, "That's nice." But everything about Kirkly had made him happy. He had called him the day after he received the letter to thank him for his words of encouragement and to find that relationship he had implied with Shelly Clarke. The phone was answered, and Gerald said hello and announced himself. There was a hesitation on the other end of the line. Kirkly was trying to recall. That was obvious. But was it understandable? He had just written the letter, after all. Gerald felt insulted or hurt or pained or possibly just annoyed that Kirkly had not jumped on his cheery hello with an equally eager greeting. Gerald nudged him.

"Oh, yes, of course. How are you, Mr. Downing?" Now it was eager, but now was it true? Gerald talked, somewhat nervous, gave his thanks, then told Kirkly about the Conception Reception and how they would like to invite him to be the guest of honor. Kirkly was reluctant about it at first. Hesitant, like a customer not sure this was the television for him. Unwilling in that compassionate way, not wanting, necessarily, to say the hurtful No. Gerald had never learned to pounce on such reluctance as other—as successful—salesmen did. He had always taken it as the uneasy No it was and backed off, relieving the customer of his pain. But this time, it was a product he truly wanted to sell. This time, the "commission" meant something to him. This time, he pounced.

"I understand your feelings, of course, since we discussed them. And I explained to the Jan Lawrence Society that you wouldn't join or endorse them due to your policy. But, they feel, and I agree with them, that you eloquently state a view on No-Birth that they happen to share, and they feel that they would like to meet and talk with you."

"Well, have them send me an invitation, and if I can make it, I will be there. But understand this, Mr. Downing. They are not to use me as a drawing card, for I may be unable to be there."

"Well, I'm not sure they have any plans like that, but would it be okay to say that your appearance is tentative?"

There was a pause. "Yes, I guess that's okay."

Gerald excitedly called Shelly Clarke with the news of Malcolm Kirkly's tentative acceptance. She was happy but very businesslike over the phone. She took down Kirkly's address and asked Gerald if he was coming.

"Well, yes, if I can be of any help," Gerald said, half hoping he could go in an official capacity. He would like to have a reason and a purpose. He would like not to have to pay the donation.

"We don't need any help with the party. I mean, do you want an invitation?"

"Oh, sure. My name's on the list, in fact."

When the invitation came, he wanted it to have magic, to dazzle and stir excitement, to be a real prop in this play of importance. But he had to face a disappointment, for it had instead the tinge of a bill about it, a rather fancy statement of account due. He struggled to put the five hundred dollars together. He called up his ex-wife and asked forgiveness on part of that month's child support. "Things are just a little bit rough right now. Can you manage?" He decided to suffer a second notice on the car payment due in two days. But he got it all collected, in the bank, and ready to come out through a flourish of his pen at the party. Once committed, it seemed right and proper, an obvious action and all anxiety over the deed wore off.

***

Dr. Kurtz's apartment, where the party was being held, was in the East 70s off 5th Avenue, which was to Gerald, despite being a near-native of Manhattan, like a make-believe land, a fine and delicate invention of a mind prone to the clouds. It was in books, and it was in films, and, despite its inclusion in the non-fiction of his newspapers, it was as distant to Gerald as it might have been to a Midwest boy itching to get out of small-town America. He had, of course, traveled the streets before. He had walked them, looking at the buildings, gazing up, seeing the windows, wishing to see through them, past the panes to the rooms decorated instead of just furnished. But what was that but fantasy in 3-D? You still couldn't touch.

But now he could touch. And did, eagerly, the elevator button, the doorbell, the hand in shaking.

"How do you do? I'm Doctor Kurtz."

"Uh, hello, I'm Gerald Downing."

"Mr. Downing, you're our first guest. Welcome."

He was on time. Exactly. Which somehow, now, seemed wrong, as an unoccupied, large room greeted him with a cold stare. It was a space well filled with the fine—a room *decorated* as he had expected. But more than that, it was more set, as if to plan, for exhibition, as if it was a party at the Frick House, which was not too far away. Two maids passed through carrying dishes for the buffet, causing the room to blink. Then they were gone, and Gerald stood alone, for Dr. Kurtz had excused himself and left. He walked over to the buffet table against one wall and looked at the food. He found it architectural in setting, almost painterly in color, a true life still life. He could have, but he did not touch.

"Hello!"

Gerald turned around. It was Shelly Clarke, beautiful as he had expected, yet, somehow, surprisingly so. All her lines were sharp, from her face to her dress (a contrast to her usual jeans) to the simple but elegant jewelry she wore on her wrist and around her neck. Gold. Thin. Unobtrusive.

"Gerald Downing, right?"

"Yes."

"Ah, good. I'm happy you could make it. The others should be arriving soon. And I've got excellent news for you. Malcolm Kirkly RSVPed."

"Oh, great!" But he had to think to be thrilled by that. He was becoming numb; the room, the food, her.

The doorbell rang.

"Look, let me greet some guests. We'll talk later."

Gerald moved to the center of the room, feeling naked and exposed. He took a deep breath. He thought he needed it. People started to arrive and fill the room. In couples, in groups, one at a time. At first, Shelly would come in with them and introduce Gerald to them as an associate of Mr. Kirkly's, then run off at the sound of the now repeating doorbell. Gerald quickly corrected what Shelly had said, truthfully relating his association with Kirkly, using words open to interpretation. Soon, though, more people were coming faster, and Shelly had little time for introductions. After the first hellos, people moved on. Gerald soon found himself alone again, still in the middle of the room, though now surrounded by people talking, people smoking, people drinking and eating, people kissing hello, shaking hands, laughing. One small group pushed close to him, unknowingly forcing him into inclusion. But he quickly extricated himself, feeling unwanted. He finally moved to the side, to the buffet, to find the food attacked, devastated, and, somehow, now more accessible. He ate. Gladly. It occupied, engaged his hands, mouth, even his mind.

"Nice party." Some man said to him as he picked up something edible and popped it in his mouth.

"Uh, yes," Gerald said, maybe wanting to say more, but the man moved on.

Who was there? Suddenly, he wanted to know. It occurred to him that he had not closely looked. They had only been forms moving through space, variously colored and shaped. But who were they? Here, he was in a place he had always wanted to be and wasn't paying attention. He had *stared* at pictures, movies, and words that formed images that showed this very thing he was now glancing at. And now he was *not taking advantage, letting opportunity slip, losing the moment.* He quickly started to look, concentrating on what he saw. He was, after all, a writer, an observer, and he should feel no discomfort in looking.

He saw some people he had seen at the meeting, but certainly not all. They were mainly young, probably all students. They stuck together, and none came up to him. Others at the party were older.

But youthful looking, nonetheless. They were all very well dressed—they suited well being suited well—and they all seemed familiar. Not in any particular way, but in general. Except—yes—there was a TV personality on the other side of the room. Gerald recognized her immediately and felt himself almost move up and out as if suddenly inflated. But then he was calm, taking it as a simple fact. He found quick pride in that.

But where was his celebrity? Where was Kirkly?

After looking, he listened. He heard chatter and talk, jokes and tales of time abroad, causing quick, dumb pangs of envy. But where was the talk of No-Birth? Where was the "Action-oriented conversation?" There seemed to be no control, no center to the thing. Just people eating and drinking, talking and laughing while they faced various directions—from true north, through east, south, and west. But maybe that was okay. It was, after all, a fundraiser. Maybe Shelly just invited sources of money instead of motivation. But still, he wanted to talk about it. He wanted to discover how these people felt about it. He wanted to see concrete ideas for action come about. Something he could get all excited about. He wanted to bring up the need for a publication.

Someone blew smoke in his face. It was a woman, now with the cigarette hanging from her mouth as she scooped food onto a plate. It had been an accident she had not even noticed, as she had been talking, now mumbling, to the man behind her. Gerald moved on, side-stepping through people, excusing himself, trying to find an out, to a hallway maybe, to the restroom eventually.

Shelly was suddenly there. "Oh, hi! Isn't it going great? Oh, Malcolm Kirkly called. He's going to be a little late."

"Oh."

"This will give us a good fund to work with."

"Are you going to lead a—well, I don't know, a discussion, or something, on No-Birth?"

"What do you mean?"

"Well, uh, I just thought we were going to talk about what to do about No-Birth."

"We will. Don't worry about it."

Shelly was a little annoyed by the question. So little that it passed before it registered within her. But Gerald felt it. It pushed him back slightly, and he had no answer. He wanted to explain his concern, take away the tiny evil that had annoyed her, but she left and went across the room, stopping and talking to almost everyone, and Gerald stood at the edge of the room now, once again, alone. He looked down the hallway. There was a strangeness there, without even the brief familiarity he now had with the party room. But he decided to brave it, walk unarmed, let intuition guide him to the right door, and find refuge in a restroom. With concentrated confidence, he walked, guessed, turned the knob of a door, opened it slightly, and was rewarded with success. He went inside and shut and locked the door. It was large, clean, carpeted, and beautiful. Things shone. He noticed that first. Then, he noticed and appreciated the muffled party noise and the lack of smoke. He breathed in the various delicate smells. The bathroom in his home, the home he had grown up in, the house he had come home to, was small and always full of fallen hair, dried soap foam, and talcum smells. The toilet bowl was merely functional, the sink stained, and the mirror-fronted medicine cabinet had little organization but, being metal, some rust. Brushes laid haphazardly around, and a hook on the door had almost always supported a shower cap and an enema device, hanging ready to use. It was a comfortable room, and he had done a lot of reading in it.

This bathroom was immaculate. But it didn't seem to be just for show. It seemed naturally flawless. The walls were painted a subtle salmon color, and hanging from them were small, original—he looked, touched, and verified—oil paintings of Paris. A tall plant with huge leaves was sitting in a beautiful pink pot in one corner. The towels were somewhere between pink and salmon and had a fullness about them Gerald truly admired. Over the sink and covering the top half of the wall was a mirror in which Gerald's reflection looked straight ahead and concentrated. He was looking for the bulge of his wallet. He thought he saw it—damn it!—but, no, he didn't see it at all—thank god! He was pleased and took the time to relish where he was, feeling better about it than he had in the room with the food and the people. He breathed in, again smelling sweet smells, and looked at his image surrounded by the cool, clean, salmon and pink environment. He met his own eyes and knew the rightness of their placement.

Someone said something close outside the door, and he quickly moved his concentration from his eyes to his groin and realized that, yes, indeed, he did have to urinate. So he did, being very careful to hit the bowl—also salmon colored and finely crafted—dead center. He finished, rinsed his hands—unable to accept the implied dare to use one of the sculptured, untouched mini bars of soap that sat in the sculptured soap dish to the side—and went to dry his hands. He stopped. He knew what wet hands did to a towel, especially one of light shade: dark spots of water, if not darker spots of dirt, and the drape disturbed. He reached around to the back of a towel, the part that did not show, and used it gently so as not to soil and not to spoil, as if they would know it was his dirt, as if they would accuse him hatefully as if they would never invite him back.

He left the restroom, assuring himself into a straight stance, ready to enter the room well. *Naturally* well, he hoped. As he re-entered the party, he noticed a difference in sound and tone. Then he saw the reason why. Malcolm Kirkly had arrived. People were paying attention, talking to him, listening to him talk. Dr. Kurtz and Shelly were making introductions. Gerald started towards them but then detoured to the food, noticing that Shelly had not seen him but acting as if—in case she had—he had not noticed them. He ate with his back to them, concentrating on the food. He could hear Kirkly's voice, which was loud and flamboyant after much practice, commenting on No-birth in much the same words that had appeared in his column. He talked of Jan Lawrence and showed approval that her name was being used this way. "Although, by my self-imposed rules, I must remain objective and unattached to all things, and therefore cannot join the society. But I will certainly follow your progress and possibly comment on it."

"Well, that's pretty good in itself, Mr. Kirkly," Shelly said.

Others came up and talked to Kirkly, and that pleased him. He had always had some small following because of his column and had received attention from readers many times upon meeting. But ever since he started appearing on TV talk shows of varying intents, he had gotten more and different attention from his readers, who now took a proprietary pride in him. Even those who never read his column, who may have cursed his broadcasted face and opinions, nearly fawned over his face, if not his opinions, live. It was a curious phenomenon. But Kirkly had read about it long before he had experienced and expected it. He did not take it seriously, though he did take it. We are always the center of our attention. And if we are honest with ourselves, we take pleasure from that attention. A like pleasure, if not a heightened pleasure, accompanies being the center of another's attention. Kirkly accepted this as a given.

Gerald finally went over to Kirkly. He came close and stood on the border of a conversation where Kirkly comfortably talked to two students.

"Are your feelings indicative, do you think, of most students?" Kirkly was asking.

"Well," one of the students started. "That's hard to say. I don't think so right now because students are always apathetic at first. But I think they can get riled up. I mean, look at the Vietnam thing in the Sixties. Look what the students did then."

The students finished the conversation and started to move away. Gerald stepped closer but was still to the side and had to touch Kirkly's arm to get his attention. Kirkly turned to face him.

"Mr. Kirkly, hello." Gerald held out his hand. "Gerald Downing."

"Of course, Gerald; good to see you again. Do you consider the party a success?"

Gerald Downing, who it was good for *Malcolm Kirkly* to see again, said, "Oh yes, I think so. Shelly, uh, Shelly Clarke seems to have done a great job."

"That's the young girl who lives here?"

"Uh, yes. She organized everything. I want to thank you for coming."

"Well, thank you for the invitation. I can't stay much longer, though, I have a late appointment. But I was happy to come. No-Birth must be defeated somehow. Maybe this is one way. I'll certainly be interested in following your progress."

"We all appreciate that."

"Well, good to see you again," Kirkly repeated his pleasure, then excused himself to move on, smiling broadly, shaking hands warmly, then exiting for the night.

"Did you see Malcolm Kirkly?" Shelly had come up to him.

"Uh, yeah, we just talked."

"Thanks again for your help in getting him here.

"Oh well, that's okay. I was happy to do it."

"Maybe he'll write something about us."

"Possibly. You know," Gerald threw out the words, trying to aim true, as he saw Shelly ready to move on. "We really should have some kind of, uh, you know, of a publication or something of our own. Something to get our views across."

"You mean like a magazine?

"Sure, yeah."

"Well, maybe. I can see that. Maybe we should talk about that later."

"Yeah, uh, I think we should. I mean, I've been thinking about it, and, uh, I could try to help, and—"

"Good. We'll talk later about it. Right now, I've got to start collecting money. You've got yours?"

"No. I mean, I have to write a check."

"Fine, that will do. Make it out to W.T. Kurtz, MD. We haven't got a bank account yet." Then she raised her voice. "Everyone! Hello! Donation time, everyone. Let's make JLS strong."

Wallets and checkbooks whipped out as people seemed tickled to donate, and Shelly took their names. When that was over, the party broke up, with many of the older guests saying goodbye and what a good time they had, hoping the money would help, and the few younger ones staying on, plus a professor or two. Dr. Kurtz and his wife went out for a late supper.

Gerald stayed, wondering what would happen now, slightly uncomfortable as the group relaxed with drinks and some drugs to watch Shelly count the money.

"Should we register to be a lobby in Washington?" someone asked.

"What good would that do? That's stupid. Politicians won't change until they hear the people clamoring. We've got to get to the people."

"Don't be surprised by Jack; he's taking Butler's Intro to Con Law course."

"Oh god! Does he still have that American flag tacked to the wall?"

"Yeah."

"Stupid bastard."

"Look, we didn't get that kind of money anyway. This is just for operating expenses.

"So, what are we going to do with it?"

"Well, you know, Gerald here—you all remember Gerald?"

"Yeah.

"Sure."

"Hi."

"Gerald has suggested a newsletter or something to get our point across."

Gerald was shocked. She had remembered! She had taken note and listed it down somewhere on a mental agenda as if it mattered.

"Yes, that's obvious, isn't it?" someone said. "But that's expensive, isn't it?"

"Depends, I suppose, on how elaborate you get. We could do something simple, Xerox it. Couldn't we, Gerald?"

No! No! Gerald wanted to shout. Xeroxed? Like some ancient third-grade project for the parents? No! Uh, "No, uh, I mean, I think we want to be taken, well, seriously. And that means, I would think, a fairly nice, uh, sort of, um, classy, or, maybe, classic, presentation."

"What do you mean? You mean a full-blown magazine?"

"Well..."

"Shit! That *is* expensive. Not to mention the work. That's a lot of work."

"Well, I'll, uh, be happy to do it," Gerald said.

"Do what?"

"Well, edit it, I guess, or something."

"That's not the thing though. It's the production, it's the paper and the printing that costs time and money."

"Oh, hell! Those are just practical matters," said one of the professors. "Do it with Desktop Publishing. You can make a beautifully slick publication."

"Wait a minute! You've all got a damn magazine printed here, but what do we write about?"

"I think that's fairly obvious," said another professor. "You would use such a publication for an information organ, for one, letting people know who to write to, their congressmen and such, and what's going on regarding meetings, rallies, and such. Also, you use it to disseminate news about and document the struggle against No-Birth. I see one thing right away: a follow-up on Kirkly's article. I mean, that's all been sort of dropped. So how about an interview with a psychologist or two on how feasible it is that Butchko's actions, which affect us all, are based on, or is, in a way, his way of coping with a personal tragedy? Or how about something about the trauma of women being forced to have abortions? I can see all sorts of possibilities."

Yes! Yes! Gerald thought. He understands!

"Would you be willing to be the editor?" someone asked the professor.

No! Thought Gerald. Shit! That's not my idea at all.

"I'd be willing to contribute, certainly. But I would hardly have the time to be the editor."

Good.

"Well," said Shelly. "Let's keep thinking about this. I think it's a good, long-range goal. But what about now? We need to call attention to ourselves now. The speech did some of that, but now we need something else. And we need it soon."

"Uh, well," Gerald pushed into the conversation, "just on the magazine idea real quick before we leave it. Uh, as I said, if we get it started, I would be happy to edit it. I think what he—" He hated saying, "He," but he didn't know the professor's name, he had not been introduced, or, if he had been, he had not remembered. "—was saying was that it's a bit of a job, being the editor of something, and takes a lot of time. Well, I could, you see, do that."

"Gerald has been working with Kirkly," Shelly said.

"Oh, really?" someone said with interest.

"Well, kind of. In any case, I would love to do it. I mean, I could quit my job if there was some salary or something available. But, but if not, I would do it, I guess, on my own time. But it's important, I think, so I would be glad to do it."

"There would be no money, that's for sure."

"Well, that's okay. I can, like I said, do it on my own time." Shit!

"Okay," Shelly said. "Let's think about it. But again, what about now? We should have a demonstration or something."

"Like what?"

"We've got to protest the law."

"How?"

"By civil disobedience, I would think. Right? Protest the law by breaking it. That's how all great movements made their point. We should do what Vivian Pavin called us to do. I suggest we all get pregnant."

"That's easy for you to say," said one young man to a couple of laughs.

"Wait a minute, wait a minute. I agree with that," said a young woman. "I think Vivian Pavin was right. If we could convince a lot of women to get pregnant, they can't abort us all. But that's hardly a demonstration. I mean, in an event sort of way. You can't get pregnant in one afternoon during a rally or picket or something."

"Yes, you can."

"Be serious, Shelly. It still takes nine months, as far as I know."

"Not to *get* pregnant. It only takes a moment to *get* pregnant."

Everybody was quiet. Shelly smiled. "I propose that we have a demonstration of mass conception. I suggest that we get as many of us as possible, pair off male-female, obviously, and in one mass demonstration, have the males do their best to impregnate the females."

A professor smiled.

Several sets of eyes got wide.

Someone said, "You're talking about a goddamn orgy."

Gerald fought back a hard-on, embarrassed that his body took so frivolously what his mind took so seriously. But he had to admit; his first image was of him and Shelly in the middle of a mass of couples leading the crowd by leading the beat.

"Shelly!" someone said. "That's shocking!"

"That's the point! Can you think of a better way to get attention?"

"Or arrested."

"Of course! We must get arrested. That's what it's all about."

"Yeah, but will we get arrested for denying No-Birth or for just plain indecent exposure."

"Oh, they wouldn't do that! That would be so obvious. They will have to arrest us on a No-Birth charge."

"And then throw us all into an abortion clinic.!"

"No, I don't think so, not right away. We'll be too prominent."

"That didn't help Vivian Pavin."

"Yeah, but there's more of us. And even if we do get aborted, we just do it over again. More headlines! We can really get people thinking about the injustice of No-Birth."

There was a moment of quiet, of no one speaking.

"Look," Shelly finally sliced through the silence, "it's just demanding the right of personal freedom. This will be a basic American civil disobedience protest."

"Where would we have this protest?"

"Well, Central Park's too cold right now, so I suppose inside somewhere. A hall or something. Something with enough room so that the press can get in and TV cameras."

"Wait a minute, you want us to do this in front of cameras?"

"Well, we've got to get coverage."

"Yeah, but we'll be laying there fucking, for god's sake!"

"May I make a suggestion?" said one of the professors quietly. "First of all, it's not a bad idea. But I think you'll be defeating yourselves if this comes off as a Roman orgy. You won't receive any support for that; you'll just turn off the blue noses. We're fighting for the sanctity of individual freedom *and* privacy. We don't want to make a circus out of it. Yet you must make a very noticeable and notable demonstration of your views. So, consider this: renting a hall, partitioning off that hall into private areas where couples can copulate out of sight, and inviting the press to attend to witness the fact of what each couple is doing, if not the act. After that, the press can interview the couples. If any couple wishes to allow cameras into their private area, well, that will be up to them, and the JLS will not be held liable for any indecent exposure charges. To conclude: Demonstrate but do it with some style and grace."

"Yeah, that sounds good."

"Yeah!"

"Okay, I like that."

"Well," said Shelly, "that's not what I envisioned, but I can see your point. Do you think it can be as effective as just doing it?"

"More effective, I would think."

Agreement spread throughout the group, and possible dates, times, places, and particulars were discussed. Gerald mentioned that if they could get the magazine or paper out quickly, it could be the first headline, which might cause a stir. Maybe so, but they wanted to think about it. Gerald then volunteered to find someone to donate a bunch of mattresses.

Soon, the talk led to other things, general things, regular things. Shelly put on some music, and a few couples danced.

Gerald sat back and watched, sank into his chair, and looked and wondered how this evening of planning the fight for a cause could end with dancing as if they were teenagers. As if this was after the planning of a prom. He hated dancing. He always had. He hated it because he could not do it. Or, rather, he had always felt stupid doing it, had always felt like an ass when he had tried. He had no grace or rhythm, and he did not have that simple quality of not caring how things looked that allowed others to dance ill-timed, poorly executed steps. He didn't mind looking at the girls. Girls dancing was almost always attractive, for there were layers of movement to watch, a certain erotic quality to appreciate.

On the other hand, despite the few with grace, men always looked stupid to him, doing the steps, swinging their hips, and trying for an attitude in their looks. All he wanted was to avoid the stupid. His opinion on dance was a minority one. He knew that. Most everyone dances. In high school, in college, socially, and later in life, almost everyone jumps in with the crowd. And they usually don't like people who don't, people who stand back, hold back, stay back. They tell them it's easy; they tell them there is nothing to it, you step here, step there, following the beat of the music, come on, it's fun, you'll like it, let go like everybody else. Gerald hated that, the push, and the press. This is where he truly understood the concept of individual freedom of choice.

The music was loud, hitting out beats. The dancers started expressing themselves, making moves that communicated things mostly basic to human existence. Gerald wanted to leave, but how? The simple taking of his leave did not occur to him. To come here had been so important. Just getting up and going seemed somehow not the proper climax. To do it just now seemed a too-soon rush of the evening into history.

Shelly came up to him like a good hostess. "Gerald, do you want to dance? Come on, you don't look like you're having fun."

He was thrilled that Shelly was asking him, but—

Fun? We're in a time of crisis, and you talk about having fun was a possible answer to Shelly. Or—

Shelly, my dear, "Fun" is a very individual concept. Just because I am not bouncing around like some tribal warrior, do not assume I am not having fun. Or—

I certainly wish I could accept the honor of your invitation, but, sadly, I cannot. Doctor's orders, You understand…, he could have mysteriously said. But instead, he said:

"Uh, well, yeah, sure."

Shelly took him by the hand and led him to the center of the room. She immediately started to dance, self-assured and comfortable in her moves. Gerald desperately tried to find the beat, make his legs work, and do something that wasn't crude and awkward with his arms. He failed. He danced without grace or definition. He felt like an ass. But he smiled, assuming that would say that he was having "fun," hoping it would convince him of the same. But it didn't. So he had to think of other things; he had to place himself somewhere else—sitting at a desk—doing something else—writing words of power—being someone else—*The controversial editor of...*—to console himself while he danced, while he was an ass.

20

Wednesday, February 15

FUTURUS

The Journal of Future History
Circulation 325

A NEW GENERATION GAP?

By Leslie Berny, Ph.D.

When a nation takes its destiny in hand, so definitely, as this nation has done by its initiation of Birth Cessation, it is an act of extreme courage, and thus, a rare act indeed. Nations are more prone to wait and see, argue during consideration, or, in various ways, pass the time, hoping that time alone will heal the problem needing attention. Strong and swift acts to effect change, even when the need for change is more than obvious, are not often a national norm. I suppose this is because no one is ever assured that the change—just because it is a change—will solve the problem. It might aggravate. It might hinder. It might have no effect at all. In any case, someone must take responsibility for the result. There is the potential for glory in that. But there is also the potential for shame. The fear of shame, I believe, is a far more powerful motivator toward inaction than the love of glory is toward action. So when action is taken, strong and swift, we have no other recourse but to admire the courage it took. But we must not let our admiration of the courage displayed shroud our duty to examine the action taken. Was it proper? Was it intelligent? Was it indeed the most effective action to take?

According to Darryl Butchko (director of the Birth Cessation Agency and, indeed, the architect of it), Birth Cessation is most certainly an act of intelligence, thus proper and therefore right. He has always stated this view plainly and precisely. Our nation has only so much livable room and a finite amount of resources. There are also too many people demanding shares of that room and those resources, so they are bound to be discontented, eventually, over the size or lack of shares. History teaches that such a situation causes internal conflicts, usually violent ones. There are two solutions: an increase in room and resources, accomplished in the past through war and imperialism, or a decrease in the demand, meaning people. War is an alternative we have avoided for too long—for obvious reasons—to consider now. Imperialism is a dusty old relic of a method we were never good at. Decreasing people, thus demand, seems the only solution.

But how? Some form of intra-national mass murder? Of course not. Not only is it inexcusably inhumane, but it is also simply not practical. Who would you murder? The old? The infirm? Peoples of specific ethnic derivations? More trouble than it is worth. No, Butchko proposed, and we accepted, not death, but the simple lack of births, to allow for a natural pruning of the national tree, as President Henshaw has expressed it, so that which remains can grow strong and healthy. Simple. C follows B, which follows A. No argument, it seems, except by those emotionally committed to one ideal or another. And their opinions can undoubtedly be discounted, given the facts.

But are there other facts Butchko and we need to consider? Butchko's facts are facts of the moment that speak to the problem at hand, which is not necessarily a negative. Butchko's well-tempered consideration of those facts has led to our courageous act. But what about facts that speak to the future and its flow, which will become history once completed and recorded? Is it a flow that can be disturbed, altered, or damaged? Are there specific forces of future-becoming-history flow that could be adversely affected? I believe so. And I think that the disturbance of that flow might impact human history more devastatingly than the problem of too few resources and too much demand. I speak most notably of a disturbance in the flow and ebb of the conflict of generations, which the Spanish philosopher Ortega y Gasset felt was the fundamental ruling concept of history. I speak, then, of a disturbance in the future of history.

Ortega y Gasset saw that conflict between generations was the generator of history—of progress, of movement forward. Not precisely delineated generations, one neatly following the previous, but of overlapping, generations, active at the same time, but from different and differing perspectives. Gasset felt that a generation is approximately 15 years long and that the only pertinent generations at any one given time are those between the ages of 30 and 45 and individuals between the ages of 45 and 60. For, "The boy and the old man hardly intervene in history, the former not yet, the latter no longer." But "From 30 to 45 runs the stage in which a man normally finds all his ideas, the first principles, at least, of that ideology which he is to make his own. After 45 he devotes himself to the full development of the inspirations he has had between 30 and 45." The conflict comes when the 30 to 45 group, which is actively engaged in trying to make the world over—as the young are wont to do—butt up against the 45 to 60 group, which has just completed making over the world and would damn well like to see it remain stable for a while. They, the 45 to 60s, of course, always conveniently forget that while they were making the world over, they used to butt up against their elders, offering not a little amount of instability. And rightly so. Humankind and its drama called history cannot remain stable or static, for that which is always still is dead and heading for rot. Conflict here, far from being harmful, is the rubbing together of ideas new with ideas solidifying which causes friction, which causes warmth, which gives life to humankind's story. It is a must. It is necessary. It is natural. For humankind, as Ortega y Gasset says, "Is drama, destiny, but not thing." Humankind is its drama, and drama feeds on conflict. Take away the conflict, you destroy the drama, you destroy humankind.

That is the potential Birth Cessation has. Those are the more profound facts of the matter. Birth Cessation will force a gap between the overlapping generations, diminishing the conflict, friction, and warmth, thus the proper flow of future-becoming history.

Consider: When the last group of children born before Birth Cessation reach the age of 45, the age they start to dominate society, the time they must turn around to defend themselves, there will be no one of the age of 30, the age of challenge. There will be 20-year-olds who will challenge, but not with the maturity needed, so they will not be effective. The 45s will have ten years before the 20s mature to the point of real challenge. A moment they will just be entering, as opposed to the 45s (now 55s) position, that of comfortable dominance. The 55s will have had ten years to have amassed influence and strength. They will be the practiced dominators of ideas, mores, and the ways of life, facing unseasoned challengers still determining their new ideas, thoughts, and perspectives. This will lead to a rigid conservatism, a solidification of society, and a slowing down of the conflict flow that might prove irrevocable harm in the final analysis.

For even with a brief ten or so extra years of dominance, what might the 45s accomplish? Perhaps a new constitutional convention and the rewriting of that thin but remarkably strong piece of paper that has so effectively protected us. Would such a rewriting lead to a dictatorship? Not so hard to imagine. I believe that most American citizens today would favor a dictatorship—as long as they agreed with the dictator. Of course, no dictator can be all things to all people; on the contrary, they usually strive to force the people to be all things to them. But they are good at agreeing with the masses long enough to establish power. Dictatorships often inspire violent revolution. But not immediately. A new dictatorship in this country could be long-running, unchallenged, or not well-challenged for years. As happens under such rule, free thought would be hampered, thus innovation, invention, and the forward thrust of human growth to a more humane level. Since the American democratic experiment has meant so much in that thrust, for a dictatorship to happen here, it would be tragic on a much larger scale than just a national scale.

Butchko has pointed out that without Birth Cessation, our immediate future would be challenging. I want to submit that all futures are challenging. Can we afford to compound that difficulty by removing the stimulation of the conflict of generations that might provide the innovation that could successfully deal with the challenge? Is it a moot question? Birth Cessation is a reality, after all. But realities, I remind you, can be changed. Indeed, that may be the definition of man himself: The changer of realities.

***

THE REST

The Magazine of Tomorrow
Circulation: 2.3 million

COMMENTARY

By Cynthia Jones-Mark

America has, once again, as has been its too terrible habit of late, bungled an excellent opportunity. Faced with a shortage of resources and a glut of people, it has decided to scrap the people. Not reorder priorities, which America has planned to do for years, search for complementary resources, or even grab a decades-old opportunity to exploit space to solve earthly problems. No, America, the land of the free and the home of the Butchko has decided to just TC—that's, "Trash can" to the uninitiated—25 years' worth of humanity. Sorry folks, full up, no more room at the inn; try calling for a reservation next time.

Talk about wiping the slate clean!

Talk about sweeping the dust under the rug!

But what the hell! Something had to be done, right? Birth Cessation is better than a poke in the pocketbook with a sharp stick, right? Especially since our collective pocketbook can hardly take any more poking.

Sure, everybody likes Birth Cessation. You don't see too many people protesting it, do you? Oh, the odd moralist here, the even odder female industrialist-wanderlust there. A few college kids now and then (but then, college kids always protest. It's taught in freshman orientation). But essentially, no one else. So, the people have spoken. The people want more resources. The people want fewer people. But that's what's wrong with the people; they always want more or less, never better or the best.

It is not Birth Cessation we should be—desperately—utilizing to solve our current and many problems. It is Birth Regulation that we should be—intelligently—applying to not only cut or trim the population but better it, make it stronger, wiser, and of greater all-around quality.

Birth Regulation? Yes, damn it! Let's get smart, shall we? If we, as a nation, can have the audacity to order the cessation of births for 25 years—a unique step in the history of man—for the general good, why can't we have the smarts to amend that radical idea and allow for—well, there's no other term for it—some selective breeding to assure talented, quality people to grow up and offer solid advantages to the general good? We shouldn't just throw out 25 years of humanity without first looking at and salvaging what may come in handy someday. Yeah, I know, I'm an incurable pack rat. But you never know when you could use a genius, a great artist, a sublime musician, a brilliant mind, or even a damn fine athlete. Twenty-five years without new people does not dismay me. But 25 years without any new geniuses, artists, thinkers of merit, etc., does.

Well, Jones-Mark, you're a bit of an elitist, aren't you?

Yes, there is no doubt about it. I certainly am. But then, I'm a historian, and what is history, real history, actual moving and shaking history, but the record of the elite in thought, art, and politics? (Discounting those French Mundanists, of course.) Is it hard to understand that I find that hard to give up?

But we do not have birth regulation. We have Birth Cessation. That seems pretty set—at least for twenty-five years. But what about year twenty-six? May I suggest that in year twenty-six, we institute a Birth Regulation? That we select before we breed? Why not? We selectively breed cattle to get juicy steaks. Why don't we try to gain some control over our population to get quality people? I'm not limiting the idea of quality people to geniuses, artists, etc. Starting in year twenty-six, I would also be happy to see some just plain well-adjusted people. How about allowing no child to be born to parents who either:

1. Do not want the child.

2. Can't afford the child.

3. Are children themselves, no matter what their age.

4. Have little in the way of a nourishing environment or heredity to offer the child.

Is that an outlandish proposal? What if starting with year twenty-six, the only people allowed to have children are ones we are reasonably sure will give the child good, intelligent, authentic, and warm love; a good, clean environment; respect for others in society; a sense of right and wrong? What would be the effect of that on the country if only good people—diverse in many ways, but all essentially good—were allowed to give birth? Could it have any effect but a good one?

It is an exciting prospect. First, decrease our population to a manageable level. Then, nurture it to strength.

A good gardener does not just prune; he cultivates.

21

Wednesday, February 22 — Near Oodnadotta, South Australia

Vivian Pavin Handlin read Cynthia Jones-Mark's commentary and was furious. At first, the words were fine; the whole first paragraph was right on the mark, but then the force of her words, casual yet powerful, became mocking, revealing a smirk. Vivian felt used, her thoughts had been caricatured, made broad for satire. Then the comment hit her, "... odder female industrialist-wanderlust..." The bitch! What the hell is she getting at? Then Jones-Mark got at it, and Vivian knew the truth, another damn dumb totalitarian fascist master race proposal. It wasn't bad enough that the government invaded free women's bodies; this woman wanted them to set up shop and run production their way. *For the greater good*, of course.

Vivian steamed at the inhumanity of the woman. Dean Harry was preparing for the taping and had to listen. "Strange thing, Vivian," he finally said. "You are one of the most competent—no, there should be no euphemisms between us—you are one of the toughest, maybe most ruthless businesspersons today. In all dealings, you are cold, unemotional, strong, factual, unbending, demanding, and not very compassionate, I assume, towards the loser in any competition you've entered. But mention a tough, fact-based, unemotional *social* deal making a pact with reality for a higher social profit, and you become a blubbering bleeding heart, decrying about somebody's *in*humanity as if there was something innately good about humanity. Vivian my dear, *think*, will you? All acts ever committed in the history of man that you would label as inhumane were they truly aberrations? Or were they not more the norm? War, persecution, religious intolerance, genocide, slavery, murder, mass or otherwise? Hardly a year has gone by without an abundance of each. All performed by humans. Yet we persist in calling these acts 'inhumane.' And, despite their regularity, each new occurrence will shock us. But the odd thing is, Vivian, so will any effort to change the causes of these acts outside of prayer and 'morality.' Offer a simple plan to manage society competently—as you competently manage your business—to attempt to do away with such atrocities, and the cries of 'inhumane' are just as strong as if you were stoking the ovens and laying in the gas. Well, you're right. It is inhumane. But rather, we should be this inhuman than the human we've been all these years."

Vivian moved in her chair, looking for comfort. "Very nice, Dean, very dramatic with a nice flare. Like you. Like your house. I know what is human. And I know what is inhuman. The fact that one outweighs the other means nothing except that we must strive to alter the balance. I have nothing against managing. It's the managers that bother me. There are no benevolent dictators, Dean. Nor philosopher-kings. Only wielders of power. Give all power to one man or a few; they will invariably misuse it. Spread that power out by recognizing the rights of people; then no one will have enough concentration of power to do any harm."

"I've never known the 'people' to do much good."

"They haven't had much of a chance, have they? They've been too busy trying to prevent the harm."

"Ah, Viv, multi-millionaire, topflight brilliant woman of business. And yet, you are so naive."

Vivian laughed. "Isn't that funny? I was preparing to say, 'Ah, Dean, scientific genius, innovative inventor. And yet, you are so naive.'"

"An impasse then, I would say."

"Agreed."

"Well, then, let's make a TV show."

Vivian had read other things besides the Jones-Mark commentary. She had read everything written on Birth Cessation in preparation for her first broadcast. The pro, the con, the smart, the smart-assed, the considered, the prejudiced, even the simple-minded. Dean Harry's inflow of information was marvelous. He had "friends" all over the world who fed newspapers and magazines in total—articles, ads, columns, and come-ons—and all television and radio broadcasts into computers linked with his own, which *read*, *watched*, and *listened*, gathering all the information, cataloging, cross-filing and storing it all, ready to retrieve any of it, any significant to minor, major to insignificant bit of it at a moment's notice. It was like having the most wonderful, huge head to scratch. For four weeks, Vivian had entered the communications room each morning and punched keys on a keyboard, instructing the computer to tell her what the world was thinking about Birth Cessation that day. She then spent the rest of her day reading, note-taking, and writing. She rarely went into the Victorian section of the house anymore except to sleep and eat; she now found the white and silver room more comfortable.

Most of the information was of no value. Reiterations mainly. Some were of personal interest: accounts of the investigation into Vivian Pavin Handlin's fugitive flight and her husband's arrest on a charge of obstructing justice. Some were fascinating, such as other nations' and peoples' views of Birth Cessation. "A bold experiment," said the Prime Minister of Great Britain. "About time," said the People's Daily in Beijing. And "No comment," said the Pope in Rome, which seemed odd but understandable. For this Pope was the first from South America, and he had long, first-hand experience with overpopulation and its attendant problems. Since donning the Shoes of the Fisherman, he had quieted the Vatican's usual and constant declarations against birth control and the total sin of abortion. He would continue to disapprove—dogma is difficult to drop—he just made a holy office assumption that God had more important matters to attend to. That's a blow, thought Vivian, who had once welcomed this change after fighting the right-to-lifers and Catholics but now could use their support.

Some of the information was odd. A report of a food panic riot at a supermarket that ended in several deaths. Birth Cessation was mentioned in the rationalized context that such indications of food shortages were further evidence for the need for "pruning." But Vivian did not doubt that the panic was started by false conditions controlled by somebody's sure hand and that such panics would be used to keep the populace in fear of themselves.

Some of the information was of simple interest. There was the complete text of a new publication called *Birthright.* It was the official publication of the Jan Lawrence Society, which Vivian remembered as the sponsoring organization of her Fordham University speech. However, it slipped her mind again — who was Jan Lawrence? She was amused to read in this Vol. 1 No. 1 that the JLS had held a "very successful Conception Reception to raise funds for the society" and that they were planning a series of protests against Birth Cessation, the usual ones, of course, but also the unusual one of, "public copulation and conception to drive home the point of Vivian Pavin's message that women should, *en mass*, 'Get pregnant!'" *Good for them*, thought Vivian. *I'll give them a boost.*

Some of the information was infuriating. Especially about Butchko. Profiles, interviews, commentary. He had his critics, but few. It seemed he was rapidly becoming famous as the "Architect of Birth Cessation" and so a sort of savior. There had, at first, been shock over his involvement in the writing of the law, his possible psychological reasons, and his Machiavellian maneuvers. But the shock subsided, and he became admired for it. He became a star of the nightly news. The president had won points for bringing him into the government and, more importantly, for putting him in charge. Vivian found it all perverted and strange. People were admiring Butchko for robbing them of freedom. How stupid! But, of course, they didn't see it that way, bless their simple little minds. The people had for so long been without "Leaders," "Men of Action," and "Strong-Armed Helmsmen of the Ship of State" that anybody with any melodramatic plan to alleviate the dual problems of overpopulation and dwindling resources was bound to be admired and, unfortunately, followed. Hitler simply called his people "The Master Race," and they loved him for it.

"Do you want to rehearse before we tape?" Dean Harry said when he was ready with the camera.

"No, let's go." Vivian moved to the warm wood and brick library set and sat at a desk.

"Okay, when you see the light."

The small red light on the camera came on.

"Hello. I'm Vivian Pavin Handlin, and I am a fugitive from 'justice.' My crime? Life is growing within me. My husband, Edgar Handlin, is sitting in a jail cell in Los Angeles. His crime? Conspiring with me in the conception of that life. In the not-so-distant past, it would have been said of us that, 'They are having a baby.' And our friends and family would have celebrated. Instead, now our friends and family are forced to say, 'They are committing a crime.' And that gives them nothing to celebrate. My husband and I have shared the most precious and personal act a man and woman can share. That of the conception of another human being. It is an act that has been honored for many millennia of humankind's existence. It is an act now condemned by the current government of the United States of America. Through a process of abortions and sterilizations, this, let me point out, *ephemeral* government is trying to halt a process of millions of years of biological tradition. Why? We can only imagine that there is a special thrill in the wielding of such radical power and that we have in place in our government individuals addicted to that thrill. Certain men have always strived for the power to affect and alter history. They usually claim a special providence allowing them to do this. Caesar, Alexander, Napoleon, Hitler, Stalin, Mao Tse-Tung. But their strivings have always affected not just history but people. Ordinary, everyday individuals like you and me.

"And the effect on the people has usually been a suffering one. Pain, loss, and even death have been the lot of the people while those addicted to the thrill of power strived to fulfill their 'destinies.' But what is happening now knows no precedent. For what greater suffering can there be than being denied the right to birth?

"As you may know, when Birth Cessation became the law, I protested publicly. I became pregnant and announced it openly. I did this knowing full well that it would lead to my arrest for the 'crime' of conception and to my eventual prosecution for that crime in a trial by jury. My lawyers and I planned to use that trial as a forum to consider Birth Cessation's ramifications rationally and objectively. Ramifications that we felt could only lead to eroding the personal freedoms of every man, woman, and child in America. What we did not expect, though, was the hideous speed with which the government would rush me through the legal process to rip the child from my body.

"It was an action on the government's part that did, I confess, confuse me and lead me to consider the radical options of fight or flight. To remain in America to fight meant having my child aborted, the concrete symbol of my protest. To leave America to save my child meant leaving the fight, exiting from the battlefield before the battle had begun. Going meant that my child would live, but my protest would die. Staying meant just the opposite.

"In either case, the government would win. In the end, I chose flight. I did not come to this decision through rational means but rather allowed the growing mothering instinct within me to dictate my actions. What became of utmost importance to me was the survival of my child. Above all else, I knew that my child must survive. As selfish as that may seem, I'm convinced it was the right decision, for it was a thoroughly *natural* one."

Vivian got up from the desk as Dean went for a wide shot, getting a full view of the library set. Vivian then crossed to the front of the desk and sat on its edge.

"Nevertheless," she continued. "Once I settled into my current location, I was saddened that the protest I started would now end. I would have my child and fulfill my biologically directed role as a mother, but America would be burdened with an unjust, freedom-robbing law. That was my first reaction. One that I have since reconsidered. I realized that in this world today, physical attendance is not required to make your presence known. Through electronic communication, I can talk with you, state my case, air my views, and ask you, the American people, to make a choice. Freedom or slavery?

"The Birth Cessation law allows the government to reach not only deep into our lives but, literally, deep into our bodies, the temples of our souls. From now on, each time an instrument enters a woman's body to destroy her child, that is an instrument of the government. Each time those minor cuts are made on a man's testicles, the government wields the blade. If we allow the government to reach so publicly into our private bodies, how soon will it be before they ask permission to control our minds? And will we give them our permission? After being conditioned to give our bodies, we may be too weak to deny them our minds.

"That frightens me. For people must be free to think."

Vivian stood up, returned to behind the desk, and stood behind the chair, placing her hands on its back. Dean zoomed in for a close-up of her face.

"That is why I protest. That is why I ask you to join me."

Dean pulled back now to a medium close-up.

"A while back, during a speech I gave at Fordham University, I suggested that other women get pregnant, as I had, as a show of protest. I still suggest it. But if the government's actions towards me are any indication, you must be prepared to have your pregnancies aborted. But, if there is enough of you, if there is a mass of you, maybe the strength of numbers will prevent their butchering or, at least, significantly slow it down. In either case, it will be a protest; no one can deny the seriousness of it. It will bring to the American public's attention the fact that some of us will not and that all of us should not, tolerate this barbaric infringement upon our basic, God-given right: the right to reproduce. It will be a call to action that I do not doubt will be answered in great numbers. I understand that some plan to do as I have suggested. Follow their lead."

Another zoom to close-up.

"Finally, to my husband, Edgar, if they allow you to view this broadcast, please remember that I love you very much. We *will* have a fine, healthy, and beautiful baby.

"Providing that the government, providing that Darryl Butchko does not censor me, I will be talking to you again in the very near future.

"Thank you."

22

Wednesday, March 1 — Cleveland, Ohio

Entry in the Diary of Frederick Lewis Howard:

I GOT MAD WHEN I HEARD THAT VIVIAN PAVIN GOT TO GET TO BE ON TV. WHY? I NOT HER I DROPPED THE BLOOD I DROPPED THE BABY PIG. I WAS THE FIRST TO PROTEST. BUT SHE GETS TO BE ON TV. PEOPLE BURN PEOPLE FUCK THEY GET ON TV WHY? I DID IT FIRST. YOU TOLD ME SAMMY. YOU KNEW BECAUSE YOU READ THE BOOKS. THEY ARE OUT TO GET US YOU SAID THAT AND I UNDERSTOOD SEE EVEN IF YOU DIDN'T THINK I DID. SO I DID IT. I DID IT WITH YOUR KNIFE. AND THINK THAT WAS GOOD. DO YOU THINK SO TOO? SHE'S PRETTY THOUGH SAMMY LIKE ON HER BOXES OF WHICH I HAVE SOME. I WAS HAPPY WHEN SHE SPOKE BEFORE SHE LEFT I THOUGHT MAYBE SHE HAD HEARD ME. BUT THEN SHE LEFT. SHE WAS SUDDENLY GONE AND NOBODY KNEW WHERE SHE WAS. DID YOU KNOW SAMMY? BECAUSE YOU ARE UP THERE AND I THOUGHT MAYBE YOU COULD SEE. YOU SHOULD CONTACT ME SAMMY AND TELL ME. SHE GOT ON TV AND SAID IT WAS WRONG. YOU KNOW LIKE YOU USED TO SAY. BUT SHE DIDN'T MENTION ME OR THANK ME EVEN THOUGH I CALLED HIM BUTCHER FIRST. I'M MAD AND I DON'T WANT TO BE. SAMMY SHOULD I DO MORE SAMMY SHOULD I TRY SOMETHING ELSE. LET ME KNOW SAMMY OK LET ME KNOW.

***

New York City

He was amazed to suddenly know that time, indeed, was relative.

For the five years Gerald Downing had sold appliances, each day had been structured like the last. Each began at the same time, with specific set wake-up duties, leading to breakfast and dressing, a little talk on TV, and a drive to work, usually stopping at the same stop lights and pulling up to park in the same general area in the lot. Punch in. Count money. Turn the TVs on. Wait for customers, pitch them, write up the occasional sale, check your watch for break time, same time each day, as was lunchtime, as was the time to close, all waited for, anticipated, expected. Turn the TVs off, count money, put the day's total into the safe, punch out, and go home. Each day had its particular events, some disparate but most familiar, all taking place within a 9-hour period that seemed stone. Weeks also had this quality and months, and, sadly, he had begun to realize, years. True, seasons broke things up—hot, cold, wet, dry—but always annually, always in the same pattern.

Then he quit. Or was fired. Or quit. And time changed immediately. It happened soon after coming in one morning. Then he was suddenly driving home accompanied by an oddly placed sun and a different quality of sound from the traffic, if not a different sound itself. He got home and explained things to his mother and, still a little stunned, sat down to watch soap operas with her. Soon, they were over, and the day was over, not sooner than he expected, nor later, but over here instead of over there. Or something like that.

"Well, just what happened?" his mother asked.

"Well, I guess I left a whole stack of bills out overnight lying on the counter instead of, you know, putting them in the safe. I guess I was so anxious to get home last night because of, uh, the reception, and I guess I must have forgotten. Well, anyway, Mr. Gilbert, he's that new assistant manager I told you about, he's a real bastard—"

"Gerald!"

"He found the damn money this morning and called me in and read me the riot act, you know, I mean, he treated me like some damn high school kid, you know, summer help or something. I mean, hell, I've been there five years. I never made one mistake, and he treated me like I did this all the time. Well, I went back to the department and fumed for a while, but then I just, you know, got mad and decided, hell, if that's the way they want to treat me, well, fuck it!"

"Gerald!

"Sorry, so anyway, I just went up to Gilbert and told him that and punched out and left."

"So you quit?"

"I guess so, yeah?"

"Well, I guess you'll have to look for a new job."

"Yeah, I guess."

That night, he called Shelly. He found an excuse. He decided to tell her that now that he was out of a job, maybe he would have more spare time to start the JLS magazine, or whatever, if you want to start it, even though he would have to look for another job at the same time, of course, because he knows, of course, that there's no salary, or anything, that can be paid for this.

"Why don't you go on unemployment?"

"What?"

"You get on it for six months. It might give you enough money to get by. And then you could work on the paper full time."

"But I quit."

"So what? Tell them you were forced to. Sounds like it to me."

"Yeah, but don't you have to keep looking for another job?"

"You fake it. There are so many unemployed people right now; they don't have the time to check up on you."

"Well, the store might fight it."

"Look, just give it a try. I talked to one of my teachers today. You met him last night, and he said he's already drafted some commentary for the paper, so I guess he's just assuming that it will be done, so let's do it. It is a good way to get some exposure for our mass conception. I've got a laptop and printer we can use. So, if you want to be the editor, you can since you might have time to work on it. I really think you should get over to unemployment on Monday."

Which he did, feeling like a cheater, a fraud, suspecting all the time that they could see right through his flimsy ruse. But all went well. He even received the highest benefits allowed on unemployment. He met Shelly that night, suggesting and winning her approval for the name *Birthright*, and started working on the publication the next day out of a small space rented by the JLS.

And time became stranger still.

He woke up differently. Different time, but also, differently, more leisurely. He did not drive to work, fighting traffic, but took the subway to Manhattan. He found the place, met Shelly between classes for an "editorial" meeting, was introduced to people, got a copy of the professor's commentary, made a list of potential articles and topics for the editorials he would write, got hungry later than usual, ate lunch, almost dinner, at some small coffee shop where he read the professor's copy, making editorial notes. However, he had already read them and noted before, but he wanted to look busy and occupied, as an editor should look in the busy town of Manhattan. He returned to the JLS office, worked late, long after dark, and then took the subway home. It was a long day but fast, instead of a short day but slow.

He sat in the subway, amazed at the relativity of time.

***

Gerald remained amazed two weeks later when the first edition of *Birthright* came out. Cheaply printed and handed out free, it had commentary by professors, a declaration of intention, an editorial by himself praising the work of Malcolm Kirkly, and a call for mass conception on March 1. It had only been two weeks, but the stone routine of life and work in the store seemed years ago, more like a memory of a life read instead of lived.

He entered the third week much like the other two but was looking forward to the fifth week—the week of March 1.

"The bachelor president and his barren assistant," Gerald called Henshaw and Butchko in his editorial in Vol. 1 No. 2 of *Birthright.* He was proud of that. He liked it. He read it to Shelly soon after he wrote it and asked a new volunteer assistant (spurred to action by the first issue of *Birthright*) what she thought of it. He wondered what Kirkly thought of it—as a turn of phrase, a use of words, and a philosophical stand. Kirkly was receiving *Birthright.* Gerald mailed them himself, adding a cover letter to the first issue—*your kindness in considering my work and your encouragement that I should continue with it has had no small part in my current situation. I am only disappointed that my writing skill—if I have any—is not yet up to appropriately expressing my profound thanks to you*—but he had not yet heard back from him.

The fourth week was very comfortable. He rose, breakfasted with his mother, and talked and told her about his doings. She listened and liked that he was happy but did not like the particulars. She had no strong opinion on Birth Cessation, nor public conception, except that it seemed silly, but was worried over what his child, Laura, would think, someday later when she was older, or even now, when questioned by schoolmates, if he became known for what he was doing.

"Think of the child, Jerry. Is it fair to her? Why ask for trouble?

"Christ, Mom! Trouble is everywhere; you don't have to ask for it."

"But why put her through that kind of trouble?"

"Look, I hope she'll be proud of what I'm doing."

"But still, to put her through that trouble. You know, she might get kidded in school."

"And she might come out stronger for it."

"Well, maybe. I always think kidding is cruel. Why put her through it if you can avoid it?"

"Mom, don't worry about it."

"I'm not worried about it. I'm just making a statement, that's all. Can't I even make a statement in my own house? Whenever I express an opinion, you say I'm worried. It's just a statement, that's all. I just think you ought to consider the child."

"Okay, Mom, I'm considering her. But this is something that has to be done. You know what I mean. And, like I said, I think it will be okay in the long run. I think Laura is strong enough to take any trouble. She's a tough kid."

"Well, I hope so."

He would always leave after the rush hour to sit in the subway and read. It was a pleasant walk from the station to the office, which was not fancy; it had a thrown-together look. But his desk was a nice sight, despite the nicks and stains and one corner knocked off, rounded out, and painted over. He sat alone most of the day, with the occasional volunteer in after classes. Still, he talked on the phone a lot, arranging articles, talking "the philosophy," and taking care of things for the upcoming mass conceptions, like the time and place for the last planning meeting of the mass conception committee, where Shelly had asked:

"How many couples have we got?

"Four.

"Is that all?"

"Well, we've got a lot of guys volunteering. But a lot fewer girls."

"No shit!"

"Look, we've got to convince some more girls."

"Well, did you hear about Vivian Pavin?"

"No, what?"

"I heard it just before I came over. She's going to be on TV."

"What? When?"

"The night before our thing."

"Really?"

"Yeah, I guess. That's what the news said. TV stations all got this letter that said that a satellite transmission of Vivian Pavin talking about all this would be coming, and, uh, they can pick it up and air it if they want. No one knows where it's coming from."

"Wow! I wonder what she'll say?"

"I don't know, but I'll bet she hasn't given up the fight. She may say some very inspiring things that might get the people to come out for mass conception, you know, in general and our thing in particular."

"I think our problem is that girls don't want to fuck in public."

"Some girls don't want to fuck, period."

"Hey! Let's watch the tone of this conversation."

"I mean, you know, they only want to make love to someone they really love and all that."

"Well, tell them to fall in love quick."

"Look, this is something bigger than love. They've got to understand that," Shelly said. "In the few days we've got left, let's concentrate on the girls, really get in there and recruit them. We can pair them up with the guys on the day of the protest. They don't have to make love here; just get pregnant. Or, at least, make the attempt. That, at least, would be a symbol. Gerald, can you concentrate on that in the next *Birthright?*"

"Sure. We can make the whole issue on it." Gerald answered quickly and with command. He liked that. It felt good. Plus, he agreed with Shelly. The cause was too important to let some shy, demure women screw it up. He would write something full of gentle logic. He would persuade them.

"Plus, we've really got to spread the word about Vivian Pavin. That may be the key. Gerald, some box announcement on that?"

"Sure."

"Good. And we should all be out there just telling everybody."

After the meeting, Gerald asked Shelly if she would participate in the mass conception.

"Well, I was going to run everything out front. Take care of the press and police and all that. But I guess I really should, huh?"

"Yeah, it might look—" He swallowed. "—a little bad if you push this on a bunch of people and then don't do it yourself."

"Yeah, I've thought about that a little bit. Well, I suppose I could leave Mary in charge and get back for a quick one sometime during the day. Or do you think maybe I should start it off? You know, be one of the examples."

"Yeah, maybe. That sounds right."

"Yeah, guess I should."

"Have you got a, you know, a partner? I mean, if you weren't planning to do it, I figure you didn't line anybody—uh—up."

"No. You're right. But they said we've got plenty of guys who volunteered, so I don't figure I'll have any problem."

"Yeah, well, you're right, but, uh—" Shelly was putting her coat on, checking her purse, getting ready to leave. "—I thought I would volunteer for that."

"For what?"

"For—uh—you know, being your partner on this."

"Oh." Shelly paused and looked Gerald over, maybe for the first time. "Well, okay," she finally said. "Fine. That will save some hassle. You'll be there early anyway, right?"

"Yeah."

"Good. Okay. Well, see you later."

Then she left.

Gerald was very excited about the meeting. Things were being accomplished.

***

Gerald got the third issue of *Birthright* out. It was an easy one, with the front page taken up with a large box reminding people of Vivian Pavin's upcoming TV appearance. Page two was boxed as well, a boxed editorial by Gerald— "An Appeal to the Ladies." Gerald sent this issue to Kirkly as he had the others, enclosing a short cover note saying, "Any comments?" He had been reading Kirkly's column first thing each week, assuming that he would mention *Birthright* and the work of the JLS. But he hadn't yet. A few of his columns touched on Birth Cessation, but most covered other subjects that Gerald found interesting but frivolous; they weren't pressing or essential to the future of mankind the way Birth Cessation was. Maybe Kirkly was waiting until after March 1, the day of mass conception, the real test of the JLS and, thus, of *Birthright*. In which case, Gerald could see the logic but would have loved a preview nonetheless and even dared to assume some right to one, if not the strength to fend off much annoyance and some anger when his assumption was not shared. He felt his short note to Kirkly was pithy and would wound him slightly.

The night of Vivian's broadcast, Shelly invited several people over to watch it with her and the Kurtz's. Gerald showed up early and tried to help where no help was needed until he readjusted the TV set for better color, making a joke that no one laughed at about his recent profession. It was a large screen television covered by a fake bookcase when not in use, and Vivian loomed over them when she came on. They applauded.

"Shhh!"

Vivian began to speak, and Shelly was happy to hear her words. They confirmed much that she had felt about Vivian and bolstered the defense she had had to make for her. When Vivian mentioned Fordham University and her speech there, Shelly leaped in spirit, breathed in, and touched someone close to her. She leaped again when Vivian mentioned their plans for the next day, and when she said, "Follow their lead," the whole room broke into applause and a mixture of individual vocalizations, all of which quelled in time for them to catch the end of Vivian's message to her husband, which they all found moving.

"Ah. That's the essence of it all, isn't it?" said one of the young first-year instructors who had recently joined the JLS.

Vivian's broadcast was followed by commentators commentating, assessing, and even joking among themselves as they displayed their professional comradeship over the air. The history of the broadcast was recapped, Vivian's location was reported as still not known, and a report on the Justice Department's attempt to stop the broadcast was given, followed by an editorial defending the First Amendment in defense of the network's decision to broadcast Vivian's statement even though she, "is a fugitive from the law."

They had some little things to eat and talked about the broadcast. Enthusiasm was high, and they were happy to hear that more people—more women—had committed themselves to tomorrow's event.

"Mrs. Godfrey wants to do it."

"Good god!"

"No, seriously. Even though she's long past her childbearing years, she wanted to be, at least, symbolically, counted 'among the troops.' I think she sees herself as some sort of earth mother."

"Well, she is, I'll tell you, a damn fine person."

"But, you know, she's so old?"

"What's that got to do with it?"

"Well..."

"But who's going to do it, you know, to her?"

"She says Professor Kingsman has volunteered."

Laughter broke out.

"Well, you better have a coronary unit around."

More laughter.

"Hey!" Shelly loudly stopped the talk. Gerald was grateful. "If they want to do it, that's just wonderful. We need the support of people of all ages. I don't appreciate your jokes. And I'm sure that Kingsman and Godfrey wouldn't either. They're human too, even if they are old."

"Okay, okay, Shelly. Don't get upset. It's just a funny sort of image, that's all."

"Are you taking this thing seriously or not?"

"Sure, of course."

They got on to other matters, and the evening ended with good-byes and see-you-tomorrows.

Gerald hung around till the last. "Well, do you think it will be a success?" he asked Shelly.

"Oh yeah, sure. We've worked hard for it. You've worked especially hard."

"Well, I hope."

She was pensive, giving something some consideration as she moved about the living room straightening things. "Look," she finally said. "Do you think that I'm really needed if we've got plenty of women showing up now? I hate to give up that front post for even a minute. I've got to handle the press and the police when they come to arrest us. I'd hate to be, well, occupied when they come."

"Well," Gerald slightly panicked, "that's a good reason to do it early. The police will probably wait a while."

"You think so?"

"Sure."

"Well..."

"Look, like it or not, you've taken on the role of leader of the movement. You must lead by example sometimes. Like Vivian Pavin."

"Yeah, I guess, but...

"And me, what about me? I sit in that office and write about defying the law in pretty words, and then I don't do it myself?"

"Well, you can still do it."

"Yeah, of course, but you and I, you know, we were going to do it together."

"Well, there's others now.

"Yeah, but—look, Shelly, I wanted to do it with you. I mean, especially."

"Oh, that's sweet." She seemed genuinely moved. "Well, okay, I guess I should. But first thing, huh? I want to be upfront when the police come."

"Okay, I'll be there early."

"Okay then, see you tomorrow."

He wanted to kiss her good night, which seemed fitting, seeing how he would make love to her in the morning. But she offered him no encouragement, and he had little courage of his own. "Good night," he responded to her, then left, walking directly to the luxury elevator, descending, exiting, riding, and, finally, home.

***

They had rented a hall and a lot of partitions, and many small "rooms" were created with curtains to pull for privacy. Banners and posters had been made.

JAN LAWRENCE SOCIETY
MASS CONCEPTION

CONCEIVE FOR HUMANITY

TO CONCEIVE IS OUR MOST
NATURAL RIGHT

GET GOVERNMENT OFF THE

FRONTS OF THE PEOPLE

BAN BUTCHER BUTCHKO

ABORT BUTCHKO
NOT BABIES

REPEAL BIRTH CESSATION

STOP CRIMES AGAINST OUR BODIES

OUR BODIES ARE PRIVATE PROPERTY

Gerald showed up early, but already onlookers were standing around outside. That pleased him. The message had gotten out. The door was still locked to the curious, but Gerald was allowed admittance, which tingled his reflexes, causing his posture to improve quickly. "Where's Shelly?" he asked someone as if it was a question one *had* to answer.

"Uh, oh, over that way, I guess," said the someone.

Gerald found her checking things out, looking at the placement of the banners, going over the list of who exactly would be doing it to whom and when and in what little curtained room. "Hi!" Gerald said, smiling, hoping his new slacks, shirt, and sweater followed suit.

"Hi," Shelly said, preoccupied.

From the other side of the room, Gerald heard certain unmistakable sounds: the moans of a woman in the pain of pleasure, the occasional grunt of a man trying to find his joy, and—most obviously—the wet slap-slap sound of human male-female copulation. "Uh, someone's started?"

"Yeah. Tom and Susan. They wanted to check out the camp beds we got. Make sure they were strong enough."

"Oh."

"Listen, we're ready to open. Do you want to get started and get it over with? I've got a lot of work to do.

"Yeah, I guess. Sure, whatever you think."

"Mary!" Shelly yelled out, calling forward Mary, who had become her lieutenant. "Here, take this. Gerald and I are going to get started. Once we're in it, get the others to their camp beds, then open up. And keep an eye out for the press and police. I'll be upfront as soon as I can." Then she hurried to a curtained cubicle, Gerald following close behind.

He entered and closed the curtain. The camp bed had a clean white sheet and a pillow with a clean white case. A little stand next to it held a change of sheets and little packets of pre-moist disposable towelettes, the kind you get with fast food fried chicken. Shelly had thought of everything.

She started to get out of her jeans, which stopped Gerald for a second. The sight of her slipping out of her pants was terrific; the exposure of leg and the slick undies did much to define by shape and line, *woman* as opposed to *man*.

"Well, come on," she said.

"Oh, yeah." He moved into action.

She turned around and started unbuttoning her shirt. Gerald slipped off his coat, then his new sweater—

"There's not much heat in this hall, but we'll just have to put up with it," Shelly said.

—His new shirt, his new pants, his—

Shelly had taken off her bra, still had her back to him, still had on the slick undies. "You ready yet?"

—new store-white briefs; no dullness, stains, or lack of elasticity. He stood up straight. "Okay."

Shelly slipped her thumbs into her undies and pulled them down quickly, relieving herself of them. The move had grace, and the view of buttocks revealed; the sight of a side of breast appearing stirred Gerald's blood—or some such chemical—and he wanted to breathe hard but subdued it.

Shelly turned around, lay on the bed, spread her legs, and said, "Okay, let's go."

Gerald took surreptitious glances at her body to see if she was viewing his as he brought himself down and prepared to enter. Shelly wasn't looking anywhere but up to the high, featureless ceiling. Her breasts were pointing that way as well.

"Ouch! Jesus!"

The attempt at entry was dry skin against dry skin.

"Ow! Christ! Here, wait a second; let me get lubricated up."

Gerald moved awkwardly out of the way but still directly above her.

"No! Move! I mean, get off!"

"Sorry." Gerald swung to the side, getting off, but landed his knee on her thigh.

"Ow!"

"Oh! Sorry."

"That's okay. But move over more."

"Okay." Gerald moved to sit on the edge of the small bed.

Shelly reached down to her pubic area to masturbate. "God, it's all dry!" She moved her fingers around and, gingerly, in. She sighed slightly like she was waiting for a bus. "Damn! Nothing's happening."

"Here, let me try something."

"No! Wait a minute."

But Gerald was on his way down.

"What are you doing?" Shelly's voice raised slight panic.

"I want to get it wet," came Gerald's muffled reply as he started to lick her pubic area, concentrating on not just providing moisture but aiding Shelly's natural biology to pitch in.

Shelly leaned up on her elbows. "Oh, okay. But hurry—Ooooh."

Gerald had made a subtle point.

"Ahhh, yeah, I think that might do it, Gerald, ahh, ahh!" Shelly leaned back and allowed her body to trust the bed, to fall into its support. "Ahhh! Yeah! Ooooh! That's right! Jesus, that's… Ooooh! I, uh, I uh, like that! Ah! Ah! Ah!—"

Gerald could feel his success flow down to his face, treat him with that particular taste.

"Ah! Ah!" Shelly expressed as her hips gyrated to an age-old beat. "Aaaaahhhh!" She trailed off, pulling Gerald's head towards and away from her.

Gerald lifted his head and smiled, loving that his face was wet, that maybe it glistened. He wished he could see it. He swallowed. Shelly swallowed between breaths. Their eyes met. Finally, thought Gerald. "Do me," he said.

"What?"

"Do me. I mean, you know, like I just did you."

"What, you mean...?"

"Yeah. Here." Gerald moved up, trying to place himself in the proper position.

"You want me to eat you?"

"Yeah."

"God damn it, I can't get pregnant giving you head! We're here to conceive, not to have fun."

"Well, you just enjoyed yourself."

"That was hardly my fault!"

"Look—I like it."

"I don't give a shit!"

"I mean, what I'm saying is *I really like it.* I mean, it's my favorite. It's really the only way I ever come. If I get inside you, I may not come."

"What?"

"But if you get me all, you know, hot, then I'll be able to get in you at the last moment and come inside."

"Why didn't you tell me this before? Damn it!"

There were sounds: moaning and moist slapping, driving Gerald crazy. And sounds of people out front, maybe the press, perhaps the police, giving Shelly the call.

"I've got to get out there."

"But we're not finished."

"Damn it, Gerald, this is important!"

"So's this. I mean, *this* is important. This is what we're here for. Look, I'm really turned on now. It won't take long."

"Meanwhile, I'm drying out."

"Here." Gerald shot his hand down and started masturbating Shelly, taking her by surprise. "Ah—oh—okay." She leaned over and started to suck Gerald's penis.

"Oh, good, yeah, that's good," Gerald said, dropping his masturbating chores to engage in introspection. "Ooh, good. Oh, Shelly. That's great. Yeah! Ooh, ooh! Oh, Shelly, I think—I think I love you."

Shelly disengaged and raised her head. "Look, Gerald, let's not get mushy, okay? Just let me know when we make the move."

The shock of this coldness immediately affected Gerald, losing length and breadth in her hands.

"Oh, fuck!" she said, plunging to pump away with hand and mouth furiously.

Gerald tried to concentrate only on this sex and not the disappointment in himself and his rotten handling of his declaration of love and in Shelly—the bitch! But it wasn't quite there; he wanted to, or his body wanted to come, but as a small tear ran down his face, he realized that he would fail. So he thought back, fantasized a factual love-bout between him and his wife, ran it through as dirty as he could, forbidden almost. It worked. Suddenly, he knew he would reach a climax. Damn! Despite everything, it felt good! He loved it! And he wanted so badly to come in Shelly's mouth; he loved coming in girls' mouths. But he knew he mustn't. That would make Shelly mad. "Oh, oh, yeah, okay, I'm going to come now," he said, giving Shelly fair warning.

In a beautifully executed and graceful move, as if it had been choreographed and rehearsed, the two moved and merged their bodies into the most efficient of sexual couplings. Gerald came, filling Shelly with sperm that moved towards its target with less political motivation than she may have desired but eliciting from Gerald the manly grunt-moans of success that he was determined to wear as the acoustic badge of honor—despite Shelly's desires.

He finished. She pushed him out, grabbed a towelette, wiped, patted, and cleansed as furiously and thoroughly as possible, then slipped on her undies, jeans, shirt, shoes and headed out to fulfill the responsibilities she had suffered guilt over neglecting.

Gerald laid quiet for a moment.

By the sound of it, quite a few couples were still protesting.

He even heard moans coming from obviously aged vocal cords. Godfrey and Kingsman, no doubt.

There were also sounds of another protest, an official protest. And sounds of notation and recording of the protest, and the protest of the protest.

Shelly's police and press had arrived, he assumed.

The mass conception would be a success.

He was awfully happy about that.

23

Thursday, March 2 — Transcontinental

Darryl Butchko liked leaving the earth. He liked to fly. He saw it as an escape, as a de-rooting. It was only a symbol; he knew that. For gravity still tethered him to the sphere. But at least his feet were not planted so firmly on the ground, and his head was in the clouds, the thesis and antithesis of all adolescent arguments with his father.

Who won those arguments?

Neither. Butchko concluded one day that his ideals for himself, and, more importantly, for mankind, could best be reached only through practical, hardheaded actions: synthesis. The ideal was to ascend, but you can't ascend by thoughts alone. You climb, you assert effort. It was the drag of others who were less ideal, jealous of your ideal, or opposed to your ideal that was the tether pull of gravity. You've got to cut it mercilessly to complete your assent.

The government plane was over the Midwest, and Butchko was on his way to secretly meet with Ed Handlin. Vivian had made a nuisance of herself again, and Butchko wanted to appeal to Ed personally for the information about her whereabouts that he had been withholding.

They could stop her broadcasts—maybe. Since the total deregulation of communications, there wasn't much that couldn't be broadcast on television. But a woman advising people to commit an illegal act was not the now normal boldness of bare tits and ass, so they might be able to get a judge to say, "No more." If not, they had to find her, extradite her, abort her child, and put her on trial. The fate of the nation, Butchko felt, depended on it.

"That goddamn thing," George Mays said, referring to television. "We all grew up with it, related to it, experienced life through it. It talks, we listen, and we let it shape our thinking. I hate to think the impact Pavin could have if she got on it regularly."

"You think so?" Butchko said, offering a challenge.

"Yes."

"Based on her performance the other night?"

"Yes."

"But you're not taking something into consideration."

"What?"

"Vivian could be a flop. She could get poor ratings. Despite what you may think of the viewing public, they do not accept passively everything put on TV. Most things fail, don't they?"

"But look what succeeds. Mindless crap."

"Exactly. Is Vivian mindless? That's what we must ask."

"I don't follow."

"Didn't you think that Vivian's broadcast was a bit boring? Too—well, intellectual? Who is she going to appeal to? College students and some of their professors, maybe. But will she appeal to the man on the street sitting in his easy chair? This was not one of her TV commercials where you see the sexy Vivian frolicking in a glamorous world. You know, nightlife, bistros, sandy beaches, fast, rich cars. She was not offering anyone little pieces of dreams. She was in a goddamn book-lined den talking straight into the camera. She could have been selling life insurance. Or worse, she could have been a politician."

"Then you don't think she's a danger?"

"I didn't say that. What I think is that she's such a pompous ass that now she thinks she can hold people's attention just by the force of her personality and what she sees as the 'rightness' of her cause. But I also think she's too smart to let that arrogance get in the way once she sees that she's not having as much of an effect as she thought she would. Pretty soon, I imagine she'll start broadcasting shows with a little more emotional appeal than intellectual. First off, she'll start using catchphrase language. Then she'll show you the progress of her pregnancy, the glow of impending motherhood, and bring you to tears over the fact that 'Butcher Butchko' wants to rip her kid out. Eventually, she'll show films of abortions and aborted fetuses in bottles and contrast those with films showing beautiful children at play. Once she stops taking herself so seriously, she'll call forth all the practical ability that made her such a commercial success and then really do a TV number on the American public. That's when she'll be a danger. I want to stop her before that."

"A cynical view. But not incorrect, I suppose."

"I've learned a lot in the past months, George. I've learned that you can only reason with reasonable people. And I've learned that most people aren't reasonable. Maybe because they're too busy just trying to survive daily to give their minds the exercise of thinking, a prerequisite, I would think, for reason. Or—and I sadly suspect this is the true case—they just don't have the ingrained, inherent, gene-encoded ability to be truly rational. Most people are people of the moment, not people with a rational sense or perspective of past and future. Therefore, they are only concerned with what is happening and how they are feeling *now, at this moment.* Remember to appeal to the moment if you are courting the people, George. Concern yourself with daily bread. We've got the people now because they have a lower quality of life than they desire; they have a vague notion that it was once better, and they greatly desire it to improve. Birth Cessation appeals to me, to yourself, I assume, because it is logical, workable, and a *rational* plan. I thought at first that was why it appealed to the public. I was under the impression that rationality was always naturally appealing. I was wrong. Birth Cessation does not appeal to people. The potential for comfort appeals to people. If you are hot and uncomfortable, take off, get rid of a jacket, a sweater, or something, and make yourself comfortable. It's instinctual. The people are allowing us to 'take off' some future population because they have the instinct, the *correct* instinct in this case, that it will make them individually more comfortable. Not because they have reasoned it out as something for the greater good.

"Now, along comes Vivian Pavin, trying to reason with them about individual rights, government interference, power-mad men, and the endangered freedom to think. Why should most people care about the freedom to think, George, when most people *don't* think? Most people are more concerned with freedom from want. That's all. Take away that freedom, and then they'll fight.

"But what's also relevant to this case is that there is also an ingrained, inherent, gene-encoded instinct to reproduce. If Vivian gets bright enough to make an emotional appeal to that, then, as I said—that's when she'll be a danger.

"Now, I believe you have a report for me?"

Mays gathered his notes and made them neat. "First, here's some stuff on the so-called 'Mass conception' arrests."

"Christ! What a spectacle."

"Yeah. Something, huh? Anyway, some, oh, twelve couples were arrested, including one Shelly Clarke, whom we've identified as the leader of this Jan Lawrence Society, who sponsored the, uh, affair."

"Got anything on her?'

"Yeah, some stuff. Step-father is a prominent doctor in Manhattan. Moneyed family. Law student."

"Okay."

"At our suggestion, all twelve couples were arrested on lewd and lascivious conduct charges and not conception charges."

"Good. What's the public reaction so far?"

"Mixed. Some people seem amused; some don't care. Some are outraged, of course."

"Of course. It was a damn public orgy, right?"

"Yeah."

"I mean, Jesus, they clean up 42nd Street, and then this happens? Let's play that up. This is a repulsive thing they've done, fucking in public and all that. Let's emphasize that. Lewd kids, no respect for decency."

"Sounds good. Of course, there was one elderly couple."

"Yeah, I know. Saw that on the news."

"Can't write them off as punk kids."

"So? Old fart college professors, right? Ivory tower sorts are not tuned into reality, into day-to-day reality. Believe me, it's true. I know the type."

"Okay."

"Now, let's make it clear, again, that they were arrested for lewd conduct alone, solely for being grossly rude to society. If we're asked if there will be charges under the Birth Cessation law, make it clear that there won't be at this time as there is no evidence of conception, only of public lewd conduct. But we will be monitoring the parties involved. If conception becomes evident, then appropriate action will be taken, arrest warrants will be issued, pregnancies will be aborted, and the full measure of the law, as far as penalties are concerned, will be applied."

"Okay." Mays made notations.

"With luck, maybe only two of the twelve took."

"Yeah."

"Brings down the numbers."

"On other matters, we've got another report of a food riot at a supermarket."

"When?"

"Just happened this morning."

"Anybody hurt?"

"Yeah, lots. Plus four dead."

"Christ!" Butchko looked out the plane's window and saw clouds below and the sky taking up the balance. He put his mind to the matter. "What seems to be causing them?"

"Rumors. Little ones that become big ones. And what's worse is some evidence backs them up. People have been smart enough to see the shelves thinning. If not, they certainly hear it on the news every night. We know, of course, that there is plenty of good stable food left or producible for the time being. But, you know, when certain items are suddenly not up there on your local market's shelf, it's easy to imagine those shelves completely empty. There's been a lot of stocking up too. And a boom in freeze-dried foods. Cellars are packed with them. In California, they're digging holes."

Butchko thought for a moment. Calm, order, things working well, that lovely feeling that "All's right with the world" seems always, but a small, insubstantial distance from chaos or stagnation or whatever makes it wrong. Take a car—everyman's tool. It's a sleek, swift power that takes us here, takes us there, then back again, comfortably, smoothly, in style for some, just plain conveniently for others, while we sit, relaxed, exerting little effort, our whole body feeling benign, all being well. Then, one little thing goes wrong. Something as silly and simple as a battery cable popping off, the fan belt breaking, or the voltage regulator suddenly becoming horribly irregular. Then, the once swift, comfortable, convenient friend to man becomes nothing but a big hunk, a lump, a glob of very heavy metal. It might still be a beautiful car—streamlines, brilliant color, flashing chrome—but it is now just heavy and useless—a waste. Of course, it can be fixed. Put the cable back on, replace the belt, or regulate the regulator. And that was Butchko's point. Fix things. All of history is fixing things. If things go wrong, fix them. That was Butchko's definition of the glory of man—*Homo fixit.* People are calm, people are happy, people are moving along. Then daily bread becomes every other daily. Cups don't run over; they struggle just to be filled. People, unlike cars, do not then come to a halt. People lose control. But in either case, things are very, very wrong. So—fix it.

For god's sake, that's all I'm trying to do! Butchko thought.

"Look," Butchko said to Mays. "We've got to use this. It might be our strongest counterpoint. We've got to ask the president, get the president to go on TV and talk about it. Right? He goes on with the cold, hard facts. Which he feels it is his duty as president to do. He's there to calm fears, of course. There's food enough for now; the riots were false alarms. But he points out that they were indications of a genuine problem, that they just back up and make a successful birth cessation program even more relevant and important. So you should all do your duty and comply with the law, or, God forbid, food riots will become a common occurrence. Right? What do you think?"

"Yeah, sure. I think it's okay."

"Make that a memo for me and call for an appointment when we get back, okay?"

"Of course."

"Anything else?"

"Just that all the arrangements to get you into Handlin are now set. It will be as secret as we can make it. I think we're okay. As you know, we've got you on some speaking engagements, which gives the press a reason for the trip. And we've scheduled the meeting when you, and all rational people, would be expected to be fast asleep. So I think we're okay."

"Good. When do we land?"

"Uh," Mays checked his watch. "Soon. Within the hour."

"Okay. I think I'll work on this speech then. It might be nice to have something to say at these speaking engagements.

24

Friday, March 3 — Los Angeles

He was enjoying his captivity. They had arrested him for withholding evidence and obstructing justice, then threw him into jail to punish him, to make him remorseful. But he sat there and smiled. Jail wrapped around him like an old, known, warm sweater. It was comfortable, and he wore it well. Ed Handlin was not, of course, the average, hardened criminal well suited to society's cesspool, and he was not being treated as such by the county prison officials who thought his imprisonment absurd but had no potent means to question it. So they made him a home to feel at home in—a clean cell away from other prisoners, climate-controlled air, a comfortable bed, shelves, and cases for his books, a TV, good, hot meals, and some companionship.

Nevertheless, he was captured, caged, and confined; the sweet air of freedom was not his to breathe, a definition of punishment for most people. But Ed didn't give a damn. Freedom held no allure for him. Or, rather, his caring captivity, from his perspective, was freedom. He did not see the locked steel door to his cell as an instrument of confinement but simply as design, part of the decor, and he appreciated the symmetry of its clean, simple lines. He found a deep love for the fast familiarity of his small surroundings: bed, bookcase, shelves, TV, desk. They all sat solid, placed, as he directed, in certain corners, up against particular walls, reflecting his choices, thus himself. He claimed this room/cell as his own, as his territory, as his domain. If he could have, he would have painted a picture of it, so much did he love it and want to express it. It had been just over two months now, and his office at the State Department held no real bone-deep memories for him, and his room in Vivian's beautiful and large house had passed into dust.

He was innocent. He had no idea where Vivian was, so he had nothing to withhold; he had nothing with which to obstruct. But he made no such claims. He remained silent and allowed assumptions to protect his newfound freedom.

Imprisonment was the true escape. Not just from the world, but from the world in conflict and its stupid combatants, the dummies on the side of Right vs. the dummies on the side of Right, the evil idiots against the evil idiots, retarded forces of wrong battling retarded forces of wrong. The world is a conflict of mirrors. And he, Edgar Handlin, the only genuine conscientious objector that he knew of, had never had a choice but a life spent in flight dodging the draft, hiding out in the State Department, following the orders of this party and that party alike without prejudice or favor, taking refuge in Vivian's home and, at times, in her arms, a woman too busy with outside conflicts to bother him, appreciating the fact that he did not bother her. He had been a man on the run by staying put, but ever afraid of capture, that some controversy would find him out. But now, finally, after years of flight—true freedom. He could sit and read and watch TV and think, and if he dared to express an opinion about what he read, saw, or thought about, there was no one to counter it, say it's not so, or declare it wrong. Freedom was a pure, rarefied vacuum for his opinions, where they could exist untouched, his only to look at, like, take in, or discard as he saw fit, for he did enjoy expressing opinions. He was, after all, not inhuman.

He had even once thought that expressing opinions would be the most suitable occupation for himself, and he had started training at his hometown community college for such an end. He wrote a weekly column for the college newspaper. Funny, he hoped, satiric, aware, biting, so wise for his age, 19 years old! So well thought out; so destined to be so well thought of in the future. Where his perceptions were made even more apparent by the ease of hindsight. But, as some astute pundit would inevitably point out, "Handlin, at the time he wrote these pieces, had no hindsight, just pure, glorious foresight." He had been encouraged to write his column by the journalism teacher in the small hometown community college. Mr. Essex liked his writing and allowed him to write the column, which Ed took as a deserved compliment. Essex also wanted him to take Journalism 1A—"Learn the basics"—but Ed had refused. His column would be little bits of literature, *not* journalism, *not* who, what, when, where, and why objective reporting. He was going to become a writer, not a reporter. And it was his opinion that you cannot teach a person how to write. A person either can do it or he can't, and he could do it. Therefore, there was no need for Journalism 1A. So he wrote his columns, and Essex praised them, offering mild criticisms at times, which Ed never took seriously. Essex was a small man with white hair and pale, nondescript features. He was not well-liked nor greatly respected on campus. Ed liked him well enough, though, most of the time.

Ed prided himself on the fact that, unlike most college newspaper writers, he rarely covered campus topics but concentrated on social issues of national importance. One week, he decided to cover the conflict between the races. In recent years, the years that first noticed dwindling resources, minorities were suffering again at the blatant hands of the majority instead of their subtle minds. Migrants from south of our borders, from sunny islands, from across the Pacific, were targets of bitter regret that we had not closed our borders, like all other, more sensible, countries. Rude names were more common than not, so common that they hardly seemed rude. New ghettos were created in once calm Dick and Jane suburbs, soon becoming the last areas to receive essential city services. Some of the migrants came over poor and remained poor, causing resentment. Some came over well-financed, ready to start traditional refugee businesses of restaurants and laundries, and that caused resentment as well. Some came over ready to work hard, which they did, and that caused the most resentment of all. There was violence. There was the eroding of rights. The Supreme Court, most of its septuagenarian members placed there by a septuagenarian president, proved to be no friend to the migrants, ignoring petitions to over-rule the findings of one local lower court after another that had found its sense of justice in days gone by. The first generation of migrants, having come from countries far more practiced in injustice, said nothing and did nothing but went about their business building up their lives. But their children, born to the availability of not just network but multi-channel cable television, were unwilling to accept passive acceptance. They saw shares handed out, and they wanted theirs. They said so, loudly, as Children of Migrants (COM), hurting the ears of some of the majority, some of whom erected armed summer camps and taught their kids to kill, claiming it was to protect them against the migrants who had come over here armed and violent in the first place. Violence among the races was the expected next six o'clock staple. Ed wrote about all this this way:

ED'S CORNER
COM...COW...CRUD?

Recently, because of friction in race relations in this country, many activist groups have grown up on both sides of the opinion fence. One such group on the extreme of one side is the Children of Whites (COW). The following is a verbatim account of a recent meeting of that organization:

PRESIDENT: *This meeting will now come to order. The first order of business will be recommendations about what to do with the migrants.*

OUT-OF-STATE MEMBER: *Well, if ya want my opinion, boy, I say, I say, keep 'em happy, boy, that's all ya got to do. And to keep them happy ya just got to give them something theys naturally love doing. Now I says this; get yourself a plot of land out yonder somewhere and plant some cotton. Then ya can put these people to work picking the cotton. Whooee! Can't ya just imagine how happy theys going to be out there bending over in the hot sun picking cotton and singing their spirituals? They do still sing spirituals, don't they, son?*

BLUE COLLAR WORKER: *Well, that's the dumbest goddamn thing I've ever heard! Everybody knows that will only work for blacks. Look let's be real smart about this here thing and try to do something that will last. Take the slanty-eye ones, for example. What's their main problem? That they got slanty eyes, right? Okay, so, it's simple, we get rid of their slanty eyes. I say give them all plastic surgery until they look like us.*

INTELLIGENT-LOOKING MEMBER: *Somehow I don't think yours is a very considered opinion, for had you really given it some thought you would be forced to conclude that a man's look, or even the color of his skin, is no indication of his worth. The migrants would be worthless no matter what you make them look like. No, I think we need to look at the realities and decide based on that. Now, it seems quite evident to me that all these migrants came from places that seem to spend an inordinate amount of time in revolutionary war. In other words, their basic instincts are to kill each other off. Considering that, the solution presents itself. Take the migrants and place them into a stadium and let them kill each other off, while providing some simple amusement and divertissement for the rest of us. In other words, let's make the migrants our national sport.*

PRESIDENT: *(Standing up in rage) I refuse to listen to you people anymore. I thought you were going to come up with constructive ideas instead of this display of stupidity. If you had given the matter any real thought, you would have come up with the right answer. You would have realized that the only possible solution would be to put all the migrants on one big boat, or a lot of little boats, and send them to*

Russia. Let the Commies worry about them. Meeting adjourned!

NEWS ITEM - Several members of the activist Children of Whites (COW) organization were found dead in their homes today.

On the days such columns would appear—columns that he designed to hit responsive chords—Ed would get to school an hour before his first class, sit in the student lounge with a cup of coffee, and wait for reactions. He always expected a surge, but usually, the most evident would only be the ripple of his few friends who knew he wrote "Ed's Corner." "Oh, hi, Ed, liked your column today," they would say in passing. Nonetheless, he assumed that other students, strangers to him, were sitting around the lounge reading his words, getting his allusions, and subtly nodding their heads in agreement with thoughts they'd never been able to put so effectively into words. He enjoyed sitting, sipping his coffee, and watching them. The day this column appeared, he never made it into the lounge for his coffee; he was stopped by the president of his college's chapter of COM.

"Hey man, I think we have a problem!"

He was a pretty good guy, the COM president. He and Ed had worked together on a project in biology, getting a D, where they most likely both would have gotten Fs separately. He liked and found him an engaging, dramatic person, like certain current TV personalities. "What do you mean?"

"This damn column of yours. The members are taking it seriously."

"What?"

"They think you want to turn them into gladiators."

"What? That's silly. Hey, it's satire."

"Things are sensitive, man. It's no time for satire. And look at that damn title you put on."

"I didn't put that on. One of the newspaper staff did."

"It doesn't matter who put it on, man. All that matters is it's on. You mentioned COM. The members think you're calling us killers."

"But I'm not saying that. Shit, COM has nothing to do with what I'm talking about. This is silly."

"Yeah, well, in any case, they think you're attacking them."

"But I'm not attacking them. I'm attacking the people who are attacking them."

"I know that, Ed. I understand. Nevertheless, they're angry as hell.

Look, I'm going to try to calm them down. But if I can't, I will have to let them let some steam off."

"What do you mean?"

"A protest of some kind. A demonstration against you."

"Hey, let me talk to them."

"You crazy? They'll kill you! Look, just let me handle it. It will be okay if they can just let some steam off."

Letting some steam off amounted to storming the newspaper office, breaking down a locked door, ripping the phone out of the wall, gathering all the copies of the offending newspaper they could find, taking them to the student fire pit, and setting them to flame.

"Let's find the guy who wrote this and throw him in the fire," someone was heard to say.

"No, let's take him to the stadium and kick him around like a ball," someone else said.

The whole scene was reported in the next week's edition of the campus newspaper:

Most students gathering around the fire pit seemed to sympathize with the COM students. After briefly glancing at the article, several students grimaced and threw their papers into the fire. It is unknown whether they were really against the article or just going along with the crowd.

As each new stack of papers was thrown into the fire, the crowd giggled and cheered with glee.

The paper did have some supporters, though. One student, a veteran just back from the South American war, stated, "When I saw 'responsible' ASB leaders throwing the paper into the fire, I thought to myself, with student leaders acting like immature preschoolers, why bother voting in the school elections?"

One of the student leaders throwing papers in and shouting for Ed's burnt flesh was Tracy O'Casey, the president of the Associated Student Body. She was the cheerleader type (although these were the first cheers she had led in college), beautiful, bouncy, and bright, the daughter of two white CPAs. She was a sociology major because she wanted "A career helping people," and she was active in all phases of campus life. Her listing in the annual would be extensive. Just before coming to the fire pit, she had attended the noontime ground-breaking ceremonies for the new college theater. In fact, on the front page of the paper the next week, in a photo right next, but unrelated to, the story of the paper burning, she could be seen, shovel in hand, breaking ground with a local state assemblyman, the chairman of the college's board of trustees, the president of the college, and a faculty representative. It was the other big event of the day.

Ed was also at the ground-breaking, and in the distance, he could see the smoke rising from the "letting off of steam." From the groundbreaking, it was suggested that he go to the Dean's office for protection. The threats were getting stranger. Several hours later, he was taken home in a sheriff's car, which surprised his mother, and an hour after that, he got a phone call.

"You Ed Handlin?"

"Yes."

"The one that wrote this newspaper thing."

"Yes. Would you like to talk about it?"

"No, man. We just wanted you to know we know where you live."

It was late Friday afternoon, and a bully had just threatened Ed, and now he had the whole weekend to suffer through. School bullies had that habit. They would threaten you on Friday, predicting your death on Monday so that you would sweat on Saturday and Sunday. But Ed was 19, Ed was in college, not "school," and Ed tried not to sweat. He did not wholly succeed.

Nevertheless, he returned to campus the following Monday, boldly walking into the student lounge. Do with me what you will, he thought. I will stand up to you.

But in the main, he was ignored. Not consciously shunned, he was not being ostracized. It was just the usual unconscious lack of awareness of Ed's existence that most, except Ed's few friends, displayed. Once, during the day, in the student bookstore, he rounded a corner and came shoulder-to-shoulder with two COM members. His heart reacted, as well as other various organs and glands. But the two passed politely, looking beyond him. He was just not visibly known as the writer of the column. Even after insulting a whole sub-culture of people, he stood out no more than he ever had.

But his column did. It was still a "Hot" issue, as the student paper called it in their news account. Sociology and Political Science teachers dispensed their course plans to spend class time denouncing the column. Students wrote Letters to the Editor calling Ed's column "A gross indiscretion in light of the inflamed times." They claimed, "Our time is not the time for this kind of subtlety and obscurity." They demanded an apology for "This tasteless and tactless article." Long gatherings were held in the student lounge where one speaker after another got up to demand this or that control over writers and the paper. They wanted review boards or administration "censors," although all avoided that word. Others just wanted Ed's blood, considering that more satisfying than present apologies or future controls.

The paper did not apologize. Instead, the editor wrote an inspiring editorial calling on and defending the First Amendment. He also stated, "In conclusion and in defense of Mr. Handlin, many migrants and the sons of migrants will testify to his unselfish and untiring pursuits to work in their interests." Which was a complete lie. Ed had never done a thing to hurt any migrant or son of a migrant, but he had also certainly never lifted a finger to help. Except to write the column, of course, trying to point out the dangers of extremism. But the only real help he had intended here was to help people to his wisdom.

The paper did not apologize but did not allow Ed to answer his accusers in print. "Look, I've written this editorial to calm them down. I don't want you stirring them up again," the editor had said when Ed turned in his copy.

Nor did the Sociology and Political Science teachers invite him to their classes, where they denounced him.

Nor was he ever asked to join the proceedings during the mass meetings in the student lounge when speaker after speaker came to the mike to share in the attack, even though he may have had a few things to say on his behalf. He even sat through one of the meetings anonymously, ignored.

No one seemed interested in any words of truth from him to spoil their fun. This was a controversial situation, an event of issues where passions and blood could rise, heated by the active declarations of wit and wisdom or indignation (righteous, of course) or anger at barbarism still displayed by humankind. It was exciting. Everybody, or close to everybody, was having their say, and their say was being applauded. They would dispense with half-time and continue the game; they enjoyed themselves so much. They didn't want it to end; they wanted it to continue forever. Heroes are born in such times!

Stupid, goddamn fools! Ed thought. *Give me a chance. Ask me why. Allow me to defend myself, and I'll give you words so powerful you'll find yourselves rooted in place; you'll find yourselves unable to move against me. My words will be so clear, so correct, and so right!*

Ed thought that. But he never said that. Instead, he would storm out the goddamn doors, striking them, dramatically forcing them open, and marching out and across campus to one location or another with words zinging throughout his head.

The real absurdity, of course, was not the events but the locale. A stupid two-year community college in a dumb and dull little suburb of Los Angeles. Not a major university, all brick and vines and rambling acres flowing with pre-law, pre-med, pre-Ph.D. students shocked and stunned—as only students can be—over this injustice, or that, and so a place where crises and conflicts over questions of the day were natural and normal and made the news, made up images, made the cover of magazines, made people mad, made reputations. Ed's college was, instead, a more than minor campus attended by the next generation of court stenographers, dental assistants, cops, and high school teachers who, nevertheless, felt a kinship with their bigger brothers and sisters on the Cable News coverage of campus political protests, and who wanted to grow up and be just like them. But they were just indistinct shadows of those students whose names were all becoming well known to the American public, whose shouted-out demands were amplified, recorded, beamed to satellites, shot, and spread around the world. Hell, this campus was a microcosm of a microcosm, a third-generation image, a bad copy. Yet it went on. Stances took place. Speeches were made. Poses were struck. Like bad actors in stock pretending Broadway is the next step.

Absurd!

Ed quit college.

He had to have an operation, anyway. They wanted to take it out of his hide. A cyst. So he rolled over on his belly, and they cut and carved, and they got it out and sent him home to heal.

The healing took time, long months of lying about in his small room in his parents' house. He was closed in but comfortable, a mile from the college geographically but miles away in every other sense. Books to read, TV to watch, occasional pain, and discussions about his future with his father.

"Are you going back to school?"

"Yeah, sure, I guess."

"Here?"

"No. The university, I think."

"Well, you know your mom and I can't help you go there. It's too expensive."

"I'll work. I'll find a way."

"What are you going to major in?"

"I don't know. Something."

"What's 'something'? You've got to know what you want to be."

"I don't want 'to be' anything."

"You've got to be something."

"Why?"

"Don't be an idiot! You've got to live; you've got to earn a living."

"Don't worry. I'll find a niche."

"Have you thought of the Civil Service? I mean, it's always secure."

"Yeah, I've thought of Civil Service."

Healed, he went to the university. Not because it was any less absurd than the community college—Ed was now seeing most things as absurd—but simply because it wasn't "that" college. He worked, took general liberal education courses, became interested in several subjects, kept most interests to himself, and fell in love with Vivian Pavin.

It was a strange and silly love, but Vivian soon came to appreciate it. He did not quite worship or idolize her; he was not a sycophant, but he did take a subservient position that both he and she were comfortable with. He let her talk, listening to her with interest, with direct eye contact. Occasionally, he mentioned some small interest of his own, which she rarely noted. They graduated as good friends. She was mildly surprised to learn that he had gotten a job at the State Department—clerk-typist, or something like that—and had moved to Washington. But they kept in touch, seeing each other when they could, at Vivian's convenience. It was almost five years after graduation that they realized that they had been, all this time, "lovers," if that term applied.

Ed had to admit that the only thing he missed, now that he was in residence at the county jail, was his occasional nights of lovemaking with Vivian. By any usual standards, they were probably not worth the missing. But he had some slight affection for them.

***

It was almost one a.m., and Ed was still awake. Not by choice, he had been asked to stay up. He was to have a visitor.

"At one a.m.?"

"Yeah."

"Am I being naive in thinking that even in jail, that's a bit unusual?"

"No, it's unusual, all right. But we're getting used to that since you've been around."

"Who is it?

"Can't say."

"Oh."

"I mean, I don't know myself. The word is, you know, a high government official."

"Oh, a mystery, huh?"

"Yeah."

It had to do with Vivian, of course. It couldn't be someone from the State Department needing to know something vital and mysterious concerning his old duties there. He had never done anything vital and mysterious. The visitor was to come to his cell. It was isolated, and the visitor could be safely snuck in and snuck out. At 1:10, the visitor was announced, the cell door opened, and Darryl Butchko walked in.

"Holy shit! It's a high government official!"

"Hello, Ed. How are you?"

"In jail."

"Yes, I know that. How have they been treating you?"

"They whip me daily."

"Ed—I'm trying to be seriously concerned."

"Too trying, I would say."

"Why do I feel this has been a false start?"

"Because it started with false emotions. You don't give a damn how I am. So why ask?

"Social graces?"

"Out of place."

"Yes, I guess you're right. May I sit down?"

"Sure, if you'll stop being polite to me. You've never been in the past."

Butchko sighed. What else could he do? He sat down.

"You know, this is pretty dramatic, you coming here at one a.m. Did you bring me a pardon from the president?"

"I just wanted to talk to you, Ed."

"Really? We've known each other for twenty years, and you've never wanted to talk to me. I've tried talking to you before, but somehow, I always felt that you weren't listening to what I had to say.

You weren't, were you?"

"Ed, I—"

"Why, suddenly, do you want to talk? Why are you, I assume, prepared to listen? Are the acoustics better in jail? Or could it, by any chance, have something to do with my wife and your old friend, Vivian Pavin—uh—Handlin?"

"Yes, it's about Vivian."

"Oh. Then it is a visit not born out of any great concern for me and your contribution to my being here?"

"Despite what you may think, I am concerned about you. My contribution towards you being here could not be helped, but it does not lessen my concern for you. Especially since you could be out of here so easily."

"Oh, bullshit! Let's cut this crap and be honest. Why don't you just come out and say, 'Ed, I've always considered you an insignificant little shit, I've never understood what Vivian saw in you, but I need you right now, so I'll just have to tolerate your company?"

Darryl looked at Ed, wondering when the change had happened. He was different than he had ever seen, more forceful, less subject to control. He looked around the cell. He saw Ed everywhere. He realized whose territory he was in, on whose ground he sat. He looked back at Ed and looked him in the eyes. "Ed, I've always considered you an insignificant little shit, I've never understood what Vivian saw in you, but I need you right now, so I'll just have to tolerate your company."

"Ah, the fresh air of honesty. Well, for the record, I've always hated your guts. I've always considered you a self-centered, pompous ass son-of-a-bitch, determined as hell always to get your way like some spoiled little kid. You're a snot, Darryl. That's the only word I can think of for you." Ed smiled, satisfied.

Butchko smiled, amused. "Feel better?"

"I feel great! It's better than booze."

"I'm glad."

"Yeah. I think you may be. Now, what the hell do you want?"

"Where's Vivian?"

"Somewhere, I suppose."

"Do you know where she is?"

"How's Bobbie? I haven't seen her since the wedding. How'd she bear up under that crap from Kirkly?"

"Bobbie's fine. I'll give her your regards. And she took that 'crap' like a trouper. Is Vivian out of the country?"

"I don't like Kirkly. I don't like columnists in general. They get to feel that people hang on to their every word as if their words are that much better than anyone else's. Pretty good writer, though, don't you think?"

"We're pretty sure she's out of the country."

"How's Birth Cessation going? Except for a few glitches, I hear it's a success."

"Damn it, Ed! You're such a frivolous little bastard. You're playing a game here, but this is serious. Now, what the hell is your problem?"

"What? I'm sorry. Do you mean you take all this seriously? I'm sorry. I guess I just assumed that you were all suited up and ready to play."

"You know, I always thought it was your personality I didn't like, but now I realize you don't even have one. You don't really care about anything, do you?"

"Should I?"

"Yes."

"Why?"

"What's your opinion of Birth Cessation?"

"I have no opinion of Birth Cessation."

"What's your opinion on abortion?"

"I have no opinion on abortion."

"What's your opinion on government intervention or interference in citizens' daily lives."

"I can take it or leave it."

"Ed, you're a vacuum."

"Are you telling me I suck?"

"Shut up! You're an empty person, Ed. You have no opinions. You have no self. You have no ego."

"You're telling me you must have opinions to have an ego?"

"Yes! A man's ego is nothing more or less than the collected mass of his opinions."

"Then that should make his opinions very *suspect,* shouldn't it?" Ed said firmly, loudly, shocking Darryl, breaking the rhythm of their exchange and allowing Ed to continue. "Did you hear what you said, Darryl? Men are their opinions. Opinions are men. Men are flesh and blood, so opinions are cells with nuclei, DNA, and proteins. Opinions are biology! Well, what biological unit is better than any other biological unit? The taller ones? The stronger ones? The more handsome? The better suited? The more adaptable? Is a rose more right than a cactus? The rose is more beautiful, but the cactus is heartier. What the fuck do you mean, Darryl? What is your *opinion* on this?!"

Butchko had to think to breathe, and the breaths came in short. "Well," he finally said, "I guess I was wrong. You do seem to have some opinions. You do seem to have given some things some thought."

"Nice of you to notice."

"How could I ever have noticed before? You never made your opinions apparent."

"I have never felt the need to burden people with my opinions. And I have never cared to be burdened by other people's opinions."

"Why?"

"Because they are, so often, so stupid."

"All opinions?"

"Most. Handlin's Law, revealed here for the first time: "*Most people are wrong, most of the time.*""

"You believe that?"

"Emphatically! But, of course, I may be wrong. What do you think? Not that I care."

"I think Handlin's Law is well stated. But, by its very nature, allows that some people are right some of the times."

"Yes, indeed, it does. And I bet you think you're 'some people' all the time."

"Emphatically. How else could I act? How else could I get the courage, drive, and energy to accomplish what I think needs to be accomplished?"

"What if you accomplish the wrong thing?"

"Who's to say? Ed, despite your law, in every conflict, somebody must be right."

"Why? That's stupid! It's perfectly conceivable that two equally wrong wrongs could battle it out."

"Okay. Let me restate it. In every conflict, one side must prevail."

"There must be a winner?"

"Yes."

"Why?"

"Because conflict is stagnation. The end of conflict by one

prevailing leaves that one to take action, thus ending stagnation."

"To the victor belongs the spoils."

"No. To the victor belongs the right of action."

"What's wrong with stagnation?"

"It brings on death and decay."

"What's wrong with death?"

"Nothing. It's just that most people do not choose it. We tend to act to delay it."

"So, if Hitler had prevailed in World War Two, he would have been given the right to take action?"

"Yes."

"And everything would have been right with the world?"

"Not necessarily. But things would have moved—"

"The trains would have run on time?"

"You know I don't mean that. Things would have moved; for better or worse, they would have moved. Hitler may have turned the whole world into an ordered, totalitarian system—"

"Ah, the blessed state of decisionless life. It appeals to me."

"But it doesn't appeal to others. In a totalitarian *world*, resistance to that action may have grown slowly, but maybe more surely. Eventually, another conflict, a period of stagnation, and, finally, once again, one side prevailing. Perhaps freedom this time. But, possibly, freedom more highly cherished and more widespread, for the whole world would have had to be converted. As it is, since World War II, most nations have been totalitarian in one form or another. But this totalitarianism has been fragmented, with freedom coming only of late. But it's a strange freedom. Almost freedom achieved as vacuum filler when totalitarianism petered out. Not hard-won freedom, thus freedom truly cherished. I worry about such freedom. I think it's very fragile. If totalitarianism had been solidified, if Hitler had achieved world domination, and when conflict arose again, it would have been conflict on the same world scale. If that had happened and then if Hitler or his heirs were defeated, then, maybe, true *worldwide*, hard fought for freedom would have prevailed. And perhaps that would have been a much stronger, more vital freedom—a freedom truly for the future. Maybe, in any final analysis, it would have been better for mankind if Hitler had won the war. It's all speculation, of course.

"Yes, professor, it certainly is."

"But do you get my point?"

"Emphatically."

"In this conflict, someone must prevail."

"It seems to me that you are. I mean, Vivian hasn't done you that much damage, has she?"

"It's her potential I wish to prevail over. Opposition to Birth Cessation is small and weak. But it's there. Feed it, and it may grow. Vivian as a symbol may be the nourishment the opposition needs."

"And what if the opposition were to prevail? Then, they would be the ones to 'take action.' If that's all you're concerned about, action would be taken."

"But less effective action."

"Why?"

"Because they would be burdened with overpopulation and the violent scrambles for resources that would cause. All their actions would be spent trying to deal with that."

"And if you prevail?"

"We would bring the country into a state of management, freeing us to take actions dedicated to advancement."

"Advancement to where?"

"To the future."

"It seems to me we're going to get there in any case."

"To the future more on our terms, then. A future more suited to our needs. A future of maturity as a species."

"And you think it's okay to kill off a bunch of babies to get there?

Butchko laughed. "I wondered when rhetoric would creep in.

"Sorry."

"I think it's okay for us to try to manage our entry into the future rather than just letting 'come what may' dictate things."

"I see. So you would rather be the dictator."

"You're getting clever again."

"Doesn't a man and a woman have a right to have a baby? I mean, extend their line?"

"Doesn't a species have the right to take action to extend its line?

"Isn't the individual more sacred than the mass?"

"I don't know. Is the individual more sacred? Is the mass sacred at all? What the hell is sacred? A man? Mankind? I just look at the facts. If we continue making more people non-stop and, at the same time, have fewer and fewer resources to offer them, what good is that for any one individual? Not to mention the mass. But, if we get control of things and bring the population down in line with the supply of resources, then, along with fewer people, there will be less *individual* suffering, thus less mass suffering, plus the time and freedom to grow, mature, and better our existence."

"But what about the fact, the simple, biological fact that a woman will want a child because she's instructed by something inside her to want that child? But you prevent it. You cause her to deny this biological fact. Isn't that wrong? Or, at least, sad?"

"For each case individually, certainly."

"Why should we fight biological facts, then? If anything is right in this world, it's a fact of nature. To want and to have a child is a fact of nature, and therefore as right as anything can be."

"Cancer is a fact of nature. Does that make it right? No. We strive to eradicate it. We are the only species on the face of the earth who are not slaves to such facts of nature because we know the facts of nature. Indeed, we discovered them, worked to understand them, revealed their laws, and used those laws to our advantage. We have been shaped by nature to shape nature. Other species do it by accident. We do it by design. The true conflict here, Ed, is that all human conflict revolves around the question of what design we will choose. Maybe, in the long run, it doesn't matter which is chosen, but one *must* be chosen. *That* is the ultimate biological fact. We have developed the rational capacity to choose. Thus, we *must* choose. Not choosing is the only 'wrong' in our nature, for it contradicts our nature."

Both were quiet for a moment. Then Ed said, "And I have chosen not to choose. That's a choice, isn't it?"

"I would like to be broad-minded and say that it is. But I don't believe that it is."

"So that is why you hate me."

Darryl was going to say, no, that he didn't hate Ed at all. But: "Yes. That is why I hate you."

***

Los Angeles International Airport - Three A.M.

Butchko boarded the plane, went to his seat, and sat. He yawned as he settled into the comfort of the chair. He closed his eyes. To sleep would be nice. He usually considered sleep an intrusion into activity, a regrettable lack of forward motion. But there were times when he did not resent it when, indeed, he welcomed it. For rest? For escape? It was debatable. He heard soft movements, padded footsteps, the brush of a coat against a chair back, the fold of a body sitting next to him. He opened his eyes, and George Mays was in view.

"About ten minutes until take-off," Mays said quietly.

"Okay. Good."

"How'd it go?"

"Hard to tell."

"Handlin wasn't cooperative?"

"Nor uncooperative."

"What?"

"Noncommittal is the word here."

"He refused to talk?"

"He did not talk. I don't know if that is the same as refusing."

"Uh—let me try another approach. You didn't find out where Pavin is?"

"I didn't find out where Vivian is, correct."

"Handlin wouldn't tell you?"

"No, Handlin didn't tell me."

"You offered him his freedom."

"He has found his freedom."

Mays looked down and saw a gravy stain on his pants from the speaking engagement luncheon the afternoon before. It was the color of his pants but not the shade. He looked back up at Butchko. "I may sign up for a class in Zen after this."

Butchko smiled. "Sorry, George." He paused for a moment. Then, he paid in explanation what he owed Mays. "Ed Handlin is—a very strange man. Or maybe there is no Ed Handlin. There doesn't seem to be a core there or a center. No—thing there. No essence that is Ed Handlin. But, of course, that's absurd. What seems to be cannot be. So what we see as missing must just be hidden. Submerged, suppressed, whatever you want to call it. Ed Handlin has been so overpowered by events, and certainly by Vivian, that he has shrunk to nearly nothing. But today, he has faced that fact—hard—maybe for the first time. Maybe with that fact in hand, he can find the strength to bring himself out."

"And how does that help us?"

"I don't know if it does. He may find the strength to oppose us instead of just being passive. Or he may find the strength to oppose

Vivian, who has been more his subjugator than us. I hope it's the latter. But it's hard to tell. I have a feeling—it could be instinct or wishful thinking—but I feel he will eventually do something to help us get at Vivian. I don't know what. I couldn't even begin to guess how."

"Well—"

"Well—"

The FASTEN YOUR SEAT BELTS sign came on with a ping.

"Well—let's fasten our seat belts," Butchko said.

***

L.A. County Jail - Six a.m.

Ed Handlin lay on his bed in his cell; his head cradled in the stiff, institutional pillow; the prison blanket, lightweight but obvious and felt, covered him. The lights were out, but he could see. Not colors, but shapes, forms, sizes—grays having presence but no solidity.

He was frightened.

His eyes were opened wide, not scrunched closed, trying to shut out fear by shutting out the view of it. Handlin knew too well that it was there, seen or not, and not seeing would not make it any less frightening. He was compelled—by command possibly, but just as possibly by choice—to open his eyes as wide as possible, to take in what light was left, all the light available, making the fear even more sharp and delineated.

The fear was a monster, a personal Gorgon, a sister to Medusa, here and now. But not a monster to be conquered by a high-flying hero of broad dimensions with a graceful sweep of arm and sword; a hero, not larger than life—nothing is truly larger than life—but of large life, life so constantly aborning in the center that the surface glows with the excess. Not to be conquered, but to conquer, the monster was self-assured, for its opposition had never opposed, had never won, had never lost, had prevailed only over the occasional, superfluous, unknown, unseen insect, too slow under an unaware foot. Not to be conquered, but to conquer, the monster became the blanket, the pillow, the bed; the beast became the gray presence, no color; the monster laid on, down beside, supported beneath; the monster surrounded, permeated; the monster became matter sparse as space; dense as diamond; the monster was unavoidable; the monster prevailed.

Lights came on. A guard looked in and saw Handlin awake.

"Hi. I wanted to check. It's six a.m. I know you were up late. Do you want breakfast? I mean, now? Or do you want to sleep some more? They said you could sleep some more if you wanted to. We can save you some breakfast. But if you want it now—"

"No." Handlin did not move. He did not turn to look at the guard nor stir to stretch to acknowledge that he had been still and so now stiff. He spoke, but even his mouth did not seem to move. "No breakfast. I want no breakfast."

"Oh, okay, sure. Get some sleep, then. I'll see you later about something to eat." Handlin was usually very amiable, an exchanger of pleasantries. He had been a change, a nice break in the routine of dealing with the "scrots" who made up a prison population. But no pleasantries came.

"God! Wiped out," the guard thought as he walked away.

25

He was not as nervous as before and happy about that. Not that Gerald was not nervous at all; he was taking part in his first news conference, and that had put him on edge. But it was nerves derived from altogether different anxieties than what he had ever experienced first going to Malcolm Kirkly's apartment or his first meeting of the Jan Lawrence Society. He was anxious about his performance, not about whether he had any right to perform, the former being natural and honorable, the latter being the unavoidable worry of alien progeny. Alien no longer but fully assimilated, Gerald felt more at home with shared nerves.

It had been a weeklong sharing. Ever since the arrest, the group of them being quickly clothed and handcuffed—chaotically and not too well—by the police as the press snapped pictures. Shoulder to shoulder, Gerald still shirtless, he and Shelly were caught by a flash flood of light, reflecting it to effect emulsion, shaping it to order, the order later fulfilled in print, pressed, front-paged, headlined, and captioned.

(Evidence of being integral.)

They were all charged with lewd and lascivious conduct, then released on their own recognizance without bail. Gerald called his mother. Far from upset, she seemed excited about it all. He put Shelly on the line, who wondered what she was doing there but was friendly and pleasant to Mrs. Downing, who offered supportive words.

They re-grouped—although they had never really been separated, it seemed an appropriate concept—Shelly and Gerald and the other members of the JLS, as it was now always referred to, including Godfrey and Kingsman, the senior partners in the crime. They met and plotted and worked things out and considered the next steps. Gerald read aloud the draft of his next editorial for Birthright, and they applauded—although they also corrected some of his faulty sentence structure—and, in effect, clapped him on the back. One art student member proposed an emblem he had drawn up. It was adopted by acclamation and with great enthusiasm. Slogans were discussed. FUCK

FOR FERTILITY, causing the most heated comments:

"It's crude!"

"Yes! Exactly why it's effective."

"Too smart-ass, it'll just turn people away."

"Oh, hell! We've screwed in public. If they can accept that, they won't be bothered by a little profanity."

"Who said they accepted it? We could be on everybody's shit list."

"For now, yes, maybe for now. But we've shocked them. That's good! That awakens people. We need to keep shocking them and be outrageous. It will make them think, and they will realize that we're right, then it won't matter."

"Oh, bullshit! They won't think at all because we've offended them."

"Look!" said Shelly firmly. "We must emphasize conception, procreation, pregnancy, and birth, not fucking. Fucking is not our point! We have a right to conceive and bear children. That is our one and only message. Let's not cloud the issue."

Gerald agreed. It was sound. This was a bright woman. He looked at her and smiled. She saw and looked away. Why? Was she still mad? *Jesus, I should talk to her, straighten this out*, he thought.

"Look, I was a little, you know, turned on the other day," he later said when they were alone. "I get a bit crazy in, you know, situations like that. So I'm sorry about saying things. I mean—uh—don't—uh—well, don't let me scare you."

"Oh, no, don't worry about it. I was preoccupied. I wasn't mad. I, well, you know, reacted funny. Uh—it was unexpected."

"Yeah, I know, I'm a klutz sometimes."

"Well, let's forget it, huh? We've got other things to be concerned with. We've got a lot of work to do.

"Yeah, okay. So—uh—we're still friends though?"

"Sure." She said, then thought, then said, "Well, yeah. I mean, certainly comrades in a cause."

"Oh."

"Which is better, right?"

"Yeah, sure, I—"

"Well, bye!"

And she was gone.

Shit! thought Gerald.

***

Gerald returned to the office the next day and worked on the next issue of *Birthright.* He got there early, at 6 a.m. He wasn't sleeping anyway. By 9 a.m., the phone was constantly ringing—people commending, people condemning, reporters wanting to know (or, rather, wanting a quote).

"Our positions will be fully stated in *Birthright,"* he repeated to all. "Yes, that's our publication. I'm the editor. Downing. Gerald Downing. D--O--W--N--I--N--G. Yes, I did. Yes, I was. Look, I'll be happy to send you a copy."

Shelly burst in. In an instant, Gerald plotted a romantic scene of reconciliation. But…

"God damn! I've been trying to call you all morning!

"The—uh—phone. It hasn't stopped."

Shelly sat down. She was beaming. "Guess who called me?"

"Who?"

"Malcolm Kirkly."

Why? Why you? I'm the one with the link to Kirkly, came quickly into Gerald's head. "Oh?"

"He wants to help now. He's really angry with them, really going to take our side. We've got a meeting with him in one hour."

"We?

"Yeah. He asked for you, of course."

Of course. The satisfaction was quite satisfying.

***

Everything was different now about the building where Kirkly lived. The doorman, the elevator, the hallway, and Kirkly's apartment were all as they had been before, but Gerald no longer felt that the building resented his presence, that, if he touched—invaded—the building, it would reject him and turn him out.

"Sit down," Kirkly said. "Look, here's what I've been thinking..." He outlined what he thought he could do and why he was breaking from his usual non-participatory role.

Gerald sat next to Shelly and listened and leaned back in one of Kirkly's outrageously comfortable chairs and crossed his legs and took notes in a notepad and commented on what Kirkly said and commented on comments of Shelly's and said, "We" a lot in referring to he and Shelly. Then Shelly had to leave, had to get home. She was very excited and thanked Kirkly for "Joining the troops. By the way, how are we going to announce all of this? I mean, in your column or what?"

"Well..."

"It's obvious," Gerald broke in. "We'll have a press conference, answer questions about the mass conception, and introduce this."

"Yes, that's wonderful. That's brilliant, Gerald," Shelly said.

"Thank you. I do try."

"Is that okay with you, Mr. Kirkly?"

"Of course."

"Good. You coming?" Shelly said to Gerald, who didn't quite know. He hated leaving her side; he wanted more time with her. But he knew—taking the time not to kid himself—that she would break away from him once they were on the street. And he wanted some time with Kirkly if Kirkly would allow, so: "Well, I have a few questions yet, so I guess I'll see you later."

"Okay." And Shelly left, suddenly unsure she should, but not knowing how not to, now that she had announced she was.

"Mr. Kirkly—" He kept expecting him to say, "Call me Malcolm," but he never did. "I—uh—just wanted to know if you've received your copies of *Birthright* all right?"

"Oh yes. No problem."

"Good. Uh—I was wondering what you thought of them?"

"Well, considering that it's a political publication, or, shall we say, a one-issue-oriented medium of communication, it's not bad. Considering the circumstances you've had to put it together under."

"Yeah. I wish it were more professional."

"Well, in this case, you're better off having a more amateur—although that's not quite the right word—uh—look to it. That is, you want the reader to know of your concern and dedication to your issue and not necessarily be impressed by the professional slickness of your publication. The message here is far more important than the medium here."

"Yes, of course. That's how I envisioned *Birthright* when I created it. What do you think, though, of—uh—of the writing?"

"Well, I was impressed with some of Dr. Halliday's articles. But then, I've always admired his work."

No! Gerald did not even know that Dr. Halliday had work to admire; *I mean* — "Yes, I've enjoyed editing his work. What about though—well, I was wondering what you thought of the editorials?" *My editorials!*

"You wrote them?"

"Yes, most. Well, I've written all of them so far."

"Yes, they're good—

(Ah, blessed day!)

—As were those other writings you showed me. I remember them being pretty good."

"Yes, you wrote me a nice note on them. I appreciated that. You said, though, that they were—uhm—not publishable."

"Did I? Well, I think they were probably a bit rough around the edges. Your editorials for *Birthright* do show improvement. But, of course, as I've said, you're writing about only one issue. The true test of your writing will be in seeing how well you can write about other subjects."

"Oh, yes, I agree. The thing is, of course, I'm so—uh—tied up with this right now, so dedicated to it that I tend to concentrate on it."

"Well, it's an important issue."

"Yes, but I guess you're right. I should write about other things. Do you have any suggestions of things you think I might try?

"No."

(God, that word stings!)

"Subjects are something each writer must find for himself. My suggestion is to write about what interests you."

(Heard that before.)

"Of course. Of course, fighting Birth Cessation is my main interest right now."

"That's your problem then if it is a problem. You must decide if you're a writer or a fighter."

(Or a writing fighter. Or a fighting writer. Or a—oh, what the hell!)

***

Gerald checked the JLS banner featuring the new JLS emblem and found it hung just right on the wall behind the table where he, Shelly, and Kirkly would sit during the press conference. The press wasn't there yet, but they would be, he assured Shelly, although he had no way of knowing. But they came to the mass conception, didn't they? They would follow up on that, wouldn't they? The hint about Kirkly would certainly bring them in, wouldn't it? He felt sure about it. Sort of. He marveled at how quickly the banner had been made up, plus the gross of T-shirts with the emblem printed on, one of which he now wore, one of which Shelly wore—quite well, he thought. The emblem featured a graphically interesting simple line drawing of an infant—sitting cross-legged and straight-backed in front of a bright red, orange, and yellow graphic representation of fire. It was meant to be Jan Lawrence's child, and so a symbol of all the children being victimized and destroyed by the government. JLS, in a bold typographical style, was under the child and the flame. Gerald looked at the banner, then dropped his eyes to his chest, then looked back up at the banner again, then back down to his chest, quickly getting two views of the emblem: straight on/down upside down/straight on/down upside down, sewing the connection between the banner and his chest, his chest and the banner. Shelly walked in, checking something. His eyes detoured to now take in the banner/Shelly's chest/his chest/the banner/Shelly's chest/his chest, adding another stitch to the connection.

Uniform. There was something about the uniform, wasn't there? Something seductive about sameness connecting the different; like covering the unlike. The even balancing out the odd.

The disparate should not despair when they are paired.

Oneness. Wasn't that it? Whole more important than the parts; the parts more impotent than the whole.

Band. Bound. Braced. Balanced.

Tommy and Timmy are twins together in tweed. How precious! How cute!

Looks good! That can't be denied.

Symmetry.

In line. Alignment. Enlightenment?

"Here is who I am," The uniform states, "I am them."

Malcolm Kirkly walked in wearing his well-known velour jacket, bow tie, and fedora.

"Oh, hi, Mr. Kirkly," Gerald greeted him.

"Things about ready?"

"Yeah. We're set if the press shows up."

"They're coming. I saw some in the lobby. They tried to get an exclusive, but I put a stop to that. What's this?" He was looking at the banner.

"Uh—our new emblem"

"Mmm." Kirkly seemed to be considering it.

"We have T-shirts too!"

"Yes. I see."

"Shelly has one on as well."

"For the occasion?"

"Yeah. We thought it might be effective. Uh, we have one here for you if you would like. I got you a large—"

"No, thank you. I never wear undergarments as a display. When you put that burning baby on a simple but elegant lapel pin, I will wear it."

Doors opened, and the press flowed in in a rush. Equipment was set up quickly. Lights, video cameras, sound. Shelly crossed behind the table and motioned to Kirkly and Gerald to do the same. Together? Tommy and Timmy? It would be nice! They came around the table and sat with Shelly, one on each side.

"Uh—ladies and gentlemen," Shelly started. "I'm Shelly Clarke, representing the Jan Lawrence Society. To my right is Gerald Downing, editor of our publication, *Birthright*, and to my left is a man I'm sure you're all familiar with, columnist Malcolm Kirkly. Mr. Kirkly's presence here will be explained shortly. But first, I would like to make a statement. Then, if you have any questions, you may ask them.

"As you are aware, last Wednesday, March 1st, the Jan Lawrence Society had a Mass Conception in protest of the new Birth Cessation Law, which we believe is unconstitutional. At this Mass Conception, couples, always shielded from each other and the public, engaged in acts of copulation in a conscious effort to conceive. Conception now being a criminal act, we would not have been surprised to have been arrested under the new Birth Cessation Law. But we were not. Instead, we were arrested for lewd and lascivious public behavior. This came as no surprise either. Indeed, we expected it. We knew that the government would be too cowardly to have this law challenged so soon in the public eye and, later in the public courts, as it would certainly have been the case had any of our members been arrested and charged for conception or attempted conception. The government has taken the easy way out. And in so doing, they have sidestepped a basic tenet of our democracy. The charge that we were arrested under will not, of course, stick. Everything that we did during our mass conception was done in private. There was no public display of lewd and lascivious behavior. I will admit that some of the sounds evident that day were—uh—provocative. But if that is against the law, thousands of criminals are now hiding in thin-walled apartment buildings all over this city, and I suggest the authorities investigate the matter."

The press laughed and shifted in their chairs and scratched their noses. Shelly was pleased.

"No," she continued, "our 'crime' was the conscious act of conception, of impregnation, of lack of contraception. The government can deny that now, but they will not be able to deny that later as members of the JLS become visibly pregnant. Then, they will be forced to make arrests under baby killer Butchko's immoral law. Then, we will challenge this law. Vigorously and with all our energies. But not with all our pregnant members! We will offer up to baby killer Butchko only our strongest women, only those willing to go through the abortion he will most certainly order, and only those willing to go through the long process of trial, appeal, and trial. Our other pregnant members will go into hiding as soon as their pregnancy is confirmed. They will be protected by a Conception Underground that will see them through term, that will provide for a healthy and proper birth, and that will continue to hide them and their children. This is our true challenge to Butcher Butchko. Babies! Through a series of Mass Conceptions, some in the open and some done in secret, we will follow the line first espoused by Vivian Pavin, who is now pregnant and in hiding. We are going to get pregnant! We are going to put babies here. We are going to put babies there. We are going to put babies everywhere. And we will continue to do this until the country comes to its collective sense and repeals the repressive, anti-human, inhumane Birth Cessation Law."

The press strained to ask questions, but Shelly held a manner about her that did not indicate that she would welcome them at this time, and with a mere beat between her last words and her next, she was introducing Kirkly for a second time.

"... his reputation for impartiality in causes is well known, yet you see him up here with us. I think that is a clear indication of the concern starting to be expressed throughout the country and between social lines about the immorality of Birth Cessation. I will now ask Mr. Kirkly to speak."

Kirkly had sat dour-faced throughout Shelly's comments. An impression used to hold the line against expression in a small effort not to upstage Shelly, which he knew he could easily have done, and in a significant effort not to reveal himself, not to flag his opinions of the things Shelly had said, supportive or non-supportive, for if he was going to "join the troops" it would be as an associate soldier at best; he would give no orders, nor would he take any. But now it was his turn. Now, he smiled in a friendly, fraternal manner. "Some of you in this room have known me far too long to completely accept Ms. Clarke's assessment of me as 'impartial' regarding causes. I have been damn partial at times, and I would be stretching a point to infinity not to admit it. But I think you would agree that I have, in the main, tried to be as objective as possible towards all the subjects I have written about in a long career of public commentary. But it is true that I have never joined, given endorsement, or lent my name to any organization whatsoever supporting any idea, cause, or charity, for that matter. Nor, in the 27 years I have been somewhat of a public figure, have I ever called or participated in a press conference. So, what am I doing here today?

"Today, I recognize that there are times when one must do more than objectively assess. More, even, than give subjective support. Sometimes, one must act according to one's conscience to effect changes to make things right.

"Or maybe the word is, 'react.' For things once were right. This once was a land of freedom, a land of choice. This once was a land of God-fearing individuals who held life—each life, theirs and others—to be precious and sacred. But now it is a land of mass, of society, some amorphous gathering of units once known as individuals but now just dispensable parts of a whole. At least, that's how our government under President Henshaw and the influence of Darryl Butchko seems to see things—as they have made very clear in the drafting, signing, and implementation of the Birth Cessation Law. We the People are no longer people in their view. We the People are a tree, with limbs and branches to be hacked off if inconvenient to the whole. Without regret. Without remorse. With hardly a first thought, let alone a second. If we were a tree, then I suppose everything would be fine. Limbs and branches would fall without protest, and the laws of might and gravity would be accepted without question. But We the People are not a tree.

We are not a collection of offshoots going in various directions but connected to a central trunk that feeds us, or not, as it decides. We the People are individuals, separate entities that have a common government that was instituted by our Founding Fathers to act as an umbrella only, a shield to protect us from harm, to keep us healthy so that—protected and free—we, as individuals, may grow to the best our abilities. The government was not set up to surround us or to be the feeding trunk, core, and center of our existence.

"Nor to dictate existence itself. To say when and where existence may or may not come forth. Our government has stepped boldly into an area once reserved for God—dominion over life and death. That is wrong! And I believe that the perpetrators of this transgression know, in their hearts, that it is wrong. Their current actions prove that, for they are not accepting the protests of the JLS and others well. They try to suppress and quiet them by seeming to ignore them in public but actively working against them behind closed doors. Why? They had enough faith in their law to railroad it through Congress; why do they not have enough faith in it to welcome all challengers? Because they know that it is unconstitutional. Because they know that eventually, the highest court in the land will so rule and that their precious scheme to prune humans off the face of the earth will be stripped of its power; the puppet strings they have tied to us will be cut.

"But they are so self-righteously sure that their actions—unconstitutional or not—are right that they are trying to get as much of their plan into effect as possible before they are stopped. They are determined to abort, butcher, rip out, and slaughter as many children as possible before We the People force them to repeal the law. They are determined to vasectomize, to spade, to neuter, to fix as many males as possible before their sham of a law is seen for what it is, and We the People force them to dump it. They are determined to affect their vain, selfish will on as many people as possible before We the People can truly exercise our will.

"A strange course of action. True. But it is understandable if we remember one important fact. Birth Cessation was born in the academic mind of a university theorist, Darryl Butchko. It used to be merely an idea, an amusing little concept, an intellectual conceit with no practical reality. But it was a fun idea to play around with in between classes, a 'what if?' as bright and colorful as a new beach ball. But then Butchko was taken out of the Groves of Academe and thrust into the

Corridors of Power, bringing his destructive little ball with him. What fun, he must have thought, to be able to make everyone play my game, to make them play ball with me.

"The American population has become the victims of an experimenter. Butchko has turned America into the world's largest laboratory, and vivisection is his primary tool.

"This must be stopped! And this is why I am here before you today. While I am not announcing an official association with the JLS or any other organization, I would like to announce the formation of a justice fund that I will head up and actively solicit donations for, that will be available to members of the JLS and any others who wish to challenge the Birth Cessation Law. I call it a justice fund as opposed to a defense fund, for our purpose will not be only to provide for legal expenses but also to force the government to make the proper charges against these protesters and to bring them to trial with all deliberate speed. We do this to counter the government's stalling activities. We want this law, this gross experiment, openly examined in court and, more importantly, by We the People so that we may see what evil Butchko has fostered upon us and so that Butchko's mad experiment may finally be rejected before it goes too far.

"One man, *one* man is forcing this country to commit unspeakable, immoral mass murder. He must be stopped!"

Was Kirkly finished or just pausing? He relaxed his shoulders, which had been stiff, and thrust forward, and then everybody knew it was over. The press started to ask questions. Shelly began to call on reporters, but then Gerald jumped in.

"Excuse me, but I would like to make one quick statement." With a microphone and amplification assistance, Gerald was heard and heeded, which surprised him a little. Shelly looked at him, annoyed. Kirkly also looked as though looking behind at the nipper at his heels. "I'm, of course, in full agreement with Mr. Kirkly that Birth Cessation is certainly a form of mass murder. And I agree, of course, with the JLS position that the government has no right to invade, to violate, really, a woman's body and take from her, her child. But there is another thing here, another violated right that I think is equally important. That is, a person's right of descendants, of, well, of a family line. If Birth Cessation continues, if you and I are not allowed to have children for 25 years, then there is a good chance you and I will never have children, or any more children, if we are already parents. For many of us, that means an end to our family. The discontinuing of a particular line of Downings, Smiths, or Jones. It seems to me that continuing your line is one of the most basic and natural rights. With the violation of this right, the condoning of mass murder, and the invasion of women's bodies, Birth Cessation shows itself to be totally out of step with reality, a completely unnatural concept and law. Therefore, no one should be surprised that these protests have come about. It seems obvious that they will eventually carry the day, and Birth Cessation will be ended. The JLS will protest long and hard, both in action and, from my end, in print. We applaud Mr. Kirkly's commitment and welcome his support. We, in turn, support Vivian Pavin's struggle, and she should know that we are here if she needs us. We will win. We will win even if we are not allowed our day in court. The American people will not stand for the unnaturalness of Birth Cessation for long. The American people are our hope."

How did that sound? Gerald wondered. *Did that make sense?* He tried to play it back in his mind, missing the first two questions from the press, but they had not been addressed to him anyway.

***

Later, when it was over, Gerald and Shelly walked back to the office. "Was my statement okay?" Gerald asked. "I mean, I hope you didn't mind, but I felt that it was something that should be brought up."

"Oh, no, it was okay. Yeah, sure, it was fine. I wish you would have told me beforehand that you wanted to say something."

"Oh, well, it just occurred to me there."

"Oh."

"Just, I don't know, it just occurred to me as something important, so I thought I would bring it up."

"Yeah, well, I guess it was okay. I mean, it was an interesting point and all."

"Yeah, I thought so. I think maybe I'll expand on it for the next editorial."

"Yeah, that would be good."

"Did you think—uh—it was okay giving the support to Vivian?"

"Yeah, I did!" Shelly smiled. "That was neat!"

Back in the office, Shelly did some work, and Gerald did some work, and one would get up now and then and cross the room, passing the other, the other maybe noticing; sometimes they would get up together, their heads bowed into work as they walked, almost bumping into each other—"Sorry"—"That's okay"—Gerald made a pot of coffee and offered a cup to Shelly—"No thanks"—but she got up ten minutes later and poured herself a cup—"In the cabinet"—"What?"—"Sugar. It's in the cabinet"—"Oh. I don't use it."—"Sorry, I thought you did."—"No. Bad for you." Shelly went back to her desk with her coffee, and Gerald resumed typing on the laptop, sending the sound, the quiet TAP-TAP-TAP, out into the room.

It could have been a better sound. Gerald would have preferred sending out through the flurry of his fingers that now ancient, noble sound of the purely manual typewriter. A sound of thoughts—CLACK-CLACK-CLACK—being pressed—CLACK-CLACK—down onto paper. A sound—CLACK-CLACK—of something being accomplished CLACK—by a bright mind. And so—CLACK—CLACK—CLACK—CLACK —an awe-inspiring sound, one much finer than the cold hush-fall of a computer keyboard. But Gerald felt that CLACKs would have bothered Shelly, she not being, he had pretty much decided, a romantic.

"Hey!" Gerald finally said as he saw Shelly prepare to leave. "Let me ask you something?"

"Well, I've got to get—"

"What are we going to do if you get pregnant?"

"What?"

"I mean, what do you want to do? Do you want to go to court, or will we go underground?"

"*We* are not going to do either."

"Well, I would be the father."

"No, I meant that I'm not pregnant."

"Oh. Can you know that already?"

"Yes."

"Well, what about next time?"

"If there is a next time, I still won't get pregnant."

"But, if we keep having mass conceptions, eventually, you know..."

"One: I may not participate in them."

"Ah, well, you know how I feel about that."

"I don't give a damn how you feel, Gerald! I make my own choices on this."

"Yes, I know, I mean—well, look, if it has to do with—what happened, you know, what I said and all that, well, I told you to forget that. It won't happen again."

"What makes you think you would be my partner again?"

Gerald had no answer except the fall of his face.

"Look," Shelly said, "I can't get pregnant. I've had my tubes tied."

Gerald's face came back up, animating into a question.

"When we started all this." Shelly continued. "When we saw that we would have to fight this by getting pregnant, I went to my doctor and had them tied."

"That doesn't make any sense."

"Yes, it does."

"No, it doesn't! Why don't you just join Butchko in Washington? You could be his example of the perfectly compliant citizen."

"You don't understand—"

"I understand that you're a damn hypocrite, asking everybody to get pregnant but not willing to do it yourself!"

"I can't, Gerald!"

"Why not?"

"Because I've got to run the JLS. I'm the leader; I organized it and keep it going. Now, how am I going to do that if I'm pregnant and go into hiding?"

"You could have the abortion; you could go to court."

"And take up all my time with one case instead of overseeing all the cases?"

"You could be the symbol—"

"The martyr? Not me, Gerald. Jan Lawrence did that. Vivian Pavin's giving it a good shot. And the troops have been effectively inspired. But I'm the—the general, Gerald. I must be free to lead, to plan, to organize. I am not going to get shot up at the front lines."

"The general?"

"Well, yeah, sure."

"Are you a patriot? Or just a mercenary?"

"What do you mean?"

"I mean, are your great military skills for sale; would you fight just as hard, *mon general, for* Birth Cessation if it was lucrative?"

"I'm not getting anything for this! You know I'm not getting paid!"

"Sure you are. I hope the rank of general is payment enough for you."

"I resent that, Gerald."

"I don't give a damn what you—"

"I am committed emotionally, spiritually, and mentally to fight Birth Cessation. I loathe it!"

"Then get pregnant!"

"I can't!"

"Get pregnant!"

"I won't!"

"Get pregnant!"

"Fuck you!"

"That's the idea!"

"Bastard!"

"Bitch!"

"Who the hell are you to talk to me like this?"

"Your comrade. Remember? Your comrade in a cause. I believed in you. You inspired me from the first time I saw you on TV. I fell in love with you then. Yes, I will say it because I'm out of love now, so you have nothing to fear. I fell in love with you, not just because you're attractive or any of that natural boy-girl biological stuff, but because of who I thought you were—inside—a particular woman with a mind, bright and intelligent, caring, dedicated to what was right. You were one of the first; that's what so impressed me. You were one of the first to see the evil of Birth Cessation. You organized the JLS; you invited Vivian Pavin to speak, took a stand early, and didn't wait to see if it was a safe position. I thought you were as true a person as I could ever find. And now—now I see what you were—are; just a rich bitch with vainglorious dreams of power, a little demagogue willing to talk the troops into sacrifice but not willing to share that sacrifice."

"Gerald, where the hell did you come from? I mean, what are you doing here? Who let you in? I mean, I have to think about that. You're just this little shit refrigerator salesman who walked in the goddamn door and started volunteering right and left, right? You're no world-famous writer of note, are you? I mean, you never did show us a resume or anything, did you? No, you're an appliance salesman from goddamn Queens, for Christ's sake, who lucked out by getting involved in a movement that by the power of its rightness is going to grow and make an impact and change things and take *you* along for a great ride! So shut up and enjoy it because you don't understand shit! Of course, I want power! How can you do anything, make any changes without power? I need the power to direct this movement toward success. I believe I can do that. I believe I deserve to be able to do that. I want power, not for its own sake, but for the sake of the movement. Movements do not move on their own. Movements are led! And what do you want, Gerald? You've been getting off on being able to do all this writing, haven't you? Shit, suddenly you're a big fucking deal, aren't you? But how the hell did you get there? Merit? Track record? Previous well-regarded writings? No, you got there by being the only one to volunteer."

"Kirkly likes my writing!"

"So what? You're getting more out of all this than the selfless thrill of fighting for what you believe in. And what's all this bullshit about loving me for my mind? Look, all you want is to get your cock up my cunt—no, sorry—in my mouth. That's the way you like it, right?"

Gerald couldn't help himself. He began to cry.

"Oh, Christ!" Shelly said.

"I'm—I'm sorry," Gerald said between sobs.

It had just happened. Tears were suddenly there in his eyes, filling up, ready to overflow. There was no way to call them back. You could wipe them and get rid of them quickly, but that only called attention and did not necessarily stop the flow. You could let them run out, trickle down your cheeks, hoping they were overlooked. But they would drip down onto the floor, onto the desk, dropping onto paper, spreading out, making themselves known. You could hold back as long as you could, but the cry would eventually come in sudden, quick, staccato, taking in breaths, and that's when it's noticed. "Oh Christ!" someone says, and then you really start to cry.

"Come on, Gerald. Stop. Jesus, it's not that big a deal.

"I'm—I'm sorry—I'm…"

"There's nothing to be sorry about. I mean, I'm sorry, okay? I didn't mean to make you cry."

"You—you—you didn't—make me—I mean—I don't know—what—what—it's just—I—"

"Don't talk, Gerald. Catch your breath. Calm down. Come on now, breathe slowly."

"I'm—okay—I'm sorry."

"Cut it out, Gerald. Stop talking for a minute. Christ! Let me get you some water."

She got him the water, and he got a hold of himself, the crying discontinuing, the inhaling sobs dissipating, the tears wiped dry.

"Are you okay?"

"Yeah. Sorry."

"Look—"

"I don't know what brought that on. I—"

"It's okay."

"Do you understand?"

"I guess."

"I mean, it was just upsetting—I mean, why were we arguing? We're supposed to be on the same side."

"Yeah."

"I don't know, it's just—"

"You don't have to explain it."

"Well, I really think we should—"

"I'm really running late, Gerald. I've got to go."

"Yeah, but you understand. Maybe the emotion of the press conference today—"

"Sure, of course."

"Fighting Birth Cessation is important to me. I'm not just doing it for—"

"Sure, I understand, you're right. I just got a little heated. I really must—"

"And I apologize. I didn't mean any of that. I was just taken by surprise by what you said. I agree with you, of course, about being free to lead. I mean, that's what I meant. I was sincere about that. You might not believe me, but I was. I mean, the qualities in you that I fell in love with are leadership qualities. I really did fall in love; I don't just want to get into your pants or anything like that."

"Yeah, I know."

"Really?

"Sure. I'm sorry about that.

"No, it's okay. I mean, not that I'm not attracted to you also physically, I mean—"

"Well—thank you."

"I mean, you are beautiful, Shelly."

"Yeah, well, thanks.'

"It's just that I also see the inner you, and that's what's important."

"I know, I believe you now. And I really am sorry about all this. You are doing a good job with *Birthright*; it was your idea. I want you to know I know that and appreciate that."

"I do."

"Good. Well, I really must get going. Are you leaving now?"

"No. I think I'll stay awhile. I want to write that editorial. You know, the one I told you about about the right of descendants."

"Yeah, good! That's a really neat idea. That is a good point. Okay, I'll see you tomorrow then, I guess, so—uh—take care."

"Okay. Bye."

"Bye."

And then she left.

Gerald sobbed one last sob, then put his hands on the laptop and started to type.

TAP—TAP—TAP

The first sentence was brilliant.

TAP—TAP—TAP

Wait a minute! Why didn't I say to her...

TAP—TAP—TAP

Oh hell, no, she's right!

TAP—TAP—TAP

But goddamn it! I could have said...

TAP—TAP—TAP

Four paragraphs done!

Jesus, this is great!

TAP—TAP—TAP—TAP

Wait till she reads this!

TAP—TAP—TAP

TAP—TAP—TAP

She'll see!

TAP—TAP—TAP—TAP—TAP—TAP—TAP—TAP—TAP—TAP—TAP—TAP—TAP—TAP—TAP—TAP....

26

Thursday, March 9—Washington, D.C.

News is so damn prevalent, thought Butchko. You have it reported to you on TV in the morning almost the same time you read it in the papers during the commercials. The day's main item comes at you again later over the car radio as you drive to work, where someone on the staff mentions it. Someone brings it into the conversation at lunch, and as you walk back to the office, you'll pass a headline about it at a newsstand. The early evening news covers it again, updates between TV entertainment will flash on it, and the bedtime reporters will recap it. By the time you are ready for bed, you are prepared to be rude—"Yes, I know, I've heard it already!"—though any such declaration would fall on deaf ears. We, the industrialized, live with news events—world, national, local—a terrorist attack in Angola, a significant shift in the economy, a four-alarm fire—thousands of miles away, hundreds of miles away, several miles away, yet always, in their strange reality, within arm's length. The town crier is now a world bellower. And he does it in your ear.

Butchko was fully aware of, nearly permeated with, the news about the JLS-Malcolm Kirkly press conference. By the end of this day, he knew that others would be fully aware of, nearly permeated with the news of his response. For he would have to respond, the news would demand it, so it was inevitable. He was forced to be an Act Two to an Act One, which he had no control over. But he might be able to influence Act Three by an Act Two response geared not so much for the pad and pen or the mike and lens as for that which laid beyond those recording tools: the receptors of the playback, the audience. Then he would have to sit back, re-joining the audience, and wait for Act Three to work its magic, will, and effect. Then, coming back up from the audience...

Eventually, the acts would end, and the play would climax. But there were no limits to the number of acts; there was no standard. Except there could never be just one act; there would always be at least one more.

The phone rang.

The answering machine clicked on. Bobbie's voice sounded:

This is the Butchko residence. I'm sorry but we are unable to come to the phone right now. But if you will leave a message, we will be glad to return your call. Please leave your message at the sound of the tone.

The tone sounded.

"Mr. Butchko, this is Durant from the Times, leaving my sixth message at the tone. You know what I want. Thank you."

Excellent machine, thought Butchko as he stared at the source of the sound, not moving, just registering. It is a marvelous tool. He enjoyed and sincerely appreciated the machine. Important messages were not missed, which was a great aid in communication. Superfluous messages were always avoided—also a great aid in communication.

The phone had rung all night; the machine had toned in answer, recorded out of courtesy. The late news stated that Butchko had been "Unavailable for comment."

The phone rang.

The answering machine clicked on. Bobbie's voice sounded:

This is the Butchko residence. I'm sorry but we are unable to come to the phone right now. But if you will leave a message, we will be happy to return your call. Please leave your message at the sound of the tone.

The tone sounded.

"Mr. Butchko, good morning. It's Donald Carr of the Post. I really would appreciate being able—"

Butchko picked up the phone, and the answering machine automatically shut off. "Hello, Don."

"Oh, hi! Is that you, in person?"

"Yes."

"Been trying to get a hold of you since yesterday afternoon. A lot of us have."

"Well, I'm sorry, Don. I was in a private conference most of yesterday and well into the night. Was sleeping in a little this morning."

"Did the conference have to do with the JLS and Malcolm Kirkly?"

"No."

"Well, I assume you have heard about their press conference?"

"Yes, I'm aware of it."

"I would like to get your reaction then."

"Maybe I have no reaction."

"You're saying, no comment?

"No, I most definitely am not saying that. When you guys report, 'No comment,' you put far more than two words in people's mouths."

"But you're refusing to comment."

"No, I'm not. I commented. I said, 'Maybe I have no reaction.' Aren't I allowed that? Maybe I have no reaction to the press conference. Maybe it didn't stir me one way or the other. Maybe it was just somebody's press conference that I have not paid much attention to."

"And maybe it has made you madder than hell."

Butchko chuckled. "Maybe."

"So maybe you have no reaction to the press conference and so no comment of note to make. But, at the same time, maybe you've had, shall we say, a strong reaction to the press conference, so any comment you have would be very interesting to our readers."

"Sounds like a fair assessment."

"Well, Mr. Butchko, the latter fits all available facts. The former is pure fantasyland."

"Well..."

"So, a comment or no comment. I don't know what other choice there is."

"Where are you now, Don?"

"A block away from your house. Which, as you can see, is pretty much surrounded."

"Yes, I've seen them. Do they know I'm in here?"

"They're not sure. There's a bunch at your office also."

"Don, spread the rumor that I'm heading towards the White House for a meeting with the president. There will be a car leaving my garage and heading there. Then go to my office. My secretary will quietly let you in. I will be there eventually and give you an exclusive."

"Thank you, Mr. Butchko."

"Don't mention it."

***

When Butchko walked into his office, Donald Carr was there."

"Hi!" said Carr with the greeting of a happy conspirator.

"Hello." Butchko sat down. "Let's get started."

"Do you have a comment regarding yesterday's JLS-Kirkly press conference?"

"In general, nothing beyond acknowledging it as an exercise of their freedom of speech, with the note that most of what they said was inaccurate."

"Okay. Let's get to the particulars. Shelly Clark, spokesperson for the JLS, accused the government of arresting her for lewd and lascivious conduct, as opposed to arresting them under the Birth Cessation law, to forestall any legal challenges to that law. Is that view inaccurate?"

"Highly. In this country, it has always been the tradition to arrest people for a crime you feel you have sufficient evidence to convict. To convict under the Birth Cessation law, we must have evidence of conception. So far, we have no such evidence in this case, so we have no right to arrest them for violating that law. The evidence, on the other hand, for lewd and lascivious conduct seems rather substantial. Based on that, the local authorities took the appropriate action."

"But the JLS openly declared they were breaking the Birth Cessation law."

"You do not arrest someone for a crime on their say-so alone, do you? For example, you could walk into any police station and declare that you have just murdered your brother. Now, the police might well hold you in custody while they investigate. Still, if they found that your brother was alive and well, or that you had no brother, or even that you had a brother, that he was missing, but that there was no evidence of murder, no body found, they could not arrest you and would not, even if you continued to declare vehemently that you had murdered your brother. Our criminal justice system does not work that way."

"And yet, Vivian Pavin was arrested under the Birth Cessation law basically on her say-so, wasn't she?"

"No, not at all. If you check the records, you'll see that she was arrested for advocating an illegal act publicly."

"But she was ordered to have her pregnancy terminated."

"Yes, that's true. But that order came directly from Judge Ramirez, not from Washington. His position, I assume, was, if you are pregnant, then comply with the law and terminate it."

"If any of the women who took part in the mass conception become pregnant, will you charge them under the Birth Cessation Law?"

"Certainly. If we have the evidence."

"Will you watch them to see if they become pregnant?"

"No! Absolutely not. This country has not and will not be instituting Big Brother. At least not until 1984."

"A joke?"

"Well, a feeble attempt at one."

"How will you know if they become pregnant then?"

"How do you know about any crime? When evidence of it becomes apparent to the authorities."

"Then the JLS plan to send some of their pregnant members underground could keep them safe from arrest and, it has to be assumed, conviction."

"Depends on their success in setting up such an underground network. I would think it's tough to hide pregnant women."

"Do you have any concern about scores of illegally pregnant women disappearing into this underground and successfully defying the Birth Cessation law?"

"None at all. I doubt highly if there will be scores."

"You think the numbers will be negligible?"

"Definitely. Also, the more there are, the more likely the authorities will discover them. Again, how do you successfully hide a pregnant woman? Especially now when such a person would be a rare exception. And let's say a woman is successfully hidden, and she comes to term and gives birth. How, then, do you hide the child? Pretty soon, infants will be rare. The cry of one lone infant will be a loud sound indeed."

"What about the men arrested at the mass conception? If they had not yet had vasectomies, why were they not arrested?"

"Well, you know, there's a real odd part about that. It turned out that some of the males had their vasectomy certificates. Odd they participated in such a stunt then, don't you think? And the rest had not yet been called up, based on their social security numbers, to be vasectomized. So we had no call to arrest them on any Birth Cessation charge. If they fail to report when called, we will take the appropriate action."

"So, to sum up this point, you are not acting to forestall any legal challenge to the Birth Cessation law?"

"None whatsoever. What would be the purpose?"

"According to Malcolm Kirkly, you know that your law is unconstitutional and will eventually be struck down and that you are trying to accomplish as much birth cessation as possible before that happens."

"Well, first, it is not *my* law. It is the law of the land supported by a huge majority in this country. Second, Kirkly's little scenario is absurd, of course. If the law was eventually declared unconstitutional—which is highly unlikely for Birth Cessation is one of the most constitutional laws to come along in years—but, anyway, let's say it was declared unconstitutional. Then, every male in America would have the right to have his potency restored, and soon, births would be back up to their old levels. What would those of us who support Birth Cessation have gained? Nothing."

"But there would be no way to reverse the effects of the abortions."

"Yes, that's true. But I don't think the population reduction achieved from abortions alone is worth the trouble Mr. Kirkly seems to think the government is taking."

"Then why are they worth the trouble at all? I mean, why didn't Birth Cessation operate through sterilization alone?"

"Ah, well, that's another matter. In combination with the sterilizations, the abortions add greatly to the effectiveness of the effort to reduce our population quickly. That is, with abortion, the positive effects of the law will be seen in this country far sooner than they would have without the abortions. I think you will agree that time is of the essence right now. Certain current events make that very clear."

"You mean the food riots?"

"Well, yes, that and other things. The water problem in the Southwest, for example."

"What do you think of Kirkly's justice fund?"

"It's within his rights."

"You stated earlier that Birth Cessation is 'most constitutional.' Can you explain that?"

"I shouldn't have to explain it. I found it funny that Kirkly should accuse me of being an experimenter. Because what were our founding fathers if not experimenters? They revolted against control from England, but that did not dictate that they had to set up a system different from England's. They could have become independent from England but still set up a system no different from England's with a monarchy, titles, parliamentary law, and everything else. As you know, there were strong sentiments to do just that. After all, it was not the British system that most people resented but British rule. And to follow what was known would have been easy, simple, and clean. But strong minds prevailed. And they said, no, let's do something different, experiment and try to improve government, to make it grow or mature as an institution. Let's try to—what?—'Form a more perfect union.' Right? They wanted to establish justice and domestic tranquility, promote the general welfare, and secure liberty for ourselves and our posterity. Well, I submit that the extreme overpopulation in this country is threatening all of that simply because the numbers are becoming too large to manage. So, in an experiment as bold, I would like to think, as the one our founding fathers conducted, we are trying a new approach to the problem; we are trying to take the facts at hand and reshape things to our benefit, to the general welfare. It was obvious to me, the president, and Congress that this meant drastically reducing the population of this country over the next several decades. Now, how does one do that? Do you go out and start indiscriminately killing people to cut down the excess? No, of course not; that's unthinkable. Do you, say, get rid of the old, the infirm and the inferior? Or maybe a particular race or religious group? Obviously not. The only choice was to control the population at its source: birth. To try to eradicate any of the existing population, now that would have been immoral!"

"Malcolm Kirkly has stated that Birth Cessation itself is immoral; is a form of mass murder."

"He has a right to that opinion. I am afraid I have to disagree. I don't think most people in this country agree. One thing is for sure, though: If we do nothing and allow the population of this country to rise by even one-tenth of one percentage point, or even allow it to stay at its present level, then Mr. Kirkly will eventually see mass murder on a scale that he couldn't even begin to imagine. It will occur in the streets, people's homes, everywhere. And far from being murder by the government, it will be murder the government will have no power to control or stop."

"It was also mentioned at the press conference, something about the right of descendants—"

"Ah, yes! What the young man brought up. That was the most interesting thing stated there; it was the only real idea stated. I sympathize with that concept and agree that, for twenty-five years at least, this government will deny that right to its people. But I think what must be considered is a larger right. The right of this nation—as a whole—to have descendants. That is, *eventually*, to have descendants.

If we, as a nation, through overpopulation combined with a lack of resources, destroy ourselves, then we destroy our descendants. I think the young man's point must be seen with that larger field of vision. And, in fact, larger still—what about our species' right of descendants? We are talking about the whole world here, aren't we? What we are doing here in America, this experiment, if successful, will be, I sincerely hope, adopted by the whole world, for we are all so interdependent. This problem is a worldwide problem. Eventually, we must solve it—peacefully—on a worldwide scale. If we don't, men will become desperate for their needs and resort to violent means to secure those needs. All evidence of history and current events alike leads to the conclusion that those violent means will finally become swift, horrible, irrevocable, and total in their destruction of mankind, the destruction of our descendants. So, I'm saying, while the young man is concerned with the right to descendants, Birth Cessation is concerned with the rights *of* descendants."

"You consider Birth Cessation, then, essential to the future survival of mankind?"

"Of course. Obviously. I thought that was clear. I've always stated such anyway."

"With so much at stake, do you see the JLS and opinion makers like Kirkly and even Vivian Pavin as your enemies?"

Butchko did not answer right away. It was the first missed beat in the flow of question and answer. "No. Just as people who have a different opinion on the matter. A very minority opinion, I might point out. I want to point out also, that so far, 97 percent of all people called to terminate pregnancies or for sterilization have complied. I think that demonstrates that the people see the necessity for Birth Cessation despite the opinions of some."

"And you have no concern over the dissenting three percent?"

"None whatsoever."

"Well. Good interview. Thank you, Mr. Butchko."

"Am I now off the record, then?"

"If you want to be."

"I want to be."

"Okay. You're off the record."

"Off the record, do you know who my real enemy is?"

"No. Who?"

"You."

"Me!"

"The Press, I mean."

"Well, yes, we've been accused of that before."

"With justification, don't you think?"

'No, not at all. We are tasked to find the facts and report them as news."

"Is the opinion of a deviant three percent of the population news?"

"Yes, of course."

"Worthy of, say, 50 percent of your endeavors and coverage?"

"Well..."

"Aren't you overemphasizing the protest of the JLS, of Vivian, of Kirkly?"

"That's a matter of interpretation."

"But your interpretation prevails."

"Would you prefer yours to?"

"Emotionally, yes, of course. Intellectually, no, never."

"Seems an honest answer."

"Thank you."

"For years, in many countries, differences of opinion were not emphasized at all, much less reported. It was a hard-fought battle."

"I know. I've used that same argument myself when I was an academic."

"But now that you are a player."

"Exactly. So—"

"So you feel it when the other side gains a point. But that's the price of a free press."

"True. But what has discouraged me is discovering that a free press does not guarantee a quality press."

'Whatever made you think it should?"

"I don't know. The child in me, I suppose."

"Well, growing up ain't easy."

"True."

"You seem more sad than angry."

"Really? I would much rather be angry."

"Why?"

"Sadness causes reflection. Anger causes action."

"What do you really think of the JLS?"

"Still off the record."

"As long as you like."

"A damn bunch of smart-ass college kids who don't know from shit. I've had my experiences with them in the past; I know them well."

"Kirkly?"

"Professional pisser and moaner. He has never done a damn thing in his life but complain about one thing or another."

"Vivian Pavin?"

"That's Vivian Handlin. You must remember, she is married now."

"That's right, that reminds me. What do you think of what her husband is doing?"

"I don't understand. What is he doing?"

"You really must have been sleeping in. It's just been reported. Ed Handlin is on a hunger strike. It seems he has been for about a week now."

***

"I know why he's doing it."

"Who?" George May asked Butchko, who had entered his office talking as if in Mid-conversation

"Handlin."

"What? The hunger strike?"

"Right."

"Why? I mean, he hasn't made any statements."

"Right. That's why I know. Remember, I told you. Remember, I had a feeling."

"Yes?"

"He's found his core, and he's opposing Vivian."

"Aren't hunger strikes traditionally a prisoner's protest against his jailers?"

"Yes. But usually with accompanying declarative statements."

"True."

"Handlin has said nothing, not a word, and doesn't seem to want to."

"Yeah? So? I don't get it."

"You see, Vivian loves him. God only knows why, but she loves the s.o.b."

"Really?"

"Always has. It's a strange, weird love, believe me, almost an unemotional love."

"I can't imagine such a thing."

"But it is real, and it is sincere. And Ed knows it. It's been the power over him."

"He's a strange duck, then."

"True."

"But now?"

"Instead of being subjugated by it, he's turning it against her."

"How?"

"I think he has no idea where Vivian went."

"So he's not refusing to tell; he can't tell."

"Yes. But maybe he can get her to come back."

"By starving to death?"

"Sure. Or at least attempting."

"A bit melodramatic, don't you think?"

"In a way, I suppose."

"Isn't he being very presumptuous in thinking she cares for him enough—"

"To come back to save him?"

"Yeah."

"But he's right. As cold as she is, she'll panic when she hears what he's doing."

"And will rush back to him, to his waiting if emaciated arms?"

"Yes! No matter what it risks. I mean, he *is* the father of her child."

"He would do this to help us?"

"Maybe. Maybe I got to him in L.A. Maybe I convinced him."

"Well, you can be persuasive."

"Maybe he just wants the thrill of finally opposing and besting Vivian."

"Do you care?"

"Not if it gets the job done."

27

Tuesday, March 14th—Near Oodnadetta, South Australia

Vivian was beginning to resent her child. Although unborn, unseen, not yet in her arms, gaining nourishment from her breasts, the child had a presence that seemed fully formed, finalized, real, and intrusive. That morning, Vivian woke up nauseous and weak, threw up, and then laid back down feeling drained. It had been a review of the morning before and a preview—she was sure—of the mornings to come. But this was a minor part of the resentment, which was a secret resentment, hidden from Dean Harry, hidden from his staff, and, at times, forcefully out of sight to herself.

It had been three months of this new life, one unlike any time she had ever spent before, one far less active and energetic, far less full of control and command. It had been her choice, of course, but still, the growth inside her, the fetus forming into child was the cause. "Get out!" it occurred to her that it would be a relief to shout. "Get out and let me be. Let me go back! Get the hell out of my body! Who said you could squat there, claim space, tap into my system, and suck my strength? Vampire! Feed off somebody else!"

Who the hell am I doing this for? Why am I going through this?

Her first videotaped speeches to the nation had yet to have the impact she had hoped for. Those who had been protesting Birth Cessation were still protesting—the JLS, Kirkly—but were there recruits? A few, not many. Some, not a lot.

No legions this trip.

Why? She had asked, seeking an answer.

Why not? Dean Harry had asked rhetorically, offering it as an answer.

"Because they are cowards with no blood to fire!" She finally answered herself.

"Ah," Dean Harry said. "An interesting thought. Might just well be true."

"So I'm doing this for them?"

"Doing what?"

"Sitting around here in a God-forsaken part of Australia, twiddling my thumbs, watching the breeze blow, occasionally talking to them, but to no avail."

"Yet."

"Yet? I've been on three times!"

"And I'll be willing to wager that last night's broadcast had a greater impact."

"Yes, possibly. Due to your films, I'm sure."

They had been films of newborn babes and infants under six months of age, and they had backed up Vivian's words:

What is an infant? The pure expression of a man and a woman's love for each other and every man and woman's right. What is an infant? Pure potential, untapped if unallowed. What is an infant? Our continuing statement of This is who we are! This is our identity!

Dean Harry could not talk her out of the words but insisted on the films. "You are trying to appeal to them, are you not? Then, capture their attention with something appealing, instantly recognizable as warm, wonderful, and worth saving. Something that will get to them in their hearts and stir them up."

"My words should do that."

"You're not Winston Churchill, Mrs. Handlin, and no one is bombing America."

"They might as well be."

"Philosophical bombs have little impact. The rabble needs rubble to react."

"Cute."

"Speaking of which, that's what you need to sell. Think of it as if you were making an appeal to save baby seals. You've got to rely on their cuteness to do your selling for you. Babies are like that; they're like dumb, cute animals, so we automatically love them. Babies are like pets."

"That's absurd!"

"No, far from it. Infants and pets share the same attributes: a roundish need for nurturing, sympathy-inducing cuteness, and a total lack of substantial opinions."

"What?"

"Do you think, Vivian, that a pet's play on our mothering instinct is enough to turn most of us into doddering, cooing fools when they purr, wag, or fix their liquid round eyes on us? Certainly not. It is the simple fact that they do not argue with us, that they do not ever counter one of our various precious beliefs, that makes them very comfortable to be around; that makes them—whatever we want them to be. And so they charm the pants off us. That's all a baby is for the first six months to a year: a cute, charming pet. But let the child get a little older; let it develop an individual personality with the potential to defy you, to hold an opinion opposite from your own, even if it only amounts, at first, to him believing in noise and movement while you hold fast to faith in quiet and stillness, then you'll see how soon the precious little cute baby is suddenly not so precious, and not so cute. Haven't you ever wondered why a precious child, by the time he reaches the age of two years, is suddenly being described as 'terrible?' So, we'll show films of babies, all under six months, and use cute appeal to sway the masses. It works. It works damn well."

"You can be a very depressing person, Dean Harry."

"Truth is not always a stimulant, my dear Vivian. I know it's a crude psychological tool, but I'm willing to do just about anything to get you out of here."

Dean Harry did not want her there. She did not want to be there. Why was she there? The baby? The cause? The baby was the cause. The cause was the baby. The red and plush and wood and marble of the Victorian rooms no longer held comfort for her; they were merely the interior's shapes, colors, and textures, all seen out of the corner of an eye, even when fully faced. The white and silver of the labs no longer signaled the excitement of preparing to speak, or researching, of thinking, of getting it all in to consider, of composing it to her view, of stating it firmly. The *single* concentration on birth and Birth Cessation was just not enough. She had a company to run. She had *companies* to run. She had things, a multitude of things to do. How did she find herself here? A passion for freedom? But now, she was almost a prisoner. A passion for a child? So? She could have gone to England or France, set up corporate headquarters there, done what she does so well, and had the kid. She had the right, didn't she? She had the right of her wealth that gave her the freedom to have her child when all around her found theirs entering the world dead.

Damn!

She would not take the privileges of wealth when her less fortunate sister Americans were forced to suffer!

Very noble.

But did her less fortunate sister Americans give a damn one way or the other? It seems not. But that doesn't make Butchko right! Government invasion of a citizen's body is wrong! It must be stopped! No one else may see that, which is sad, but it must still be stopped. She felt it imperative to try, even if single-handed and alone on the field. Why? For some martyrdom?

Not if I win! Winners are never martyrs. And I intend to win!

But now, this minute, she wanted to be on the phone overseeing, developing, preparing, planning, or finalizing and not standing still, not sitting quietly with this growth floating in its sack, forming itself into one of Dean Harry's "cute" human pets with all the potential of being "terrible" two years down the line.

The nausea faded slowly.

***

Dean Harry walked into her bedroom. "I have more information about your husband." He did not knock as he entered nor say "Hello"; he did not take any preliminary actions.

"Okay," Vivian said weakly.

Dean Harry noticed her pale face. "You've been sick again this morning," he declared.

"Yes, thank you. I had noticed."

"The arrival of the doctor tomorrow is well timed then."

"No, the doctor's arrival last week would have been well-timed."

I've explained the delay."

"Yes, you have, and I thank you for your concern. What about Ed?"

"The latest reports are that his hunger strike continues, he is losing strength, and he has yet to make any statements. They also state, of course, that the authorities are powerless to interfere and force-feed him due to the Prisoner's Right to Protest Law and the Right to Die Law. As far as I can investigate, these reports seem perfectly correct. I'm afraid I must disagree with your first conclusion about all this."

"You don't think the government would lie about this?"

"Oh, yes, if they needed to. I don't think in this case they need to."

"They are not trying to lure me back?"

"Do they want you back?"

"Butchko does. Butchko knows how dangerous I can be. Well, if they're not lying about it, then I suppose that Ed really is on a hunger strike. Well—well, that's marvelous, isn't it?"

"I don't know. I've never met your husband. How improved will the world be without him?"

"No, damn it! That's not what I meant! I mean, it's marvelous that he's doing something, that he's taking some action in support of me. I think he's standing up for something for the first time in his life."

"What?"

"Me, of course. He's protesting that I am being hounded like a criminal."

"And yet, he has not made any statement to that effect."

"Or the government hasn't allowed his statement to reach the public."

"Vivian, his lawyer sees him daily and reports nothing but silence from the man. Do you think he's in collusion with the government?"

"No. Harrison wouldn't do that."

"So, I think we can accept no conspiracy theories and must accept as true what has been presented: that your husband is on a hunger strike but has not explained why. I wonder if the word 'strike' really applies. It implies protest. I'm not sure that's what he's doing. Maybe he's just not hungry."

"That's absurd, Dean."

"Yes, it is. There's a severe reason why he is not eating. Can you be so sure that this action is for your benefit? Could it be designed to harm you?"

"You mean he wants me back?"

"Possibly. It could well be that he disagrees with you on this political question."

"He probably does, I suppose. But he wouldn't act against me. He loves me."

"Do you love him?"

"Of course—in my way. Which is a way I wouldn't expect you or anyone to understand."

"I don't need fancy theories of modern love, Vivian. Do you have any feelings for him? Do you care for him?"

"Yes—yes."

"Does the fact that he is not eating and may well starve to death bring you any pain and consternation?"

"Yes, I'm concerned, naturally."

"Even I'm *concerned*, Vivian. But does it twist your guts, by any chance?"

"Yes, of course, I told you I love him. But it's always been an effortless love. There's never been any threat to it."

"There is now."

"Yes." Vivian became silent. Dean had forced her to admit to a common bond, and she did not like it.

"You should go back."

"No! I can't! They would butcher me, kill my child! You just want to get rid of me!"

"Please, Vivian. There is some reason, something wrong that your husband has perceived, that is causing him to starve himself. I believe it could be associated with the fact that he has always been peripheral.

"Always on the outside."

"Exactly."

"By his choice."

"But now you have placed him into the middle, not by his choice. You have put him in a position he was never meant to occupy. I don't believe it is a thing he can cope with."

Fighting such a clear-cut command from nature, Vivian almost shouted, "Was I *meant* to occupy the position I'm now in?"

"From the moment of your conception."

"Bullshit!"

"Then why are you here?"

"Because *I* want to be!"

"Granted. Just understand there is more to an *I* than you can imagine."

"But you, of course, can imagine it."

"I don't have to. I've seen it."

"How do you know about Ed anyway? How do you know about my relationship with him?"

"Vivian, I know just about everything. When will you accept that?"

"God, you're a pompous ass bastard."

"True. And with every conceivable right to be so. If the insults are over, let me deal with the facts. Your husband, Edgar Handlin, is starving himself to death, not for any political commitment one way or the other, but because he has been placed in a position that exerts pressure on him that he cannot tolerate. If things remain as they are, he will surely die. The only thing that can save him is the alleviation of the pressure. Only you can do that, and you can only do that by returning to America, placing yourself squarely in the center of the pressure, displacing your husband, and assuring him that such has taken place. I'm sure that that will return his appetite. And, of course, you will be much happier, the center of pressure being your natural habitat. Despite your illegal flight, I'm sure Mr. McNeil can arrange bail. You will be free to return to your corporate duties, which I am convinced you gravely miss, and to continue fighting Birth Cessation from the front lines themselves."

"But they will kill my baby!"

"True. But is the baby real to you? Or is it just a symbol? Maybe you should consider its sacrifice. Your husband's life is at stake. Your commitment to fight Birth Cessation is at stake. A fight you can wage so much more effectively in person. What is the JLS doing? What is Malcolm Kirkly doing? Fighting on the front lines using the weapons you first conceived. What are you doing? Offering videotaped moral support. If you stay, and if you listen to me, we'll make those videos more and more effective. But they can never be as effective as you among the troops. Stay, and you may eventually win; you will have a babe in your arms, but you will return home to a dead husband. Go now, and you can join the troops, fight the good fight, save your husband, and breathe deeply into the kind of life you like. You will lose a child, true. But if you win this fight, you can have another. If you so wish."

Vivian left her bed and the room, saying, "I don't care to talk anymore."

"As you wish," Dean Harry said to the empty room.

***

Vivian sat in a form-fitting white chair in the white and silver communications room. She had ordered the computer to print out all the day's worldly comments on Birth Cessation. She had thought she would work. She had thought that that was possibly what she needed to do: to work. She held the printouts in her lap. She turned away from the computer console and its desk. She pushed the chair close to the center of the room. She wanted to see the white and silver around her, the nondescript nature of the non-color white, the hard, unforgiving bluntness of the silver. She wanted their cool touch, automatic in their comfort, no half second of getting used to it. She wanted the clarity of their lines, the whites in place, the silver, as borders, delineated and delineating. She saw the white as her mind and the silver as her instincts, the purity of her knowledge, and the quick catch of light gleamed back of gut confirmation. No colors, No shades. No tones. No primaries blending to form colors, the others mixing into an eventual mud. No emotions. The attempt here was for an atmosphere for decision-making, guided by her only rule: use your head and your guts, and never use your heart. Use your head for the accumulated knowledge you trust; use your guts for their sensitivity to truth; keep your heart out of it; send it to a movie to cry buckets at some tried and true plot line: boy loses girl, girl loses job, kid loses dog, dog loses life, all somehow regained at the end; tears of joy, catharsis completed, a cleansed heart returns opinionless. Could an instinct be mistaken for an emotion? Could the heart feign knowledge?

She had always done it easily, allowing her two favorite companions their say, saying the final word herself. But who's talking now? Industrialist Vivian? Political activist Vivian? Mother Vivian? One to the others? Two at a time? All three setting up a din? One plotting? Two conspiring? All three fighting? She had a mind to build, the instinct for freedom, the heart of a mother. Free to build? Build towards freedom? Bear a child to receive what's been built?

It should be so god damn simple! she thought.

"It should compute!" she said aloud, seemingly accusing the computers in the room.

Colors suddenly mixed..

Ed.

"Oh god!"

The computers were still punched in to print out the latest; one pinged a warning: a fact, statistic, or opinion on Birth Cessation was coming in. Vivian pushed with her heels and found herself by the console, watching the printout slowly slip out, first short and stiff, soon longer and limp. Then everything stopped, the current and the mini rat-tat clack and the waves of the sheet. She took the printout, forcefully separated it from its source, and started to read.

SACRED SONS, DIVINE DAUGHTERS

by Gerald Downing

I am a father. I want to tell you how proud I am about that. But I'm not sure I have the skill, or, if I have the skill, I'm not certain words in any combination are adequate to the task. I need to patch into you and let my feelings on this flow into you naturally, coming to you in a raw and pure state, unrefined by words.

Take the word "proud' for example. To say, "I am proud to be a father" is almost a family snapshot sentiment. Every father can use it because it is such an appropriate thing to say, as well as the expected thing to say. All caring fathers say it. But so do many uncaring fathers. As with a snapshot—father and the kids standing there smiling for the inexpensively priced Kodak or Polaroid—it is impossible to tell, without intimate knowledge, if sincerity exists. A frozen fraction of a second that shows smiles, and so—one assumes—love, happiness, and caring is no evidence that minutes, hours, and days are also full of smiles. The simple, inexpensive statement "I am proud" is also no evidence that the deep feelings indicated exist beyond the words.

But what else can one say? What are the alternatives? "I am happy to be a father"? "I am greatly satisfied to be a father"? "I love the idea that I am a father"? They all have as many problems behind them as "proud" does. Not all fathers truly feel proud, happy, loving, and satisfied. But most all feel the need to make such statements. Why?

Because some other feeling, something like pride, but more profound; something like happiness, love, and satisfaction, but far more complex than those, and, yet something so essential we should be able to find a simple way to state it, is in evidence here. For some, a need tied to this feeling causes men to become fathers.

It has to do, I'm sure, with survival. Not the survival of ourselves, our bodies, the trunk, arms, legs, head, and organs that are us, but with the survival of ourselves, as represented by our genes, by the code that is our signature, by the unique sequence of whatever it is in our DNA that is uniquely us. That survival, of course, occurs not without some slight alteration to ourselves—we must combine our genes with another's to form a composite that is us, but not wholly us—but we have, from time immemorial, known that instinctively and have accepted it as a price that must be paid.

This seems obvious to one like me, hooked on popular science magazines. But how easy would it be for me—for anyone—to say: "I'm proud that a piece of me will survive. I'm happy, I love the idea, I'm satisfied that a piece of me will survive"? Not easy at all. For it is too cold, too selfish sounding. But is it not closer to the truth? Not all men become fathers because they want children to love. But all men—by nature—want children to receive and carry their selves into the future.

All men want descendants.

Indeed, all men are decreed by nature to demand, through their mating actions, descendants.

So, even to bad fathers, uncaring and abusing fathers, their sons are sacred, their daughters are divine. Because nature so demands.

But Darryl Butchko demands the opposite. Darryl Butchko, who blithely rewrites the laws of man to conform to his views, is also audacious enough to attempt to rewrite the laws of nature to conform to his views. But it is an action doomed to fail. You cannot rewrite the laws of nature, for they were written by a hand far steadier than that of mere men. Butchko tells us that it is now against man's law to have descendants. But it is nature's law that a man should desire and deserve descendants. Which law will prevail?

If every man has a right to live—a fundamental American premise even Butchko would not dare to deny—then surely every man has the right to ***live on*** *in the lives of his children. Birth Cessation attacks this fundamental, inalienable right. This is why it must be struck down. This is why we fight as hard as we do. This is why our cause is so eminently just.*

Vivian understood. She did not want to be a mother, but she did want to have a child. She could hate the growth inside her yet fight for its survival. She could resent it yet revere it. She could be tempted to take the action that would relieve her of the "thing" she hated and resented, yet find the strength not to take that action.

She understood, and in understanding, she could decide. Vivian pushed an intercom button. "Dean!"

The intercom responded, "Yes, Vivian?"

"Let's prepare more broadcasts."

"You're not going back?"

"Later."

"Your husband will die."

"No, he won't. He could never stand being hungry. He'll give it up. If he doesn't, we'll have to chance that he will survive until I return."

"Which will be when?"

"After the 24th week of my pregnancy."

"So they can't abort?"

"Exactly."

"But they will take your child away."

"Maybe. If they do, they will have to return it when we win in court. If we lose, the child will be so famous we will not lose track of it. Once it becomes of legal age, it can resume its position as my child. In either case, I get what I want."

28

Wednesday, April 5—San Diego, California

Quitting time! At least at the A & V clinic. Six hours there, almost non-stop, but now eight hours, maybe twelve, upstairs in the true practice of medicine. "Practice." A good term, since half the time he wasn't sure he knew what he was doing. But he would get it right yet, he was sure, for Dr. Hoss had always wanted to be "Doctor Hoss." In his adolescent fantasies, though, he had always seen himself mature, experienced, and well-heeled.

Doctor Hoss, not this somewhat clumsy, insecure, struggling intern Dr. Hoss. "Getting there" was nowhere near half the fun; it was a damn nuisance. "Being there" was when it would be an absolute ball, he maintained.

He rode up in the elevator, exited, and walked straight down the corridor, surrounded by hospital sights, sounds, and smells as he stepped each step, loving being a part of it all instead of some scared outsider waiting to hear bad news. He entered the men's room, crossed to the urinals, and took one next to Dr. Lavelle.

"Hi, Hossy!"

"Hi there, Tom. How you doing?"

"Fine. You just come off A & V?"

"Yeah. Six straight hours."

"Abortions?"

"No. Vasectomies. If I see one more cock, I'll go nuts."

"Then don't look down."

"Oh, well, mine, I don't mind. I like mine."

"Glad to hear it."

"Yeah, I'm kind of attached to it."

"One would hope."

"Mother gave it to me for a birthday present."

"Oh yeah? And I bet you play with it all the time.'

"Sure. If I don't, who will?"

They zipped, washed, dried, and left, both heading for the doctor's lounge, entering with some expectations of relaxation.

"Coffee, give me coffee!" Hoss said as he entered.

"That stuff's bad for you," said Dr. Baker, rising from a supine position on the couch.

"Yeah, great. And the major cause of death is life. Leave me alone, will ya?"

"Just looking after your health."

"Look after your own, Baker. It's either coffee or dope; something's got to keep me going."

"Sorry," Baker said with feigned offense.

"Don't mind him," Lavelle said. "He just came off Prick Patrol.

"Christ, you don't need coffee, you need booze."

"Move your ass, will ya?" Hoss gave Baker a little nudge with his knee. Baker complied, and Hoss sat down, stretching out his legs.

"When do you go on duty?" Baker asked.

"In twenty."

"Going to eat?"

"No. No appetite. I'll grab a sandwich later."

"How many did you do today?"

"Who counts? I tell you, it's getting to be a hell of a drag. Why can't some of the residents take some of the load?"

"Be realistic, Hoss."

"Well, why not? They're going to kill a whole generation of new, young doctors with this overwork."

"Interns have always been overworked. It's part of the training."

"Yeah? What interns have ever had to go through something like this? I mean, god damn, that's assembly line work down there. It's boring and tedious, and—and dehumanizing. Why can't they certify nurses to do it? Or paramedics?"

"Ah, quit your bitching."

"No, damn it! I mean, fuck, I mean it. We may only be interns, but is it not true that certain lives are in our hands each day? Are we not important and integral medical community members trying to keep people alive? Don't we need to be at our best for that? Isn't this forced slavery sapping the best from us?"

"Hossy, all slavery is forced.

"Well, you know what I mean."

"Yeah, we know what you mean," Lavelle said. "So, write your congressman. What do you want us to do?"

"I don't know. Just wasn't too well organized, that's all."

"Hey, it's a government program; what the hell do you expect?"

"Not to mention the increase in emergencies. I mean, what the hell's going on here? Did you read the statistics? Why the hell are people suddenly beating up on each other?"

"Well," said Baker. "I don't think it's so sudden. It's been coming. Slowly, but it's been coming."

"What?"

"A buildup of tension due to the food thing and the water thing."

"Ah, that's all a figment of somebody's imagination. There's plenty of food."

"That's a damn lie, Hossy, and you know it," Lavelle said.

"Doesn't matter if it's true or not," Baker continued. "People are beginning to believe that it is, so it causes tension, so that causes violence, so that causes our emergencies."

"Ah, bullshit! The statistics are too large for just that."

"Okay. Add the crowding, the pushing together of people. Look at San Diego. We're now a major urban density center. It wasn't that way when my grandparents moved here."

"So?"

"So, Hoss, all I'm saying is, it's tough times. We're overcrowded and under-supplied, and that's bound to lead to tension, which leads to violence, which leads to our emergency load."

"So keep working hard down there on the Prick Patrol," Lavelle said. "And all will be rosy in the end."

"Exactly," Baker stated. "For we are the blessed and chosen ones, the Royal Gardeners of King Henshaw, making the garden neat, trimmed, and manageable once again."

"Very eloquent, Baker."

"Thank you."

"I don't want to be a gardener; I want to be a doctor."

"Then think of it as the removal of a deceased organ so that the body may live."

"All Hoss is thinking about is his country club membership."

"Hey, I want to make money! Is that a sin?"

"Hossy, if things don't improve in this country, there will be no country clubs. People will be camping on the grounds for a place to live."

"That's ridiculous!"

"Whatever you say, Hossy. I give up trying to talk to you."

Hoss got up and poured himself more coffee, adding powdered cream and sugar substitute. "Listen," he finally said. "Do you guys really think food is going to become scarce?"

"Depends," said Lavelle.

"Sure," said Baker. "But I'm not worried."

"Why not?"

"My old man was a survivalist. I've got dehydrated and freeze-dried food up the ying-yang."

"Really?"

"Yeah."

"Hey, how much? Can I buy some?"

"I thought the shortage was a figment of somebody's imagination."

"Never hurts to be prepared."

"Well, I only got enough for my family."

"Where do you get it, then? Where can I buy some?"

"I don't know. Dad had all this literature, but I never went in for it. I just inherited all this stuff."

"He's dead?"

"Yeah. Shooting accident. With one of the guns that he bought to protect himself when the crash came. Dad was a real ass. Anyway. If you can find the food, I bet it's really expensive now.

"Yeah?"

"Yeah."

Hoss turned on Lavelle. "Hey, Tom, let's go in together; let's get some of the other doctors; we'll get up a mini-corporation and buy up a bunch of the stuff."

"Are you serious?"

"Sure. You know, just in case."

"Count me out. I'll take my chances."

"Why?"

"I'd rather starve than live on paranoiac fear."

"Well, what the hell! You're the one who was telling me I was wrong, that there was a shortage coming."

"I know. It's just the way you go about things, Hossy. Why don't you just do your duty quietly, and maybe we can get past the shortage problem."

"Ah, jeez, I was just trying—"

"To cover your ass. I know. That's all you're ever trying to do. I've got to go."

Hoss looked at his watch. "Jeez, me too. But—what's wrong with trying to cover your ass. I mean, that's just smart, isn't it?

They were out the door. Baker, alone again, stretched out on the couch, placed his hands on his abdomen, started to pace his breathing, closed his eyes, and prayed for solitude.

***

Los Angeles

His work week ended on Wednesdays, giving him Thursdays and Fridays off. Almost every week, he would find an occasion to announce to someone with a smile that he was being "sprung from jail" or that he was "Getting time off for good behavior," maybe said with a chuckle as he talked with the cashier as he was buying the beer he hoped would last for the next two days. Then, a weary climb into his compact car, needing to catch a quick breath before putting the key in the ignition, turning to spark, catching with gas, shifting for backward movement, backing out slowly, swinging the car to position for its forward move out of the parking lot, onto the street, then on to home.

Home was a four-bedroom suburban stucco-covered tract house he and his family shared with another family. His being a wife, two kids, and a third from a previous marriage visiting on the weekends; theirs being husband, wife, and three kids, all three always there. Duo Family Habitation. It was the only way to get a house these days, to get some equity, to get out of those damn apartments. Or so it seemed if you read the papers, watched the news—and believed them. Two or more families would form a homeowner's corporation to buy the house, splitting shares and voting stock. Decisions had to be made together, after discussions, sometimes arguments, and eventual votes. It was a pain. It was inconvenient. But, what the hell, anyway, got a house—semi-private—got a back yard—semi-private—got a pool—semi-private—got 2 1/2 bathrooms—hardly ever private.

He pulled into the driveway, parked next to Bill's car, grabbed his beer, got out of the car, and headed for the house. Birds were chirping. There were lots of trees in the neighborhood and lots of birds in those trees. Their sound had always meant peace to Sam, giving him a sense of calm in the shade and green, unlike work in downtown L.A., in the downtown central jail where he spent his time guarding scum, scrots, blacks, greaseballs, gooks, fags, queens and, sometimes, like recently, fascinating people, God-only-knows-why-they-were-in-jail. He stopped before entering the house; he listened to and noted the birds, trying to record their songs in his mind for later conversion into pleasant memory when he would need it among the hard steel doors and dull walls of peeling paint and people always pissed; mad at him, it seemed, for being in jail, although, hell, he didn't put them there, the bastards, they put themselves there. He opened the door. A wife and mother was screaming at a kid, maybe two. At first, he couldn't tell which and whose, but finally saw that it was Sally, his, yelling at Shannon, theirs.

"Damn it! I'm not telling you again, Shannon! Set the table, or I'll slap your little face off!"

Sally was known to friends as sweet and always exchanged pleasantries in her soft female voice at the market and such places, causing smiles and little laughs, for there was always humor in her small talk. But at home, she rarely spoke below a shout to her kids; their kids, it didn't matter. The kid joined in the shouting, as Sam did naturally as he entered. "Shannon, you heard Sally! Set the table!"

"I set it for Henry yesterday. It's his turn!"

"Well, Henry's not here right now," Sally said, "so set the damn table!"

"Hi honey," he said to Sally.

"Hi." She took the beer from him and put it in the refrigerator.

Shannon banged a plate on the table.

"Shannon! You break a plate, and I'll break you!"

"Where's Bill?"

"In his bedroom watching the news."

"Sam opened the refrigerator, grabbed two beers, and headed for Bill and Mary's bedroom. "Hey Bill," Sam said as he entered.

"Yo," Bill said. He was stretched out on the bed, watching a small portable TV placed on the dresser.

"Brought you a beer."

"Hey, thanks, man."

Sam pulled a chair from Mary's vanity, sat, and rested his legs on the bed. They both opened their beers and drank.

"Shannon being a problem?" Bill said more for the need to say something than any need to know.

"Yeah. You would think table setting was a major chore."

"Well, just smack her one."

"Well, hell, Bill, she's your kid."

"So what? We got to have some order around here." Bill took a long fill and deep swallow of beer.

"Well, maybe she resents taking orders from Sally."

"I'll resent her. She's been told that Sally is the kitchen authority and to do what she says. There's no excuse."

"What's on the news?"

"Same old shit. I'm just waiting for the sports. Hey! Your favorite prisoner was on there."

"Oh yeah? Handlin?"

"Yeah. Showed him in the hospital. Not doing well."

"Well, fuck, you wouldn't either if you hadn't eaten in a month."

"Jesus, what an idiot."

"Yeah. Nice guy, though. The best damn duty I ever had. Got me away from the scrots for a while."

"What a shit pile! I don't know how you stand it."

"Just grin and bear it, I guess. It can get you down, though. I mean, these are real lowlife bastards, a bunch of creeps. But hell, I'd like to see more of them in there. There're too many creeps out here."

"Tell me about it. I almost got a route through East L.A. and Compton. No, thank you, man! I almost quit over that."

"Yeah, I remember."

"I don't know. I sometimes think there are more of them than us."

"They should have stayed on the damn boat."

"Yeah."

"And if it ain't the migrants, it's the blacks and pimps, and if it ain't them, it's the gang members or the goddamn queers; God, they're a bunch. In fact—Jesus—something hilarious happened today. We got his new girl in working the property room, a clerk, and she's a real innocent see, I mean she's real sweet and nice and all that, but real naive, you know. Well, anyway, this fucking queen is getting let out, see, and this girl is told to release his personal property to him. So, there she is handing back to this guy, see, all this female stuff he had when he was picked up, which she thinks is weird, right? Anyway, I mean, I don't even know if she's ever seen a friggin' queen before or even knew they existed, right? But, well, anyway, she's trying to be cool, handing back the dress and slip and wig and all the make-up stuff, but she's taken back by all this. I mean, it's her first day, right? And maybe she thought she'd see some weird stuff, but not this, right? Well, she's doing, basically, okay, handing back this stuff and checking it off the list when she comes to a pack of birth control pills, right? Well, that really floors her, and she blurts out—I mean, this sweet, innocent little girl who's been trying, all this time, really, not to even acknowledge that she's got this flaming fairy queen in front of her—she blurts out, 'What do you need these for?'

Well, the fag just gave her this look that was just classic, I mean, so indignant as if to say, you know, '*WELL!*' or something like that, and he just grabbed his stuff and got the hell out. And then I cracked up, and then George—you know George?—George cracked up, and she turned, I swear, beet red, I mean, you know, this *real* red. And we tried to explain it to her, but she didn't get it. She knew men don't take the pill, and anyway, how could he get pregnant anyway and, anyway, why doesn't he report for his vasectomy? And we just laughed some more and had to explain things."

"Wow, that's a crack-up."

"Yeah, it was pretty funny. Anyway, that's the insanity going on all the time there. That's why Handlin was such great duty."

"Yeah. I can't figure that guy at all." Bill drank the last of his beer. It was more than a mouthful, but he managed.

"Yeah, hell, he had everything. Boy, I'll tell you, if I were married to the richest woman in the world, I sure wouldn't starve myself to death."

"But she went off the deep end, you know, with all that protesting shit. It was her fault that he was in jail. That couldn't have been easy to take for a guy like him, being in jail and all."

"You think so? Hell, we've treated him like a damn king. I mean, it was asinine, him being in jail. And he didn't seem depressed about it at all. I mean, he was taking it well. It didn't bother him at all."

"Well, maybe he thought his wife would come back and get him out. And then she doesn't."

"Yeah, that might have something to do with it. I don't know."

"Which reminds me. Before you came, they said that she's going to be on the tube again tonight. Knocking off something good, I'll bet you."

"Yeah, football is on tonight."

"Oh, shit! You know, I'm getting real tired of that dumb bitch."

"Maybe Handlin's got a good reason to kill himself."

"Yeah, she's a real pain. Who the hell does she think she is with all this TV stuff."

"Well, she's got a right, I guess. But what gets me is why all the damn stations have to carry her like she was the president or something. I mean, you know, somebody may want to watch something else."

"Yeah."

"Well, I'll watch her. She might say something about Handlin. I would like to hear her new excuses for not coming back."

Shannon burst into the room. "DINNER! DINNER! DINNER!" she shouted, then ran out.

"God damn it, Shannon!" her father yelled. "I swear, someday I'm going to kill that kid."

29

Tuesday, April 18—Cleveland, Ohio

It had been his brother's baseball bat. A prized one, one he had been proud of, his brother used to keep it beside him as they talked in their shared bedroom, feeling it up and down, finger tracing the cut-in words that gave the brand and the endorsement, balancing it on his open palm. His brother had been a hero with this bat, *his* hero with this bat, the most valuable player, gripping this bat, squeezing it tight as he prepared to slug a ball out of the park to cheers, to his cheers. This bat had his brother's body oil in it; he could feel that. This bat contained some of Sammy.

Nevertheless, Frederick Lewis Howard had hacked this bat in half.

He now sanded the raw end, bringing out a smell of wood and leaving light wood dust on his floor. He wanted it smooth so it wouldn't snag.

Vivian Pavin was coming home. She had said so, she said last night, on TV, on the *Vivian Show*, or *The Adventures of Vivian*, or so he variously called it, it almost being a regular goddamn series now.

He had written in his diary, SHE'S ON AGAIN SAMMY. ON TV. SHE DIDN'T MENTION ME AGAIN. BUT I KNOW WHY SAMMY, YOU TOLD ME SAMMY. SHE'S A FAKE. IS THAT RIGHT SAMMY? A FAKE. WORKING FOR BUTCHKO. RIGHT? SHE'S NOT REALLY PREGNANT THAT'S WHY SHE HAD TO GO AWAY SO NO ONE COULD CHECK. IF SHE'S PROTESTING THEN EVERYBODY THINKS THERE'S PROTESTING SO THEY DON'T PAY ANY ATTENTION TO ANYONE ELSE. THEY JUST HAVE TO WATCH THE TV BABE, THE TV BITCH VIVIAN AND LET HER DO IT AND NOT HAVE TO DO ANYTHING THEMSELVES OR LISTEN TO ANYONE ELSE. DID I UNDERSTAND THAT RIGHT SAMMY? TELL ME SAMMY. HOW DO WE PROVE THAT SAMMY? WHEN SHE COMES HOME HOW DO WE LET

THEM KNOW WHO THE REAL PROTESTER IS? WE GOT TO BUST HER BALLOON SAMMY. BEAT IT UNTIL IT POPS, RIGHT SAMMY? BUST IT RIGHT THERE ON TV. POP POP POP POP POP POP POP POP POP POP POP POP POP POP POP POP POP

Vivian would return on Monday the twenty-fourth. "I will turn myself over to the authorities in Los Angeles," she had stated during her last TV broadcast, and he knew that he had to get there by then; he had to get from Cleveland to California by then. But he had no money for a plane, there were no trains anymore, buses were packed, always, you needed long advance reservations. But he knew he would find a way there.

SHOULD I STEAL A CAR SAMMY?

The end of the bat was becoming smooth; his hand and the sandpaper ran over it quickly back and forth/back and forth. He stopped. He looked at the end. He ran a finger over it. A little more. Then it would be okay. Just a little more. Then it would work okay.

***

Washington, D.C.

Darryl Butchko was mad, and he wanted to rant. But his secretary was gone for the night, and as she was the cause of his anger and the ideal object toward which to direct his ranting, he just sat and stewed in his own juice, as his mother used to say. Earlier in the day, his car had been vandalized, he had spilled red wine on his slacks, and he had slipped on the Capitol steps. Then he returned late to his office to find memos not typed right and a call informing him that his secretary had failed to make another call to inform someone else that Mr. Butchko was sorry, but he would have to cancel lunch. She was new, which could be an excuse, but there were no excuses, Butchko had always declared.

He gathered some papers together to staple and, in stapling, found a finger in the way. Just a tiny piercing and little blood, but he damned everything in sight. He sucked on his finger, self-nursing the wound.

Vivian Pavin Handlin was a bitch! That was all there was to it. A bitch! A televised bitch.! A satellite bitch! An electronic bits bitch!

As he had predicted, she had become more emotional, less philosophical in her appeals to the nation. Contrary to his prediction, she had not come running home to hubby Ed, now near dead. She had held on somewhere—where was she?—in her little outpost of outcry, becoming the "Conscience of America," as some punk pundit of the media had stated (Malcolm Kirkly wouldn't like that!). Just plain "Con of America," Butchko preferred to think. Like puppy dogs, television networks ran her speeches. Like a purring cat, the news ran clips from her speeches. Jesus Christ! She was not only the event; she was the event's coverage! Why? Because she was a pretty woman who sold perfume? Because she was a glamorous woman who made movies? Because she was a ruthless woman who made little machines of destruction? Because she was rich? Because she made magazine covers? But where was the validity of her ideas? There was scent there. There were images there. There was death there. There was money there. There was exposure there. But where were the ideas? Where were thoughts worth musing on? Why should she become the country's conscience or even be allowed to con it? Did she have an effect? The polls showed only slight movement in her favor. What help was she getting there from the other protesters, the public fuckers? She seemed a folly, an impotent folly.

But Butchko knew it could turn and that it could turn with sudden and swift effect. If she could just hit one right note, send out one right signal, her side, her team, her troops might, eventually, win. So—he stops her. Simple. It had been his only plan.

She'll be back on the twenty-fourth with her baby safely tucked inside her womb and the law. They can't destroy it now; they must let it come to term. Fine. Baby can be born then borne away, out of her sight forever, nonexistent as far as she is concerned. If they can hide mobsters, if they can conceal killers, dopers, fiends, and squealers, they can hide one baby. That takes care of that; it is proper partial punishment. But she'll want her day in court. Fine. But not while still carrying the precious growth. The government has far too much concern for her health for that. And maybe not right after; perhaps she'll need time to recover. We are concerned about that. We understand the trauma. We can do nothing about taking her child. THAT IS THE LAW, but we can understand what she is going through; my god, we're not monsters; we're human, after all. So later,

later when the docket is not so full. *In all criminal prosecutions, the accused shall enjoy the right to a speedy and public trial...* Yes, that's true; she'll sue, and the government will concede. It did not act hasty enough. Well, sorry, we were wrong. Good-bye.

She'll go back on TV, of course. The woman who was treated with compassion and got justice from the government. How dare she attack! Spoiled rich bitch! Her baby's better off in the nice, solid, middle-class family it is said to be now residing with.

Welcome home, Vivian.

Butchko stopped sucking his finger.

***

New York

Gerald Downing was beginning to receive praise. But was it his words and how he connected them, manipulating them into thoughts, ideas, and well-stated opinions? Or was it the packaging? *Birthright* had gone from a Xerox, stapled handout sheet to a nice, well-designed tabloid on good paper stock. People were impressed. Gerald had almost regretted it. There was a romance to Xerox, to copies of your raw, self-printed words placed before the eyes of others. Malcolm Kirkly had told him, "The message here is far more important than the medium," recognizing but appreciating the amateur look of the publication. But the tabloid was good, too. Gerald appreciated its professional look; he enjoyed the professional stance he had to take to edit it, to get it published; there was the better form to live up to, more content—many now wanted to write for *Birthright*—to edit; better distribution to keep an eye on, all paid for by the increased donations to the cause, *Birthright*'s share of which was his to manage. And there was the praise. There was being taken seriously. But for what? What he wrote? Or, of equal importance to him, how he wrote? Or how it was so well printed and published?

People are impressed by looks, not by what they see.

His mother was impressed, which surprised him. But she seemed to enjoy the "notorious" reputation coming down upon him and did not mind that it may reflect on her. Her warnings of the potential hazards were gone, outside of an obligatory "Be careful" now and then. Instead, she offered to help and "Get pregnant!"—even though that was biologically out of the question—offered to do filing in the office, an offer accepted by Shelly before Gerald could discourage it. It was embarrassing for the first few days—bringing in his mother from Queens—but soon the JLS took to her, liked her, then loved her, making her the mascot of the cause, which she loved, which Gerald found to be silly and uncomfortable.

His ex-wife seemed impressed. She had seen him on TV and saw his picture in the paper and thought that was neat and told her friends, some of whom thought he was weird to be involved with a bunch of dumb college protesters. But she defended him and watched for his appearances on TV.

Shelly seemed constantly amazed that Gerald was becoming impressive; even she was impressed. But she allowed herself to believe that she had "discovered" him, making it a more comfortable conception. Still, she would not date him.

But what about his words, his actual work, that thing that he did? Did anybody like those? Was anybody impressed by them?

"Better" would be Kirkly's one-word assessment when Gerald made a concerted effort to get an opinion out of him. *The old fart!* Gerald would think afterward while wondering why he bothered. He *wouldn't rave if he loved it more than his own life. Too afraid of competition. He knows damn well I'm getting good. I am good!*

THE POET LAUREATE OF THE MOVEMENT was the term Gerald felt the media was—any minute now—ready to apply to him. He had been mentioned, his writings were being quoted, and it seemed the next logical occurrence if things ran as they usually ran. That would indicate—wouldn't it?—that his words were good.

He had work to do. He had to stop thinking about all this and get to it. He had an editorial to write, a welcome home message for Vivian Pavin *Handlin*. He made sure to emphasize the "Handlin," the married "Mrs. Handlin," the mother-to-be "Mrs. Edgar Handlin," the widow-to-be "Mrs. Handlin?" What sacrifices the woman was making! With Shelly, he shared the conviction that Vivian Pavin Handlin was a sincere fighter for the cause who did what she did because she *had* to do it. She explained herself well in the broadcasts and eloquently and movingly stated the basic views and feelings that he, Shelly, and the JLS shared. He felt toward Vivian as one might an exiled general or religious leader, the focus of one's endeavors for the good. Although he had not met Vivian as Shelly had—as Shelly kept reminding him—he felt as if he knew her. He had been touched when he saw her on

TV speaking to the Fordham students. They were connected in an almost mystical way, he felt. Kirkly still thought of her—and some agreed—as a dilettante protester, seeing this as just another world to conquer. Kirkly was wrong! He was sure of that. But his justice fund had been great. Certain members of the certainly wealthy had been tapped to their delight, and the flow of cash had been large enough to pay for all the bail and other legal fees.

But Kirkly would allow no portion of it to pay for the trip.

"It's a fund for legal defense, not for trips to sunny Los Angeles," he gave as his reason.

So, other plans were made, and different ways to get to L.A. were figured out. He would be there. As would Shelly. Boosted with the L.A. JLS chapter of 45, they should show decent support for Vivian, and they could organize others.

He and Shelly were going to drive. It was the only way to get there in time. Finding a seat on an airline with such short notice would be far too expensive, even for Shelly. She needed a driving partner. Gerald's importance to the movement was too well established, so he was the only choice.

Gerald was excited. As Shelly drove, he could do some writing—concentration furrowing his brow, his pen speedily scratching across paper. As he drove, they could talk—about the fight against Birth Cessation, of course, but maybe also about him, about her, about him and her. Perhaps they would fight, spat a little, barbs not too sharp going back and forth, ending in—it would be nice—mutual laughter and smiles and eyes (and more) meeting. Maybe. He turned on his laptop. It would be nice.

***

Malcolm Kirkly wasn't quite sure what to make of Vivian Pavin Handlin's return. He had followed her TV broadcasts and found not one word she said debatable, even if he felt that a few others, one being "God," should have been mentioned. But he didn't like the feeling he got from these "Letters from Abroad," assuming she was abroad. Somehow, he couldn't take seriously the words of a movie mogul/arms manufacturer/perfume purveyor jet-setting queen. She was everything crass about current culture, everything he tried to warn against as "Argus." And now here she was as protester, rebel, liberator.

But all from behind the TV screen, like the worst of late 20th-century religion. She was nothing but a media protester, a regularly scheduled, prime-time TV star rebel, a good guy-gal ready to shoot it out with bullets or lasers of truth. Her truth. But his truth also, and that's what was so damn infuriating about it.

Where was the grace of the old days, of the respectable vocation of adding to the marketplace of ideas? Where was pen to paper, paper to reader? In *his* hands, of course. But who has more readers, or should it be said, *viewers*? Vivian, of course.

So, how could you argue?

But, still, he wanted to.

Many more people now know of the evils of Birth Cessation than when he was the lone voice crying out. He should be grateful to Vivian for that. But are those people convinced? The way he convinces—when he does. Or have they been *moved* to knowledge? And, if so, could they, just as quickly, be moved to other and opposite knowledge? Next year, would Vivian not be a top-rated, top-ten propagandist, and would the cause lose points with her? Can truth be made dull by overexposure? Is she returning to America to establish her umpteenth corporation, Martyr, Inc.? Is she planning to revamp her show, stop shouting propaganda, and suffer persecution instead in the hope of forestalling audience impatience, quelling their itchy fingers on the remote controls? And what should he do about that? Support her and so support the cause? Point out her cultural shabbiness—one of the duties of his life—and possibly hurt the cause? Just continue with his campaign against Birth Cessation and ignore her? How could one ignore Vivian Pavin Handlin?

His syndicate had suggested that he go to California on the twenty-fourth and "Do an interview" with Vivian. He considered the suggestion an insult. He was a commentator, an essayist, an editorialist, not a reporter, not someone who "Does" interviews. And, anyway, what for? Everything she's had to say she's said on TV, what was he supposed to ask? Well, they tried to explain their idea. You're well known for your viewpoint on this, and so is she. The combination might be exciting and boost a day's circulation for some of our more important clients. But we have the same viewpoint, Kirkly explained patiently. That's true, but it's different also, they diplomatically replied, meaning, but not saying, "You don't like the woman, everybody knows that. Getting the two of you together will create make interesting copy." They figured readers, informed by the drums of print and the trumpets of the airwaves, would also think so.

But I am not a lackey reporter. If you want to offer to send me out to L.A. to have a conversation with her, with *both* of us expressing our views and *equally* being reported on, then I'll think about it."

They so offered. And Kirkly accepted.

30

Monday, April 24—Los Angeles, California

Vivian Pavin Handlin returned home on the same plane she had left on. She sat in the same seat, facing the opposite direction. Parker was at the controls and was happy to be flying her home. He did not like dealing with Harrison McNeil, he preferred Vivian as a boss. He wasn't sure he agreed with what she was doing and with what she was saying, but he also wasn't sure there was any need to. There was only the need to fly. To check the plane and instruments and declare them safe and operable; to start the engines, to taxi, to speed forward and take off; to lift into the air and let the exploitation of some basic physical laws rush a particular and powerful sensation through. A pilot for fifteen years: commercial, private, personal; jets, props, classic biplanes, he never tired of that sensation. To fly was important. Most everything else was not.

Dean Harry had seen her off. "Good-bye, Vivian."

"Wish me luck?"

"Certainly not! Luck has always needed you more than you have needed luck."

"You're right, of course. Luck has always been too slow for me. I'm going to miss you, Dean. But not much."

"Still, a far more feeling response than my own."

"Do you really hate me?"

"I have tried my best to have no emotions concerning you whatsoever. I just dislike guests in general. In the particular, I have always considered our relationship to be one of honor. I would be happy if you feel that you have been treated with honor during your stay."

"A statement I wouldn't refute."

"Good, then keep sending money."

"It's arranged. No matter what happens, the money will always come. Harrison has taken care of everything."

Harrison took care of everything. The plane would land in secret and a car of no luxury would transport Vivian to the U.S. courthouse in downtown Los Angeles, the arrival time agreed to be at Vivian's discretion. Once in the building, where formalities would finalize the future relationship between Vivian Pavin Handlin and the government of the United States in a deal negotiated by Harrison. The media would be informed of the exact time she was expected to come out of the front door, free on a substantial bail that would be a news item in itself.

***

He had gotten space on a bus. It was a fluke. He had taken a chance and gone to the terminal and inquired just as a cancellation came in and the clerk felt it too much of an annoyance to call the stand-by.

"Thanks, Sammy," he said aloud looking up.

"I'm sorry?" the ticket man said thinking he had been addressed.

"Oh, nothing. Talking to myself." He smiled and took his ticket and went home to pick up a few clothes and other essentials for the trip.

***

After a while the drive became monotonous. Gerald felt at first the need to entertain Shelly, to keep a constant conversation of wisdom and wit flowing. It was hard. He could tell her nothing about the evils of Birth Cessation that she did not already know; she was not interested by anything about his personal life; comments on the countryside all seemed shallow. For her part, Shelly seemed to prefer sleep over talk during those times when Gerald drove, and when she was at the wheel, she declared concentration on the road ahead more important than conversation. Each quiet minute seemed outrageously long and empty compared to any minute filled with talk. During silences he would try to occupy himself with the road or the scenery, a book or writing. But he was acutely aware of every move Shelly made, every sound she expelled. He was totally aware of her body being there as a physical thing, achieving glances at portions he liked. And of her mind as an elusive mental state, probably critical of this whole situation and him. And how the hell could he turn that around? It was not pleasant, wanting the pleasure of Shelly's company.

In Arizona the car broke down.

"Of course, god damn it! I knew we couldn't get the fuck through this trip without some kind of tragedy. Shit!" Shelly declared to the desert.

"Hey, calm down. We'll get the car fixed."

"Shut up, Gerald!"

"Hey—" he tried to put his hand on her shoulder.

"Don't touch me, god damn it!"

"Well, then, fuck you, *Clarke!* Jesus Christ, all I've ever done is try to help."

"Help yourself, you mean."

"Are we going to go through this shit again?"

"No, no, for god's sake, no! I don't want you in tears again."

Shelly was suddenly ugly. Gerald stood there and stared at her and realized that she was ugly.

You know, now we're going to get to L.A. late." Shelly declared.

"So?"

"So? So, I wanted to get there in time to meet Vivian."

"Is Vivian expecting you?"

"You know what I mean. I wanted to be there when she makes her first appearance."

"Well…" Gerald looked at his watch. It was 12:02 am, they were at an all-night gas station next to a motel, a promise that the car would be fixed by 5 pm tomorrow fresh in their ears. "That's sometime later today. How you going to make it?"

"I'm going to hitch a ride on a truck."

"What?"

"Why not?"

"Well..."

"Look, I'll give you the credit card, you get the car fixed and meet me in L.A. later."

"Well maybe I'd like to get there on time too."

"Look, someone's got to stay with the car."

"It's your car."

"Gerald, please. This is important to me."

"And it's not to me?"

"Look, I know Vivian."

"You met her one night."

"Well, you've never met her at all."

"God, you're childish."

"Look, I'm going to hitch a ride, period! You do what you want."

Gerald thought for a moment. "Okay, give me the credit card. I'll stay with the car."

"Good."

"I'd like a night without you."

"Well—fine. You've got it."

Shelly grabbed her most important bag, walked to the edge of the road; stuck her thumb up into the air—as proud of it as she was of anything—and stopped a truck within minutes. She climbed high into the cab and disappeared.

Gerald checked into the motel and slept without that certain tension that had been, recently, ever present.

***

Malcolm Kirkly could never get used to the ugliness of Los Angeles from the air: flat land with blemish marks smeared with smog. There was not one point on the land that signaled or indicated excitement or stimulation of any sort. Once on the ground there were some points of interest, he knew, he had been dragged to them, shown them proudly; but from the air: nothing. The basic natural geography was uninteresting. And most of what L.A. Man had done to augment it was equally dull. Kirkly's criticisms were not unique, and he had never once in his column discussed L.A. in any light, negative or positive. It was too easy of a target, evidence by the volumes of criticisms his precursors and peers had written. He could find nothing truly revelatory to say about the place so he preferred to say nothing at all.

But was there any "sense" of L.A. he could work into anything he might write about his upcoming encounter with Vivian Pavin Handlin? Some L.A. surface, shallow show biz reference by analogy, bringing a clear-eyed view of Vivian as performing protester to his readers? *The plastic protester from the plastic city* ? It was a solid temptation; he would have to see how his encounter went.

Kirkly's plane landed and he was met by the driver of the limousine the newspaper syndicate had arranged for his use. It was a luxury unit with wet bar, TV, stereo, audio and video cassette players, phone, fold down desk, lamp, and other writing utensils. Kirkly knew this model and slipped comfortably into the back seat, finding it and its luxuries familiar.

He brought the writing desk down and started making notes of points to raise during his conversation with Vivian. Her lawyer had arranged everything. He assured Kirkly's syndicate that Vivian would soon be free on bail and able to talk to Kirkly, and that they would bring her to his hotel for the conversation as soon as they left the courthouse, and as soon as they had gotten some television exposure. He reported that Vivian was delighted with the opportunity to be able to talk with Kirkly even though he had expressed public reservation regarding the sincerity of her actions. "Mrs. Handlin is sure that Mr. Kirkly will have no questions about her sincerity after they have talked." *Fine*, Kirkly thought. *I'm willing to give her a chance.*

"Mr. Kirkly," the chauffeur's voice sounded over the intercom. "If you want to turn on your TV, you'll see coverage of Mrs. Handlin. It seems she's in the courthouse now."

Kirkly turned on the set. All the major channels were covering the event. All there was to see now was the front entrance to the U.S. Courthouse. All there was to learn was that Vivian Pavin Handlin was reported to be inside, that no one else was being allowed inside, and that she was expected to exit by the front door and would at that time talk to the press. The fact of her impending exit, the press took to be confirmation that the judge would indeed grant bail, which, it has been rumored, could be as high as 15 million dollars.

***

Having been informed, the press waited on the steps outside the entrance of the U.S. courthouse. In turn, the press had informed the public—which was their job—and members of the public who cared, and who could get there, were there. Shelly Clarke was now among their number. She had just gotten there wondering if it was too late, relieved to find out that it wasn't. Everything had been fast and hectic since she pulled into L.A. earlier in the cab of a cross-country truck, and had called an L.A. member of the JLS who lived in The Valley and found out that The Valley was miles away from downtown L.A. But, they managed to get together, nonetheless, to gather some other JLS members and make it to the courthouse, and they now waited outside ready to show loud and visible support for the actions of Vivian Pavin Handlin.

Also among the public's number were some not intending to offer support for Vivian. They had the opposite in mind. They gathered around two big black busses parked in the street, both covered in the red lettered legend:

BIRTH = DEATH
NO-BIRTH = LIFE

Shelly thought them to be obscene. But they were there and far more visible than the JLS—*they should have thought of something, this L.A. chapter, damn!*—and prepared to be just as loud, if not more so. A sense of impending combat arose in Shelly.

The doors of the courthouse opened, the press and public rushed forward. Vivian Pavin Handlin, flanked by Harrison McNeil and a large, muscular man and several crowd control cops, emerged.

ABORT THE BABY!
ABORT THE BABY!
ABORT THE BABY!

Came immediately from the guts and lungs of those who had come in the big black busses.

GET PREGNANT!
GET PREGNANT!
GET PREGNANT!

Shelly and her friends countered.

The Press started to ask questions. Vivian raised one hand. And her stern and sad look quieted everyone.

"Before any questions. A statement, please." It was not clear whether she was aware of those calling for the death of her unborn child, or of those standing and shouting in support of her. She just looked straight ahead into the battery of video cameras aimed at her. "While in the courthouse taking care of legal formalities, I was informed that my husband, Edgar Handlin, died this morning of self-induced starvation."

Silence. Brief. Then a question: "Did Mr. Handlin make any last statements?"

"My husband was in a coma and unable to make any statements. But I believe that this brave and self-sacrificing act of his is statement enough. Indeed, it is the most eloquent of statements; to take your own life as a show of opposition to the repressive acts of a government. His child will be proud of him."

"Are you free on bail?"

"Yes."

"How much was the bail?"

"A substantial amount."

"What will you do now?"

"What I've been doing. Fight against the evil of Birth Cessation."

"Are they going to abort?"

There was a flash of sound from the black bus people: "YESSSSSSS!"

"Shut up!" Shelly Clarke shouted.

Vivian looked their way, then back to the press. "No. I am now legally protected from that."

"Will you let them take your child away?"

"Never. I assure you it will never happen."

He was close enough to her now. He had mingled among them all: The black bus people, the JLS, the curious, the press. He was comfortable among them and they seemed not uncomfortable to have him. He had made up his right arm in a sling and covered it with a large navy pea jacket which he wore over his shoulders. He held the bat in his right hand. It was warm and Vivian wore no overcoat, just a beautiful, understated, self-designed business suit. Good. No real padding. Just as Vivian was starting to make a statement about the irony of standing here on the steps of the U.S. Courthouse, across the street from the *Los Angeles Children's Museum* (of which she had always been a benefactor), he unbuttoned his coat with his left hand, reached in and felt the end of the bat he had smoothed, then slipped his hand down slightly to get a good grip as he moved his other arm out of the sling. With a sudden push through the Press the pea coat slipped off revealing the bat just as he pulled it out of the sling and pulled it back—swift—and then forcefully shoved it—hard—into Vivian's abdomen. There was, of course, a grunt from her, the expelling of breath and a questioning look in her eyes, which had quickly shifted to fall on him alone. He smiled and once again, in a jerk of back/forward motion, slammed the smooth end of the bat into her belly. He noticed her start to double over just as his head was being forced back by a strong arm and his arms were being grabbed by others. The bat fell and made a particularly wooden sound as it hit the steps, soon followed by the indescribable sound of his head hitting those same steps.

Vivian was grabbed and rushed to a hospital. Frederick Lewis Howard was turned over to the police and the paramedics and taken away. Shelly Clarke, who saw it all, sat on the steps and cried uncontrollably. A member of the black bus group had the poor taste to applaud the action.

***

SAVE THE BABY!
SAVE THE POPULATION!

They gathered that evening outside the hospital where Vivian Pavin Handlin was undergoing emergency surgery. There were four groups essentially. Those very much for something. Those very much for something else. Those who came to watch. And the police who came to control them all. But with discretion. No one wanted any more violence. "Just let them shout," some authority had said. "Hospital Zone or not, just let them let the steam out." More people had been black bussed in. There were more people on the streets concerned with the "good of the whole population" than with that of Vivian and her fetus. But that just made the others, the JLS under the leadership of Shelly Clarke, shout louder and stronger.

SAVE THE BABY! Shelly and her JLS comrades shouted out.

SAVE THE POPULATION! The black bus crowd shouted out.

SAVE THE BABY!
SAVE THE POPULATION!

They took turns. They seesawed. They competed.

SAVE THE BABY!
SAVE THE POPULATION!

But soon they tired of that, for the purpose here was, in all reality, not to out shout, but to overcome. What *they* wanted, they both felt, was just, plain, wrong.

SAVE THE BABY! *SAVE THE POPULATION!*
SAVE THE BABY! *SAVE THE POPULATION!*
SAVE THE BABY! *SAVE THE POPULATION!*
SAVE THE BABY! *SAVE THE POPULATION!*
SAVE THE BABY! *SAVE THE POPULATION!*
SAVE THE BABY! *SAVE THE POPULATION!*
SAVE THE BABY! *SAVE THE POPULATION!*
SAVE THE BABY! *SAVE THE POPULATION!*

SAVE THE BABY!   SAVE THE POPULATION
SAVE THE BABY!   SAVE THE POPULATION!
SAVE THE BABY!   SAVE THE POPULATION!
SAVE THE BABY!   SAVE THE POPULATION!
SAVE THE BABY!   SAVE THE POPULATION!
SAVE THE BABY!   SAVE THE POPULATION!
SAVE THE BABY!   SAVE THE POPULATION!
SAVE THE BABY!   SAVE THE POPULATION!
SAVE THE BABY! SAVE THE POPULATION!
SAVE THE BABY! SAVE THE POPULATION!
SAVE THE BABY!SAVE THE POPULATION!
SAVE THE BABYS!AVETHE POPULATION!
SAVE THE BABSYA!VETHE POPULATION!
SAVE THE BASBAYV!E THE POPULATION!

31

Thursday, April 27—Los Angeles, California

The cameras had been there, and the cameras had caught each image: the swift violence, the shock, the confusion, the moves to action. The cameras had witnessed the aftermath: The car with Vivian racing away, the blood of Frederick Lewis Howard on the courthouse steps, the tears of some. Captured, these images, prized by their owners, were put on display for all to see. The videotape ran forward, and it happened all over again. Then rewind-rerun/rewind-rerun/rewind-rerun throughout the day, sometimes in slow motion, sometimes frame by frame—"Yes, you can see the bat in his hand here"—Vivian was seen suffering the assault again and again.

And then other images were caught:

Outside of the hospital, the protesters gathered.

The corridors of police headquarters and someone answering questions—who was the man with the bat? Was he working alone? What was his motivation?

Malcolm Kirkly, in the hotel suite where he was to meet with Vivian, commented on the regrettable act.

Gerald Downing, who had finally made it to L.A., the car radio informing him of the acts as they happened, joined the JLS outside the hospital to become one-half spokesperson; Shelly was there as well; Shelly was caught.

Business associates and famous Hollywood friends denounced the shameful act.

Harrison McNeil, shaken, tired, his voice, his eyes telling all that it was late, very late, announcing the death of Vivian's child in the making and the fact that a hysterectomy—an illegal hysterectomy, as far as he was concerned—had been performed on Mrs. Handlin. He was outraged, and the cameras caught that outrage.

Doctors stated that there was no way to have saved the child whatsoever, and yes, the hysterectomy was medically called for. Yes, they were aware of the basic biological fact that this meant that Mrs.

Handlin would no longer be able to bear children, in answer to a reporter's statement (was it accusing?) of that fact.

Not caught:

Butchko. But he issued a statement deploring the violence.

President Henshaw also deplored this unwarranted act of violence—through a press representative.

***

The members of the JLS returned to their spot outside the hospital the next day and the days after. They brought plenty of food and held a vigil in memory of the dead child and sympathy for Vivian. They sent flowers and notes of condolence and support. In the late afternoon, Harrison McNeil came among them.

"Is Gerald Downing here?"

"Yeah," Gerald said, looking up from a pad of paper.

"Can you come with me, please? Mrs. Handlin would like to see you."

"Should I come too?" Shelly Clarke eagerly stepped forward.

"No. Mrs. Handlin has only asked for his gentleman."

"Oh, well, please give her my best. I'm Shelly Clarke, we met at Fordham. I arranged for Mrs. Handlin to speak—"

"Yes, I remember, Miss Clarke. I'll give her your message."

***

Gerald expected to see a weak, drained woman in a great deal of pain. Instead, he found a vigorous Vivian sitting up in bed, on the phone. Someone had been in and done her hair and make-up. She finished the phone conversation with a strong request, waited for positive assurances, and then hung up. She looked at Gerald, into his eyes, across his face, down his form. "Sit down, Mr. Downing."

Gerald did so, sitting in one of two metal and plastic visitor's chairs. Harrison McNeil sat in the other.

"Mr. Downing, thank you for your kind note." She held up a small piece of paper. "And your supportive comments on TV. I'm very appreciative."

"Uh—well, they were sincerely given."

"Yes, I know they were, Mr. Downing. But they are the least of the reasons I have asked you here. Do you know what has happened to me in the last several days?"

"Well, yes..."

"I have become a victim, Mr. Downing, a victim of the arrogance of one man and a victim of the government he represents. I have lost a husband. My baby has been murdered. I have been brutally sterilized. Why? Because I became a threat to their 'master plan.' They were rightfully afraid of that threat. I just didn't realize they would go to such lengths to stop me."

"You mean Howard?"

"Yes. Do you doubt that he is an agent of Butchko's?"

"Well..."

"Do you doubt it at all?"

"Well—" *What to say, my god, what to say!* "—uh, I wouldn't be surprised if the evidence led to such a finding. But there doesn't seem to be any—"

"That the public has been made aware of. But what else could explain the attack?"

"Well..."

"And they have sterilized me, Mr. Downing. Butcher Butchko reached in and cut my womb out because it frightens him so deeply."

"It seems to me that was unnecessary, yes."

"Of course it was! Butchko attempted to neutralize me. The fact of this is too obvious to be denied. Has he succeeded, Mr. Downing?"

"Well..."

"Here I sit, without my husband, without my child, without the capacity to bear children. Am I neutralized, Mr. Downing?"

"Well—not if you don't want to be, Mrs. Handlin. I mean, you could still be a very effective spokesperson for the anti-Birth Cessation movement. Especially—well..."

"Yes?"

"Well—especially now that you have become a victim."

"Exactly, Mr. Downing! So, where do *we* go from here?"

"Excuse me?"

"Mr. Downing, I knew of you before your little note and TV appearance. In my exile, I had the occasion to read *Birthright*, to read your columns—"

The rush was fantastic, a beating in the center of his chest, the flow to his head.

"—I liked them all. I was especially impressed by your piece on the right of descendants. It seems to me, Mr. Downing, that you are a first-rate thinker on this question. I want to take advantage of that thinking. I want you to join me in a strong and, finally, I'm sure, successful effort to overturn Birth Cessation. I want you to edit and write for a publication I will publish and distribute, and I want you to be one of my advisors in a national protest organization."

"You mean, like the JLS?"

"No, I do not mean like the JLS! This will not be a school club for extra-curricular activities. This will be a political organization of scope and power, and it will be extremely well-funded and well-managed. It will be an organization for adults, Mr. Downing. Once we get started, there will be no need for the JLS."

"Well, there are some very dedicated people in the JLS."

"Anyone that you recommend will be invited to join us. What's your view on this, Shelly Clarke?"

"Uh—" He wanted to breathe very fast and very hard; it all seemed like a quick burst of running speed and easy leaps over once too-high obstructions. "—Well, Shelly is, uh—well, to be honest, Mrs. Handlin, I've never been that impressed with Shelly. I mean, she organized the JLS and all that, but I've always sort of looked upon her as a little rich girl playing games—"

"*I'm* a little rich girl, Mr. Downing!"

"Uh, yes, but you earned yours, didn't you?"

"Thank you."

"Shelly is a dilettante, I guess you would say. The JLS to her is sort of a, well, a school play."

"I'm glad you'll be with us, Mr. Downing. Your assessment of Ms. Clarke matches my own."

Gerald smiled.

"Now, you live in New York?"

"Yes."

"You will move to Los Angeles."

"Oh. Well, sure. Okay."

"Any family?"

"Uh, no. Well, I mean, I have a daughter, but she lives with her mother. We're divorced."

"Are you close to your daughter?"

"Yes, very."

"We'll bring her out here."

"Well, my ex-wife has custody."

"There will be no problem, Mr. Downing. You will have your daughter out here. Any other family?"

"My mother."

"Any need to move her out here?"

"None that I know of."

"Okay. Mr. McNeil will give you a check today. You are working for me now, Mr. Downing."

"Well—thank you."

"Are you staying in a hotel?"

"No, at a member's house."

"You can move into my house. There's plenty of room. Your daughter can live there as well. What's her name?"

"Laura."

"How old is she?"

"Almost six."

"I will enjoy having her around. Goodbye, Mr. Downing. Mr. McNeil will take care of everything."

"Goodbye, Mrs. Handlin. And, uh—thanks."

"You're welcome."

Harrison walked Gerald out and gave him a check that surprised and delighted Gerald and Vivian's address, stating that he should move in tonight. He then returned to Vivian's room.

"You do your research well, Harrison."

"Who are you adopting, him or his daughter?"

"Shut up, Harrison!"

"Look, I'm just not sure this is—"

"Harrison, I have great use for Mr. Downing. I want no more opposition."

"Don't you think this is getting out of hand? It's not just a court case anymore."

"If it is out of hand, it is because of Butchko. I am just reacting in kind. We will defeat Birth Cessation in any way we must, from propaganda to subversion. You do not have to participate if you do not wish. But I prefer that you do."

"I am your lawyer."

"Good."

***

Gerald Downing could think of nothing better to do than to take a walk. He did not know L.A.; he did not know any particular way to go except not back to the JLS. He just wanted to walk. When he felt like stopping, he would figure a way to get to Vivian's. Los Angeles had some bus service left. He could thumb a ride. He could, he supposed, take a taxi, no matter what the outrageous expense.

But where were the trumpets?

A slow, measured blaring for his procession would be nice.

Or a hard, quick drum beat of triumph might be more to the point.

He wanted to feel the enormity of what had just happened.

The major significance of it

The historic trembling.

The momentousness.

He felt a great need to be melodramatic.

But the warm spring air was all that he could feel. The few steps just ahead were all that he could see. Now and then, blasts of traffic communication were the only horns he could hear.

He supposed it was now time to think about what he could do instead of just amusingly feeling about what he would do. The security and comforts of daydreams were over. The fun of preliminary games was over. Actions now had meanings and consequences. Life would now be facts.

He knew, but he could not yet see nor feel, that he would be very famous by this time next year. He knew that he would have, at least, the pretensions of wealth. He knew that he would know few who were not also famous and most likely wealthy. And he knew that he would travel without effort among them.

Facts. Their edges were well-defined. Their bulk was solid. Their weight could be measured. But was there to be no excitement at all?

He smiled broadly, forcing a lift of flesh and feeling.

He stepped up his walking pace, forcing his pulse to beat faster, causing a quick oxygen rush to his brain.

He would have his joy, damn it! He would have his joy!

32

Friday, April 28—Washington, D.C.

Darryl Butchko knocked two quick raps on the president's door, heard a muffled grunt giving permission to enter, and found that the only light in the president's working office emanated from a small work lamp on the president's desk.

But the president was not at his desk. There were several pieces of paper on the desk, centered and stacked, and an open briefcase, but the chair was unoccupied.

"Hello, Darryl," the president said from a visitor's chair to one side in the dark. "How are you?"

"Oh!" Darryl was a bit startled and hated it. He hated being surprised. "Fine, Mr. President. Yourself?"

"Fine. What have you got?"

"Well—" His eyes were adjusting to the level of light, and he was beginning to make out the president. "—he seems to be a mentally disturbed individual obsessed with the idea that Vivian Handlin had usurped his authority to be the premier campaigner against Birth Cessation, an authority that seems to come, in his mind, from his deceased brother. He has a Joan of Arc complex and seems to have feared the competition."

"He was the young man who dropped the bag of blood and pig, was he not?"

"Uh—he takes credit for it."

"And coined the term, Butcher Butchko?"

"Apparently."

"That's good for you."

"I suppose."

"They are shouting conspiracy, of course."

"Yes, sir. Several theories are being floated."

"But only Vivian Handlin's is of any importance to us."

"Yes, sir."

"The doctor who performed the hysterectomy?"

"Yes, sir?"

"I have a report that he is your long-time personal friend."

"That—uh—that is true, Mr. President."

"A coincidence?"

"Absolutely."

"Knew him at U.C.L.A.?"

"That's right."

"Do you know his views on Birth Cessation?"

"I believe they are substantially the same as ours."

"I sincerely wish they weren't."

"I understand."

"What are the plans for Mr. Howard?"

"Since the child died, he will be charged, I suppose, with murder. Maybe manslaughter."

"Interesting."

"Sir?"

"He only did what you so desperately wanted to do. Yet, he may go to jail for it."

"I'm sure his lawyers will plead insanity."

"No doubt. Are you scared, Darryl?"

"Sir?"

"For the first time—truly for the first time, Birth Cessation is in jeopardy."

"I don't see it that way, sir."

"You've always seen it that way, Darryl—when it came to Vivian Handlin."

"Well, I'll admit I've been concerned over her potential influence."

"Substantially greater now, I would say."

"I hope not."

"Well—we'll see."

"Do you have an assessment, sir?"

"We know she will launch a major propaganda campaign: TV commercials, motion pictures, lectures. We know she's gained a lot of sympathy. She is naturally attractive. The people like their major players attractive. She has as great a possibility to shape the democratic process to her will as any propagandist has ever had. She should not be taken lightly.'

"Yes, sir.'

"She is going to pound upon us daily from now on."

"I know.

"The American people will get her message."

"But will they agree? I have faith they know what's right for America."

Darryl, cut the rhetoric when you're alone with me in this office."

"Sir, I wasn't—"

"Never mind, Darryl."

The president got up and walked over to his desk. He put the stack of papers in his briefcase and closed it.

"Mr. President?"

"Yes?"

"What about you, sir?"

"What about me?"

"Regarding re-election."

"Oh, I'll be fine. There is still quite a majority on our side. It won't dwindle—if it does—quite that fast. Our party's candidate who succeeds me will have the problems, though. Five or six years will not be nearly enough time for the positive effects of Birth Cessation to become apparent. But it's plenty of time for the opposition to grow. The People will look around them, using their poor, weak eyes, and see no apparent change and wonder, why? Why are we suffering through this? Why can't we have babies, those cute little bundles of joy we all want to cuddle so badly? Why should we allow this to divide the nation? Our opponents will answer their questions with slogans that smack of logic, and The People will suddenly see an alternative, and quite a few may decide to support it. Some intelligently. Some emotionally. Some ignorantly. It doesn't matter. They will support it because it is, at least, an alternative, a change. When dissatisfied, participants in the democratic process never vote for a person, Darryl; they vote for a change. And they are ever hopeful that their dream of change will come true. Voters are dreamers, Darryl. That is their particular charm."

The president picked up his briefcase. "Well, it's Friday—end of the week. TGIF, as the common working stiffs of America say. Time to put our cares behind us and relax with the purity of athletic competition and beer." He walked to the door and opened it. "I suggest, though, that you work through the weekend."

The president walked through the doorway, stopped, turned, and said, "Be sure to turn out the light and lock the door when you leave, will you, Darryl?"

"Yes, sir," Darryl Butchko said in response. But the president had already shut the door behind him.

The End

AFTERWORD

In the early 1970s, I sold major appliances at a discount department store in Southern California called Zodys. I am not kidding about this store's name; it was indeed called Zodys. Why? I don't think I ever knew. Nor did it matter so long as the paycheck cleared. In any case, there was a chain of Zodys Discount Department stores throughout the Southwest United States. And Michigan, for some aberrant reason.

Occasionally, my duties took me to another nearby Zodys to pick up some items not in stock at the location where I toiled. It was always a surreal experience. The interior of each Zodys was laid out in the exact same way, with each department in the exact same location in each store. But each store, of course, had its particular way of displaying and decorating, not to mention a different staff than the ones I knew running around in their awful little blue vests serving customers.

So I would walk into this store, so familiar yet so strange, and my head would spin for a moment, my equilibrium would be thrown off, and the theme music from *The Twilight Zone* would trickle through my mind. As I said, it was surreal, disconcerting, and, at least momentarily, discombobulating.

I hope this is how you felt when you started reading *Right: A Portrait of Controversy,* which takes place in a 1980s that never happened, even if the landscape seems familiar. And the controversy that I endeavored to portray certainly never happened, nor could it have happened. And it will certainly never happen today nor in the future. I hope.

Why have I discombobulated the reader with this ahistorical novel? Outside of the fact that I love the word discombobulated. The clue is in the subtitle: A Portrait of Controversy, not: Portrait of A Controversy.

If I had decided to portray an actual controversy from the 1980s or thereabout, or a current controversy, then readers would come to the novel with, in most cases, their minds already made up, their positions set, their absolute faith that they have chosen the *right* side of the controversy. Therefore, it would not be a portrait but a Rorschach test.

Creating a controversy that didn't exist then and doesn't now and yet has certain familiar elements was the only way I could attempt to portray Controversy as a thing itself and not the questions the controversy is about.

I leave it to the reader how lifelike—or abstractly revealing—the portrait is

ABOUT THE AUTHOR

Photo by Amanda Martin

Before publishing eleven critically acclaimed works of fiction, award-winning and Amazon Bestselling author Steven Paul Leiva spent over twenty years in the entertainment industry as a writer and producer. He worked with such talent as Academy Award-winning producer Richard Zanuck; director Ivan Reitman; literary legend and screenwriter Ray Bradbury; *Star Wars* producer Gary Kurtz; Looney Tunes legend Chuck Jones; and Animation Feature Academy Award-winning director Brad Bird. He even lent his voice to the Academy Award shortlisted (placing in the top ten) animated short, "The Indescribable Nth."

Leiva produced the animation for the original *Space Jam*, starring the very tall Michael Jordan and the relatively short Bugs Bunny. For this production, Leiva put together an ad hoc animation studio for Warner Bros and executive producer Ivan Reitman in three days over the phone

During this time, he wrote novels and a play, *Made on the Moon*, which premiered at the Edinburgh Festival Fringe, receiving a four-star review from *The Scotsman.*

After *Space Jam*, Leiva decided to concentrate on writing novels. Since 2003, he has published ten novels, a novella, and a book of essays.

His work has been praised by literary great Ray Bradbury, Oscar-winning film producer Richard Zanuck, *New York Times* bestselling author and Pulitzer Prize finalist Diane Ackerman, *New York Times* Bestselling Author Jonathan Maberry, comedy great Phil Proctor of The Firesign Theater, *USA Today* Bestselling Author Jean Rabe, *Star Trek: Enterprise* actor John Billingsley, Australian philosopher Russell Blackford, and British physicist and author Stephen Webb. He has received the Scribe Award from the International Association of Media Tie-in Writers

You can find Steven Paul Leiva on Facebook and read his blog, The Emotional Rationalist, at **https://tinyurl.com/ydgpkps8**

BOOKS BY STEVEN PAUL LEIVA

Blood is Pretty
The First Fixxer Adventure

Meet the Fixxer—with wit and aplomb he works the fruitful fields of Hollywood fixing the sins and correcting the stupidities of the denizens therein. In *Blood is Pretty* he comes to the rescue of "the most beautiful woman I have ever seen" to extricate her from the grip of the soul-sucking sexual desires of a producer born in slime, and takes on the task of buying off with money and muscle a film geek who won't cooperate with a director of minuscule talent who simply wants to claim "V"—the geek's "Holy Grail" of a film treatment—as his own.

Hollywood is an All-Volunteer Army
The Second Fixxer Adventure

What those in the know in Hollywood really know is that if they need a dark deed done, if they need a sticky personal or professional problem "fixed," they can call upon the mysterious and dangerous Fixxer. Whether you are a successful comedy film director whose "Art" has never truly been appreciated because the country's most important film critic has held a grudge against you since college or you are a neophyte and naïve screenwriter who resents the professional blackmail she has just suffered, you call upon the Fixxer.

Traveling in Space

A unique first contact novel from the aliens' point-of-view. The last thing the factfinders—who call themselves Life—expected to find while traveling in space in "The Curious" on a mission from their planet, The Living World, was other life. But one day, they stumble upon the third planet out from a backwater sun and find it teeming with a vast diversity of life, including one sentient and cognizant, if primitive, species that they dub Otherlife. Being not only from The Curious but inherently curious themselves, they begin to study the Otherlife and their alien culture, discovering such strange things as marriage, intoxicating drinks, weapons of minor and mass destruction, the gleeful inhaling of toxic substances, two-parent families, layered language, genocide, non-nude bathing, and—the strangest thing of all—religion.

This first contact between Life and Otherlife, disconcerting for both, has moments of humor and moments of horror—and neither escape the encounter unchanged.

12 Dogs of Christmas
A Novelization

Winner of the Scribe Award from the International Association of Media Tie-in Authors

Based on the beloved independent family film.

12-year-old Emma O'Connor is sent to live with her "aunt" in the small town of Doverville. Emma soon finds herself in the middle of a "dogfight" with the mayor and town dogcatcher. In order to strike down their "no-dogs" law, Emma must bring together a group of schoolmates, grown-ups, and adorable dogs of all shapes and sizes in a spectacular holiday pageant. *The 12 Dogs of Christmas* is a fun, heartwarming story featuring a diverse canine cast and is perfect for all those who love dogs, kids, and Christmas.

By the Sea
A Comic Novel

A modern comic adult fairy tale with an ensemble cast of Cinderellas. Instead of a kingdom by the sea, our story takes place in and around a residential hotel by the sea. The architecturally eclectic Briers Hotel is situated on Leech Beach, a not particularly inviting beach that is often fog-bound and always scruffy. But it's the perfect setting for our Cinderellas, male, and female, who put up with the scruffiness of life while striving to make it through their various personal seaside fogs. Theater; art; antiques; old movies; sex; more sex; death; fast and slow cars, chicken shit, and cow poop; military bearing and erotic emissions—not to mention the wicked witch, the sea serpent by the sea shore, the village ogre, the village idiot, and several Prince Charmings—all figure into this merry tale with a multitude of happy endings.

IMP
A Political Fantasia

Thomas P. Powell's ascension in politics was both unusual and yet very American. From traffic cop to Vice President of the United States, his climb up the ladder of public service was often due to the push of random acts and not-so-happy accidents—although Thomas held the opinion that it was due solely to his singular innate moral authority. What matters is what's within, that's the Powell political philosophy. Then, on the cusp of his grasping the last rung of the American political ladder, something truly within suddenly appears. A horrible homunculus, an impetuous imp, climbs out of Thomas's right ear to bedevil his nights, confuse his days, and take him on a crazy, wild, nauseating, and nuclear journey. It's as if *The West Wing* was done as a *Twilight Zone* episode.

And you thought our last political nightmare was surreal.

Journey to Where
A Contemporary Scientific Romance

When a radical experiment into the nature of time is sabotaged, the scientific team finds themselves in an alternate universe where humans never became the dominant life force. Instead, dinosaurs evolved into intelligent bipeds, developing language and societal structures.

The scientists must learn to communicate with this alien species, who view them as unusual pets, and figure out how to recreate the original experiment in a non-industrialized world so they can go back home—assuming there's a home, or even a universe, to return to. But the scientist who sabotaged them is trapped in this new world with them. And he's looking to rise to power, even if his quest means the death of his traveling companions.

A contemporary scientific romance in the tradition of H. G. Wells and Jules Verne

Creature Feature
A Horrid Comedy

There is something strange happening in Placidville

It is 1962. Kathy Anderson, a serious actress who took her training at the Actors Studio in New York is stuck playing Vivacia, the Vampire Woman on Vivacia's House of Horrors for a local Chicago TV station. Finally fed up showing old monster movies to creature feature fans, she quits and heads to New York, and the fame and footlights of Broadway.

She stops off to visit her parents and old friends in Placidville, the all-American, middle-class, blissfully normal Midwest small town she grew up in. But she finds things are strange in Placidville. Kathy's parents, her best friend from high school, the local druggist, and even the Oberhausen twins are all acting curiously creepy, odiously odd, and wholly weird. Especially the town's super geeky nerd, Gerald, who warns of dark days ahead.

Has Kathy entered a zone in the twilight? Did she reach the limits that are outer? Has she fallen through a mirror that is black? Or is it just—just—politics as usual?

Bully 4 Love
A Rather Odd Love Story

Adolphus Seruya is a happy, middle-aged, unambitious bachelor and a history professor at a prominent community college. Then suddenly SHE walks into his classroom. Lavinia Carson is beautiful in a unique yet compelling way. And radiant almost beyond description. Thus begins a rather odd story of love rejected, love ignored, love found—and cuttlefish pizza.

Extraordinary Voyages

What if a man wanted to go to the moon from the time he was an infant? Not a toddler, not a child, not a young man, but a babe in his mother's arms?

What if Baron Munchausen traveled from 1790 to1641 to take Cyrano de Bergerac to Mars?

What if the man who wanted to go to the moon from the time he was an infant wrote some rude poems?

What if the author of this book wrote his own Wikipedia page that he was sure Wikipedia would never publish?

What if you bought this book and found out?

Includes the critically acclaimed novella *Made on the Moon.*

The Reluctant Heterosexual
A Tragicomedy in Four Movements a Prelude and an Interlude,

With *The Reluctant Heterosexual,* Steven Paul Leiva concludes his thematic trilogy: **The Love, Sex and Pursuit of Happiness Novels**. All three novels look at these essential aspects of the human condition, with each novel focusing on one of the three. *By the Sea: A Comic Novel* looks at our unease when unhappy. *Bully 4 Love: A Rather Odd Love Story* takes a skewed view of this most revered emotion. And now, *The Reluctant Heterosexual*, as the title predicts, concerns sex, which is not always the same as love, nor is it always a happy situation.

Subtitled *A Tragicomedy in Four Movements a Prelude and an Interlude,* each section of the novel, as in a musical composition, has its own tempo, mood, and form as it tells the story—and stories—of Robert Leslie Cromwell and Sandy Smith. Two *Homo sapiens sapiens* surviving and striving in the late 20th century.

Robert and Sandy are intelligent, creative, not unattractive, wealthy, married to each other, and in love. And yet their procreating bodies might as well be standing naked on a savanna in Africa in the late Pliocene Era.

It's the sometimes comic conflict between ancient bodies and modern culture. Can there possibly be a happy ending?

Right
A Portrait of Controversy

In a 1980s America different from our own, both familiar and not, Congress passed and President Henshaw signed the Birth Cessation Act. Once it became law, no one would be allowed to have a child for twenty-five years, any woman under 24 weeks pregnant was required to have an immediate abortion, and all men were called up to report for a vasectomy.

"Conscious regulation of human numbers must be achieved." Dr. Paul R. Ehrlich wrote in his 1968 bestseller, *The Population Bomb.* By the early 80s, the government had statistical projections that the population growth was outpacing the available resources needed for all in America to live a comfortable and secure life. A situation that would inevitably lead to the chaos and violence of extreme civil unrest.

Most Americans, liking comfort and security, supported the government's action. Most, but not all. And those who didn't, including a world-famous female billionaire entrepreneur inventor film producer, a major appliance salesman from Queens, a well-to-do Manhattan college radical, an unwed mother in Los Angeles who protests most horribly, America's premier pundit-columnist, and a young man who talks to his dead brother, became loud enough to start a fresh new controversy in America.

This is a portrait of that controversy.

Searching for Ray Bradbury
Writings about the Writer and the Man

Includes the title piece written for the *Los Angeles Times*, and "The Man Who Was Himself," Leiva's memorial appreciation of Bradbury commissioned by the Science Fiction & Fantasy Writers of America for the Winter 2012/13 edition of their quarterly magazine, *The Bulletin.* Other pieces were originally written for *Neworld Review*, KCET.org, and his personal blog.

With a special foreword by Hugo and Nebula Award-winning author David Brin.

THANK YOUU FOR READING

RIGHT

A PORTRAIT OF CONTROVERSY

www.ingramcontent.com/pod-product-compliance
Lightning Source LLC
LaVergne TN
LVHW041106080826
845145LV00007B/1699

* 9 7 8 1 7 3 5 2 9 8 5 9 7 *